# an ANCIENT TRAP

# TITLES BY PAUL E COOLEY

# an ANCIENT TRAP

## Paul E Cooley

**SHADOW**
PUBLICATIONS

Paperback ISBN: 978-1-942137-15-3
eBook ISBN: 978-1-942137-16-0

Visit our website at https://shadowpublications.com

To stalk Paul on social media:
  Mastodon: @paul_e_cooley@vyrse.social
  YouTube: https://youtube.com/paulecooley
  Email: paul@shadowpublications.com
  Mailing List: http://mailinglist.shadowpublications.com

Printed in the United States of America

Cover art, cover design, and internal layout by Scott E. Pond
Scott E. Pond Designs: www.scottpond.com

10 9 8 7 6 5 4 3 2 1

*For the Dead Robots' Society:*
*For keeping me writing,*
*For keeping my sanity,*
*For the love of story.*
*For Friendship.*

# an ANCIENT TRAP

# PROLOGUE

*P*rospector-9C512 entered the system weeks ago. The autonomous vehicle found the first three large celestial bodies and quickly discounted them as mere ice giants. It made note of their location, their likely future orbital shifts, if any, possible deleterious effects on the bodies or simulated collision points, and various other data.

Water in the system was abundant. In addition to the three ice giants farther in, *9C512* discovered an entire ice belt orbiting the dying star's outreaches. *Prospector* had been trained to know how precious water was and that significant sources might mean life of some kind. With that in mind, *Prospector* began scanning for radio signals or signs of artificial power.

It discovered thousands of signals originating inside the system. Most appeared to be radiation music cast by the remaining inner planets. In the final stages of its life before it flickered out of existence, the star cast a wan glow over its system.

After passing through another 20 million kilometers of space, *Prospector* discovered a trio of objects trapped in the gravity of an unremarkable gas giant. Massive debris fields filled the space between the large planetoids or satellites. Metal. Rock. Minerals.

*Prospector* decided this system, the third it had visited in its forty-five-year service, was worth exploring. Specifically, the trio orbiting the gas giant. The triplets might once have been identical but no more. For instance, one of them had obviously taken a hit from an asteroid or some other body, causing it to spin at a dizzying speed. *9C512* determined the target to be impossible to explore. The second of the triplets was incredibly radioactive, so much so that *Prospector* didn't dare get any closer than necessary to travel to the third object.

The third, the prize, held a stable orbit, was spherical in nature, and had a third of Earth's gravity. Perfect for exploration, especially after *9C512* had spent weeks aligning itself to orbit the satellite and discovered seven different sites of interest. *9C512* went into prospecting mode.

First order of business? A designation for the object. *Prospector* had already computed a hash based on the object's location in the system and the system's relative position to that of Proxima, but it loaded its list of approved names, and chose one at random—MacReady.

*9C512* fired four of its remaining twenty pods at the target satellite, each pod destined for a site of interest. Pods 1, 2, and 4 all headed for craters while pod 3 made its way to the base of a rocky peak.

Pod 3, a spider-looking thing, bounced gently on its ten spindly legs before lowering itself to the moon's surface. A slot retracted in the pod, and a robot crawled out from its belly.

*Prospector* monitored the dog-sized robot as it trundled over the rocky surface and to the twenty-meter-high cliff wall.

The robot extended a sensor array, placed it against the stone, and activated the tool. The array sent out a powerful burst of energy against the rock, waited for echoes to return, and transmitted the results to *9C512* using its pod's comms. *Prospector*, not sentient and therefore incapable of excitement, marked the results as "Extremely Likely" and continued monitoring the four robots and analyzing their conclusions.

With every analysis, *Prospector* continued to update its recommendations. After five days of testing, it sent its findings in a single quantum message, which was all it had the power to initiate. In order to fit the message into the minuscule bandwidth, it reduced the fidelity of the reports to their most basic assumptions and evidence, leaving out extraneous information and speculations.

The report said nothing of the other objects that shared MacReady's orbit. The report said nothing about the debris field or the ice giants. The report contained no warnings. Because of the loss of fidelity, the report didn't even contain robot 3's record of a micro-radiation burst from inside the peak.

# CHAPTER ONE

The *Kirkland* had been decelerating for weeks, its engines pointed in the opposite direction of its travel, the reactors humming along at sixty percent power. Once it entered the target system, it flipped and resumed a sane burn. Two weeks later, it awakened its sleeping crew of twelve—they were less than a week away from MacReady.

Jordan and the rest of his prospecting team had climbed out of their stasis pods, vomited a few times, showered the gunk and puke off their bodies, and stumbled to the galley, wearing fresh jumpsuits, boots that had last been worn over one and a half solar years ago, with their bellies rumbling and a desertlike thirst.

After supping, the dozen members of the team began taking care of chores. The starboard shield had taken a hit from a meteorite at some point during the journey, and three sensors had gone dark on the port side. In addition to all of that, they had a leak in the reactor shielding. Quite the list in addition to all the other madness that had to occur before they arrived at MacReady.

With breakfast finished and the Captain's Time over, Jordan was free to do his job. Unfortunately, that job meant climbing out an airlock, attaching to the hull with magnetics, and walking the starboard line to repair the damaged shield. Joy of joys.

Jordan climbed into the EVA suit and waited for the pressure checks to finish. When they did, he blinked through status menus on the visor's interface, looking for warnings or other unexpected statuses. Like the kind in which you forgot to actually charge your suit or refill its atmosphere and ended up going into the deep dark for a total of two minutes before struggling to get back into the airlock to escape freezing or burning to death, or simply dying from asphyxiation. No, that had never happened to Jordan. Never.

"Hey, Jordan?" Captain Til called over the radio. "We've spotted some debris out there. Nothing too close, mind you, but there might be some things we can't see."

"Um, Cap, you do realize I'll be on the hull, right?"

Til snickered. "Get below the shield, walk in the shadow, and fix the damned thing."

Jordan sighed. Of all the parts of his job, this was the one he hated the most. "Aye, aye, Captain Til!" he said with mock respect.

"Hey, Jordan?"

He turned to the left and saw Aryana already suited up and laden with supplies. She was almost always ready before him, usually owing to some last-minute chore he needed to take care of or dealing with a drive-by question or concern.

"Guess you're ready," he said.

Aryana grinned beneath her visor. "Always ready for a walk."

"Good," he said. "Then I'll let you take lead."

"Beauty before age," she said and tromped to the airlock, the welding torch's handle sticking out of her belt. The armored pack on her back contained fuel for patching as well as other tools.

Jordan pulled his pack from the wall and attached it to his back. After securing his own welding torch, he followed Aryana and entered the airlock.

"Cap? We're ready for the EVA," Jordan said.

"Acknowledged. Get 'er patched up so we can get back to relaxing."

Jordan rolled his eyes, wondering how many times Til had found himself walking on the hull of a ship moving at thousands of kilometers a second, especially when there was debris lurking about. He had a feeling Til had never done it. Lucky bastard.

"Copy," Jordan said and switched to the EVA channel. "Ready?" he asked Aryana.

She tapped the stud and the airlock closed. A beat later, all atmosphere was sucked out of the airlock, vacuum established, and the light turned green. Without waiting for Jordan to say anything, she tapped the other stud and the airlock door opened.

Jordan stared into a perfect rectangle filled with stars. "Wow," he said.

Aryana, normally chatty, only breathed into the microphone. "Wow."

"Okay," Jordan said, "get moving, 'beauty before age.'"

"Got it, boss."

Aryana stepped past the lip of the airlock and onto the short platform. With her magnetic boots and gloves activated, she easily crawled onto the hull and descended out of view.

Jordan took a deep breath, reminding himself of all the times he'd done this before, that he'd only had two incidents in all his years, and this was simply routine. It didn't help. After exhaling in a long, uninterrupted stream, Jordan stepped forward and into space.

Aryana walked twenty meters aft and toward the ship's keel. The shield, a massive disc of metal jutting from the actual hull, was one of eight. While they didn't provide complete protection from debris pounding into the metal at high speed, they cushioned the impact and, in all but serious cases, kept space flotsam from perforating the hull.

This shield, number five, had taken a serious hit. The ship's hull cameras had shown a deep divot along with crumpled metal. They didn't exactly carry replacement shields—they were far too large and unwieldy for a few humans to move into position, much less attach while away from a dry dock. Instead, the *Kirkland* carried plenty of temporary plates.

Aryana quickly moved beneath the shadow of the battered disc, and Jordan followed her, his suit's HVAC immediately adjusting for the temperature change, although in truth, this far away from MacReady's star, there wasn't much of a difference.

The cameras had shown him the damage, but it was truly difficult to appreciate until you saw it for yourself. Whatever had hit them must have been relatively massive. This hadn't been a micrometeorite—this had been something as big as a hover car.

"Who the hell hit us with a sledgehammer?" Aryana asked.

"Would have been a big one," Jordan said. The massive divot in the steel protruded at least half a meter from a rough, four-meter circumference circle. "We can't pound it back into shape, so all we can do is reinforce it."

Aryana made the thumbs-up gesture she'd been trained to always use even when comms were available. She placed one knee against the hull and sent the command to the automated storage door. It slid aside with a minuscule puff of dust and a rack of plates ascended.

Each 2x3 meter rectangular plate had been treated with a nano-bonding agent, and once they added enough heat to the temporary plate, the two materials would effectively merge, becoming a single, albeit still stressed, piece of metal. "I think four should do it," Jordan said.

Aryana pulled the first from its slot and carried the unwieldy plate aft to the shield's edge. Jordan made his way past her and stood just inside the shadow. "You ready?" he asked.

She grunted and carefully mag-walked around the shield into the dim starlight. Jordan followed a moment later, careful not to crowd her or let her get too far away. Magnetic boots and gloves rarely failed, but when they did, someone needed to be around to help. Buddy system. Rule of the company and the most important rule of the ship.

He looked past the hull and out into space, where a brilliant blue nebula hung on the horizon like an abstract, translucent mural. Jordan was struck with wonder at first, and then his lizard brain reminded him that he was standing outside the shield on a hull with debris in the area. That was enough to snap him out of it.

Aryana held the first patch in place while Jordan activated the torch and heated the metal. A moment later, the plate seated and bonded with the steel. Aryana pulled the scanner from her belt and ran it over the patch. "Secure," she said.

"Okay," Jordan said as he turned, "three more to go."

Thirty minutes later, they had all four patches installed and seated. The shield looked as though it had been partially cleaned and sanded while the discolored portions were scarred and pockmarked.

"That's ugly," Aryana said.

Jordan nodded in agreement. "Yes, yes, it is."

As he turned to get back under the shield, something whizzed by his head and into the darkness. His brain froze for an instant. While he couldn't possibly hear its movement through space, his imagination conjured the sound of a ricocheting fléchette.

When his mind shrugged free from the fear, he moved as quickly as he could behind the shield while his skin thrummed with electricity, and his heart threatened to leap out of his rib cage.

Once safely in the shield's shadow and meters away from the disc's edge, he stood still and did his best to calm himself down.

Aryana appeared from around the corner and slowly walked to join him.

"That was close," she said, sounding more excited than afraid.

Jordan tried to speak, but his voice was indiscernible, even to himself. After clearing his throat and somewhat sure his voice wouldn't quiver, he said, "Yes. It was."

Aryana closed the patch rack and stood to face him. "We done here, boss?"

"We are," he said. "Cap? We're done."

Til responded immediately. "Didn't know we were a low-rent scrap heap."

Jordan rolled his eyes. "You haven't seen the rest of the hull."

Til laughed. "Get inside."

"Copy," Jordan said and gestured to the airlock. "Beauty before age."

"Got that right," she said and walked to the airlock.

Jordan turned in place and let his eyes take in the portion of the nebula he could see. God, it was beautiful. He'd have to go over the ship's video logs and find all the records with that image. It was too damned gorgeous to be forgotten.

# CHAPTER TWO

The Captain's meeting, held nightly after dinner, usually included friendly banter, jokes, and the occasional stern warning about something Til didn't think was up to snuff. He did his best to keep the meetings short, and while Jordan certainly appreciated that, even Til could be long-winded.

The Command meeting, on the other hand, the meeting in which the three section officers got together to discuss things? This meeting always went long.

Jihi, the leader of the mining team, sat with a cup of hot tea in her thermal mug, eyes glittering. Jordan guessed she had seen the full report from the prospecting satellite. Judging by the look on her face and from experience, he knew she was excited about something.

"Heard you had a close one," Jihi said to Jordan, the pair of them still waiting for Til to show up.

Jordan harrumphed. "Close enough."

"Can't tell you how much the idea of hanging off the hull of a traveling starship scares the shit out of me," she said quietly.

Jihi, the terror of the miners, afraid of a little space walk? He'd watched her stand tall in the face of a collapsing tunnel, confident the structure above her would hold. He had thought she was fearless. Was good to know she was human after all.

"Was just the shield, luckily," he said. "Aren't too many places on this ship where you don't have some protection out there. But percentages are percentages. Sooner or later, you're going to get one in your face."

She nodded, blew a cloud of steam from the top of the mug, and took a sip. "Kind of like mines, I guess," she said.

"Yeah," Jordan nodded. "Kind of like mines."

"Sooner or later," Jihi said, "you get unlucky. And sometimes, you just fuck up the easiest, safest thing in the world and"—she snapped her fingers—"it's over."

"What's over?" Til asked as he walked into the room and leaned against the bulkhead, looking bored and sleepy. The man had another two hours on his shift, as did Jihi and Jordan. In truth, though, the trio were always on shift, at least until the mining got underway in earnest.

Jordan rubbed his hands together. It was cold in the captain's room. Til liked it that way.

Jihi shrugged. "Just talking about fate and chance."

Til cocked an eyebrow. "Two words I don't like."

"Got that right," Jordan said.

Til picked at his thumb with his index finger, something Jordan had seen him do more and more lately. "What did *Prospector* have to say?"

"That we hit fucking pay dirt," Jihi flashed a toothy grin. She tapped a few icons on the table's holo interface, and the display came to life. A map of the star system quickly appeared and hung in the air like a specter.

She tapped the interface, and three large objects appeared on the screen. "These are the ice giants we passed by on our way in. They left quite a bit of a mess in their wake, dozens or hundreds of unremarkable moons, and not much else.

"However," she said—and the interface panned farther in system until it showed three round objects—"*Prospector* found these beauties."

Jihi touched the interface, and the first of the objects filled the screen. The object's image had a slight blur to it.

"This is the first of MacReady's brethren. It's roughly the same size as MacReady, but it's currently spinning so fast that it would be impossible to land on, much less mine."

"It'll make my head spin?" Jordan asked dryly.

Jihi glared at him, but Til snickered.

"Anyway," Jihi continued, "*Prospector's* readings estimate a ninety percent chance that this twirling dervish of rock has the same general makeup as MacReady. Which means it has the same potential amount of riches."

"They're just unreachable," Til said.

Jihi nodded. "Unless you have a way to mine in 40Gs or slow down a large moon, they might as well not exist."

"And the second one?" Til asked.

"The second," Jihi said—and the holodisplay changed to show another moon nearly identical to the first but without the spin—"is also estimated to be about ninety percent of the same minerals and metals as MacReady."

"Let me guess," Jordan said, "this one has aliens?"

"Might as well," Jihi said. "The moon is one giant ball of radiation. I don't know what caused it, but it would fry your suit if you came within five thousand kilometers."

That made Jordan sit up in his chair. "What the hell could cause that?"

Jihi shrugged. "I'm a geologist who mines shit. Unless the entire moon is made of a radioactive metal, I don't have a fucking clue how that kind of radiation happens. I only know it's bad news."

"That's putting it mildly," Til said. "So that one's out."

"Right," Jihi said. "*Prospector* couldn't even send a pod there—the rads would have killed it long before it could have landed, let alone explore."

He hadn't ever heard of something that radioactive. Not a whole goddamned celestial body. Portions? Sure. That happened all the time, even to ships. But for an entire moon? The idea made no sense.

"And now we're on to MacReady," Til said.

Jihi's grin reappeared and made Jordan smile. The holodisplay flickered, and a moon looking much like the first two filled the screen. It rotated slightly, and four arrows with labels appeared, with two of them blinking.

"This is MacReady. One-third of a G, temperature and pressure well within the tolerances of our mining suits, and holy shit, is it loaded." The display zoomed in on the first arrow, which became a snapshot of terrain.

"Wow," Til said. "That's a nice mountain."

"The technical term is 'bluff.' We have one cliff wall here, which is where *Prospector* first discovered proof of the metals."

The image darkened, and lines of text appeared.

"Tungsten, tungsten alloy, titanium, titanium alloys, and"—Til paused—"holy shit, iridium?"

Jihi rapped her knuckles on the table. "That's just what's at the surface. No telling what's inside."

"Inside?" Jordan asked.

"Inside," Jihi said emphatically. The display changed again, and the rock rising from the surface turned translucent, thick lines of gray and silver threading through the shape. "Those veins are at least several meters thick at nearly all portions returned from the sonic scans."

"Um, that's a lot of ore," Jordan said, trying to imagine just how long it would take them to level a mountain. Sorry, bluff.

Jihi flashed her manic smile again. "More than I've ever seen in one place. If it's as rich as Prospector thinks it is, we might be heading back home with a galactic fortune."

Til rolled his eyes. "You're assuming it's easy to refine."

"I am," Jihi said, "but I'm the one that's supposed to dream big."

"Uh-huh," Jordan said. "And I'm the one that has to figure out thrust-to-mass ratios." She mock glared at him before sticking out her tongue. Jordan smiled.

"So, is that spot where you want to drop?" Til asked. "Right at the base there?"

Jihi slid her fingers across the interface, and a new diagram appeared. "We drop the orbital line here, half a kilometer from the site. That will give us enough room to maneuver and keep things close to the ore."

Jordan whistled. "That's a bit too close, isn't it?"

"Why?" Til and Jihi asked at the same time.

"Um, because of safety margins?" Jordan said. "If we have a problem with the orbital, get a failure of some kind, or get a swing when we're sending shit down, we—"

Til frowned. "A swing? What are you talking about?"

"Ah, the swing," Jihi said and stared at Jordan, a sneer on her lips. "You ever seen 'the swing?' Or is it just some kind of nightmare engineers swap when they've had too much to smoke, vape, shoot, or drink?"

Jordan remained smiling, but his eyes hardened. "The swing, Cap," he said without breaking his stare with Jihi, "is what happens when we drop a platform connected to an orbital and get unexpected wind shears, other atmospheric phenomena, or just plain old gravity that causes the line to swing."

"And have you ever seen it happen?" Jihi asked.

Jordan ground his teeth. "Not personally, no."

Til looked confused. "Why would this be a problem at MacReady if I've never even heard of it before?"

Jordan took a deep breath doing his best to remember Til hadn't been on too many of these. "Does *Prospector* have the sensors to determine gravitational flux? Do we have enough information regarding MacReady's orbit? Do we know if there's something else we don't know?"

"Fuck's sake," Jihi muttered. "Exactly how do you expect to recover if a line snaps?"

"I don't," Jordan said. "But if a line snaps and whatever's on the crawler gets fucked, so be it. If that line, however, pulls on the *Kirkland*, we're all fucked."

Jihi and Til exchanged a look. Til cleared his throat and stared back at the holodisplay.

"Just something to keep in mind," Jordan said softly.

"What distance would make you happier?" Til asked.

"Three quarters to a full klick."

Jihi sighed. "Fine. I'll give you a kilometer, okay?"

"Thank you," Jordan said. "I'm not trying to be a pain in the ass, but—"

"But you are one," Jihi said. "Even when you're probably right."

Til grinned. "So that's settled, I guess. We've got two more days of travel to get to MacReady. *9C512* has been running in low-power mode since its QE blast, so it's only been passively scanning," Til said. "We still have to go through the astronomical observations tomorrow and build up a threat analysis. But as far as the find itself goes, I think we're in business."

"Excellent," Jihi said.

Til nodded to her. "Do we have any information on the pod bots?"

"Last known positions," she said. "The pods ran out of juice quite a while ago. In case you hadn't noticed, there's not a lot of starlight out here."

"Speaking of," Jordan said, "how dark is it?"

"Dark twilight. Another reason I want to use that cliff face is that it's constantly facing the star," Jihi said. "It'll be about as warm as it's going to get. The other sites are either in complete shadow and receive no light at all, or are closer to those areas than I'd like."

Til brushed something off his jumpsuit. Probably a crumb.

"So this site is both rich and convenient?" the captain asked. "Why do I get the feeling there's a 'but' coming?"

She shook her head. "No 'but' coming, Cap. We can drop the platform and begin setting up for the first horizontal shaft."

Til glanced at Jordan. "What do you think?"

Jordan leaned back in his chair and clasped his hands behind his neck. "Sounds too good to be true. But," he said, "unless the astronomical data shows us something to be worried about, I don't think there's really anything else to do."

The captain turned to Jihi. "Can we get *Prospector* to fire another pod?"

"We can," she said. "It probably has more than enough power to handle that. Why?"

Til scratched at his stubble. Unlike Jordan, the man didn't seem to like a beard, yet he was hardly ever clean-shaven. Jordan still couldn't figure out how he did it.

"It's been a while," Til said. "I'd like to make sure I don't send you down into a rad trap or something else."

Jihi chuckled. "*Prospector's* been taking images, Cap. We'd know if something had changed."

"Humor me," Til said. "Just this once?"

"Okay, fine," Jihi said with a smile. "I can have that done tomorrow morning. Any specifics?"

Til looked confused. "Specifics?"

"Yes, as in, is there anything you want Prospector to look for?" Jihi asked.

"Oh." Til pointed at the map of the bluff. "I want a recon of the drop area and as much information as we can get about the surroundings."

"Okay," she said. "Full kilometer radius?"

"Make it two," Jordan said.

The pair looked at him.

"Two full klicks?" she asked and held his eyes for a moment. Hers softened, and she nodded to herself. "Two it is."

"Thank you," Jordan said softly.

Til yawned and nearly failed to cover his mouth. "Sorry," he said. "Getting to be about that time. We've got two days before we reach orbit with MacReady. Since we're not near any celestials at the moment, I suggest we knock off early tonight."

"Thank the stars," Jordan said.

Til smiled. "And our head of engineering needs to recover from nearly being decapitated."

Jordan raised a middle finger and waggled it at Til, but smiled as he did it.

The captain growled, "Get out of my ready room."

Jihi and Jordan both stood, each saluting with a snap of their heels.

Til pointed at the exit. "Rest!" he yelled.

Laughing, Jihi and Jordan left the ready room and headed into the main corridor.

"You seem a little on edge," Jihi said as they walked, their mag boots clopping on the steel deck. "Something I need to know?"

"No," Jordan said. "It's just that, well, we usually have to scratch and claw for every cubic meter of ore. This is, well, unprecedented. Isn't it?"

She shrugged as they neared the personnel module. "I don't know about that. Every once in a while, someone comes across a mega find, like a massive ball of rare metals or minerals. And sometimes you come across a major vein that just seems as though it will never play out."

This was Jordan's seventh mining tour, and he'd yet to see anything like what MacReady promised. The universe didn't hand you that kind of gift without a price.

Jihi continued through the module intersection, Jordan on her heels. She took a right at the first hatch and entered the galley, probably to refresh her tea. Jordan followed in her wake, suddenly wondering if those were butterflies in his stomach or if he was just hungry.

Sure enough, she headed to the dispenser. Jordan decided he wasn't hungry but needed something of his own, something sugary that would lead him to a serious crash and help him sleep. He chose a fruit-flavored pouch from the cabinet and stuffed it into his jumpsuit for later.

"Is that what's got you spooked?" Jihi asked as she poured fresh hot water into her cup. "That it's too easy?"

Jordan crossed his arms. "Three," he said softly and suddenly knew why he was so disquieted. "Three."

"Three?" Jihi asked as she replaced the lid on her mug. "Three what?"

"Three MacReadys," Jordan said.

Jihi turned to stare at him, a question on her lips.

"Three moons," Jordan said, "one spinning like a top, one so radioactive it practically glows, and another that is a miner's erotic fantasy?"

"Erotic fantasy?" Jihi laughed. "I'm into rocks and money but not quite like that."

"You know what I mean," Jordan said. "Why are there three of them? And why are the other two the way they are?"

"Well," Jihi said, "I'll grant you it's odd. But it's not like they're completely identical. Just quite similar."

"But how does that happen?" Jordan asked. "Accretion? Something shattered because of weird gravity or something like that and formed three balls of rock and ore?"

Jihi sighed and blew away a curl of steam that had drifted from the lid's opening. "I don't know, Jordan. I'm not an astrophysicist. Maybe we'll know more when Chu gets a chance to finish analyzing the astronomical data, which he should finish first thing in the morning."

*Should have had it done today,* Jordan thought, but didn't say. He knew that wasn't exactly fair. The first day after waking up from stasis, all you wanted to do, ironically, was sleep. Real sleep. The kind where you toss and turn and dream and, well, feel human. Struggling through a single shift was difficult enough, but doing it while having to bring the rest of the ship online, repair the usual wear and tear that happened during stellar travel, and try to figure out what the fuck you were doing here? You just couldn't get everything done in ten hours.

Tomorrow would be different. No excuses. Everything balls to the wall until they finally dropped the orbital and sent down the platform. Once it touched down and secured, they could take a day off before beginning the week's first exploratory shaft. Which, if Jihi and *9C512* were correct about, would become their main shaft and the path to a hell of a bounty.

"Fair enough," Jordan finally said.

Jihi took a few steps toward him, her eyes looking up into his. This was his third time out with Jihi, and he knew her a little too well. This was her "don't worry" look. She still hadn't figured out he was immune to it.

"I promise to be cautious," she said, "if you'll promise to be a little open-minded."

"Okay," Jordan said. "I'll try not to piss all over everything."

"I'd appreciate that," she said. "Not one of my fetishes."

He laughed at that. "Time to rack?"

"Time to rack," she said and headed for the hatch.

Jordan followed her out of the galley and to the cabins. He hoped sleep would bring up the rear.

# CHAPTER THREE

A mining ship is a massive beast of a thing. Although it doesn't have anything to do with actual mining, it carries enough equipment to set up automated mining facilities, staff miners on the surface of any celestial body, and, most importantly to the company, store refined ore before heading home.

With only two engineers on board, Jordan and Aryana were on the hook for everything from engine malfunctions to clearing stopped-up septic systems. Fortunately, there were only ten other human beings on board, and two of those were the captain and copilot. Eight roughneck miners couldn't possibly fuck shit up that easily.

Fortunately, they didn't and hadn't. Jihi's crews were always filled with relatively bright, dependable people. She never ended up with the juice chasers or the slackers that constantly complained. She chose the best people, lobbied for good pay, and treated her team right. These miners didn't know how lucky they had it. Or maybe they did.

Jordan and Aryana spent their morning shift dealing with a few shorts, a broken junction box, and a CPU that had lost its mind and gone into some kind of infinite loop. When resetting the damned thing hadn't worked, he'd ended up tossing it into the recycler and grabbing a replacement from the supply cabinets.

That finished, several systems that had reported minor malfunctions all went green. Aryana had looked pleased with herself—she'd said that would happen. Jordan ended up having to grudgingly admit she'd been right. Her being right was happening more and more. Maybe soon she'd be ready to be chief engineer on her own ship.

Ah, to be young again and only on your second tour. She still had dreams of striking it rich and retiring before thirty and before a third or fourth tour became necessary.

The pair spent the afternoon checking the equipment and mining bays, tightening restraints that had loosened during the flight, and running status checks on the mining gear itself. They'd found two inoperable pieces of equipment out of the hundreds checked that had most likely been dead before they'd been loaded back at Proxima. Jordan and Aryana recycled both and printed new ones. After another round of tests, Jordan pronounced it quitting time.

"Good thing," Aryana said. "I'm hungry. Oh, and it's quitting time anyway, you tease."

He blinked at her before checking his comms band. Sure enough.

"Oh, for a whiskey," he said.

"Come on, boss," she said and headed past the raw ore refining unit that stood nearly ten meters tall and with the same width and length. The massive cube could process dozens of metric tonnes of ore per day, separating the gabbro, or rock, from the desired minerals and metals.

Jordan glanced back to the other refining units, the ones that didn't travel down to the site. Those massive bastards were for printing the metal into stackable slats or cubes, depending on the metal and its quantity.

If the find was as rich as Jihi claimed, those units would be running round the clock, so to speak. Each trip up the elevator would bring more and more ore to the hungry refineries. He wasn't looking forward to the next six months and the constant wear and tear on the elevator, the orbital lines, and whatever mining equipment malfunctioned or just plain broke.

Then again, being busy was better than being back home in a shitty apartment in a shitty block of a shitty dome. At least out here, he didn't have to worry about the next rise in the price of air or food.

"You coming?" Aryana yelled at him from the lift.

Sighing, Jordan quickened his pace, his mag-boots clopping on the steel deck. When he reached the lift, Aryana was waiting, a finger hovering over the interface.

"Something wrong back there?" she asked and activated the lift.

It jerked slightly before ascending, his mag boots holding him in place. The lack of gravity made the lift seem superfluous, but the mining bay, like the personnel bay, was capable of providing 1/3 G, and you couldn't exactly float in that. Besides, there was so much equipment in the bay, some of it rising nearly to the ceiling, that maneuvering could be hazardous. The company didn't care for anything considered hazardous. More importantly, Til didn't either.

"Not really," he said. "Just thinking about what we have to do this week. We're going to be busy."

Aryana's hands clasped together, and her fingers flexed to some beat only she could hear. "At least we don't have to worry about weather," she said. "MacReady doesn't have much of an atmosphere."

"Hardly any," he agreed. "It is going to be dark, though."

She giggled, and said, "It's dark just outside that bulkhead. Very dark."

Jordan nodded sagely. "Yup. And on MacReady, it'll be even darker in the shade."

She didn't seem to like that. "Is MacReady mountainous?"

"Not really," Jordan said. "From what I've seen, it might have low hills and bluffs, maybe a max height of 200 meters, but nothing spectacular. Just a boring rock made of profitable materials."

"Profitable," Aryana said dreamily, her eyes staring upward at the ceiling as if in awe. "Profits!" She sounded like a lunatic.

Jordan couldn't help smiling. "Yes, profits. The whole reason we're out here."

The lift reached its terminus with a slight bump, and the door slid aside. Aryana quickly walked out and to the left while Jordan slowly stepped forward to peer over the catwalk.

Billions and billions worth of credits sat on the deck, the massive metal structures true marvels of technology. Jordan loved this view of everything clean and in its place. It wouldn't last much longer. In another day or two, his neat, clean mining bay would become slathered in dust, flecks of metal and minerals, and who knew what else.

He heard the sound of Aryana's steps behind him.

"You having a stroke or something?" she asked.

Sighing, he turned and glared. "Can't you just give me a moment to enjoy the majesty of all that shit below us?"

She cocked an eyebrow. "'Majesty of shit,'" she repeated. "What planet does the Majesty of Shit rule?"

"Crapper. In the Dung Nebula."

Aryana joined him at the edge of the catwalk and looked over. He half expected her to just give it a glance, but she was slow and deliberate. Finally, she said, "Okay, I get it," and met his eyes. "Haven't you seen that so many times that you're over it?"

He shook his head. "No. Just—" Feeling like an ass, he said, "Just think of how many people spent their lives, how many credits, how much time it took to invent, engineer, and produce all those tons of machinery. Then consider the trial and error of it all, the failures, the miners and fuelers who died while the companies perfected their gear."

Aryana fixed her gaze back on the equipment. "Well, if you're going to put it like that," she said softly, "I guess it is something."

"Just like this ship, our suits, everything we use. All built by people who came before us and will continue on after us."

"Jesus, you need a drink," Aryana said. "Or to get laid."

"I'm hungry," he said. "Dinner?"

"Dinner," Aryana said. "Assuming you don't get called in for a private briefing."

"Does that bother you?" Jordan asked as they left the catwalk. "That I'm privy to more than a few things than you are?"

She shrugged. "Can't learn if I can't be involved."

"You know," he said, "you sound an awful lot like I did at your age."

"Is that a good thing?"

He said in a conspiratorial tone, "Absolutely not. You should never get caught doing any of the things I teach you to do."

Aryana giggled and said, "Why does every mentor tell me that?"

"Because it's sometimes true," he said.

They continued walking in companionable silence, the sound of the life support systems and the clomp of their mag-boots the only other noises in the large corridor. For a moment, that was.

When they reached the junction, raucous laughter punctured the quiet, and Aryana looked knowingly at Jordan. "Jihi's minions are up to no good."

"When are they not?" he asked.

He followed Aryana past the junction and into the personnel module, where the noise ratcheted up considerably. The pair stepped inside the galley where Jihi's miners sat around the table with their boss standing at the front. The miners were mostly smiling, although he noticed one of them, Shelia—he thought that was what her name was—looked annoyed.

"Ah," Jihi said, noticing Aryana and Jordan, "our engineers have arrived."

The miners waved, some half-heartedly, but they mostly seemed genuine.

Aryana blushed and walked to the drinks counter, one hand running through her short hair. Jordan thought she was blushing but couldn't be sure.

"All right, people," Jihi said. "Let's eat."

The table growled as one with hunger and left their seats. Jordan walked to Jihi as she turned off the holodisplay that had been filled with a duty and assignment roster.

"Getting everyone ready for the crazy?" Jordan asked.

Jihi beamed and said, "They're always ready for the crazy. Now they're just more informed."

"Speaking of informed, where's—"

"Oh, Til told me we'd be eating without him and Chu."

"That doesn't sound good," Jordan said.

She shrugged. "Chu ran through the astronomy data. Wasn't good."

Jordan's skin prickled. "What does that mean?"

"I believe he's planning on discussing that at the command meeting," she said. "But the short of it is that there's a nasty belt of debris between us and MacReady."

"And we just fixed a shield," Jordan groaned.

Jihi's amused smile faded into something a little more serious. "My people are all certified to go outdoors and help, if need be."

"I know," Jordan said. "Do we know how large the pieces of flotsam are?"

"Some as large as cars, others the size of pebbles."

He tried to imagine the ship punching its way through what appeared to be a cloud of dust only to discover it hid chunks of rock and metal that could perforate the hull like a fléchette through confection glass.

"We'll have to depressurize the ship," Jordan said. "Just in case."

"Agreed," Jihi said. "Although that means—"

Jordan said with a waggle of his eyebrows, "That your team will have to help clean up first."

Jihi sighed. "Well, the damned ship hasn't done anything yet. It should be clean."

"It is," Jordan said. "But regs are regs."

She stuck her tongue out at him, and he reached for it with his forefinger and thumb. Her tongue flicked back into her mouth, and she glared at him before smiling again.

"I've got it," she said. "We'll help out with whatever you need."

"Good. You going to eat?"

"Yes," she said and gestured to the miners crowding the dispensers. "Just figured I'd wait for the mob to die down."

"Good plan."

Aryana and one of the miners were laughing together, the others grinning. Jordan didn't know what the joke was, but it must have been a good one.

"Does that woman ever not make friends?" Jihi asked in disbelief.

Jordan smirked. "Not that I'm aware of. Then again, we haven't exactly spent all of our off time together. Still, she does seem to have a talent."

"That reminds me," Jihi said. "You decided which of you is coming down with us?"

"No," Jordan said. "I haven't."

Jihi nodded. "You haven't decided because you're afraid to tell her no."

"Shit," Jordan said, "I'm more afraid to say yes."

"Uh-huh," Jihi said. "And what are you afraid of?"

"I nearly got my head taken off yesterday, and you wonder why I want to be cautious?"

"Well," Jihi said, "when you put it that way, you sound downright rational. But you do know that if not this tour, next tour, she'll have to come down with the mining team for setup and supervision."

"Babysitting," Jordan sneered.

Jihi punched him in the arm, and he mock winced. "Miner-sitting. How many times do I have to tell you that?"

The indignant look on her face was more than enough to get him to laugh. "Miner-sitting. Right."

"Seriously, though," Jihi said, "it's up to you. I'm just saying I have no problem with it."

He had been fighting the urge to tell her to mind her own damned business, but that had dissipated.

"Thank you," Jordan said. "However, I honestly haven't decided. Maybe I will after we meet with Cap."

"Fair enough," she said. "My equipment good to go?"

"Of course," Jordan said, glad for the change of subject. "Found a couple of problems, but we recycled, reprinted, or replaced faulty components. Everything else checked out fine."

Jihi clapped her hands together and bowed her head. "Thank you, oh quartermaster gods, for actually doing your jobs."

Jordan rolled his eyes. "We're not on the ground yet, Jihi. It's a little early to invoke idols and deities."

"But," she said and pointed at the emptying vending area, "it's not too early for dinner."

# CHAPTER FOUR

The Captain's meeting was just the three of them again. Til had been waiting in the ready room this time, barely acknowledging Jordan and Jihi when they entered. Instead, Til continued staring at the 3D map floating before him. He finally nodded to himself and drawled, "Take a seat."

Jordan and Jihi headed to their usual places at the table. The moment the pair had finished settling themselves, the model faded into near transparency.

"And how was everyone's first full day?" Til asked. "Jordan?"

"Engineering cleared, mining equipment cleared, faulty components recycled, reprinted, or—"

"Replaced," Til finished for him. "In other words—"

"All is well," Jordan said, cutting him off.

Til smirked before flicking his eyes to Jihi. "I know most of your status already."

"Most," she agreed. "We ran our drills today, examined the films of the sites, and finalized our drop plan. You should have it in your inboxes by now."

"I do," Til said. He gestured to Jordan. "You'll take a look?"

"Of course, Cap," Jordan said.

"Good. Anything out of the ordinary?"

"No, Cap," Jihi and Jordan said simultaneously.

Til gazed from one to the other. "I know you two are completely incompatible, but you'd make a great couple."

"Well, she did stick her tongue out at me earlier," Jordan said.

Jihi crossed her arms. "I was not coming on to you."

"I don't know, Cap. Seemed inappropriate, if you ask me," Jordan said.

"Inappropriate?" Jihi screeched. "Sir? Do you know he slurps his food? Slurps! Like a four-year-old! He——"

Chuckling, Til held up a hand. "You made your point. If you two kids are done, maybe we can talk about the bad news."

"Wait." Jordan looked at Jihi. "Did I miss the good news?"

"Oh," Til said. "The good news. Right. The good news is that the ship's in good shape, *Prospector* is doing its thing, and we're getting good intel on the site. I think the drop-plan is sound."

"Ever feel like a 'but' is coming?" Jihi asked Jordan.

"But," Til said, "the bad news is what's between us and MacReady."

"Debris field?" Jordan asked.

"Big one," Til said. "*Prospector's* records indicate objects ranging in size from particulates to multiple cubic meters."

"Gabbro?" Jordan asked.

"And metal," Til said. "Lots and lots of metal."

Jihi frowned and tented her hands on the table. "What's the concentration?"

Til touched the interface, and the model's transparency solidified into mere translucence. A cloud of dust and debris appeared in the air, three large objects some distance away. Textures blinked from mere monochrome shades to brilliant color, including artificial light glinting off flecks of metal.

"Metal concentration is at about 20 percent," Til said. "Most of the debris is fairly small, but there are a few large ones out there. Chu and the ship's computer are working out the best trajectory, but our fallback plan, should we not be able to find a better way, is to go around the cloud."

"Around?" Jihi asked. "Isn't that going to——"

"Take time?" Til finished for her. "Yes. Several days, in fact. We'd have to have a hard burn for at least one minute followed by an acceleration, followed by course corrections, and then accelerating again just to get near MacReady."

"Shit," Jordan said. "That'll add like a week."

"A week?" Jihi asked.

Til shrugged. "Probably more, actually. We might need to consider putting everyone back on ice."

"Fuck," Jihi said and slapped her hand on the table. "There's got to be a way."

"If there is," Til said, "Chu will find it."

"If we do go through," Jordan said, "Jihi has offered the use of her miners for emergency maintenance."

Til nodded to her. "Thank you. I'm sure they will be pleased."

"My problem," Jihi said. "Besides, if it means they get their asses on the ground and can start drilling, they'll be happy to do it."

"Well, there is that," Til said with a grin. "Now…" He touched the interface, and the debris belt disappeared, replaced by four new windows. Each had a view of a dark, rocky surface. Portions of the pictures were utterly black rather than merely clothed in shadow. "What do we think about this?"

Jordan studied the pictures, letting his eyes relax. He knew from experience that when Til asked a question like that, there was something there you were supposed to see. Best way to see what you normally wouldn't see? Unfocus. Drift.

He sat upright in his chair and pointed at the top image. "There. That."

His finger hovered over a section of rock that had several long, sharp lines cut through it. Almost like fork tines scratching butter.

"That's one," Til said.

"What the fuck," Jihi leaned forward.

Jordan moved to the next and immediately found what he was looking for. "And there. Only those are vertical."

Til grinned. "You know, it took the computers hours to find that shit, and you more or less immediately saw it."

"What do the computers think it is?" Jihi asked.

"Impact points," he said, straight-faced. He snorted a second later. "I think the ship's computer is having a bad day."

Jordan shook his head. "No, I think the computer just confused you."

"What do you mean?" Til asked.

"Or rather, confused itself," Jordan finished, eyes still focused on the tine marks. He found them in the third and fourth pictures as well. In each case, the lines had a different orientation. "They are impact points, but that"—Jordan swallowed hard—"that looks like something a tool would have made."

"No one's ever been here," Jihi said.

Jordan glanced over at her. "That we know of." The room went silent for a moment, making Jordan feel more than just a little anxious.

"Jihi? Could those be natural?" Til asked.

She thought for a moment. "I don't see how," she whispered. "Were those the only four the new probe found?"

"Yup," Til said. "But that doesn't mean there aren't others."

"What about thermal?" Jordan asked. "Has *Prospector* found any heat sources?"

"No," Til said. "Apart from the usual background radiation and an occasional spike assumed to be from cosmic rays, or drift from MacReady's radioactive triplet, that is."

That made Jordan feel a little better but not much. His brain was still trying to put together a scenario in which the tines were the result of a natural phenomenon. He wasn't able to find one.

*Need to stop looking at it,* he thought. *Unfocus. It'll come.*

"No life signs, no heat sources," Jihi said. "No aliens."

The word sent a shiver down Jordan's spine. Humankind had been traveling the stars for thousands of years and had yet to find a single instance of life beyond that which had hitched a ride on a starship.

Still, discovering alien life, as far as Jordan was concerned, was simply an inevitability. In a nearly infinite universe, improbable was nearly the same as saying something was a certainty. Time was the only variable.

"What about the site?" Jihi asked. "Any markings near it?"

"Not near, no," Til said. "Closest one was a quarter klick away."

Jordan considered that for a moment. The miners would be down on the surface for their two-week-long shifts and ultimately get back in the lift to travel back to the ship. One engineer always supervised the mining team. It didn't leave a lot of room for redundancy.

"Jordan?" Til asked.

Jordan jerked his head to stare at him, a question on his lips.

"You, um, seemed to fade out on me there," Til said.

"Sorry," Jordan said. "Was just thinking. Can we have some bots on the ground?"

"We always have bots on the ground," Jihi said.

"No," Jordan said, "I mean stationary bots or patrol bots. Something like that."

Til crossed his arms and took a slow, deep breath. "Okay. Explain it to me like I'm a stupid captain."

"What I mean," Jordan said, "is that we construct a virtual perimeter. We repurpose a few of the backup bots to serve as a kind of warning system. That way if something unexpected happens, we might have a jump on it before it becomes a problem."

"You worried about aliens?" Jihi asked.

Jordan shook his head, although it was a bit of a lie. "I'm just being cautious."

"Okay," Til said. "Fuck it. Let's do it."

Jihi sighed heavily and narrowed her eyes at Jordan. "Okay. We'll do it."

Jordan smiled. "Thank you."

"Now," Til said, "I want to see emergency plans from the both of you on shielding maintenance and repair. Just in case. Run the drills."

"Aye aye," Jordan and Jihi said simultaneously.

"Can I get that from you first thing tomorrow morning?"

"Yes, Cap," Jordan said. "I already have everything—"

"I know you do," Til said. "That remark was directed more at Jihi."

"Oh," Jordan said.

"You'll have it, Cap," Jihi said. "Already drew up the outline and a few details once you said we had a debris belt."

"I figured," Til said.

"You ever seen one like this?" Jordan asked.

"Debris field?" Til rubbed at his beard. "Yes. But it wasn't this thick. This is just different."

"What do you think caused it?" Jihi asked.

"Well," Til said, "could have been an asteroid collision or something like that." He touched the interface, and the view zoomed out to show the debris cloud as well as a top view of MacReady and its brethren. "This one that's spinning? Something had to hit it to make it spin like that. You combine that with the cloud of debris? I think it's pretty easy to see what caused it."

"Maybe for you," Jihi said. "If it was hit hard enough to make it spin, why didn't it simply shatter?"

"Don't know," Til said. "I also don't know why we don't have a huge chunk of rock out here responsible for it. Can't imagine something that massive just disappearing back out into space."

"Well," Jordan said, "we haven't exactly done an exhaustive survey of the system."

"True," Til said. "And why would we? We normally don't come across shit like this."

Til was right about that. During his tours, Jordan had survived a few shipboard incidents here and there and had seen his share of planets, moons, nebulae, comets, and the like. But in all that time, he'd never even heard of something like this, let alone seen it for himself.

"I'm sure the eggheads back home will have an answer," Til said.

Jihi harrumphed. "When we finally have a QE message to send. And then they'll just want more information. We could be here a full year, and I doubt we'd have the answer before it was time to pack up. Shit, we might not even have an answer until we're back in the coffins or step out of them."

"Thought I was the cynical, pessimistic one," Jordan muttered.

Her eyes flicked to him, and her passionate, indignant facial expression immediately melted into amusement. "You are. So I imagine you're saying worse in your head."

"No," Jordan said. "You're probably right about everything you just said. However"—he leaned forward and hovered his index finger directly over MacReady—"once we get here, it won't matter."

Jihi leaned back in her chair and crossed her arms. "That's the most positive thing I've ever heard you say."

"Okay, okay," Til grinned. "So Chu and I will have our decision for you next shift on how we're going to do this."

"Don't want to go back into stasis again," Jihi said. "Just don't."

"I know," Til said. "Believe me—no one likes coming out of stasis. The puking, the soreness, the ache in every soft part of your body? That's a constant. I don't want to go back in, either, so let's just hope we find a way through. Okay?"

She and Jordan nodded.

"Anything else?" Til asked.

Jordan couldn't think of anything. Jihi couldn't either.

Til dismissed them and headed back to the cockpit, presumably to join Chu or maybe bring him something to eat or drink. Jihi and Jordan walked back to the personnel module in uneasy silence.

As they approached the galley, she said, "What do you think our chances are?"

"Of what?" Jordan asked.

"Of going through the debris cloud?"

Jordan shrugged and said, "Probably better than sixty/forty. Worse comes to worst, I guess we can bash our way through. The front shields are much more durable than the lateral and dorsal."

"Hope you're right," she yawned. "I'm getting another shot of tea before I retire."

"Retire?" Jordan asked. "You suddenly get Victorian on me?"

"You been reading bodice rippers again?" Jihi asked with a smirk.

Jordan blushed. "If I said no, would you believe me?"

"Not a chance," Jihi giggled. "Get out of here."

He waved and left the galley, heading to his cabin. Next shift was going to be a brutal one. Especially if Cap found a way through the flotsam.

# CHAPTER FIVE

With the ship depressurized and everyone wearing an EVA suit, Jordan felt as though he were conducting a training exercise. Except for scheduled radio check-ins, there was no discussion over the public channels. Over the private channels? He doubted anyone was being quiet.

Cap and Chu were in the cockpit together, a rare occurrence during shifts, but considering what the *Kirkland* was about to go through, it was simple common sense. Jordan knew Til trusted Chu more than the astrogation computer, at least for the in-system portions of the journey.

Still, Jordan was just outside the engine compartment, clinging to the port bulkhead like a magnetic limpet. On the other side? Aryana. Strewn across the ship were the other miners, an equal number on either side, each armed with patches and torches.

Jordan's suit had him piped in directly to the *Kirkland*'s damage control systems and engine statuses. Aryana no doubt had the same interfaces on her HUD.

"How you holding up?" he asked her over their private channel.

Aryana's normal bravado seemed completely absent. For the first time he could remember, Jordan thought he actually detected fear in her voice. "Is that a pun? If so, it's not a good one."

Jordan blinked then realized what he'd said. "Oh. You're holding up on the bulkhead. Got it. Um, I'm not bright enough to make puns."

"Whatever," Aryana said. "I think the best ones are accidental anyway."

Til's voice broke over all channels. "Crew, two minutes to the burn. I repeat, two minutes."

The moment Til finished speaking, a sensor tripped multiple times. The front shield had taken several hits, although they appeared to be from particulates. Nothing to worry about.

One of the starboard shields announced impacts as well. A moment later, the entire ship seemed to be getting pelted. According to the status reports, nothing larger than a pebble had smashed into the shields. However, there were tons of pebbles.

If the *Kirkland* hadn't looked like hammered shit before, it was certainly going to look like it now. Jordan, of course, didn't give a damn about cosmetic damage. As long as the ship functioned the way it was supposed to, it didn't matter. That said, he didn't want the *Kirkland* looking like a garbage heap. Although that ship might have sailed, so to speak.

"Um, Jordan?" Aryana asked.

The sensors were doing more than just tripping now; the fore shield glowed an angry orange on his HUD. Til must be nosing them straight through. Bastard.

The captain had told Jihi and Jordan their trajectory would take them above the worst of the field, but they'd still take some punishment. That had been no lie.

"Shields are holding," he told Ayrana. "When they turn red, then we can start talking."

The starboard fore shield lit up with yellows and oranges. Multiple impacts. Maybe hundreds of them per second.

Jordan connected to Til. "Cap? I'm seeing—"

"I know," Til said calmly. The man sounded nearly meditative in his tone. Jordan couldn't decide if Til was enjoying this or not. "Going to get worse in about thirty seconds. So get ready."

"Fuck," Jordan said off-comms. He reconnected to the private channel with Aryana. "Hey. Heads up. Things are going to get really bumpy in just a few—"

The starboard bulkhead jolted, and Jordan felt his body attempting to fly off of it, the magnetics barely holding him in place. Whatever that was had been damned big and had somehow gotten around the rear shield. Not good.

Fortunately, the object had hit with a glancing blow or Jordan might not be here to ruminate on it. Fuck, he hated this. The entire ship shuddered, and the dorsal starboard shield turned bright orange as if torched by a flamethrower. The color slowly faded to a dark yellow.

"Got a big hit there," Aryana said.

"Yeah," Jordan replied while doing his best to keep his voice steady. "The shield recovered."

"For now," she said.

Jordan didn't know what to say to that. Difficult to raise morale when you were scared shitless while waiting for a hunk of rock to come screaming through the hull.

"Crew. Ten seconds. Nine. Eight—" Til continued to countdown. When he hit the number zero, g-forces tried to pull Jordan from the bulkhead and slam him against the ship's aft. Til and Chu had ignited the main engines for a short, hard burn.

Jordan wondered if the rest of the crew felt their brains trying to slide through their skulls, saw the blurry world as he did, or felt blood welling on one side of their bodies. Were they on the verge of passing out too? Were they—

The burn stopped as quickly as it had begun, and the world righted in his mind, reality snapping back like a rubber band, the pressure in his brain and the collapsing sensation of his lungs immediately departing. Jordan groaned as a low throb started at the base of his skull. He knew from experience it would leave him alone fairly soon, but for the next few minutes, it would be an unwelcome companion.

"That was stimulating," Aryana said over the private comms.

He grinned despite the headache and the thrumming in his nervous system. "You sound as though you didn't like it."

"I didn't like the sound of all that debris hitting our girl," Aryana said.

Jordan couldn't disagree with that.

"Attention, crew," Til said. "More attitude burns incoming, but the rough stuff is over."

Jordan felt another jolt at his back. He thought maybe Til had been a bit optimistic.

Thrusters fired one at a time, the *Kirkland* rising and turning simultaneously, gravity pulling him in all directions without any sense of ground or sky. His stomach churned and alternately felt full or hollow, his throat alternately swallowing and refluxing acid. The ship took a hard hit to port, and Aryana yelped.

"Still with me?" Jordan asked.

"Still here," she said, sounding a little out of breath. "Was close."

"No perforations on my side," Jordan said after studying the sensor reports. The shields had taken a hell of a beating, but they hadn't had a single piece of debris break through the armored hull. Maybe that made the insane carnival ride worth it.

"Crew," Til said, "we'll be maneuvering for the next few minutes. Remain at your stations. Damage control on standby."

Jordan heaved a sigh. That was Til's way of saying they were through the rough stuff for real. Now it was all supposedly rote, right? Easy trip past MacReady's brethren until they set up a geostationary orbit around their target.

Somehow Jordan didn't think it was going to be that easy.

"We get ready for a disaster and nothing happens?" Aryana asked, relief in her voice.

"Better than being unprepared and—"

"Yeah, yeah," Aryana said. "When do you think Cap is going to—"

"Attention crew. Remain on alert, but you're free to move about the ship. Section leaders check in."

Jordan grinned. "That answer your question?"

"Yes," Aryana said.

"Good," Jordan said and disconnected himself from the bulkhead. He pushed off and hit the deck, reactivating his mag boots. "Now get moving. I want a check of the cargo bay."

"Aye, aye," Aryana said and pushed herself to the floor.

Jordan switched to the command channel. Jihi was already on.

"—No problems detected. I think—oh. Jordan."

"Hello," he said. "No perforations on my status board. Aryana will run a manual check on the cargo and mining bays."

"Good," Til said.

"Didn't detect anything in my section. Just a lot of vibrations and rock rain," Jihi said.

"Putting it mildly," Jordan said. "Cap? The shields took a hell of a pounding."

"I know," Til said. "We're passing by MacReady's radioactive sister.

Should reach geostationary orbit around our target in 14 standard hours or so. Will give you plenty of time to check it out."

Jordan suppressed a gulp as he remembered the rock that had nearly taken off his head. "Once Aryana and I clear the interior, we'll start checking the outer hull."

"Acknowledged," Til said. "Before you go outside, though, I want to meet with you and Jihi. Finish the interior checks and come by for a coffee or three."

Jordan didn't like the sound of that. Til would have normally let them get on with their usual duties. Him wanting to talk before they finished all repairs and status checks? Unexpected.

Jordan connected to the engine systems, manually checked each indicator for pressure loss, malfunctions, and damage, and found virtually none. The shields were a completely different issue. Most of the sensors and cameras covering those portions of the ship were either out, damaged, or destroyed. The ones that worked revealed a horror show of divots, cracks, and smashed metal. Jordan wasn't looking forward to going outside.

*  *  *  *  *

Til and Jihi were already sitting in front of the holodisplay when he entered. Til had a model of the *Kirkland* floating in the air, colored with multiple large red zones, and several yellow ones, marring the otherwise accurate image.

"Hello," Til said with a bright smile. He held a can of something in one hand. "Join us."

Jordan took the can and looked at it for a moment before smiling. "Caffeine, sugar, and real chocolate?" He shook his head before cocking an eye at Til. "Now I know we're fucked."

Jihi said, "What? Why's that?" She already had her can open and had taken a large sip, a dark mustache of foam above her upper lip. She seemed to enjoy not wiping it away.

After popping the top on his can, Jordan sat heavily in the empty chair. "Til broke out his stash," he said, eyes still locked with the captain's, "and he guards this shit. Him handing 'em out is not a good sign."

Til's smile grew, but his eyes held nothing humorous. "Take a sip and enjoy it while you can."

Jordan did and rolled the liquid around his mouth making sure his tongue was completely coated. The sugar and caffeine hit him hard, and he grinned at Til, raising the can in salute. "Thanks, Cap."

"You're welcome," he said and tapped the interface.

The *Kirkland* disappeared from the screen, a new holographic model appearing with thousands or hundreds of thousands of objects spread out across the darkness of space. The star's weak light still provided enough photons to enshroud the area in a deep twilight.

"That mess there," Til said, "is what we flew through."

Jordan held his breath as a large shape cut across the field and disappeared. "The hell was that?"

"That," Til said, "is one of several things zipping around the orbit of this star. Their orbit is different from the debris as well as MacReady and her sisters. Speed's wrong too."

"Different orbit?" Jihi asked.

Til nodded and softly bounced his can on the table. "Different orbit, different trajectory, different speed, but," he said, "the orbit is around the triplets and the field, not the star."

Jordan blinked. "What?"

"Yeah, you heard me right. It's not trapped in the gravity of the star or even one of the planets but the whole mess out here," Til said and pointed at the debris field. "It's like there's some kind of gravity well keeping those things around, which makes no goddamned sense."

"Um, is there gravity?" Jihi asked. "I mean beyond the 1/3 G of MacReady and, well, the others, I guess?"

Til shrugged. "I don't know. We haven't detected anything, but I'm not getting us close to either of the other two planets or moons or whatever you want to call them." He took a sip from his can and tapped the interface again.

The debris field faded out, and a single circle appeared in its place. After a moment, Jordan realized what he was looking at. "That's the radioactive sister," he said.

"Yup," Til said. "It most certainly is."

The image flickered, and a trail of violet light licked off the circle's surface, finally popping the shape into three dimensions for a moment.

"What the hell was that?" Jordan asked.

Til shrugged. "Fucked if I know. Looks like a——"

"Stellar flare," Jihi finished for him. "I mean, it's not one. The color is wrong. And, well, it's not a star."

The trio said nothing for a moment, their eyes locked on the dead-looking disc.

"Looks two-dimensional because it's featureless," Jordan said.

Til grinned. "Wondered when you'd say something about that."

"Holy shit," Jihi said. "Never seen that."

Jordan hadn't either. As far as he knew, no one had. Nothing could be that smooth unless it had been manufactured that way or suffered some seriously bizarre celestial event. He couldn't even imagine what that might have been.

"Has no spin at all and is the most radioactive thing in the system apart from the star itself," Til said. "At least that we know of."

"How does that affect our mining plans?" Jihi asked.

"Well," Til said, "that's kind of what I want to talk about." Jihi sighed heavily, and Til held up a hand. "Hang on. I haven't made any decisions about anything."

She relaxed slightly and busied herself with her drink.

"Okay, now you have my attention," Jordan said.

"Hoped so," Til said. "The radiation coming off that monster is mostly hitting space, although some of it is peppering the hell out of MacReady's dervish of a sister. Luckily for us, the rads don't seem to spread that far out. So long as we stay away from that thing, we'll be okay."

"I get the feeling there's a 'but' coming," Jihi said.

"But," Til said, "I don't know what the fuck those things are that are flying around."

"Any of them come close to MacReady?" Jordan asked.

Til shook his head. "Doesn't look like it. But we haven't been in the system long, and there's a lot of unmapped space out here. No guarantee there isn't something that's going to come near MacReady."

"Christ," Jihi said. "So what do you want to do?"

Til tapped the can's side, the sound strangely out of place in the quiet room. "Chu and I crawled through *Prospector's* logs and couldn't find evidence of any objects entering her space. That tells me that for one and a half years, MacReady hasn't had any visitors." He shrugged. "Good enough for me. But," he said, "it means we can't go outside for a while. As much as I want the hull patched, those little flares worry me."

Jordan couldn't say he disagreed with that. "So how long before we're far enough away?"

"That's the good news," Til said. "You're going to get about eight hours of unscheduled shut-eye and relaxation before you jump back in the suits."

"Aryana might try and kiss you, Cap," Jordan said.

Til rolled his eyes. "That said, our girl has a lot of damage to the shields and the hull. We need to get as much of that patched as we can once we get away from MacReady's crazy sister."

The strange-looking moon appeared to wink as another violet finger licked out from its surface. The sight gave Jordan the shivers.

# CHAPTER SIX

Jordan and Aryana stood at the aft airlock, the pair once again wearing EVA suits. This time, however, they weren't alone. Jihi and three of her miners stood mag locked to the deck a few meters away. Each member of the quartet wore their mining suits and carried torches and patching supplies. The heavy mining suits would offer them greater protection than the normal EVA suits Jordan and Aryana wore, but they were also bulkier and much slower. The remaining two miners served as the safety crew, ready to retrieve anyone in distress or that flew off the hull.

Rather than use Jihi and her crew to apply the patches, Jordan and Aryana had loaded them up like armored pack mules. Aryana would take one group of miners while Jordan would take the other. Jordan had already let Jihi know she was going with Aryana. Jordan's reasoning? A senior person should be there to advise Aryana. The truth, however, was quite a bit different.

Jordan liked Jihi, but he knew she'd pepper him with questions while he welded and bonded and patched damaged shields and hull plates. He didn't need that noise, especially not when they had a good four or five hours of hanging out beneath the shields when possible and scouring every centimeter they could in the most heavily hit areas.

The airlock cycled open, and the six suited humans walked inside. With all their gear, they barely fit inside the oversized aft airlock. The inner door closed, and Jordan's HUD lit up. Til had kept the ship's interior depressurized while the teams worked on the repairs, a decision Jordan couldn't disagree with.

When the outer door cycled, Aryana headed starboard while Jordan headed port, each with two miners in tow. Jordan made sure to get beneath the aft shield as quickly as possible. The miners, seemingly oblivious to the risk, dawdled for a moment as they scoped out the blue nebula.

"Come on," Jordan said over his team's channel. "Get beneath the shield."

One of the miners, named Shelia, he thought, said, "These suits can take a hell of an impact."

"Uh-huh," Jordan said. "Not from something traveling several thousand meters per second."

Shelia went silent, but she and her partner, a man named Mario, finally made their way to join him.

Jordan led them beneath the safety of the aft shield and to the port side. For the thirty meters of travel, Jordan kept his eyes swinging from the ship's hull to the shield. The aft had survived mostly unscathed, but in truth, it was impossible to discern old damage from new. He had little doubt the *Kirkland* had suffered some damage back here during the trip but also little doubt many of these marks were only hours old.

The half-bubble-shaped aft port shield had buckled like a popped piece of packing material, the massive divot marred by more than a few of what looked like close-range shotgun blasts. He stroked his gloved hand across the metal surface, feeling the damage through the glove's tactile sensors.

"What the fuck hit us?" Mario asked.

"Something big," Jordan said quietly. "We're going to need seven patches at least." He had already activated the panel containing the metal sheets.

"How long is that going to take?" Shelia asked.

"As long as it takes," Jordan said and handed the first patch to her. "Mario? Get the next ones ready. Shelia? Let's get to work."

They moved much more slowly than Jordan liked. Aryana checked in after every few patches giving him a sit-rep and a status on their supplies. Upon finishing buttressing the port aft shield, which basically amounted to slatting up a broken window, he had exhausted the emergency stash of patches. He'd have to hope the other shields weren't nearly as damaged.

That hope, however, had quickly been dashed. The other two bubbles on the port side had also suffered catastrophic damage. The midships port shield had barely remained attached to the ship, the anchor points all but pulled from the hull.

He, Shelia, and Mario, both of the miners now a little more lively and less bored, exhausted the full-sized patches. By the time Jordan's team had finished patching, the two miners' packs of supplies had practically emptied. Aryana wasn't faring much better on the ship's starboard side.

"Cap?" Jordan called over the radio.

"Go," Til said.

"Tell those laggards inside to bring out more supplies. We've run through."

"That bad?" Til asked.

Jordan snorted off comms. "Worse."

"Shit. Okay. Out."

Five hours. They'd been at this for five hours, and they still hadn't even checked the bow, dorsal, or ventral portions. At this rate, they'd reach MacReady long before they finished repairs. That wasn't necessarily a bad thing—the sooner they had the *Kirkland* patched up, the better he'd feel. Something was wrong about this system, and he didn't like it.

"Okay, team," he said. "We're heading back in for a resupply and rest."

"Fuck yes," Mario said with a groan. "Even miners get a break every couple of hours."

"Unless the ceiling is caving in," Shelia said.

Jordan grinned at that. At least she seemed to understand how much damage the ship had sustained. Mario, on the other hand, seemed as aware as a stump, but he did make sure to stay beneath the shields' shadows as they headed aft.

Aryana and her crew were waiting near the airlock but still in the shield's shade.

"About time," she said over the private channel.

"We're older," Jordan said smiling and opened the airlock. "Besides, we took our time. Our shields might actually survive another hit."

She stuck her tongue out at him as the hatch opened.

* * * * *

After an hour break, Jordan and his team once again ventured out of the airlock and made their way to the bow port shield. With half their supplies gone, he led the team to the dorsal side. Aryana and her team had already started on the ventral side of the ship.

The dorsal shields were in far better shape, although one had taken a ding hard enough to curl the metal on one edge. Jordan continued walking the hull to reach the damaged ventral midship shield when his suit flashed a warning.

**EXTREME RADIATION DETECTED**

Jordan stopped in mid-step, one foot still raised from the hull.

"Everything okay?" Shelia asked.

Confused, Jordan turned to her. "No radiation alarms for you?"

She shook her head. "No."

"Walk to me," he said.

She clumsily covered the three meters to stand next to him and seemed to flinch when she stopped. "Shit."

"You got it too?"

She nodded. "Extreme radiation. Um, call me stupid, but shouldn't we have detected that before we got here?"

He nodded. "The bottom of the shield shouldn't give us that much protection."

"Is it on the shield?" she asked.

That was a good question. "Stay here," he said and walked forward, his eyes flicking from the hull and back to the radiation status. His EVA suit could take a hell of a lot of radiation before the deadly energy started turning his DNA to mush, but that didn't mean he could take it lightly—the memory of MacReady's radioactive sister shooting off something like stellar flares made that an impossibility.

Less than a meter from the shield, he ducked beneath it and frowned as the radiation levels decreased. *Shit*, he thought. The shield was providing protection. The bottom of the shield appeared completely undamaged and unaffected. Curious.

Jordan stepped out from under the shield, and radiation warnings immediately triggered. He continued walking to the damaged edge of the shield and stopped when he was less than a meter away, mouth open and eyes staring. A jagged piece of what looked like metal had embedded itself into the shield. He wasn't sure what it might be made of, but it was definitely the radiation source.

The piece of debris, less than one-fourth of a meter in length and half as long, and no thicker than a centimeter, put off as many rads as a fuel rod. Had this come from MacReady's triplet?

Now he wanted to go over the astronomy footage from *9C512*. This had to have come from somewhere, and he was willing to bet it had been in the debris field. He zoomed in on the object as closely as he could, upped the resolution to the maximum, and took twenty seconds of video. Maybe the mining team would have some ideas about what it was, but they wouldn't know where it came from any more than he did.

"We're going to check the last dorsal shield," Jordan said, "and then we're heading to the bow."

"What is it?" Shelia asked.

He turned from the damaged shield and walked to where she and Mario stood. "Mystery for another time. Come on."

They followed him across the ship's belly until they reached the bow. The bow shield, twice as large as any of those covering its other areas, was all but smashed inward. The bubble had completely collapsed, its bottom pressing inward on the hull but not perforating it.

Jordan wasn't even sure what to do about it. Apart from using every last patch they had aboard ship and possibly printing more, there wasn't much he could do. The ship's printers were large, but he couldn't manufacture an entire shield large enough for the bow.

"Aryana?" he called over the comms.

"Yeah, boss?"

"Bring every remaining patch you have to the bow dorsal. Raid what you can from the stashes in the hull."

"Oh," she said softly. "Guess that means the bow's in bad shape."

"Putting it mildly," he said.

"We're finishing up bow, ventral. Another two patches should do it."

"Copy," he said. "We'll start without you."

"Have fun."

Jordan connected to Til. "Your bow is a mess."

"I figured," Til said. "How bad is the shield?"

"What shield?" Jordan said. "We can cover the housing, but the shield is gone. Might as well not exist."

Til was silent for a moment. "Not good for the trip home," he said.

"No, it's not. We'll do what we can," Jordan said, "but just know that we can't take many more hits like that."

He could practically hear Til nodding. "Acknowledged. How much longer do you think you'll be out there?"

"Another hour at least. Might be able to cut that when Aryana's team gets here. Just try and keep us away from the cosmic rays," Jordan said.

"Copy on cosmic rays. I'll talk to the universe and see if it'll listen."

"You do that," Jordan grinned. He connected to the team channel and gestured to Mario. "Let's begin."

# CHAPTER SEVEN

The phrase "I'm too old for this shit" had been around for millennia. Jordan had heard it often enough when he was young and had thought it funny. After as many tours as he'd completed, he no longer found it funny. He was beginning to find it to be the truth.

Walking on the hull in an EVA suit, carrying, welding, inspecting, constantly moving your calves while your feet remained locked to the deck—it all took a toll. He kept himself in good enough shape to get the job done, but he couldn't kid himself that he was capable of eight-to-twelve-hour shifts in a suit. That part of his life was over, he hoped.

The cruel ache that made his legs tremble and the frequent twinges of pain that raced down his back served as a reminder he wasn't in his 30s anymore. Or his 40s. At dinner, he'd had to take more than his normal share of analgesics. If not for the fact they were on approach to MacReady and the ship had already suffered a lot of damage, he might even have taken a muscle relaxant and faded off into the welcome abyss of unconsciousness.

That, however, wasn't a good idea. He'd be stupid when he woke up hungover, and if he had to actually repair something? He'd probably fuck it up. Too much of a risk.

Til didn't break out his stash for the captain's meeting. Instead, he and Chu, the first officer and pilot, sat at the meeting table with several squeeze bottles of refreshments locked to its surface. The holodisplay glowed blue with an empty, twinkling field.

Til looked up at him as Jordan entered. He grinned, leaned back, and clasped his hands behind his head. "You look tired."

"You look like ass," Jordan said. "At least I have an excuse."

Til's smile disappeared into one of shock and mock hurt. "Oh, the pain!"

Chu rolled his eyes. "Hello, Jordan."

"Hey, Chu," Jordan said. "He finally let you out of the cockpit?"

Chu shrugged. "You know how it is. Someone's gotta be responsible."

Til glared at his pilot. "You trying to say something?"

Chu blinked at him before glancing at Jordan and back again. "I didn't try."

Til screwed up his face into a comical sneer.

Chu rolled his eyes again and fixed them on Jordan. "Looks like you fixed up our girl."

"As much as we could," Jordan said. "Still have several cameras out and Aryana and I will have to take care of that. I'll need to print quite a few new patches and make further repairs before we even think about leaving this system."

"I figured," Til said. "What I saw of the front shield—"

"There was a front shield?" Chu asked.

Til continued after giving Chu a long glare. "What I saw of the front shield tells me you'll have to all but rebuild the bubble."

"True," Jordan said. "Hence the printing. We can't possibly print an entire bubble, so we'll have to do it in sections, carry out each section, and then weld them all together. It's going to take a while, and we might need to draft a miner or two to help us out."

Jihi appeared in the hatchway. "A miner to help out with what?"

As she took her seat, Jordan explained about the bubble.

"Pretty sure we'll do whatever you need to get back home," Jihi said. "Not a problem."

"Well," Til said. "With that settled, I just have one more thing to say before we start. Jordan? You and Aryana, with the help of Jihi's crew, did a hell of a job on the repairs. Damned fast too. Thank you."

Jihi, Til, and Chu clapped and beamed, and Jordan, not for the first time, felt self-conscious and embarrassed. He hated this shit.

"You're welcome," Jordan said the moment they stopped clapping. "What else is on the docket?"

Til gestured to Chu. "Your show."

Chu touched the interface, and windows of text, numbers, and images filled the display. Jordan tried to take in all the information at once, and it made no sense. Chu didn't give him a chance to make a second stab.

"MacReady and her sisters," Chu said, and one of the windows enlarged. A top-down view of the star system appeared and slowly zoomed in on the triplets, the debris field following in their wake like a lost dog. "I've been going over *Prospector's* astronomical logs for the system to try to get an idea of what happened here.

"The computer thinks the debris field was most likely caused by a hypervelocity collision. Something with a lot of mass hit something else with a lot of mass, and the two shattered, leaving this mess in their wake."

The view panned slightly before zooming in on the debris field. "Gravitationally speaking? Any impact that left the debris field should have scattered flotsam throughout the system. Instead, the field remains mostly intact and appears striated with radiation."

"Radiation?" Jihi asked.

"Yeah," Chu said. "Nothing our shields and suits can't handle, but they were definitely irradiated by something."

Jordan crossed his arms and leaned back in the chair as he studied the image. "When we did our walk on the ventral, I found something embedded in one of the shields. It was highly radioactive."

Chu and Til exchanged a glance.

"Is that in your report?" Til asked.

"I haven't had time to write one," Jordan admitted.

Til nodded. "Okay, so tell me about it."

"Not much to it. I marked it in my suit's log," Jordan said. "It was nothing really out of the ordinary. Didn't look strange. Just a piece of metal lodged into the tungsten alloy."

"How radioactive?" Jihi asked.

"Well, that's the thing," Jordan said. "Its range was terribly short. Like a meter."

"Range?" Chu asked. "You mean how far the radiation spread?"

Jordan nodded. "Didn't trip my sensors until I was practically on top of it."

"Strange," Chu said. "Although that could explain why our hull readings were all over the place while we were traveling through the debris field."

"What the hell could cause that?" Til asked.

"Don't know," Chu said. "When we send our first QE update, we'll have to ask."

The table went quiet for a moment, the four of them staring at the 3D model of the shatter-storm that might once have been a large hunk of rock. Or maybe two.

Jordan frowned. "Wait a second. Shouldn't the debris field be larger?"

"Huh?" Chu asked. "What do you mean?"

"Well"—Jordan pointed at the debris field—"it's a big field. I'm not saying it's not. But that can't possibly have been an object as large as MacReady or her sisters. The field would be much larger, wouldn't it?"

Chu was silent for a moment before finally interacting with the interface. "Writing a program real quick. I'll get the computer to try to rebuild a sphere from the field."

Til said, "Not going to be accurate."

"No," Chu agreed, "but it will at least give us some idea of what might be missing."

"How long is that going to take?" Jihi asked.

"To write? Not that long," Chu said without looking up from the interface. "Might take a little bit to run, though."

"Keep at it," Til said before making eye contact with Jordan and Jihi. "Since we have a moment, let's talk about our approach."

"I thought we were on approach?" Jihi said.

"We are," Til said. "Should be near when you wake up for your next shift. The duty rosters are in your mail. Jihi? You'll have to decide how to split up the work with your crew. Jordan?"

"Aryana and I will be at our regular posts," he said. "Engineering and reactors."

"Right," Til said. "Despite the debris field being behind us now, there's still some chaff out there. Expect micrometeorites and the typical junk surrounding planets with no atmosphere."

"You haven't spotted anything big, have you?" Jordan asked.

Til shook his head. "Survey appears relatively clear, but *Prospector* did find some debris once it attained a stable orbit."

"Fair enough," Jordan said.

Jihi sighed. "If it's nothing, why are you bringing it up?"

Til's face remained friendly, but Jordan heard annoyance in the man's voice. "Because there might be something relatively big that we haven't seen."

The table went quiet again.

Finally, Chu said, "Program done. Will take a few to run."

"Excellent," Til said. "Now. Chu has something else to show you."

Chu ran a hand through his salt-and-pepper flattop and seemed to gather himself. He tapped the interface, and the view zoomed out once more to show the entire star system. MacReady and her sisters were merely labeled dots on the massive display.

Something shot past the system's outer edge in the space of a blink. A few seconds later, another followed the same path just as fast.

"That," Chu said, "is not a glitch or sensor malfunction."

"Then what is it?" Jihi asked.

Chu took a deep breath. "No fucking idea. Whatever causes that phenomenon repeats roughly every fifteen days. The path doesn't ever seem to change, and the speed remains constant."

"How fast is it going?" Jordan asked.

Chu grinned. "One-twentieth of light speed."

"Fuck me," Jihi said.

"Amazing, isn't it?" Chu said. "Never heard of anything like this."

A wave of anxiety rolled over Jordan. Seeing that and having Chu tell him it was real was enough to make anyone uncomfortable. Something moving that fast outside of rift space was unheard of. Just another goddamned anomaly in this star system. There were already too many of them for his liking.

Most star systems he ended up traveling to were relatively boring. Apart from the usual phenomena like dying stars, seismic activity on planets, and the like, mining ships rarely encountered a system this unique. Jordan didn't like unique. He liked boring, routine systems and boring routine planets.

Boring meant you knew what to expect, and even the most basic training covered all of that. Non-boring systems, on the other hand, required more focus and attention and usually resulted in accidents of some kind. All it took was a moment's distraction, and they could damage the ship or the mining equipment, or pollute the find. Jordan had seen all three happen and didn't care to go through any of that stress again. Who the hell would?

"So apart from the A-word," Til said, "we don't have any idea what it could be."

"What A-word?" Jihi asked.

Chu held up his hands and shook them menacingly. "Aliens!"

He looked like a little kid trying to scare a younger sibling, but hearing the word uttered like that sent a shiver down Jordan's spine.

"It'd be a first," Til said, trying to sound nonchalant and not quite succeeding.

Chu sat back in his chair. "In all seriousness, I'm not willing to claim it's anything other than a celestial phenomenon. Any other opinion is mere conjecture."

"Well, thanks for that, Professor," Jihi said. "I'm sure that will help me sleep tonight."

"I could lie if you like," Chu said.

"No," Jihi sighed. "I just want to make sure that what you just suggested stays in this room. I don't want my people being affected by, um, superstitious bullshit."

"Superstitious?" Jordan asked. "I'd say the period and speed doesn't make it superstition. More like suspicion."

Jihi raised her hands. "Okay, okay. What I'm saying is our jobs are dangerous enough without feeling like we need to look over our shoulders for protection."

"Agreed," Til said. He made eye contact with Jordan. "Say nothing about this to anyone. Including Aryana."

Jordan immediately felt a rush of heat to his cheeks. Til was basically saying he didn't trust Aryana to keep her mouth shut. That was not only unfair but inaccurate. It took everything he had not to say so publicly. "Acknowledged," he said curtly.

Til blinked at him but said nothing. Jordan was fairly sure Til knew why Jordan reacted that way and understood it too. Didn't mean Jordan was going to pretend he liked it.

"Even if that's some kind of alien probe racing around the system," Chu said, "it can't possibly see us. I mean, think about it. No sensor could detect us before the object was too far away to get the results."

*Doppler effect*, Jordan thought. If the object fired a beam of light at MacReady on its way through the system, the light wouldn't have time to bounce off the moon's surface and return to the object. It would instead bounce back into space because the object was already long gone.

Til crossed his arms and studied Chu. "If they can move at a twentieth of light speed, I imagine they'd have sensors that work differently than anything we would understand."

The dry tone of Til's voice made Chu blush.

"I guess so," the copilot said.

Jordan didn't like what Til was saying. He also didn't disagree. "So maybe no assumption is safe."

"Right. So," Til said, "we have phenomena we can't explain coupled with two planets we can't explain and a third that appears to be loaded with riches. In addition to that, we have Chu's debris field."

"Don't blame that one on me," Chu said. "I just work here."

"I mean, I'm waiting for your damned simulation," Til said.

"Oh." Chu glanced at the interface. "Nearly done, I think."

Til yawned. "Good. Because I need some shut-eye before the next shift."

"Heard that," Chu said. "Three-hour nap at least."

"Make it four," Til said.

Jihi giggled. "How about seven like the rest of us?"

Chu and Til exchanged a glance.

"I'd kill for that much sleep," Chu said before jerking a thumb at Til. "He'll never let that happen."

Til shrugged. "I don't need much sleep, and I hate being alone."

Chu sighed. "I didn't sign up to be your wubbie."

"No," Til agreed. "That's just one of the perks."

"You two are so cute together," Jihi said.

Chu and Til looked at one another with wrinkled noses, making even Jordan smile.

The interface in front of Chu flashed. "Done," he said before swiping the touchpad.

The holodisplay cleared, and a new model of the debris field appeared. The triplets remained in the background, completely featureless and devoid of depth. As Jordan watched, the fragments of the field began moving.

Like 3D puzzle pieces, they snapped together and continued congealing, mating with others, and solidifying, the cracks and imperfections sealing together as though they'd never been apart.

Chu studied the model. "I suggested the algorithm try to piece together a sphere from the parts. I've no idea what it's actually going to give us."

The pieces continued collapsing upon one another like an explosion in reverse. When they finished, Jordan found himself looking at a nearly complete sphere somewhat smaller than MacReady. A shiver raced down his spine, but he couldn't say why. Something about the sphere just didn't make sense.

Chu rotated the artificial object, and it spun in place. The mostly finished shape had jagged edges at its top that reminded Jordan of something, but he couldn't say what.

"About the size of Earth's moon, wouldn't you say?" Chu asked.

"Yeah, I guess," Til said. "A bit smaller than the triplets, though. And it's missing a lot of pieces, although I guess that's to be expected if it exploded. Some of that shit is probably still heading out of the system."

"Plus," Jordan said, "it's a guess."

"Yup," Chu said, "but it looks like a pretty good one. I mean, this kind of suggests that the triplets used to be quadruplets."

Jihi yawned loudly and blushed when the others turned to look at her. "Sorry."

Til grinned. "No, it's time to hit the sack. Chu and I need our beauty rest before we get into orbit. We'll try to let you sleep through that."

"Joy," Jihi said. "I'll tell my crew to hit the sack. Like now."

*Fat chance,* Jordan thought. *They're either all already asleep or still playing poker. And if they're playing poker, it could be a while.*

If, that was, the last four tours were anything to judge by. Jihi was practically the only constant in the mining corps that Jordan served with. The rest of the miners were contractors. Some came back to mine again, others found new outfits to work for, and still others simply retired after their first big strike. Or they just died.

Til stood from his chair and stretched extravagantly. "Shut down. Shut-eye. That's an order."

Jordan stood and mock saluted. "Aye, aye." He nodded to Chu. "Thanks for all the hard work."

Chu beamed. "Very welcome. Have the feeling I won't be bored while the mining crew is on the surface. Plenty more data to troll. I could be at this for months."

"Let's hope it's not that complicated," Jordan said.

"It won't be," the copilot said. "See you in a few hours." With that, he left the room, Jihi on his heels.

"Hey, Jordan," Til said. "Stay for a minute?"

"Sure," Jordan said and turned away from the hatch. "What's up?"

"The front shield," Til said. "I don't like the fact it's in such bad shape."

"Me neither," Jordan said.

"If we have to take off in an emergency, we may not make it out of this system without something slamming through it and the hull," Til said. "Can we make that a priority?"

Jordan grinned. "I already had made it a priority. I figured I'll do the drop and once the miners are situated, Aryana and I can trade. She can—"

Til shook his head. "I'd rather have you up here."

"Um, why? Aryana has never—"

"Has never done a drop, I know," Til said. "She's also never printed a new shield or handled something that large—to my knowledge, that is. Correct?"

Jordan was silent for a moment. First Til had disrespected Aryana by that secrecy shit, and now he was interfering with the day-to-day?

"So?" Jordan said.

Til sighed. "It's your section, Jordan. You do as you like. However, I'd prefer if you stayed up here and supervised the repairs to the ship."

Something about Til seemed off. This wasn't like him. Not at all. Jordan finally thought he figured out why. "The object. The one that streaks through the system. Got you spooked?"

Til's face twitched at the question. "If you're not spooked, you're a fool," he said grimly.

# CHAPTER EIGHT

Jordan's eyes snapped open at the sound of the ship's shift alert. The familiar buzz immediately brought him fully awake, his mind already racing over the list of items he and Aryana had to take care of.

After quickly dressing, he headed to the galley and found Aryana already there, a mag-mug of orange-colored vitamin drink at her lips. Her eyes widened when she saw Jordan, and she smiled around the can's nipple.

"Good morning," she said and smacked her lips.

Jordan headed for the vending machines, intent on getting at least 600 calories of nutrition in his body before getting suited up. In truth, he probably needed about 900, but he'd worry about that later. Right now, something to quiet his belly and pump up his blood sugar was exactly what he needed.

After grabbing a nutrition bar and procuring his own cup of vitamins, he headed to Aryana's table and sat down. "You're early."

"No," she said. "You're late."

"Uh-huh," he said and took a sip. "You remember your orbital training?"

"Of course," Aryana said. "Not like it's rocket science."

That was true enough. The process was simple enough that even a miner could handle it if they had to. In theory, anyway.

"Good. I spoke with Cap last night, and he wants me to stay aboard during the drop."

Aryana's eyes brightened, and her grin became an all-out tooth-filled smile. "I've got the drop?"

"You've got the drop," he said, his own smile breaking over his face.

"I figured you'd be excited about that."

She sighed. "Rite of passage," she said.

"It is," Jordan agreed. "That said, however, I'll need some help getting things in place before the drop. So don't think we're getting the orbital up and then you can joyride down."

"Aye, aye," she said with a smart salute. "What was it like your first time?"

First time. He didn't want to talk about it. Not ever.

"Complicated," he said. "I'll make sure yours isn't."

Aryana knew not to pry. At least she'd figured that out last tour.

"Sounds good to me," she said. "I just want to be on the ground with the first team, get a chance to step on a world no one else has. Also? Running the lift for the first time, on board to handle any kinks? A lot of responsibility."

"So ambitious," he said softly.

She frowned. "Too ambitious?"

Jordan slowly shook his head. "No. Just remember to do your job and you'll be fine. I'll be on the comms, so I can walk you through anything."

"I know I'll do fine," she said. "I had a great teacher."

He blushed at that. "So as soon as we finish up here, we need to do the four S's."

"Shit, shower, shave, suit," Aryana said happily. "Give me another five, and I'll be on my way."

By the time Jordan and Aryana finished their breakfast and were heading for the hatch, the miners had begun filing in. He hoped they would take their time. The last thing he needed were anxious miners crowding around and waiting for something to happen.

* * * * *

The cargo/mining bay took up a significant portion of the ship and was the largest compartment apart from engineering. As such, it had wide airlocks on either end as well as ingresses/egresses both port and starboard. In short, it was made for accessibility and ease of use.

What differentiated it from the other portions of the ship, however, was the giant slot in the dorsal decking as well as a massive hatch built into the ventral deck. The slot held the orbital. The hatch dropped the other end to a celestial body's surface. With the orbital as a counterweight, alongside the occasional correction from its ion thrusters, the cable between the two remained taut enough for a climber to descend and ascend.

Jordan knew how the orbital worked, in theory, but not the actual physics involved. He only knew what to do if things fucked up. That was why he got paid the big bucks, so to speak.

"Are you in position?" Jordan asked Aryana over the engineering channel, knowing Til and Chu were no doubt listening in. Jihi might even be monitoring the channel to get a heads-up on any "oh shit" mishaps that might affect her crew. In short, he and Aryana were performers on a stage, their camera feeds simulcasted to every member of the crew that cared to tune in. Each word, each movement would be studied if there was an incident. Jordan didn't intend to skip a single step here.

"In position," Aryana said, sounding alert but bored at the same time.

Jordan could see she was where she was supposed to be, her mag-booted feet connected to the dorsal deck next to the slot. Upon a short stem sat a manual valve wheel, Aryana's hands resting on its surface. The cameras, the audio. Every step followed even if it was stupid as hell.

"Captain? Permission to launch the orbital," Jordan said.

"You are a go for orbital launch," Til said as if reading from the official handbook.

"Copy. Crew. We are launching the orbital. Please move to your action stations. In ten, nine—"

Jordan counted down, and his HUD lit up with the dorsal orbital hatch. When the count reached zero, he blinked for the interface to begin the launch process. A yellow indicator flashed before the hatch slid open above him, the blue nebula appearing as though it had been waiting for them to see it. He once again found himself lost in the shape and the hue.

The hatch finished moving and locked into place. Jordan's HUD lit up with the status, and the system announced it was launching the orbital.

"Standby for launch," Jordan said.

Now was when things would get interesting. If there was going to be a fuckup, this was when it would happen.

A massive ball of shielded, depleted uranium rose through the ventral deck to fill the slot, the connected thick tether glittering in the artificial light. Jordan said, "Launching."

A piston rose from the deck until it nearly met the ball. An indicator glowed red on Jordan's HUD, and the piston rose in a slow, smooth motion. The orbital gained momentum and disappeared through the slot at less than a centimeter per second. The tether remained taut, its length playing out as the orbital continued on its journey to its intended altitude above MacReady.

"Launch nominal," he said. "Aryana, you can move to the cable station."

"Copy cable station," Aryana said without a trace of boredom. Jordan grinned as he watched her disconnect her boots and use the manual hatch release's post as a fulcrum to send herself into a short glide to the manual cable controls. She thrust her glove forward when she reached less than half a meter from her target and came to a slow halt before clamping her boots and gloves to the station.

"Show-off," Jordan said. "Did you practice that move after last tour?"

"Yup," she said. "Just reverse the magnetics to half or full, and you—"

"I know," Jordan grinned. "I have done it before. More times than I can count."

"What? Then why have I never seen you do it?"

He sighed. "After a suit failure or two, or a misjudgment, and you experience a cracked helmet, a joint, or a malfunctioning servo as a result, you figure it's better to be safe than sorry."

Aryana considered that for a moment before saying, "Cable nominal."

"Copy," Jordan replied.

It took more than twenty minutes for the orbital to reach its calculated distance from the planet's surface. During the last minute of its ascent, the cable wheel had tightened a klick or so at a time, increasing the drag like a fishing reel. The ship, a far more massive object than the orbital itself, helped make the deceleration possible. When the orbital reached position, the ship hadn't so much as shuddered.

"Orbital in place," Jordan said. "Cap? Ready for extend."

Til immediately replied, "Go for extend."

"Copy go for extend. Aryana? Cable is managed. Move to platform control," Jordan said.

Aryana repeated her gliding trick to reach the next station. All this jumping around. He could have helped her with this, but he was standing next to the switch that could bring everything to a halt. This was his station, and since they didn't exactly have a plethora of engineers, Aryana had the other stations.

"At platform control," she said.

"Cap? We are ready to deploy the platform."

"You are a go to deploy," Til said immediately.

Here goes, Jordan said to himself. "Aryana? Deploy the platform."

"Aye, deploying platform."

The deck beneath him shuddered as seams appeared across the starboard bulkhead. A ten-meter-long section of metal and composites slowly pushed outward from the ship and into space, the orbital tether moving along with it.

Jordan watched his HUD as the elevator platform finished extending from the ship. When the mechanism came to a halt, a set of statuses filled the display. "Cap? We're a go for disconnect."

"You're a go for disconnect."

Jordan heaved a sigh. They were almost done with this part. Fortunately. "Aryana? Disconnecting."

"You're a go," she said.

Nodding, Jordan blinked through the command menus and activated the disconnect. The deck vibrated beneath his boots before the elevator platform completely separated from the ship.

The push sent the platform floating out into space until it reached nearly half a kilometer from the *Kirkland*. The platform's attitude thrusters came to life and slowed its speed until it once again stabilized its orbit.

Fuel expenditure? Ten percent of reserves. Not bad. Not good. Since MacReady had little to no spin, the orbital should stay in position without additional adjustments—"should" being the operative word. He and Aryana would have to keep an eye on that.

Company policy was to keep the orbital as far away from the ship as possible, with a minimum distance of 500 meters. Reason? Accidents. Stellar phenomenon. Gravity fluctuations. Debris. Any of a thousand things could cause the orbital to lose its place in the sky and either fall to the planet's surface or move in such a way that it could slice through a hull.

There were fail-safes, of course, but that didn't change the fact that as convenient as they were, the orbital lifts were also deadly hazards. Jordan hated them. Compared to flying down to a planet's surface every day, however, it was still the safer alternative.

"Cap? Orbital platform deployed. All statuses green."

"Acknowledged," Til said. The general crew channel came to life. "This is the captain. We're a go for the initial drop. Station chiefs report in when ready."

"Okay, Aryana," Jordan said over the engineering channel, "get with your buddy. You're going for a ride."

"Aye, aye," she said happily.

Jordan watched her disconnect from the ceiling and glide face-first to the deck. When she was less than a few meters from the steel, she flipped, and her descent slowed as she adjusted her magnetics. He grinned when she came to a less than graceful halt—she'd misjudged.

"How are those dance lessons going?" Jordan asked.

"Ahem," Aryana said as she stood and made her way to the tug.

The tug, a brick of a vehicle made to transport cargo from the ship and to the orbital, as well as corral or push away hazardous space junk and recapture lost loads, had a cabin for one. Each of its surfaces, apart from the rear that contained its powerful engines, had a shield for personnel in EVA or mining suits. The suited humans could cling to the hull beneath the shield and be protected from debris, cosmic rays, and intense heat.

Jordan connected to Jihi. "Who's piloting the tug?"

"I am," she said.

He could hear a smile in her voice. "That's not procedure."

"What's that? You're breaking up."

Jordan laughed. He'd been on enough tours to know that Jihi loved piloting the tug. He hadn't ever asked her to explain it, but inevitably, she ended up in the pilot seat every opportunity she had. Considering she spent the majority of her time on the planet, there weren't that many opportunities. Still, they were going to be here a long time. She'd have more shots.

"Tug ready to depart," Jihi said over the command channel.

"Copy," Til said. "You are clear to begin."

"Okay, Jordan," Jihi said. "Open her up."

# CHAPTER NINE

The tug transported the landing box to the platform. The landing box, a massive rectangular slab that contained kilometers and kilometers of tether along with emergency gear for the first drop, sat directly below the platform. Aryana and Mario, one of the miners that helped Jordan with the patches, had connected the tether to the bottom of the platform and were now inside the landing box, strapped in, and ready for the drop.

Jordan knew from experience—all too many experiences truth, be told—what it was like to be in the drop box. The cabin, if you could call it that, had just enough space for two bulky mining suits, two spare, unoccupied mining suits, an emergency generator, emergency shelter, and various other oh-shit equipment. The entire space that wasn't filled with tether or fuel was also a lifeboat. If the landing box crew had to ditch, either before or after penetrating a body's atmosphere, they'd have a chance at survival. In theory.

Jordan stood before a holodisplay in the cargo bay. Several windows showed different views of the orbital platform as well as the landing box and the planet below them. All statuses were green. He took a deep breath and activated the command channel.

"My board is green. Repeat, we are a go for drop," Jordan said.

"Copy, green," Til said. "Landing box?"

"We're a go," Aryana said. She still sounded as though she were grinning. She probably was.

"Copy," Til said. "Tug?"

"We're a go," Jihi said. The excitement in her voice had departed.

She was all professional now.

"Copy. Search and Rescue?"

"S&R is a go," a gruff voice said.

"Copy," Til said. "Landing box? You are a go for drop."

"Acknowledged," Aryana said. "Dropping. Now. Now. Now."

A puff of gas exploded outward from the platform and pushed the landing box toward MacReady's surface, the thick tether rolling out from the invisible spindle inside the box.

Jordan monitored the box's descent, checking for deviations in its expected attitude and velocity. He didn't have too many concerns about the drop—MacReady's lack of an atmosphere coupled with its low gravity made the process relatively simple. As long as the lift didn't descend too fast and the tether didn't get hung up, there was little that could go wrong.

*Apart from everything*, he told himself.

Still, the lift continued dropping, Aryana making a status report every half kilometer of change in altitude. The excitement in her voice had decreased with each update, boredom and listlessness slowly replacing the childish glee. She'd finally discovered the truth—drops were boring as shit unless there was a catastrophic event.

When the box finally came within two kilometers of MacReady's surface, Aryana had returned to her usual ebullient self. "Landing site looks good," she said. "Attitude nominal."

It wasn't something she'd needed to say—anyone tuned in to the landing box's feed could see MacReady's rocky surface coming into sharper and sharper definition. The landing site had been vetted more than a day ago. If it hadn't been as expected, he'd have scrubbed the mission right then and there. Any planet whose surface changed that rapidly would not be a safe place to land, let alone mine.

A tense few minutes began as the box slowly lowered to the ground. The camera jittered and shook when the metal bottom hit the surface.

"*Kirkland?*" Aryana said. "Box has landed. Green status."

Jordan smiled. She sounded out of breath and exhausted to boot. Well, now she could say she'd done a drop and survived it. That tick mark on her resume was filled in, and now she could focus on doing her fucking job. He hoped.

"Box?" Jordan said. "You're a go for unpack and secure."

"Copy unpack and secure," she said.

The cam-feed monitors flickered a few times while the box unfolded into a large rectangular platform, its left half holding the spindle with the remaining tether wrapped around it. If the orbital tried to pull away and unmoor itself, it would have to move the massive box and the spindle that held it in place. Jordan had never heard of that happening. The tether was more likely to snap first.

"Jordan?" Til asked over a private channel.

"Yes, Cap?" Jordan said.

"I figure twenty minutes for them to clear the area and test the platform. Sound right?"

"Yes," Jordan said. "Then another ten to fifteen on checks up here."

"Okay. You feel comfortable with the tug taking over the first load?"

Good question. Til was essentially asking if Jihi could drag the surface personnel module to the orbital lift and prep it for launch. Regs said you had to wait until the orbital lift had passed all its tests. Regs also said to begin mining as soon as possible.

"I'm comfy with Jihi getting it into position," Jordan said. "But she needs to stay at least 100 meters out."

Til paused for a moment. "Sounds good, Jordan. I'll let her know."

"Um, Cap? Please make sure she gets the message. You know how she is."

"Got it. Aryana did good, Jordan. She's got a good teacher."

He blushed at that. How could he not? "Thanks, Cap."

"Take a break. You haven't left your station since before the drop."

That was true. He'd barely moved his feet the past hour, and he couldn't remember the last time he'd bothered to stretch. "Aye, aye," he said and stepped away from the holodisplay and the interface.

Jihi's miners had moved the personnel module to the edge of the massive cargo bay door. With the tug already floating just outside, it wouldn't take Jihi more than a few minutes to get hooked up. Less if her crew knew what they were doing. Once she had it in place, she'd fire a few bursts and get the portable building on its way. It would be the first of many modules heading down today. It would also be the most dangerous. If they were going to experience a failure, it would most likely happen during the first lift descent.

The miners stood around the module, most leaning against its hull with their mag gloves, their feet dangling in midair in the microgravity.

He couldn't blame them for goofing off and chewing the fat on their own private channel. Loading and unloading were boring if you weren't in the tug or on the platform. Well, when you were in space, anyway. Far different when you were on the surface.

Til or Chu probably had their eyes on the cargo bay's cam feeds, watching as the miners swayed and dangled above the deck. Chu was probably shaking his head in annoyance while Til stared in envy.

Finally, Jordan's HUD flashed with a message:

**_Kirkland_ Orbital One: OPERATIONAL.**

A moment later, Aryana said, "Box to _Kirkland_. My board is green, and we're ready to receive modules."

Jordan could practically hear a Texas whoop in Til's voice. "Copy that, Box. Jihi? Let's get 'em moving."

"You heard the man," Jihi said over the general comms. "Assholes and elbows!"

\* \* \* \* \*

Once module 7 had descended near the planet's surface, Jordan finally let out the breath he didn't know he'd been holding. During the past six descents, the orbital crawler had sent multiple warnings regarding slippage. Since the loads had had no humans aboard, no one but he and Aryana even noticed the glitch.

Either the lift had a bad sensor or the grippers the lift used to travel the tether were failing. He hoped it was the former and not the latter. He didn't want to travel to the orbital platform in an EVA suit. He didn't want to fight with replacing gripper assemblies without an assistant. He also didn't want Aryana doing it by herself on the ground.

Again, it wasn't that he doubted her skill, but he'd still feel better if he was at least looking over her shoulder.

At some point, you have to take off the training wheels, he heard Til say in his mind.

The captain had said that to him more than once last tour. Aryana knew what she was doing. He just had to get used to the idea of letting her do it.

"Box to *Kirkland*," Aryana said over the comms. "Module 7 is on the ground."

"Copy," Til said. "Mining team?"

"Mining team here," a gruff voice said. "Landed gently and mustering out."

"Copy," Til said. "Jihi? You're clear to descend at your leisure."

"Acknowledged," Jihi said. "And about damned time."

Jordan grinned. Jihi and one other miner were the last two of their team aboard the ship. The others had gone down with the last module to help unload and set up for the night. Once Jihi and her partner attached the personnel box to the orbital lift, they'd descend, and that would be that until the miners actually needed something.

Right now, they were likely powering up the first of the personnel modules, the emergency reactor, and other likely needed supplies in the event of a meteor shower, stellar flare, or some other unexpected disaster. Good thing too. Every tour to a planet or moon that had no atmosphere, the modules took an impact or two from micrometeorites or larger objects.

With the system's debris field so far from MacReady, he didn't think those were much of a concern, but you could never be too careful.

The tug hovered just beyond the still open cargo bay doors. The last of the miners mag-walked expertly to the hull, clamped themselves to it, and waited a beat before the tug's thrusters puffed a cloud of gas. The tug headed for the orbital lift.

Two hours. Maybe. Within two hours, assuming nothing went wrong, he'd eat his shift's meal, shower, and crawl into his bunk for as many hours of sleep as he could. Next shift was when he'd have to be on his toes.

After a few more minutes, the tug finally reached the lift. Jihi and the last of her miners detached the transit box from the tug and slotted it in the lift, and Jihi parked the tug at the orbital lift's edge. The magnetic moorings would keep the tug from moving.

"Jihi to Cap," she said over the command channel.

"Go," Til said.

"We're a go for surface."

"Jordan?" Til asked.

"My board is green," Jordan said. "Lift is ready to rock."

"Jihi, you are a go for descent," Til said. "Enjoy the ride."

"Copy," Jihi said. She might have sounded excited while piloting the tug, but any bravado she might have had had dissipated. He supposed everyone traveling a portable orbital lift had that experience. For some reason, the idea of traveling down a tether while in a flimsy aluminum box tended to make a person tense. Even if you believed the engineers that, should something happen, the box would shatter and eject you into the safety of space, the lizard brain didn't accept the argument. Instead, it remained convinced you had entered a death trap.

"Now. Now. Now," Jihi counted off and activated the lift.

The transit box, or tbox slid through the slot and down the tether at a good clip. The tbox, far less massive than the smallest of the mining modules, could descend far faster without worrying about deceleration.

Jordan sighed heavily before heading to the port side of the cargo bay. With all the mining modules, sans two spares, on the planet's surface, the bay looked strangely empty. Had it been pressurized, he could yell and listen to the echo bounce off every surface the *Kirkland* had to offer.

"Two kilometers," Jihi said. "All is well."

"Copy," Til said.

Jordan reached the airlock with the word "Tug." The typical warning signs for vacuum and the like littered the bulkhead in luma paint, and Jordan tapped them as he hit the stud beside the airlock. The light above it flipped from red to green before the hatch opened. Jordan entered, closed the hatch, and waited for the airlock to cycle.

He entered the tug's tiny cabin and took the seat. After bringing the interface to life, he rechecked the statuses he'd already checked earlier that morning and made sure nothing had failed in the meantime. Nothing had. Why would it?

"Cap? I'm in Tug 2 for S&R."

"Copy, Jordan," Til said. "Take a nap."

"Considering it," Jordan said.

Now, he waited. And waited. And waited.

# CHAPTER TEN

The shift buzzer went off, and Jordan immediately opened his eyes. They felt as though they'd been gummed shut during the night, although he knew that had just been the result of too much dried air and not enough liquid. In short? He was dehydrated. He'd have to take care of that before he even considered donning an EVA.

He rose from his bunk with a yawn and mag-walked to the cabin's holo interface. Scratching idly at his crotch, he brought his messaging client to life and saw multiple messages from Aryana.

Fully awake now, he chose the first, read it, and laughed.

*Yo, Boss. We got the personnel module all set up and let me tell you—miners stink. Ever notice that? They reek enough to make me not want to eat anywhere near them. If you know what's causing that, you better tell Jihi. Smells like someone died.*

Ah, yes. The first day was when all the packing material, extraneous crap that held everything in place for the descent, started to decay. By tomorrow, nearly all of it would have turned into methane and $CO_2$, both filtered out by the system.

The next message, stamped two hours later, said simply:

*They tell me it's the packing material. I feel like an idiot.*

The most recent message, one that had come in twenty minutes ago, asked him to contact her at his convenience. *How professional*, he thought. *Not like Aryana to be so formal.*

Jordan rubbed at his eyes before pulling a fresh jumpsuit from the hamper and slipping into it. Certain his hair was a nest of corkscrews, he activated the interface and connected to Aryana.

A moment later, the display filled with the picture of Aryana's pinched face. The mining suit's interior camera made her features look as though they'd been squashed together by a pair of foam pillars.

Grinning, he said, "Good morning. You look as fresh as a daisy."

"What's a daisy?" Aryana asked, her voice shrill and annoyed.

"Never mind," Jordan said, fighting a chuckle. She seemed more on edge than she should be. Shit, it was nearly impossible to piss her off. "What's your status?"

"Take a look," she said.

The display flipped, and he was suddenly looking through her helmet cam. She'd focused on the orbital's landing platform. Its edges appeared flecked or maybe even rusted. It was difficult to know.

"Whoah," Jordan said. "How much of the metal is affected?"

"A lot of it," she said. "I did a tensile test, and Jihi had Mario check out the stability. Doesn't seem affected. Maybe the finish is coming off?"

Finish. They did coat the modules in a radiation-resistant glaze. But that stuff didn't fleck off. If it went, it went with the metal itself—unless something else was going on, that was.

Jordan fought back another yawn. He really needed caffeine to continue this conversation.

"Are any of the other modules affected?" he asked.

The camera view flipped back to that of her face. "Doesn't seem as though they are, but the miners are going to inspect equipment as they set up near the first site."

"Good idea," Jordan said. "You file an official status report?"

"No," she said, annoyance replacing the frustration in her voice. "Jihi's going to write it up."

*Well, that's why she's pissed,* Jordan thought. Jihi jumped Aryana's chance to file her first official status report. Christ, but the woman had ambition to spare. He fought back a smirk and said, "Is there anything else? Apart from the change in color on the metal?"

"No," she sighed extravagantly, the word dragging out several beats longer than necessary. "The stink? Why didn't you tell me that happened?"

"I thought you knew," Jordan said. "I've been around it enough times. I'm used to it."

"I smelled it before," she said, "but not like that. It was hideous."

"It is," Jordan agreed. "When do you set up for the first site?"

"In an hour," Aryana said. "I'm guessing you'll get that news from Cap."

"More than likely," Jordan said. He finally yawned and didn't fight it. The sound practically vibrated the bulkheads.

"Wow," Aryana said. "Was that a yawn or a howl?"

"Both," he blushed. "It means I need drugs."

Aryana smiled. "Go get them. I've already been in this suit for half an hour."

"And pumped to the gills, by the sound of it," Jordan said.

Now it was Aryana's turn to blush. "Guilty as charged," she said. "Okay, boss. Back to work I go."

"Aye, aye. Talk soon," Jordan said and saluted. The feed died a beat later.

* * * * *

Til waited until Jordan had finished his second energy drink before appearing in the galley hatchway. With only Jordan, Til, and Chu aboard the *Kirkland*, the galley felt haunted. That Til's voice echoed didn't help.

"Ready for a briefing?" Til asked.

Jordan smiled. "Informal, I take it."

"To an extent. Get some grub," Til said and sat across from Jordan.

Jordan had a feeling what was coming next, so he headed back to the dispensers and grabbed a pair of nutrition bars. This was obviously going to be a working breakfast.

As if on cue, the holodisplay at the far end of the room came to life with a ghostly, staticky blue. By the time Jordan returned to the table, the display had changed to show a model of the *Kirkland*, MacReady, and *Prospector-9C512*. Jordan took his seat, eyes half-focused on the display.

Jordan tossed one of the bars to Til, who nodded his thanks and ripped open the wrapper.

"*Prospector's* not far away," Til said. "Should be an easy capture for refuel and resupply."

Jordan sighed heavily. He'd known this was likely, although he thought maybe he'd dodged a bullet, since Aryana was on the planet's surface. Apparently, his luck wasn't in.

"So long as one of you two—"

Til waved away the statement. "Chu will be with you. He can pilot the tug, and you can handle the particulars."

*At least it won't be you,* Jordan thought. "Chu knows what he's doing. That should work."

"Good. It'll need—"

"New cells, replacement modules, and routine maintenance," Jordan said. "Once Chu drags it into the cargo bay, I can start fixing her up. But Cap? We're going to lose the drone feeds."

"Why's that?" Til asked.

"*Prospector* doesn't have much power left, so it doesn't much matter. But," Jordan said, "all the drones are tied to it. I can't even crack the damned things from here without *Prospector* giving me the chance."

"Lovely," Til said and tapped the bottom of the uneaten protein bar on the table. "What about in situ?"

"Is that a fancy way of asking me if I can refuel her without taking her completely offline?"

"Wow," Til said with a grin, "you're smart."

"Fuck," Jordan said. "Better to be dumb."

"Look"—Til lifted the bar and finally took a bite from the end—"you get there with a cell and whatever other comms equipment you need, hack in, and transfer the drones to us, and then you can shut it down and bring it home for the real maintenance."

"Sounds all too rational and reasonable," Jordan said.

"But?"

"But we could just as easily wait to do that until after we bring up the miners for R&R in two weeks." Jordan munched his own bar. He already felt less drowsy, brain cells more together and unified. "What's the hurry?"

Around a mouthful of crunchy vitamins, minerals, and artificial flavors, Til said, "Right now, we only have the *Kirkland*'s QE comms. If we have to phone home and something happens to our comms, we're fucked. Besides," Til said, "it's procedure. Right?"

Jordan couldn't argue with that. It was the first thing they should have done before deploying the mining team, but that had been the mission's first priority. *Prospector* had been flushed to second and the bow shield to third. Until now, at least.

"We need to get the miners to deploy their own drones then," Jordan said. "Just in case."

Til continued biting, chewing, and swallowing. "I'll tell Jihi. Now what about the fore shield?"

Jordan smiled. "I've been thinking about that. What if we take some of the refined ore and repurpose it to piece together a new shield? We'll be a galactic eyesore, but with a bit of work, including printing more massive support struts, it should handle the stresses as well as the original shield did."

Til leaned back in his chair and crumpled the now-empty bar wrapper. "Interesting idea," he said. "I take it we'll lose the ore?"

"Not at all," Jordan said. "Just means we'll be carrying it differently. I'll draw up some plans for you."

"I like that better than trying to piece one together," Til said. "Those temporaries aren't nearly as thick."

"You're telling the teller," Jordan said dryly. "Hence the overkill. I don't like the idea of waking up in a stasis escape pod."

"Me neither," Til said. "Been there, done that, didn't like it the first time."

Jordan said nothing. Til had referred to the mysterious incident more than once but had never bothered explaining it. Jordan guessed the captain would one day. Maybe.

"Anything else?" Jordan asked, desperate to change the subject.

Til stared up at the ceiling, his fingers tapping on the table. "There is one thing."

"What's that?"

Til leaned forward and put his elbows on the table. "Chu ran the numbers. You know that thing that comes zipping through here every couple of weeks?"

"Yeah," Jordan said, getting a sinking feeling.

"In about sixteen hours, it's going to go streaking across our sky."

Jordan blinked. "So?"

"So," Til said, "I'd like to get this all done before that happens. I want *Prospector* aboard the *Kirkland* and out of harm's way. If possible."

Harm's way? What was he talking about? "If I remember correctly," Jordan said, "the thing is thousands and thousands and thousands of kilometers away. How could it pose a threat?"

Til sighed and turned his gaze back to the display. He touched the interface, and the display zoomed out until the entire system became visible. An outline off to the left plotted the trajectory of the aforementioned object.

"I've been thinking about this thing ever since we discovered it," Til said softly. "I don't like it. I don't like that it's here. And I sure as shit don't trust it."

"Can't say I disagree with anything you just said."

Til smiled and said, "I figured you wouldn't."

"Sixteen hours," Jordan echoed. "We can do that, I think."

"Was hoping you'd say that. Get with Chu when you're ready. I want a flight and supply plan."

"You'll have it," Jordan said.

"And," Til said, "one last thing."

Jordan suddenly remembered Aryana. "The metal."

"The metal," Til echoed. "What do you think did that to the metal?"

"I've no clue," the engineer said. "If MacReady had an atmosphere to speak of, if it had high winds and a significant pressure, I'd say it could be one of a thousand things. But MacReady doesn't have any possible surface phenomena to explain something like that."

Til exhaled long through his nostrils. "My thoughts exactly."

"Aryana asked if it could be the glaze," Jordan said. "I guess it could if—well, if it suffered extreme heat or radiation."

Til sighed. "It's been in our bay for how long? All of these modules, all of these temporary structures? More than a year? And up until the drop, as far as I know, everything was pristine."

"I know," Jordan said. "Obviously doesn't make any more sense to you than it does me."

"No." Til sounded defeated. "It was a shot in the dark. Mario phoned in a while ago. They took some samples, and it's not the glaze."

"Do they know what it is?"

Til shook his head. "They're setting up the laboratory for today's drilling samples, so they'll have a look once they finish."

"Good, I guess," Jordan said. "I'd rather know what it is now than later."

"I know what you mean," Til said. "Anything you need to ask me before you get started?"

"Yeah. How much more of your stash do you have? Because I fucking hate EVAs."

Chuckling, Til managed, "You'll get a reward, I promise."

"Good doggy," Jordan said.

Til rose from his chair. "Plans."

"Twenty minutes," Jordan said.

Til walked out of the galley and out of sight.

Jordan's eyes slowly drifted back to the display and the model of the star system. The line representing the object's trajectory cut through the model at an odd angle. At least it looked odd to him, but he couldn't say why. Just another mystery to add to the rest of the mess.

He quickly finished another nutrition bar, slammed down another energy drink, and headed to the cargo and engineering bays. He needed to talk to Chu, but he could do that on the way.

# CHAPTER ELEVEN

The cargo bay's starboard side lay open like a clamshell. Just beyond the lip was the tug, Chu in the pilot seat. Now all Jordan had to do was cling beneath the starboard shield.

His hands shaking slightly, body vibrating like a tuning fork, he stepped forward until the tug's edge was half a meter from his grasp.

*Don't look into space,* he told himself. *Stare at the metal. Nothing else.*

Forcing himself forward, Jordan stuck a palm to the tug's hull and immediately locked himself in place. It took him a few seconds to convince the rest of his body to join it. Once he was beneath the shield, his heart slowed slightly, and he felt as though he could breathe again.

"You okay, Jordan?" Chu asked over the comms.

Jordan did his best to catch his breath. He didn't want to sound like an asthmatic over the comms. "Fine. I'm beneath the shield now."

"Okay. Hey, Cap?" Chu called.

"Go," Til said.

"We're ready for the EVA."

"You are go for EVA, Chu." Til paused a beat. "Y'all be careful out there."

"Says the guy behind meters and meters of alloy," Jordan mumbled.

"I heard that," Til said. "And it's only a meter thick. Quit bitching and go fix my satellite!"

Jordan grinned. "Aye, aye, Captain."

"That's more like it," Til said. "Get out of my damned cargo bay."

Laughing, Chu said, "Tug 2 going for EVA."

"Acknowledged," Til said, a grin in his voice.

The tug shuddered, and Jordan felt a thump through his boots. Behind the shield, he couldn't detect any real movement, but his HUD showed him all he needed to see.

The tug's cams covered all directions, including the ventral side. Jordan watched as the *Kirkland*'s hull moved farther and farther away. Another cam feed showed the blue nebula's ghostly clouds staining the otherwise empty, star-pocked horizon. The sight of it calmed him somewhat—he could look at that all day.

Across his tours, Jordan had seen various nebulae, planetoids, ringed planets, comets, and countless other phenomena. He'd even seen a pulsar from a less than safe distance. He'd rarely had a chance to enjoy them, however. Most hadn't been viewed live but via playback. Engineers didn't usually get much time to stare out a porthole.

This nebula, however, seemed different somehow. *More alive, maybe?* The thought made him shiver.

MacReady's system was dead, dead, dead. Dying star, ice giants that might once have been something else, and, of course, three planets devoid of life of any kind. Including seismic. The star system was merely dead space.

The tug continued moving away from the *Kirkland* and toward a bright spot a few hundred kilometers away. This was a hell of a hike and certainly not one he could have made without a tug. No suit he knew of had enough fuel or was accurate enough to launch from the ship and hit a target that far away. At least not one as relatively tiny as *Prospector.*

Which was not tiny at all. The satellite was the size of several rows of hover-cars stacked atop one another. It held sensor pods that contained drones and equipment, onboard ML algorithms for both interstellar navigation and prospecting, and enough fuel to travel multiple systems before requiring a resupply.

*9C512*, however, was out of fuel. MacReady was only its second find of its current tour but its fourth system. Prospectors were designed to visit up to six, but extreme distances and adjustments required the use of more fuel or stellar energy. 9C512 hadn't been near a bright star in years, and the galaxy's stellar wind hadn't been enough to keep up with demand.

If a Prospector made a find, it stayed in place and continued reconnaissance and site evaluation while it waited for the mining crew to arrive. That could take as many as three to five years, if at all. Sometimes the companies decided they didn't want the find. Either it was too expensive to mine due to environmental/system concerns, or the material price didn't support sending an entire crew.

Jordan often wondered just how many Prospector satellites littered the galaxy, orbiting their abandoned finds until the star system went nova or a stray bit of stellar flotsam destroyed it. Those derelict metal visitors would probably remain a testament to the human species long after it had gone extinct.

"How you doing, Jordan?" Chu asked.

"Fucking dandy," Jordan said.

"I remember you hating EVAs, but I didn't know they were panic attack-inducing."

Jordan frowned. "Didn't have a panic attack."

"Okay. Let me rephrase. I didn't know they made you so anxious."

"They don't, normally," Jordan said. That was half-true. He was always nervous during an EVA, and he'd always hated them. Without a fellow engineer to back him up and the other oddities that made up the MacReady system, he felt far too vulnerable out here, with or without a shield.

"Curse of MacReady," Chu muttered.

"What?" Jordan asked. "What curse?"

He could practically hear the shrug in Chu's voice. "Too many dreams, I guess. Til and I can't get that debris field out of our heads. Nor MacReady's sisters."

"Hell of a puzzle," Jordan agreed. "You have any theories?"

"None that are sane," Chu said.

Jordan smiled at that. "Okay, lay the insane ones on me. Keep me talking. It helps."

"Gotcha," Chu said. "Insane speculation number one is that MacReady and her sisters used to belong to another system. Some unknown event pushed them away from their parent star, and they wandered here."

"Okay," Jordan said. "Next."

"Next is that the planets used to be much closer to the dwarf star, but its red giant phase pushed these bodies out here, where they found a new orbit. In that case, the star fried their surfaces."

Jordan found himself nodding. Both theories made a certain amount of sense but were spectacularly improbable. "What else?"

Chu was silent for a moment. "That they're not planets."

Jordan's heart skipped a beat, and he shivered inside the warm EVA suit. "Not planets," he echoed dumbly.

"No," Chu said. "These are manufactured. What they were manufactured for, I couldn't even begin to guess."

*Manufactured. Constructed.* "Alien," Jordan said.

"Yup," Chu said. "All three are alien creations that were somehow damaged."

"Insane theory," Jordan said.

"Let's hope so," Chu said. "But I think that one might be more probable than the first two."

Even Jordan's brain seemed to shiver at that statement. Chu wasn't being facetious—the man wasn't capable of it. He was stating fact, and that was what made it terrifying.

"You don't really think that, do you?" Jordan asked.

"No," Chu snickered. "I don't. For one thing, we've detected no latent energy, the surface is as expected with other planets and planetoids of the type, and it's solid, not hollow. So what purpose could it serve?"

That was a good question. Jordan didn't think it likely that an alien civilization would spend precious resources on three massive testaments to their existence. There would have to be a good reason.

All three were the same, yet radically different. The radioactive and spinning sisters couldn't properly be evaluated, but they appeared to be identical to MacReady herself. Spin. Radioactive. Normal.

"One of these things just doesn't belong," Jordan muttered.

"What?" Chu asked. "What doesn't belong?"

"Sorry," Jordan blushed. "Just wondering how we should define normal in this system."

"Good luck with that," Chu said. "Not a damned thing about this system is normal. Fifty kilometers."

Jordan blinked. Had they been talking that long? Or had he just been thinking for that long? Maybe Chu had accelerated far more than Jordan had realized.

"Copy," Jordan said and leaned out just far enough to see beyond the shield's overhang.

Chu had hit the attitude thrusters, and now the tug's fore faced the *Kirkland* while its engines burned several times to start their deceleration. Jordan quickly ducked back behind the shield. He'd seen enough for the moment. Once the tug more or less came to a halt, he'd have no problems. Well, fewer problems.

"Hang on for a couple of burns," Chu said.

A moment later, he felt the hull vibrating gently through the gloves' tactile sensors as well as his boots. The EVA suit had some of the features of a typical mining suit but with relatively little armor and more flexibility. The onboard Suit personality, however, was completely absent from EVAs. Thank Christ.

Although he'd put up with one if it meant he had more armor. After seeing the debris field, he wasn't sure he trusted the sky to remain free and clear. Space was a big place, and it was all too easy to miss something the size of a car coming right at you until it was practically in front of you. Especially in a system with a waning white dwarf casting hardly enough light for a respectable albedo. In short, he could be taken out at any second once he left the cover of the shield.

"Okay," Chu said. "Decelerating fine with thrusters now. Going to get as close as I can."

"I appreciate that," Jordan said.

"But we might bump. So be prepped."

"Joy," Jordan said. Chu only laughed at that, but he wasn't mocking— the pilot just thought it was funny.

It was amusing. A starship engineer who was afraid to be outside the hull for any length of time was a rarity. One who was good at their job? Probably more so.

If Jordan had something to repair on the hull, he fought through the anxiety and paranoia until he was able to focus. A focused Jordan was a happy and fearless Jordan. It was the Jordan he liked rather than this shivering wreck of a human being clinging to the hull of a tug. Hell, he wasn't even in any real danger, and he was having issues.

"How long?" Jordan asked.

"Thirty seconds or so," Chu said. "Wow. *Prospector* took a beating."

Jordan focused on the aft cam-feed and immediately knew what Chu was talking about. Pits similar to what Aryana had shown him covered the satellite's hull.

"I'll be damned," Jordan said. "Looks like—"

"The damage from the planet," Chu said. "I don't like that."

"I don't either," Jordan replied.

"Ten seconds."

The artificial satellite, a massive thing five times the size of the tug itself, cast its shadow over them. Jordan felt as though he'd been plunged completely into the void. The cam feeds flashed as the tug's powerful lights came to life and banished the darkness.

"In five," Chu said and counted down.

When he reached zero, the tug jumped slightly as though it had collided with a deep sofa. Jordan yelped in surprise.

"Sorry. Sorry. Sorry. Too close."

Even if Chu hadn't hit the satellite, Jordan would have known he was too close. Even through the slit in the shield, he could make out *9C512's* damaged hull. "Worse than what Aryana showed me," Jordan said.

"From the stills I saw, I'd have to agree," Chu said. "Okay, I'm as locked in as I'm going to get. Still don't understand why they didn't design these to be dockable."

"They did," Jordan said. "But not by a modern tug."

"Oh," Chu said.

Jordan grinned. Chu was on his third tour and relatively young. He wouldn't know about the tugs from several decades ago when *9C512* traveled to its first system.

Jordan only had to disconnect from the tug and jet over to the satellite, which meant he had to get out from behind the shield. Which meant he would be vulnerable. Which meant—

"Everything okay?" Chu asked.

Jordan flinched and did his best to keep his voice steady. "Yeah. I'm ready."

# CHAPTER TWELVE

If Chu hadn't said something, Jordan might have happily stayed nearly frozen to the hull. Instead, he forced himself to get out from behind the shield. The tug's powerful lights illuminated the satellite's ventral hull, and no longer constrained by his view from behind the shield, he realized just how bad it really was.

Jordan turned, dropped to his haunches, and knelt forward, one hand sticking to the hull. He demagged his boots and his other hand and climbed down.

"How's it going, guys?" Til asked over the comms.

Chu snickered. "Jordan says it's going fucking peachy."

"I heard," Til said. "Jordan?"

"About to EVA," Jordan said as he lined up to face the satellite. If he demagged his hand and touched his jets, he'd begin a slow, gentle glide to the satellite. No impact problems, no risk of perforating his suit. Easy.

Jordan took a deep breath. "Go for EVA."

"Copy, EVA," Chu said.

The moment Jordan demagged, his body began to float away from the tug's hull. Heart hammering and adrenaline sizzling through his blood, he activated the jets for just a touch longer than he intended.

Jordan, fewer than four meters from the satellite to begin with, ate the distance much faster than he'd anticipated and panicked at the last second, doing his best to fully turn in the opposite direction with the jets. Unfortunately, he was too slow.

He slammed into the satellite with his hip, and even with the EVA suit cushioning much of the impact, it was hard enough to make his bones ache. He yelped as he bounced off the satellite and headed back out into space. Cursing, Jordan managed to get control of his attitude, kiss the jets, and touch the satellite. His mag boots and gloves came to life, and he locked to the metal like a barnacle.

"Um," Chu said, "that wasn't quite procedure."

"No shit," Jordan said. He demagged his boots and crawled hand over hand down the side of the hull. When he reached the ventral side, he locked his feet and squatted next to a shield labeled with the word Ports. He rapped it with the EVA suit's armored knuckles, and the shield lit up green. Smiling, Jordan pressed a thumb against the shield. The light flashed several times, and the shield vibrated beneath his gloves.

The thick metal panel pulled inward before sliding aside and revealing an interface. Jordan rotated the index finger on his right glove, and a small metal prong appeared.

"Chu? Going to authenticate."

"I'll be ready to pick up your charred corpse," Chu said nearly robotically.

*Fuck you,* Jordan thought but didn't say. The rumor, more like an old space tale at this point, claimed that if you didn't properly authenticate with a Prospector, you'd get a hell of a bang. As in the satellite would either expel a shaped charge designed to take out whomever had attempted to hack it, or the whole damned thing would blow.

Jordan didn't believe either, although the former was more likely than the latter. No one, not even the company, would be dumb enough to destroy all their data when they could just remove a physical pest. What better way to do that than a shaped charge or perhaps an electrical surge to disable a suit's electronics? Those were possible.

He pressed the exposed metal tip against the receiver and waited. A green light looking like a sleepy cat's eye blinked twice before the holodisplay came to life.

```
Prospector 9C512 Interface

Engineer: Jordan

Command?
```

Every satellite interface he'd seen was the same. In a way, it was a comfort. Never having to learn a new interface or new Q scripts or fight with unproven technology made life easier and made common tasks such as maintenance a well-known quantity.

It was also a testament to the Prospector's design and durability. The damned things seemed to be indestructible, and despite the simplistic interface, the pain in the ass that was the refueling and resupply procedure, they just plain worked. Jordan would take the archaic CLI (command line interface) over the fancy displays he'd seen for newer models made by other manufacturers. Sometimes simplicity truly was best.

He expertly tapped through the menu options until he found what he was looking for. The holodisplay belched blue static before bringing up the positions of all the drones on MacReady's surface. Jihi and her crew had obviously recharged *9C512's* drones, but they still didn't have any control over them. At present, they were just immobile cameras.

But not for long. Jordan went through the options and re-tasked the drones. After sending his biometrics information to *Prospector*, it relayed the commands to the drones. The holodisplay lit up with **OPERATION COMPLETE** and a slew of text statuses.

"Shit," Jordan said.

"What is it?" Chu asked.

Jordan shook his head. "Well, I fucked up and made myself root."

"Well, that's not good," Chu said. Then he giggled. "Guess that means you transferred the drones."

"And took control of *Prospector.*"

"And since you have control, whether you should or not," Chu said, "let's get this hunk of junk hooked up to the tug so we can head home."

Chu was right. Jordan had already fucked up the user account system. How much more damage did he want to do before towing it back? *Routine maintenance,* he said to himself. *Yeah, right.*

Sighing, Jordan disconnected from the interface, locked the panel back in place, and walked to the corner before climbing back onto the starboard surface. An umbilical tether, a thick cable that ended in a massive squat, cylindrical slab of metal, extruded from the tug. It hung in space like a stiff rat tail, the end barely curling.

"I hate this," Jordan said and walked across the hull to where the line dangled. He had to stretch to reach it, but with his mag-glove turned to high, the metal accelerated to him until it connected with his glove. Jordan turned, stood sideways, and kept the thick cable next to his hip. "Going for connection."

"Go," Chu said.

Jordan affixed the heavy metallic end to the satellite. It clamped with a vibration that made his fingers tingle. "Attached," Jordan said.

"Green on my board," Chu said. "Stand back."

He didn't have to tell Jordan twice. Jordan stepped a meter away. "Go," he said.

A strong electrical current flowed through the cable, and it immediately became as stiff as glass, strong as steel. The thick cable could tow something twice the size of the satellite if you had enough time and fuel. As it was, towing this sucker was going to take at least an hour, meaning Jordan would just have to sit on the hull and do nothing while Chu took them home.

*Speaking of hulls.* "Okay, getting back on the tug," Jordan said.

"Go," Chu said.

A three-meter gap. Easy. Sure, keep telling yourself that.

He demagged his boots and pushed lightly. He left the hull and floated lazily toward the tug. In a few seconds, he had his hands out to cushion the blow of contact as well as to keep him from bouncing off its surface and into space. He'd already fucked this up once today, and he didn't intend to do it again.

It worked like it was supposed to, just like out of a training manual. With his hands outstretched, he easily touched the tug's hull and clamped to it, his feet locking in a smooth motion.

*Why couldn't you do that earlier?* he asked himself.

*This time you weren't thinking about it.*

A good enough reason, he supposed. Too busy trying to re-task the drones and beating himself up for the scripting faux pas. The tug shuddered, and Jordan looked sideways.

"Retracting," Chu said.

The tug slowly accelerated toward the more massive satellite. Without assistance from its powerful engines, it was like an ant trying to tow a combat boot. When the tug was fewer than a few centimeters away, the vehicle decelerated quickly until it moved at a nearly imperceptible rate.

"In five," Chu said.

Five seconds later, the tug shook hard for an instant, and Jordan bit his lip in surprise.

"Okay, that was harder than I expected," Chu said.

"Who taught you how to pilot?" Jordan asked. "Til?"

"No," Chu laughed. "If he'd taught me how to pilot, we would have wrecked."

Til's voice broke in over the comms. "I heard that. There will be repercussions."

"Like what?" Jordan asked. "You going to threaten to come out here and help pilot?"

"That was low," Til said. "No more stash for you."

"Uh-huh," Jordan said.

Chu cleared his throat extravagantly until the other two men fell silent. "We're a go for tow."

Jordan could hear Til's grin through the comms.

"You're a go, tug 2," Til said. "Also, Chu? You have no sense of humor."

"If I didn't," Chu said, "how could I work with you?"

Til didn't have a response for that, but Jordan was still giggling as the tug's engines came to life. Once again, his bones vibrated, and his vision stuttered. Once the rockets found their stride and were actually synchronized, the vibration became little more than the occasional tingle up his spine.

"We're going to be accelerating for a while," Chu said, "so get comfy."

"Had planned on it," Jordan said. In truth, it would be easy to fall asleep here. All he had to do was convince his brain he was lying down instead of standing up. And, depending on how you were looking at things, he was already lying down.

Til's voice broke the comms again. "Hey, Jordan? I've got Aryana on the line for you."

"About time," he said. "Can you patch her—"

"Jordan?" Aryana said. "You there?"

"Here. What's the report?"

She sounded excited, happy. If she hadn't, he'd have been worried.

"Main reactor is up, and we've got two drills ready for the sample cores," she said. "I'm still at the lift site, doing some checks."

"Excellent," Jordan said. "I have control of *Prospector's* drones. Did you recharge them?"

"Of course," Aryana said. "Did that before we slipped off for end of shift."

*Of course, you did,* Jordan thought. "Good. I have control of the drones. So, if you need *Prospector's* moved, let me know the coordinates, and I'll make it happen."

"That's great," Aryana said. "We could use them. Two of our other drones kind of crapped out."

Jordan raised an eyebrow. "How so?"

"I don't know," she said. "They've got power, and everything mechanical works just fine. It's like their brains just went dead. I'm not even getting past the POST."

"You try a firmware wipe?" Jordan asked.

"I can," she said. "Just haven't had time. They don't cover the drilling areas, so I guess it's not a big deal."

"Okay," Jordan said. "Give me the coordinates, and I'll move *Prospector's* drones to cover."

"Awesome. Jihi will be happy to hear that."

"Where's she?" Jordan asked.

"She's at the south ridge drill site. She and, um, fuck, what was his name? Oh, Carty. They're taking a core on the west base."

"Sounds good. Another sit-rep in—"

"An hour," Aryana said. "Sorry I missed the last one. We were, um, a little busy down here."

Jordan knew what she meant. He'd missed a couple of sit-reps in his career too. Getting shit done was always more important than appeasing management.

*Shit,* Jordan thought. *Is that what I am now?*

"Understood," Jordan said. "Let me know if you need anything else."

"Will do," Aryana said. "You on the tug?"

"For better or worse, yes," Jordan said.

She sighed. "I love the tug, but it's better to be down here."

"I'm sure," Jordan said. Her enthusiasm, naive though it might be, was catching. He imagined her bouncing around down there, finding things to do, helping the miners as best she could, feeling useful, feeling wanted. "Out."

"Out," Aryana said.

"Well," Til said with barely a pause, "sounds like we're good down there on the planet."

"I'll try and remotely reboot the failed drones," Jordan said, "but if she can't get past POST, we'll have to replace the boards."

"Shit," Til said. "Was afraid of that. But you'll cover with—"

"Yes, I'm re-tasking as soon as she sends me coordinates," Jordan said. He knew Til had listened in on the call, so why was he asking a question he already knew the answer to?

"Good. I thought that's what you said but just wanted to make sure."

That wasn't like Til. Unless he was doing something else.

"Everything okay, Cap?" Jordan asked.

"Yeah, yeah. Just stay ready to answer some questions," Til said. "Don't fall asleep just yet."

# CHAPTER THIRTEEN

Aryana hated the fact Jordan was up there by himself, forced to do an EVA with all that debris still flying around. At the same time, there was no place she'd rather be. Maybe after a few days of the chaos of setting-up was over and things settled in, the job would become as boring and taxing as it ever was. At least an engineer always had something to do.

Her last tour, equipment hadn't failed any more often than was normal for a tungsten/titanium/corundum operation. Of course, she'd joined Jordan, Til, and Jihi for the last six months of that grind on a mine they were shutting down. She'd only seen one part of the process, apart from being involved in the orbital lift operation and reel-up.

That had been exciting, but the well-worn paths to and from the mine, the rock being abandoned because it had been all but depleted of even the difficult-to-get-at ore, and the miners worn out and ready to go home, had cast a certain gloom over it. She always felt as though she'd missed the party, or maybe the opportunity to do something important.

Jordan had been as patient with her questions as she could have hoped for. When she fucked something up, he was never angry or short. Instead, he walked her through what had happened step by step and asked her how to correct it. A good teacher. He could turn anyone into a competent engineer. He could help turn her into a lead engineer in another tour or two.

A lead engineer. Her own assistant, another captain, a new mine boss, new systems, new planets, new ore. By her biological age of 35 and natural age near 60, she could retire with her health intact and go find something else to do. Like visit New Persia and ride its waves, or maybe make her way further in, where things were a little more adventurous and less ordered.

Something like that. Who knew what it would be? She didn't, but she wanted to find out.

"Aryana?" Mario called over the comms.

"Yes?" she said. He'd already taken a sample of the pitted metal and retreated to the lab.

"You up to help take a core sample?"

She grinned as she finished packing up her tools. The lift was fully operational, and diagnostics reported everything was as expected. Unlike the mining drones, the platform's hardened, barely digital controls could survive damned near anything, including whatever was causing the strange weathering.

"Sure," she said. "Just need to talk to Jihi and—"

Mario sounded as though he were grinning. "The boss says never go alone. Boss also says you're my assistant for the day."

"Oh," Aryana said. "Okay. What do you need?"

"Bring your tools," he said. "Everything else we need is already on-site."

"Meet you at the lab?" she asked.

"Excellent," Mario said and disconnected.

Sighing, Aryana took one last look at the orbital lift. Of all the things on the planet, or moon, or whatever you wanted to call MacReady, the lift was her single priority. As long as it functioned, the team could evacuate. Without it, they'd have to rely on the *Kirkland* to drop the spare or the emergency orbital. Doing either would be a little more dangerous without a full crew on board. That was the last kind of stress anyone needed.

"Okay," Shelia said. She'd been Aryana's buddy during the diagnostics and final checks. "We good? I'm meeting Bacon to head to the west crater."

Aryana turned and saw that Shelia had already moved a dozen or so meters in the direction of the lab and personnel modules. Taking the hint, Aryana walked at a fairly good clip to catch up. In the one-third gravity, it didn't take much effort.

When she reached Shelia, the two walked down the barely visible path leading to the modules.

"Mario's taking you for a core, right?"

Aryana nodded. "I haven't been to that site, yet."

"Mario and Jihi handled that one themselves," Shelia said. "Base of the peak. That's where *Prospector* started the find."

"Oh," Aryana said. "Right."

They walked in a silence broken only by the regular ten-minute station check-ins. Company policy and one Aryana didn't intend to break again. Not with the mining team, at least.

When they reached the personnel module, Shelia stopped at the airlock and waited for Aryana to move to the lab. When Aryana reached the far airlock, Shelia waved and entered the module. After a deep breath, Aryana entered the lab.

Mario stood over one of the module's built-in lab tables, an array of chemical dispensers, microscopes, and several tools whose function she only had the barest understanding of arranged at its edges.

Although he could have pressurized the lab, he'd chosen for it to remain with no atmosphere.

"You worried about contagion?" she asked, the proximity comms coming to life.

Mario stiffened but didn't turn around. "What do you mean?"

"No atmosphere? No pressure? Wasted chance to get out of your suit."

Mario shrugged. "Got an alien rock here that I haven't yet identified," he said. "Just being cautious." He placed a plastic covering over the table and locked it down. With that done, he sighed heavily and turned to her. "Enjoying your first day?"

Aryana laughed. "Been interesting."

Mario grinned. "Let's make it more so. Come on."

After he checked in with Jihi, Mario led her to a Mule, a vehicle made expressly for mining. With the right attachments, the versatile vehicle could tow enormous amounts of ore. By design, it had enough room for two, although no form of life support. The shielded cabin provided them with extra protection from cosmic rays and other EMR. Considering how thin the planet's surface was, it made traveling across MacReady much less dangerous.

Mario expertly drove the Mule toward the far peak. Aryana didn't like the radio silence. She wasn't as bad a chatterbox as Jihi, but she liked conversation, especially when stressed or overly excited. Right now, she was kind of both.

She didn't quite understand what she'd seen on the metal, and it had left her with a strange sensation in her gut. It wasn't fear, exactly, more like a disquiet she couldn't quite put her finger on. MacReady felt strange to her, and from the way some of the other miners acted, they felt the same way. She'd heard one or two of them mention a so-called "curse" back and forth, or that some planets felt more dead than others.

That was the problem, though. She didn't know why, but MacReady had a tingle to it, as though a storm was about to break out. Ridiculous. She was inside a pressurized, walking tin can made to withstand conditions far more egregious than this relatively unremarkable little world. She couldn't possibly feel an oncoming storm through the fabric and metal even if there was one right atop her.

"You don't always get a warning when a suit failure's about to happen," Jordan had told her last tour. He'd nixed a helmet he didn't like and had chosen to reprint a new one. "If you get a bad feeling, be aware. A little paranoia can save your life."

At the time, she thought he'd been overdramatic. After a few more weeks of service with the mining corps, she'd begun to pick up on why he'd said what he'd said. Get too complacent, you die.

When you weren't paying attention, some part of you always was. Sometimes it saw or heard things or even felt things the conscious mind didn't understand. When the subconscious figured it out, it did what it could while you were awake.

Some people called them premonitions, Aryana knew, but regardless of what they were, or what caused them, she erred on going with them. She wondered if most miners and spacers had learned that lesson.

"What do you think of this place?" Mario asked as if reading her thoughts.

Aryana said in a startled voice, "It's strange."

"Fucking eerie," he said. "Nine tours and I've never seen a place quite like it. Makes sense it would have a stash of ore."

"Happen often?"

"Pretty much," he said. "If there's not something odd, the Prospectors wouldn't find them. Has to be mineable. Has to lie within a certain range of pressure, temperature, and gravity. Those are oddballs, not the rule."

"Never thought of it that way," she said.

"Same thing goes for asteroid belts. Lots of rock but no guarantee of enough metal to make it worth anyone's while."

Mario made another turn, and the Mule climbed a short incline that she realized was the other side of a crater.

"What's at the bottom of those?" she asked.

Mario sighed. "More metal, I hope."

He brought the Mule to a halt just as she made out the dim glow of the mining platform. The massive drill used a plasma burst to soften the inner ore while still providing the drill traction. Without the slag lines hooked up, the drill looked strangely abandoned despite its obvious power.

Instead of the typical plasma drill bit, it had already been fitted with a core sampler. Given the relatively minuscule test results provided by *Prospector's* drones, the larger, longer core would give the geologists hints about the potential mine's stability and purity. Those two factors would dictate how they approached the mining process itself, if it could be mined at all.

With the Mule locked down, he left the cab and approached the massive drill. The onboard computer systems were idle, waiting for both his identicode and instructions. Aryana felt as though she were walking into the shadow of a great beast. Considering how much rock and metal the drill could churn through, that wasn't a surprise.

Mario extended the control panel, and a holo-console appeared. After flashing his identicode and making a few gestures, the machine's motors began their warm-up cycle. Although she couldn't hear the sound of the giant machine, she could still feel its vibrations through the gabbro beneath her boots via its tactile sensors.

Mario gestured to her and pointed beside him. "Never done this before?" he asked.

She shook her head.

"So, what we're going to do is to take a core. I have my eyes on the drill, so I need you to watch the bluff and make sure we don't have debris coming down on us. If we do, we'll either try again after moving beneath a shield, or we'll give it up."

"Okay," Aryana said dumbly.

*Watch the bluff? The sheer rock wall that rose a couple of hundred meters virtually straight up?* If debris was going to come down on them from there, she doubted she'd have much of a chance to see it before it was right on top of them. The planet's twilight was on the deep end of dusk, not the beginning of a star's descent over the horizon.

Shadows shifted with every movement, the star's dim light casting just enough illumination for them to exist naturally. Still, with her helmet lamp oriented upward, she could see well enough. Maybe Mario's idea wasn't as insane as it first sounded.

"Boss to crew 2," Jihi said over the comms. Her voice crackled every few seconds before the static disappeared. As it continued, Aryana realized it had a pattern to it. What was causing that?

Mario paused "Crew 2 here. Go."

"Mario? I've got a big, big strike over here. We cored two meters in and found corundum! No impurities detected!"

Frowning, Mario said, "You know that's impossible. Must have a bad analyzer."

Jihi sounded offended. "Have you forgotten I'm a geologist? I know what a faulty analysis looks like. Seen dozens of them."

Aryana couldn't help but smirk at that. She imagined Jihi glaring with her face curled up in that know-it-all sneer she had somehow perfected.

"Okay. So, what are you telling me?" Mario asked.

"To only go a meter and half deep. When we finished our core, there was some kind of flash of green light. I think our drill crapped out. Carty's checking it now."

Aryana looked in the direction of Jihi's mining area. The sky there looked wrong, the stars slightly obscured by a thin film of green. Confused, she followed the horizon back to the bluff and saw the glow there as well.

"Oh, shit," she whispered.

Mario looked up from his console and followed her stare. "Jihi? Whatever you did, the sky's gone green."

The rhythmic wash of static started again. "—kidding?"

"You're breaking up," Mario said. "Jihi?"

No response.

"Jihi?"

Nothing.

He looked back at Aryana, and the camp channel came to life. All the other miners up there in space, including Til, would get the message.

"Crew 2. Anyone got eyes on Boss?"

No response.

Mario repeated the message before beginning a channel check for each of the crews. Nothing.

"Aryana? Do what I just did. Follow the sequence."

His voice sounded shaky but in control. Her own, when she started speaking, stuttered every few words. She more or less followed the script Mario had laid out and received the same response—nothing.

She took a deep breath and ran over the possibilities.

"EMR," she said to Mario. "If you and I are both affected, there's some kind of interference there. Must be localized."

Mario shook his head. "Might be right about the EMR, but it's not localized. Short range. Otherwise, we wouldn't be talking to one another."

She considered that for a moment. "Might be a downed link. Maybe we're the only ones cut off."

He nodded to himself more than to her. After glancing back at the drill, he touched the pad to power it down. It returned to standby mode, and he refolded the console. "This'll wait. What's the rule, Aryana?"

"Comms are out. Head back to camp."

"Got it in one. Come on."

She followed Mario back to the Mule and climbed inside. He lingered for a moment, staring out at the horizon.

He crawled inside beneath the shield and started the vehicle. Without attachments, the Mule's turn radius was incredibly tight, and he expertly turned them back in the direction of the barely laid road.

They trundled down the crater lip, and as they started to ascend, the green in the sky grew thicker, as though the planet itself was attempting to construct an atmosphere. Aryana knew that made no sense, but it was the thought that stuck in her mind.

"What the fuck is doing that?" Mario asked.

They crawled up the other side of the lip and onto what she'd already begun to think of as the main road. One intersection led off to the orbital lift while the other led you to camp. Of all the intersections to remember, it was the most important. No matter how you reached it, it led to safety of one kind or another.

Aryana turned to look in the direction of the orbital. The green shimmer continued growing in intensity. The thick cable rose into the sky like an all-too-distant promise of heaven. This place was no longer interesting—it was now terrifying.

"What is that?" Mario asked. He'd turned to look behind them.

She turned back to look across the crater and saw several strangely colored orbs bobbing up and down near the peak and the drill.

"Get us out of here," Aryana said.

Mario turned his head and touched the throttle. The Mule smoothly accelerated past the intersection and toward the camp. By the time they reached it, there was something else in the sky to look at.

# CHAPTER FOURTEEN

Ten minutes later, an alert appeared on Jordan's HUD. *Prospector-9C512* had officially run out of power apart from basic subsistence. In other words, it was now a more or less completely dead hunk of metal. They might as well be towing a garbage can that had a functional computer.

He'd change all of that once they finished towing the satellite to the cargo bay. Pod refills, new energy cells, a few replacement boards, not to mention inspection of whatever that shit was on the hull, and they could relaunch *9C512* in a few days, well before the first shipments of ore came up from MacReady.

Backup quantum entangled comms, more eyes on the sky and the ground, and all of that before they sent the satellite on its way to whatever system it had been told to investigate. It was worth the few days of work and the dangerous, boring tow. It always was.

"Hey, uh, Jordan? Chu?" Til asked. "Since you both have nothing to do, how about you tell me I'm crazy?"

As soon as Til finished the sentence, Jordan's suit received a file from the *Kirkland*. He blinked twice to open the file and his HUD filled with the 3D model of MacReady's star system. A line that presumably began somewhere beyond the farthest reaches of the system inched forward across the display.

"What is that?" Chu asked.

Jordan mentally plotted the line and froze. "Til? It's headed for us, isn't it?"

"Shit," Chu muttered.

"Right, Jordan," Til said. "In astronomical terms, yes, it's aimed right at us. However, it's going to pass us within 10k kilometers."

"How did its trajectory change?" Jordan wondered aloud. His mind filled with all the possible scenarios, most of which involved massive objects or gravity fields knocking the object off course. If they didn't already know the object was cyclical, they'd have no idea this was out of the ordinary.

"Ever get the feeling we're missing something?" Chu asked.

"I'm going through *Prospector's* footage again," Til said. "See if I can find another instance where it changed trajectory. I'm not hopeful, though."

"Can't have been a large one," Chu said. "Otherwise, the algorithms would have caught it."

"I did say I wasn't hopeful. Still," Til said, "doesn't hurt to take a look. Especially since the mining crew is getting their shit done."

"Heard from Jihi?" Jordan asked, only half paying attention.

"Yeah," Til said. "All's well. They're getting ready to pull the first two cores."

How much power did it take to accelerate an object to that speed? And how much more power did it take in delta-V terms to push it that far off course? And when did it begin this change?

"Hey, Chu? You still think it's natural?" Jordan asked.

"Is what natural?" Til asked.

Ignoring the captain, Chu said, "No. I don't."

The line went dead for a moment as even Til seemed to be absorbing the statement. Jordan's flesh prickled. He'd seen some strange shit over his last seven tours, but this was like nothing he'd ever heard of.

"How long?" Jordan asked.

"That's the real problem," Til said. "In about thirty minutes, that thing is going to come whizzing through here."

"Oh, fuck," Chu said. "And we're going to be out here."

"That's about the size of it," Til said. "I estimate you're still a good forty-two minutes out, if you factor in getting you on board and the satellite secured. That's a mighty tight window."

"Beyond tight," Chu said. "And I can't cut twenty minutes off our flight time."

"Right," Til said. "So I'm open to suggestions."

Jordan, still studying the diagram, said, "Til, plot the object in 3D space. Give me images of where it's aimed in relation to the *Kirkland* and the tug."

The HUD flashed a moment later, and an animated model appeared. The object would pass the *Kirkland* and the tug at a ten-degree angle. Curious. More importantly, however, it was on the far side of the planet. They didn't have time to move the ship behind the planet or out of line of sight of the object, but the tug could use the ship as a shield. Maybe.

"Chu? If we can get to the bow, we can hide behind the ship," Jordan said.

"Sure. I'll just bring a million metric tons of alloy to a sudden halt and change trajectories from midships to the bow. Easy."

"Make it so," Til said. "That's an order."

"No," Chu said, "that's a prayer. I don't think we can do it."

"It's worth a try, Chu," Til said. "Even if you don't get there, you'll be closer if you have to ditch."

Jordan hated when Til made sense, but he liked the captain's idea better than continuing to the midships during the object's flyby.

"What do you think, Chu?" Jordan asked.

The man was silent for a few beats before saying, "I'm already plotting the burns, Captain."

"Excellent," Til said. "How much did it hurt for you to admit I'm right?"

"More than I'll ever acknowledge," Chu said.

The pair's banter made Jordan grin but did nothing to decrease the bad feeling he had.

*You're just jittery because you won't be back on the ship in an hour.*

*No,* he told himself, *I'm jittery because I don't know what the fuck is going on.*

That was the truth. According to the diagrams and telemetry Til had sent, the UO had already behaved as if it was under artificial thrust of some kind. Very powerful artificial thrust.

The word "alien" kept pulsing in his mind, but it just seemed so ridiculous. All the worlds humans had traveled to and they hadn't discovered more than the simplest of lifeforms, things that were barely more advanced than single-celled amoebas back on Earth.

Amoebas don't build starships.

No human craft he knew of could reach those speeds without entering rift space, regardless of whether or not they had passengers. Although biological passengers did complicate the speed problem a bit more. Regardless, the UO moved faster than anything anyone had heard of, and it was coming straight for them.

*Who wouldn't be anxious? You think Til and Chu aren't shitting themselves?*

Jordan smirked as he imagined Til sitting in the captain's chair on the bridge, a mag-mug trembling in the cup holder as he attempted to figure out other possibilities. And, like Jordan, unable to accept any of them.

That was why Jordan's skin prickled, and his mind filled with worrying thoughts. Like what kind of power source did the thing use? Would it leave toxic radiation in its wake? Or maybe something worse? Was it traveling fast enough to create some kind of cosmic phenomenon? Was it nothing more than a strange meteor?

"Jordan?" Til asked. "What do we do in case of an EMP?"

Good question. "We're hardened against everything short of a focused military burst. That said, I don't know what happens if we get smacked with something like that."

"Lovely," Chu said. "So we could just get shut down?"

"Improbable," Jordan said, "but possible."

"Any systems I need to worry about?" Til asked.

"Yeah," Jordan said without a beat, "all of them."

Til groaned. "Seriously, J. What the fuck?"

"Get in a suit. Get ready to be on $O_2$. Depressurize the ship." Jordan took a breath after realizing he was on the verge of shouting. "Til? Treat it like you would an oncoming piece of debris that will smash through several decks."

"Oh," Til said. "That bad, eh?"

"Prepare for it," Jordan repeated. "But if I were you, I'd definitely shut everything down and vacate the air. Also? Be ready to head for the personnel module."

"Wait a minute," Chu said, "didn't we hear all this in flight school?"

"Shut up," Til snarled. "I get it. I'll make it happen. But what are you two going to do?"

"At the very least," Chu said, "I'll put *Prospector* between us and the flight path. If it can bake us through *Prospector's* hull, it wouldn't have too much of a problem broiling through the *Kirkland's*."

"Yeah, okay," Til said. "Just try to make it to the bow first. I have to get in my damned suit. Out."

Til had tried to sound flippant at the end but had failed. If Jordan hadn't already been nervous, that would have been enough to make him feel that way. Til was normally rock steady. This had him spooked enough that—

"Shit!" Til yelled through the comms. "It's moved again."

"What?" Jordan said. "Slow down."

A new image appeared on Jordan's HUD. A new trajectory lay practically atop the old one, but it was closer than it had been.

"Oh, fuck me. Is it still changing attitude?" Chu asked.

"In a word," Til said, "you're damned fucking right it is. *Kirkland* is telling me it's significantly cut the angle of approach and its current trajectory takes it nearer to the orbital."

"What?" Jordan asked. "The orbital? You have to be kidding."

"I don't—" Til broke off for a moment. "Yeah. It's the orbital, Jordan."

The updated model of the star system displayed the object in 3D space when it would be at its nearest point.

"It'll miss MacReady and the orbital itself," Jordan said, "but it's going to get damned close."

Jordan brought up his position relative to the object and turned his head to look past the shield. A blue dot glowed brightly in the distance, its hue much deeper than that of the nebula. He thought he knew what ancient man must have felt like upon seeing their first shooting star or eclipse—utter, primordial terror mixed with bewildered fascination.

"Fuck me," Jordan breathed.

"Chu?" Til said. "Whatever plan you got, you better get on it."

"Moving as fast as I can," Chu said. "I'm not driving a car here."

"Great, fine. Whatever. I'm getting into my suit now. Off comms."

Neither Chu nor Jordan said a word. Jordan wondered briefly if Chu wasn't staring up at the blue-colored object of doom approaching them at terrifying speed. The color didn't twinkle like a star but instead seemed to pulse as though it were alive.

"What the fuck are you?" Jordan said off comms.

"Alien." The word echoed in his mind again and refreshed his feeling of dread.

Aliens.

*Fuck.*

"Til? You there?"

A beat passed without an answer. The moment he opened his mouth to call again, Til spoke.

"I'm here. With a suit and a helmet. What new fresh hell have you opened now?"

"You talk to the drill crew?" Jordan asked. "Warn them we have incoming?"

"Um, not exactly," Til said. "Why don't I get back to you in a few minutes? Out."

"You know," Chu said, "he needs a minder."

"He needs a copilot," Jordan said.

"More like an administrative assistant. Preferably one that's robotic and whose programming is filled with bugs."

Jordan laughed, imagining Til screaming at a squat calendar with legs. It had a certain amount of charm to it. Especially if it had Jihi's voice.

"Hey, Jordan?" Chu asked.

"Go."

"You're a hell of a lot more exposed than I am. Might make sense for you to come up with a plan B."

"Plan B? What's wrong with Plan A?"

"A severe radiation storm, for one. Or maybe enough debris to fracture that flimsy shield you're hiding beneath."

*Shit.* Chu was right. His EVA suit was made to handle lots of rads and intense heat/cold fluctuations. It was not, however, made to withstand a bevy of impact trauma, let alone a host of cosmic rays. Whatever was headed toward them certainly had enough power to do untold damage. The only question was whether hiding behind meters of tungsten alloy would save him.

# CHAPTER FIFTEEN

Jordan shuffled to the edge of the tug's shield. *Prospector* lay directly in front of him, separated from the tug by less than a few centimeters, if that. To keep himself from being exposed to any radiation resulting from the UO's passage, he needed to mag-walk to the other side of the satellite. Yet another mag-walk he didn't want to make.

"Okay, Chu. In position."

"Copy," Chu said. "Good luck."

Instead of answering, Jordan pushed away from the tug's hull and easily clamped to *Prospector's*. With a long exhale, he moved past the edge and across to *Prospector's* adjacent side. His suit's radiation sensors flashed yellow—the rads had increased fourfold.

Jordan scanned the hull and his heart sank. Several chips of metal protruded from the hull, each glittering like quartz beneath his light. "Chu? I found more of that radioactive metal on this side."

"Wonderful," Chu said. "Keep you from staying there?"

"Nope," Jordan said. "I can cling here like a barnacle. Not much safe room but should be good enough to keep me from getting flash fried. If, that is, there's really anything to worry about."

"Oh, the best thing of all time would be for me to sit in the corner, feeling stupid," Chu said. "Cap would lord that over me for forever."

"Yes, I would," Til said.

Chu ignored him. "Okay. Stay put, Jordan. Provided there isn't some debris lingering about that we don't know of—"

"Don't jinx it," Jordan interrupted.

"I think," Chu continued over him, "you're safe as you could be. Probably safer than me."

*Probably true,* Jordan thought. He had two layers of thick titanium and tungsten alloy between him and radiation from the craft. *No,* he told himself, *UO. Object.*

"Craft." That word. Was it a ship?

*Why are you still asking yourself that question? What else could it be?*

He was beginning to run out of alternative answers to that question.

"Um, guys?" Til said. "We have a problem."

"So what else is new?" Chu asked.

"For starters," he said, "the object has changed trajectory again."

Jordan couldn't imagine something moving that fast capable of making micro adjustments millions and millions of kilometers away from its target in order to rendezvous with it or avoid it. That took a level of precision he couldn't quite comprehend. One more reason he considered Chu some sort of genius.

"Where's it headed now?" Jordan asked.

"Away. Back to its original trajectory, in fact."

"So, emergency over?" Chu asked.

Til cleared his throat in a way that made Jordan shiver. "Our scopes were focused on the object, so they saw what they saw. And before you ask, what they saw was something coming through the debris field."

Jordan raised a brow and said, "Another light? Like another object?"

"No," Til said. "I don't know what it was. It disappeared as quickly as it showed up. If it's under power, whatever's powering it casts no light and no EMR. Or at least none that we can detect."

Chu harrumphed at that. "Our sensors are shit," he said. "If *Prospector* actually had some power left, we could get better intel."

"True," Til said, "but by the time we got it refueled, or at least powered up enough to use the sensors, that thing will be far past us."

"I did say 'if,'" Chu said. "So, when are you going to give us the all clear?"

"I'm not," Til said. "Until that thing is far, far away, we stick to the plan."

Jordan couldn't disagree with that. If Chu could get the tug close enough to the *Kirkland*, both he and Chu could park the tug and its cargo against the bow, use an airlock, and get behind thick, thick, beautiful hull. But that meant continuing at this pace, one that would take far too long for his liking.

"Aye, aye, Cap," Chu said wistfully.

"Wow," Til said. "I expected more of a fight."

"No, sir," Chu said. "Unless you want to get out here with us."

"No, thanks," Til said. "I'll just stay here and—"

His voice broke off, and a few seconds ticked by without another word.

"Cap?" Chu called.

No response.

"Til?" Jordan said.

No response.

"The fuck now?" Chu asked. "We being jammed—"

Til shouted over the connection, "Chu! Jordan! We've got incoming!"

A new feed appeared on Jordan's HUD, probably from one of the many onboard telescopes. Jordan's brain tried to make sense of what he was seeing but couldn't process it. A bright blue light, waves of shimmering white either behind it or in front of it, pulsed and flashed the darkness away.

Whatever it was, it was moving at incredible speed.

"Hang on!" Chu said.

The blue comet's trajectory began deviating from its head-on course. Suddenly Jordan knew where it was headed.

"It's going to hit the orbital!" he yelled.

A second later, a lightning bolt struck the orbital lift platform. Space flashed as though hit with a high-powered strobe light, and then a flood of alerts and warnings flew across his HUD. Radiation, incoming object, collision imminent. The platform and orbital shattered as if they had been made of glass.

The camera view managed to withstand the assault for a few more seconds before a piece of debris filled the feed, and it winked out of existence. Chu shouted something over the mic, but the words were unintelligible and filled with static. Jordan closed his eyes and doubled his magnetics.

A beat later, *Prospector* vibrated like a tuning fork, and all too soon, Jordan's bones and spine joined it. His mind bounced inside his skull as though it were being pounded by an electromagnetic jackhammer. The sensation of being trampled a thousand times a second departed, leaving his head spinning.

Jordan opened his eyes while the suit's radio burped and spat static. His HUD flickered multiple times before solidifying, the stack of translucent alerts all but obscuring his vision. After blinking away the alerts, he brought up the suit's status. Right now, that was more important than talking to Chu or anyone.

$O_2$ reserves unaffected. Thrusters unaffected. Comms? Down. Magnetics? Functional.

Another barrage of broken, fractured, meaningless syllables streamed over the radio. Jordan, still facing the satellite's hull plate, turned his head slightly and saw the tug's hull glittering with what looked like quartz.

Jordan suddenly had a bad feeling. His suit's rad sensors hadn't spiked and didn't detect abnormally high background radiation, but that didn't mean those shards weren't the same material embedded in *Prospector* as well as one of the *Kirkland*'s shields. If they were, then he had to be careful. And Chu was probably fucked.

"Clear, clear, clear," Jordan said over the comms. "This is Jordan on *Prospector*. Anyone copy?"

A beat passed. Then another.

Jordan tried again, but there was no response. Either he wasn't transmitting or they weren't receiving. Or, shit, who knew? Maybe everyone's radios were fried, including *Kirkland*'s.

He crawled to *Prospector's* corner and looked at the tug's aft connection to the satellite. The hull plate looked as though it had been blasted clean, the metal gleaming and glittering in places. A piece of debris as large as his hand whizzed by the tug's bow, and another disintegrated off the tug's starboard side with a flash of light.

After pulling himself back around the corner, he tried the comms again. When he got nothing but static, he activated the low bandwidth comms and sent the tug a message. This close to the vehicle, even his suit should have enough power to send bytes of data and for Chu to receive them. Assuming, of course, any transmissions were making it through.

**Chu: Where are you?**

Jordan grinned at the message. He activated the speech-to-text interface and said, "On *Prospector*. Suit okay. No comms. Lots of debris. Safe for now."

He sent the message, and Chu quickly responded.

> Chu: Tug's engines offline. Radio comms offline. Network offline. Orbital One completely destroyed. Kirkland suffered significant damage to aft. Can see plumes. What's plan?

*Good. Fucking. Question.*

The empty reply-message button seemed to accuse him. You're the senior, it seemed to say. Use your damned training.

Too bad training hadn't covered being fired upon by aliens. Otherwise, he would.

He sent a message to Chu, asking about their position relative to the *Kirkland.*

> Chu: Off the bow, 40 km away and drifting slightly off course.

> Jordan: Drift intentional or malfunction? Does Kirkland have power?

> Chu: Unintentional drift. Impact scrambled nav computer. Adjusting by sight.

By sight. Christ. If Chu had no real sensors available, he wouldn't even be able to tell how fast they were traveling, let alone their true distance from the ship.

> Jordan: How's our orbit?

> Chu: Unstable. Too early to tell for ship.

Gravity would slowly draw them down into MacReady. Even the massive *Kirkland* would eventually succumb, crash into the moon's surface, and create one hell of an impact crater.

Jordan: Radiation levels outside tug? Kirkland?

Chu: Unknown. Unknown.

For whatever reason, the tug's sensors weren't detecting shit, meaning it was impossible for either Chu or Jordan to know if the tug's hull had been irradiated. Or if those glittering shards of metal were the same as the highly radioactive substances three meters from him. If they were, Chu might get fried the moment he attempted to leave the tug. Chu would be trapped.

*Think,* Jordan told himself.

*Prospector* hadn't had much power before the blast. Without the network, it was impossible to know if the satellite was even still online. It might have been damaged as badly as the tug. Or even worse.

Jordan would have to make his way across the hull plates and pray he could find a path that wouldn't result in him getting fried. What he really needed was a shield, something he could put between his suit and the radiation sources. If that was even possible.

* * * * *

The UO decelerated to 1/2000th the speed of light. During its last stellar run, it had picked up a signal, something different from the artificial thing now orbiting one of the five remaining fragments. When the local surveillance drone reported additional energy signatures on the fragment, ones it had waited millennia to detect, the UO responded by opening one of its many silos and launching a projectile. It knew what the sources meant—Enemy had survived.

The projectile recorded gravity, heat, dimensional drift, electromagnetic energy, and the worst thing it could find—life signs. As it flew toward the debris field and the three fragments, it continued quantum casting the information in real time. When the sensors picked up signs of life on the fragment's surface as well as in orbit above it, the UO activated one of several boring pods hidden within the debris field.

The projectile annihilated the orbital on its way to the real target—Enemy's nascent power network. When the projectile detonated, waves of gravity distortion, high-energy fléchettes, and an enormous EMP bombarded the target area. Any external power sources Enemy had brought online had now been neutralized.

Although the alien interstellar craft hadn't been destroyed, the nano-sats hidden in the debris field did record significant damage. They also recorded life signs remaining on the planet's surface.

Frustrated, the UO vowed to remedy that on its next pass. When the sensors announced life signs remained on the damaged craft and that the boring pod had successfully landed, the UO was pleased. The trap had been sprung.

# CHAPTER SIXTEEN

The shockwave rocked Til in his command chair, the magnetics and belts holding him firm against the jolts and jitters as the ship's hull trembled like a broken tectonic plate. Alerts flashed across his EVA suit's HUD.

**CATASTROPHIC DAMAGE TO HULL**

**REACTORS OFFLINE**

**LIFE-SUPPORT SYSTEMS CRITICAL**

**ENGINEERING EXPOSED TO SPACE**

**CARGO HULL CRITICALLY DAMAGED**

"Fuck me," Til drawled. "If you—"

**COLLISION WARNING**

He didn't feel the crash of whatever it was that hit the hull, but his mind provided the sound anyway. A heartbeat later, the ship's network completely died. The cabin lights flickered and strobed around him as they fought to recover from whatever had obliterated the orbital.

"Well," Til sighed, "at least there won't be any more alerts."

He knew it was hopeless, but he tried to reach Chu and Jordan. As expected, nothing but the digital version of static—connection unavailable.

Til hung his head, took a deep breath, and tried to center himself. The panicked animal that lived inside every sane life-form desperately attempted to crawl into his mind and scratch, tear, and devour him whole. He wasn't going to let it.

*Whole fucking crew is probably dead,* he told himself. Still, if they weren't, he'd do his best to get them back aboard and keep them safe. He just doubted that was even possible at this point.

"Captain's job," he said aloud and unbuckled the restraints. He rose from the dais and stepped down onto the deck. He knew it was his imagination, but the *Kirkland* now felt devoid of life, as if the engines had somehow been the ship's soul. No life now, though. Damage computers didn't exaggerate or understate. If it said critical damage, it meant something was so fucked it probably couldn't be repaired.

Til, feeling a little drunk from stress and the ship's wobbles, left the cabin and entered his ready room. He and Chu might not be engineers, but they each had emergency tool packs and extra supplies stashed in the ready room's overhead bins.

He quickly found the belt, silently thanking Chu for his compulsive ordering and labeling of everything, and attached it to his EVA. Next, he pulled a hull hammer from a slot and clamped it to his back. The tool, a thick piece of tungsten carbide with a pry bar at one end and a massive hammer at the other, with a little help from his augmented suit, could pull loose a hull plate or widen an existing perforation. As the name implied, it could also be used to bludgeon and even shape plasma-heated metal.

If Jordan and or Chu had survived, they might need help getting into the cargo bay and docked. Without a functioning network, he had no access to the ship's cam feeds, which meant it was impossible to know what kind of shape the cargo bay was in, let alone the tug docks.

"Come hell or high water," Til chuckled, "we'll get it done."

Wishful thinking, sure, but what else was there to do? Besides, it was a little early to give up, wasn't it?

Flexing his fingers and adjusting his grip, he stepped to the threshold and stared out into the cockpit. No lights. No power. Nothing.

After panning his lights around the area and somewhat convincing himself there were no hostiles, Til stepped past the cockpit cabin and headed to the corridor, locking the hatch behind him. If someone needed to go in there, they could open it. He just felt better knowing something was between him and the bridge's emergency airlock.

The corridor's emergency lights flickered but at least provided some sense of security. Til would take it. Something was wrong, though. He knew it. Felt it. That EMP hadn't been normal. Shit, nothing in this system was normal.

*Guess I should have made the call to get the fuck out of here,* he thought.

*Yeah, and lose your captaincy, waste three years of miners' lives and company resources, and find yourself unable to sustain more than a living as a janitor.*

*Besides, you couldn't have left until the engines recharged and were checked and you had a damned bow shield. What were you going to do? Risk hitting something else?*

Til flexed his fingers around the hull hammer and continued walking. The intersection of the forecastle, personnel, and cargo modules provided a strobe of shadows and less detail than he liked. Worse, when he'd first seen the flickering shadows, he could have sworn something moved by the lift leading to the cargo bay deck.

He could turn off his suit lights, switch to lowlight filters, and brave the flickering gloom but didn't dare. The filters might provide him with more details, but they wouldn't break up all the shadows nor provide him the telltale warning sign of his lights reflecting off something that shouldn't be there.

*Aliens. Fucking aliens.*

Til shuddered at the thought.

\* \* \* \* \*

The boring pod, a glowing teardrop-shaped, powered mass of exotic metal, slammed through the debris cloud forming around the pulverized orbital, and into the *Kirkland*'s damaged rear dorsal hull. The hull plates surrounding the engines had been twisted and cracked by the force of the EMR attack. The pod crashed through several bulkheads, including the one separating cargo from engineering. When it finally came to rest, it was near the back of the cargo bay.

It left a sizable impression in the deck plate, its front seemingly half-buried in the alloy. The pod jettisoned its rear casing and flung the metal slab back into engineering.

A meter-diameter orb hovered out of the pod. It bore no markings, was as dark as deep space, and moved with an uncanny grace. The orb activated its scanner, found what it was looking for, and advanced into the shadows.

The engineering bay had auto-sealed some of the damage, but the oxygen reserves were currently burning away into space. Flames flickered through the perforated bulkhead and cast strange shadows. The orb detected excessive damage from the EMR blast, estimating that some of the primitive ship's electrical systems had been destroyed. Some would come back up in time, but in essence, the ship had been disabled.

The orb's short inspection as it traveled upward resulted in a less than one percent estimate that the life-form aboard would pose a significant hazard. That was good.

The orb reached the railing that looked out over the cargo bay. From here, it could see the flames in the distance, but their light was nearly entirely lost by the time it reached the orb. Except for the ambient flashes from the malfunctioning emergency lights, the orb was effectively clothed in utter darkness, but it knew it would be seen.

It would use that to its advantage.

* * * * *

Til blinked at the lift. Regs said to use it. Fuck the regs.

He walked sideways to the railing, demagnetized, and pulled against it in a smooth, firm motion. Til rose into the microgravity at a decent clip. His lights shined on metal debris, shattered plassteel, and someone's goddamned mag-mug. He knocked it away as he headed to the ventral deck.

Til turned expertly in the microgravity and came to a more or less smooth stop, his mag-boots activating immediately. He stood there looking down across the cargo bay with an excellent view of the destroyed engineering bay.

"Fuck me." Til swallowed hard. "Look what they did to you, girl." For a moment, he forgot all about aliens, or even going home. The sight of his ship in this shape was like losing a lover.

Something moved in his peripheral vision, but that wasn't a surprise.

Everything that hadn't been anchored, including debris and shit that shouldn't ever be in a cargo compartment, floated like an asteroid belt. He'd no idea how much of the material had been irradiated. For all he knew, he was swimming in some alien EMR that his suit couldn't even detect. Shit, he could be dying.

The movement was more pronounced, and he finally turned his attention away from the flames and destruction to take a peek. A shape had risen over the railing, the occasional flicker of the emergency lights making its silhouette strobe. At first, he'd thought it was just a lightless circle, a mini black hole hovering over the deck. But it wasn't. It was metal. Or something like metal.

Til took a step backward. The orb did nothing. He took another step back, and the orb still did nothing. He walked backward another five meters before coming to a halt next to a thick hull seam support. The orb still hadn't moved.

He scrunched his eyes, trying to remember whether or not he'd suffered a shock to the head. No. And he hadn't had a moment of blackout or lack of oxygen. No gaps.

"I'm not hallucinating," he said softly. "So, what the fuck are you?"

The orb didn't answer him. Til felt his away around the support, mindful not to snag himself. Once behind it, he was sure the thing couldn't see him. At least he hoped not.

*Okay, genius, now what?*

He didn't know. He could push off and hide between the damaged modules still in the bay. Or maybe he could make a distraction.

No power, he remembered. With power, he could have started all sorts of machinery, even commanded the cargo bay hatches to open.

If only there was still a tug on board, he could—

Unless they'd been blown to shit, Jordan and Chu were on their way here. If he could get to the airlock, he could make his way to the outer hull beneath a shield and wait for them. He could figure out what to do once they rendezvoused.

Til opened his eyes and glanced at the dorsal deck, or what would normally be "the floor," and felt a brief moment of vertigo, his inner ear somehow insisting he was walking on the ceiling. Once the feeling passed, he noticed something in his peripheral vision and turned toward it.

The orb had floated past the support and was now a mere five meters away, hanging above the deck like an eclipsed moon. Til shivered as he stared at it, waiting for it to fire some kind of beam weapon and turn him into vapor. Instead, it appeared to be waiting. For him to do something?

He backed farther away, and this time, the orb followed, matching his jittering, unsteady steps with smooth motion but always halting as he did. Til looked down at the deck and saw something there that didn't belong. Some kind of egg-looking thing stuck in the steel.

He flicked his eyes back to the orb, which hadn't so much as twitched since his last step. He looked down again. If he approached at an angle, he could maybe reach the ventral deck personnel airlock. If he could get inside without that thing following, he could at least figure out what to do next. Sitting in an airlock wasn't exactly a great refuge, but as his daddy used to say, any port in a storm.

Til wanted to flex his knees, push off, travel as fast as he could, maybe goose himself with a thruster push or two just to make sure. He'd come down hard, but it would be worth it, wouldn't it?

Only problem was that his alien friend (he still couldn't quite believe it was alien) would likely follow, and he didn't know how fast it could move. More importantly, he had no idea what the thing could or would actually do. Apart from matching his steps, it had done nothing hostile. How the hell was he supposed to know if it was dangerous?

As slowly as he dared, he reached for the hull hammer and pulled it free. The orb didn't react, but Til did his best to hide the tool behind his back, even though he knew the thing had seen it. Had the orb known what it was and that Til could use it as a weapon? Would it attack?

Til ground his teeth. *Don't know until you know,* he said to himself, grinning like an idiot. He bent his knees as far as the suit allowed and pushed off, timing the cut in magnetics perfectly, and smoothly traveled through cloud after cloud of chaff, the metal and plassteel fragments bouncing off his suit like raindrops.

The deck was only seven meters away when he came to a complete stop, his brain sliding inside his skull as if he'd suffered a massive collision. There was no pressure around his body, nothing physical gripping him, yet something held him in place.

Til curled into a ball so he could see behind him, and his mouth dropped open. The orb touched his feet, its surface crackling with electricity or some other form of energy, and held him in place as he struggled to loose himself from its grip, almost as if it were patiently waiting for him to give up.

Eventually, the orb descended with him in its grasp. Another wave of energy spread outward from the orb, and he suddenly felt as though every part of his body were blanketed, immobile. He tried to move, but he couldn't even flex his toes.

The orb lowered the still-screaming Til to the deck, next to the damaged boring pod. It released his feet, but the bubble of energy remained around him. The orb hovered and shimmered above his face as a needle broke the orb's otherwise smooth surface, and descended until it punctured the suit's collar, piercing his neck.

Til, eyes bugged in horror, felt flames boiling his blood and a wave of agony he'd never imagined possible. His entire body felt as though it were covered in stinging wasps, each puncturing his flesh thousands of times a second. A sense of pressure fell over him, compressing his lungs into empty sacks of crushed alveoli.

His eyes remained open while the needle once again disappeared into the orb. It lowered itself further, its bottom nearly touching his face. A hose appeared from the pod and connected to the orb. The translucent hose immediately filled with green and yellow liquid.

Something else extended from the pod, a transparent container with something green and yellow and red. He couldn't make out any details, but it looked as though the something was twitching.

Til, panicking from the feeling of suffocation and his heart beating like a runaway machine, tried to scream.

# CHAPTER SEVENTEEN

**Jordan: Need to interface *Prospector*.**

**Chu: Y?**

**Jordan: Check ops. Drones.**

**Chu: Walk careful.**

The last text response came after a maddeningly long moment.

Jordan hadn't poked his head back around to look at the tug and didn't plan on it either. Right now, he was studying the hull plate.

There was no pattern to the flecks of glitter, which worried him. It was as if *Prospector* had found itself in a cloud of the stuff and some of it had clung like pepper on a filet, if the spice had been pressed into the meat at hypervelocity.

Jordan moved to the right for two meters until his rad sensor went off, a bright red glow at the edge of his HUD telling him which direction the energy was coming from. Instead of continuing left, he extended a glove, locked it in place, and slowly pulled the rest of his body upward.

He managed a full body length before the sensor went off again. This time, the signal was much stronger and directly above him. A quick glance told him he was beneath several shards that had clumped together. Mindful to keep himself as parallel to his former position as possible, he slowly moved left until the sources stilled.

Another body length upward and this time, he didn't have to adjust at all. Another eleven or twelve meters and he'd reach the hull plate with the interface. Another set of sources on the left side and above him. Fuck.

He moved right, but the sources didn't diminish. They multiplied both in number and strength. Just as he was thinking about backtracking, he crossed some sort of threshold and found a clear path to the near right angle formed by the hull plates.

With a sigh of relief, he crawled upward until he reached the edge. Once there, he stopped in disbelief as he took in the full view of the destruction.

The orbital was gone, as well as the platform. No trace of the tether remained, meaning it had probably been detonated along with the orbital. What hadn't been blown apart would slowly drift down to MacReady, the massive loop of flexible alloys and electronics crashing into the surface after extreme acceleration. Any miners unlucky enough to be caught in the vicinity would be pulped into spray.

The *Kirkland*'s aft was doing more than pluming—it was leaking radiation. The aft containment for the reactors must have perforated spewing steam at intense temperatures and pressures. The gas most likely burned through the rear firewall and into the engines themselves. Once that happened? Boom.

He could just make out the telltale curl of a warped hull plate, the exposed portion ripped and torn as though a firecracker had gone off inside a closed tin can. Jordan winced, thinking of all the damage done to the engines. If the *Kirkland*'s comms still functioned, his HUD would be stacked with warnings and critical failures, resulting in a veritable field of yellow and angry crimson.

The remains of the orbital had exploded outward creating a cloud bank of debris that spread for a few cubic kilometers. Jordan wondered how long it would take before the pieces began conglomerating, all pulled by MacReady's gravity to rain down upon its surface.

*Surface. Aryana.*

He walked to the interface and brought it to life. The display flickered for several beats before finally stabilizing with only a few staticky horizontal lines that occasionally drifted down from the top of the screen.

The status windows told him exactly what he'd feared—*Prospector's* sensors had been all but fried, and its power reserves had almost been completely drained. General comms with the ship and suit telemetry had been torched as well. No good news there.

However, *Prospector* still had comms with the drones, although the bandwidth was practically nonexistent. Jordan copied the surveillance footage for the last two hours to his suit's memory store, intending to peruse it later. If there was a later.

*Has to be,* he told himself. *Otherwise, the mining crew is totally fucked.*

*Like the orbital tether falling atop them wouldn't have done that?*

Jordan gritted his teeth at the interior voice's mocking, hateful tone, but it was right. Right now, he needed to worry about himself, Chu, Til, and the ship. Those were the only things he could do anything about and therefore his only priorities. Or so he told himself.

He brought up a list of all the available systems and shut down any that he considered extraneous. Scientific instrumentation, any system whose sensors had been fried, and as many others as he could find. When he finished, the only systems left were *Prospector's* brain, its low bandwidth comms to its drones, and the general comms system, which didn't function.

After waiting for all the systems to finish powering down, he checked the reserves again but this time brought up the drain statistics. This much reduced power and *Prospector* might remain semi-functional for another eight hours. If he was lucky.

He tapped *Prospector's* hull with a glove. "Hold together," he said to it and disconnected from the interface. If the comms came back on, *Prospector* would recognize him as the root user and let him do whatever he wanted. Very much against company policy, but Jordan didn't give a shit. He needed whatever edge he could get.

Jordan looked to the horizon and the *Kirkland*'s damaged aft. The midships, however, appeared intact. At least structurally. He wouldn't know just how damaged the interior was until he could get in there. If he was lucky, very lucky, the two things he wanted most in the world remained undamaged and functional. If not, they were in even worse shape than he feared.

**Jordan: Pro has 8 hour battery remaining. No comms with ship or ground. Next?**

He waited a moment for Chu to respond. After more than ten seconds, his neutral expression dissolved into a frown. Five seconds later, he started to get downright scared.

Finally, a new message appeared.

**Chu: Maybe thirty minutes to reach ship. Ready for a leap?**

*Leap. Shit.* If Chu had in mind what Jordan thought he had in mind, the pilot wanted Jordan to flip off the tug and use his jets to reach *Kirkland*'s hull. From there, Jordan could easily get inside one of the emergency airlocks even if Til was injured and had no control over the ship. Or if other infrastructure systems had been damaged.

**Jordan: U?**

Another pause that lasted longer than he liked.

**Chu: Stuck in tug until you tell me otherwise. Safety.**

Safety. If the fragments buried in the tug's hull were radioactive enough to fry a suit, Chu was stuck inside until they could actually dock the tug with the *Kirkland*. It would keep him from being exposed directly by design. Once aboard the ship, he and Chu would have to don their mining suits. Til as well. There was no telling how many hyper-radioactive fragments had contaminated the ship. The mining suits might not fully protect them from the worst of it, but they would do a better job than the EVA suits.

**Jordan: Abandon *Prospector*?**

**Chu: Good idea. Push orbit?**

*Good idea, better question,* Jordan thought. Chu wanted to know if they should try to save *Prospector* by putting it back in orbit before they disconnected. Eight hours of battery life. It might make an orbit or two.

Jordan: Yes. Keep velocity as was?

Chu: Will try.

Jordan: Heading back to tug.

He didn't bother waiting for a reply before walking to the edge. He'd have to climb down *Prospector's* hull to get back to the tug, which meant he'd have to navigate the radiation all over again.

Jordan peered over the edge and to the tug below. It'd be a relatively easy jump and thrust to make it to the tug's edge again and duck beneath its shield afterward. Only problem with that, of course, was that he'd have to actually leave the hull and travel through the emptiness.

Jordan harrumphed. This was stupid. He was standing atop a failing satellite connected to a tug rife with radioactive particles, while trying to get to a ship whose ass end had exploded, and he was worried about another spacewalk.

Twenty-five meters at most. He'd gone much, much farther before, so this should be nothing.

Jordan: Coming back to the tug. Same shield.

Chu: Be careful.

*No shit,* Jordan thought, but he grinned despite himself. He positioned himself on the edge, one hand maglocked to the hull while he aimed his legs at his landing target. When he was somewhat sure he was properly oriented, he pulled himself in before demagging and pushing away from the hull.

He glided through the empty space separating *Prospector* from the tug. At first, he'd wanted to pat himself on the back—his aim had been true, and he hadn't misjudged it. What he had misjudged was the speed.

Before he slammed into the tug's shield, he flexed his legs and waited for the crash. When it came, it was worse than he expected and made his lower spine feel as though it had been rocked with a bat. Once he caught his breath, he maneuvered around the shield and locked himself in place.

*That could have gone better,* he thought.

Jordan: On tug.

Chu: Stay shielded.

Jordan: ETA to disconnect?

Chu: 30s.

In thirty seconds, Chu would perform some thrust adjustments to point *Prospector* in the right direction, and then he'd let the giant satellite go. With any luck, it would maintain a stable orbit at least as long as they needed it, however long that might be.

The problem with having nothing to do was that it gave you time to worry about all the things you had no control over. Aryana was down on the planet still, assuming she was alive. The same with the rest of the mining team. Without the orbital lift, they were trapped on the planet's surface.

However, the miners did have provisions and air to last them for weeks. Even more, should they ration themselves. They also had something just as important as food and water—the kinds of shelter that would protect them from cosmic rays, relatively high radiation, and any other dangers the planet might hold in store. In a way, they were in better shape than him, Chu, and Til.

So why didn't he believe that?

The tug vibrated several times, although from behind his shield, it was impossible for Jordan to know what adjustments Chu had made. Jordan was just along for the ride at this point.

**Chu: Five.**

Jordan mentally counted off, and at zero, the tug vibrated hard twice and stopped.

Chu: Clear.

Jordan: All good.

*Prospector* was on its way to a new orbit. Now he and Chu just needed to find a way onboard the *Kirkland*.

**Jordan: Enough fuel for midships?**

**Chu: No. Burned too much.**

*Shit,* Jordan thought.

**Chu: Kirkland bow best bet.**

**Jordan: U dock?**

**Chu: Got plan.**

Plan? Great. Jordan was glad someone had one.

# CHAPTER EIGHTEEN

The orb held the cargo case and extruded another needle, this one with a gossamer-thin point. The needle stabbed through the case and activated the proper genetic profiles, eschewing some due to incompatibilities in physiology. Unlike Enemy, the orb's creators had had no interest in bioengineering apart from taking up arms against a common threat.

After the profiles activated, the orb tested them and, once satisfied, removed the needle. It placed the case next to the immobilized creature and watched as its cargo squirmed out of the case and wriggled to the creature's shoulder.

Vapor rose as the cargo burned away the suit with its secretions. When it reached flesh, a new kind of vapor rose. The creature trembled and seized inside the suit. In a few moments, the change would begin, and the cargo would feed. The orb waited.

# CHAPTER NINETEEN

Jordan thought he'd be counting the moments, but they passed far too quickly. Every now and then, he felt an adjustment burn from the tug or maybe the sudden vibration of a piece of debris slamming into the hull. Still behind the shield, he'd no idea what was going on. He didn't have to either.

**Chu: Get beyond shield. Orient to bow.**

Jordan took a deep breath before demagging his gloves and mag-walking just past the shield's edge. The *Kirkland*'s bow and foreships appeared undamaged, but there wasn't a single running light to be found. The rectangular metal slab of a bow looked strangely sinister in the shadowy twilight of MacReady's star.

The tug was still moving toward the bow, but Jordan could tell now what Chu had planned. Once Jordan leaped for the hull, Chu could turn and blast the engines until he decelerated enough to keep from flying past the ship. If the tug had enough fuel left, he might be able to maintain orbit near the *Kirkland* if not actually land. His chances of making it to one of the docking bays, however, were slim to none.

**Chu: Ready?**

*No,* he wanted to say. *This is stupid. I should stay here until we dock.*

**Jordan: Ready.**

He took a few more steps down the tug's hull until the radiation sensors began clamoring.

**Chu: Good luck. Go.**

*Easy for you to say,* Jordan thought, and kicked away from the tug.

The *Kirkland*, a shadowy, massive metal thing hanging above the planet, was a difficult target to miss. At least in theory. However, the tug was moving, the ship was moving, and now, so was Jordan.

The distance of 400 meters wasn't the farthest he'd leaped between ships or obstacles. That record was over two kilometers, meaning this little excursion wasn't even in the top three. But in those other instances, he'd had backup. There had been tugs to retrieve him, other personnel in suits ready to give chase, and, galaxy help him, he'd had tethers. But not here, not now.

The *Kirkland*, a giant child's toy from a great distance, now looked like a building on its side and one that he was falling faster and faster toward. *You're not falling,* he kept telling himself. *You're flying. Right, flying.*

All he needed was the wind whipping through his hair, the occasional bird drifting by, and the sound of air slicing by his body. They certainly would have helped solidify the illusion.

*I'm coming in too fast,* he thought. *Way too fast.*

He pumped the suit's forward jets twice, cutting his velocity nearly in half. Sane. Far saner.

**Chu: I see you.**

Jordan didn't turn around to look back at the tug—he was too focused on the nearing ship. Fewer than fifty meters now and he spotted the precise plate he wanted to hit. Two meters below a canopy window, he'd be able to easily crawl upward and take a peek, assuming the emergency shutters weren't in place. Considering what had happened, Jordan thought that likely, but it was still worth a shot.

He managed to properly align to the plate, although he nearly clipped the edge of a buttress for what remained of the front shield. When he finally connected with the hull, he'd still been moving too fast, causing him to almost bounce loose from the metal. Fortunately, he'd already turned his mag-gloves to high.

**Jordan: Contact. All good.**

**Chu: Excellent. Burning for starboard hull.**

He turned his head and looked out over the darkness of space and the moon below. The tug, its running lights still functional, glowed like a cat's eyes. A beat later, he saw the glare of its powerful engines beginning their burns.

**Jordan: Good luck.**

He turned back to the hull and scanned for the twinkle of the highly radioactive metal. A few shards glittered back at him, but they were mostly near the port edge. Jordan climbed upward to the two-meter-high strip of transparent aluminum that ran nearly twenty meters across the width of the bow. The shutters weren't up, but there were no lights inside the cockpit.

Cursing, Jordan continued climbing past the windows and to the top of the ship. The nearest emergency airlock lay some ten meters aft of him. A simple pan of his lights showed more of the fragments embedded in the dorsal side. Whatever that weapon had been, either it had spread more of the radioactive metal by going through the debris field or it had been made of the stuff. He didn't care for either case. If that shit was inside the ship, then what?

The old phrase, "don't borrow trouble," echoed across his mind, making him smile.

He looked out over the ship's spine and past the two shields. Even from here, this far from the aft, he could see more damage. If by some miracle he could get the engines working, he wasn't sure the far aft would hold together.

You're overreacting. Making things worse just for the sake of them being worse.

He wasn't, though, and he knew it. Curled metal, a plume of gas rising into space, and the glow of what could be fire. *Kirkland* wasn't going anywhere anytime soon.

Jordan made it to the airlock, well beneath the dorsal shield, and tried to connect to the interface. Dead. No power. Great.

After he tapped a plate above the control panel, a manual crank folded out. Jordan wound it a few dozen times while keeping the speed constant against the friction. A single indicator light came to life with a dull green. Enough power for now, Jordan reckoned.

He pressed the controls again, and the airlock's outer hatch cycled open. Jordan gripped the edge of the hull and pushed himself downward and inside. With a tap on the interior, the outer hatch closed, leaving him in a short-lived darkness. An angry red lamp came to life above the interior hatch, and a message appeared on the hardened digital control panel.

**LIFE SUPPORT OFFLINE**

**SYSTEM-WIDE PRESSURE FAILURE**

*In other words,* Jordan thought, *don't take off your helmet.*

The light turned a flashing green that changed to yellow and back to green again every few seconds. The inner hatch cycled open to a corridor lit with flickering red lights.

Jordan blinked through the menu options and scanned for functioning comms. He knew the external comms were dead, but that didn't mean inter-ship's emergency comms were too.

When he finally found a working frequency, it was in the same shape as the tug's: text only.

**Jordan: All call. In bow emergency corridor. Sound off.**

After waiting twenty seconds, he sent the message again. Another twenty seconds, another transmission sent. After two minutes of trying, he gave up. The emergency corridor led to a ladder hatch, and that would take him to the bridge level. Once there, he could figure out what the hell was going on. More importantly, maybe he'd figure out where Til was.

The ladder hatch led to yet another airlock. With as large a ship as the *Kirkland* was, it had plenty of room for as much compartmentalization as possible. More airlocks, more ways to segment the ship from interstellar and stellar damage. Design considerations Jordan very much appreciated.

After cycling the airlock, he floated down to the deck in the baleful glow of malfunctioning emergency lighting. His own suit lights were far brighter, but that didn't much matter. This portion of the bridge appeared completely intact. Well, apart from the fact that none of the main lights worked and all the interfaces appeared down.

Jordan continued down the corridor until it branched toward the cockpit. The hatch that was nearly always open had been shut. It was the only way in or out of the bridge apart from the "oh shit" cutout in the deck. In short, if that hatch was closed, no one was getting in.

The sight of the shut hatch left him cold. It was unlike Til. So unlike Til.

Jordan mag-walked to the hatch and touched his glove to the interface. It came to life with a crackle of static, but the display was mostly empty apart from an error code. Sighing, he tapped the panel, and the manual crank unfolded. He rotated it several times until a green light appeared above the crank. A single push of his glove and the hatch cycled.

Fortunately, Til hadn't put the system in lockdown. Otherwise, Jordan wouldn't have been able to get in without assistance. Considering the multiple system failures, that might have made things impossible.

**Jordan: Entering cockpit.**

He waited a few beats for a response but didn't receive one. Okay, Til, he thought, I hope you're wearing a suit.

He touched the stud, and the hatch cycled open on a pitch-black bridge. Not a single light glowed inside the cockpit. It might as well have been a tomb.

With his suit lights turned to full, Jordan stepped across the threshold and onto the bridge. A short corridor led to the captain's room while the other led to the cockpit itself. Jordan opted to check the cockpit first.

The twin daises with their optional seats stood like sentinels guarding dark and dead holodisplays, empty interfaces, and the ring of transparent aluminum looking out over MacReady. No sign of Til.

In a way, that was good. In another, it was terrible. Just to be thorough, Jordan checked the ready room and found it empty, the supply caches raided meaning Til had survived. But he wasn't on the bridge level. So where the fuck was he?

Jordan walked to the first of the command daises and passed his hand over it. The holodisplay should have flashed to life, but nothing happened. The same thing with the other. The bridge, including both the cockpit and the ready room, had no power. No power, no terminal.

Without a working terminal, it was impossible for him to even attempt to figure out what was going on with the ship. Since Til wasn't here, there was only one place to go before he headed to cargo and engineering, and that was the personnel module.

It served as the primary lifeboat and was the only other likely place apart from engineering or the cargo bay. Sighing to himself, Jordan headed out of the bridge, making sure to leave the hatch open. If Til came back and found it open, maybe he'd realize someone else was aboard the ship. If he did, maybe he'd try to reach out over the emergency comms.

As Jordan made his way down the corridor to the personnel module, he kept his eyes moving over every surface, looking for signs of, well, anything out of the ordinary.

*Like glittering metal?*

*Yeah*, he told himself, *like glittering metal.*

That stuff had been flying through space, so why was he half expecting to find it inside the hull?

*Because that's how my day is going*, he told himself with an ironic grin.

The lights above the airlock leading to the personnel module flashed to the beat of an arrhythmic heart. The airlock itself had been shut tight, although it was impossible to know if that had been an automated response to pressure loss or if it had been part of Til's prep.

This airlock, obviously, had power. When Jordan reached to touch the stud, the holodisplay controls came to life, displaying a slew of warnings.

**Personnel Module Status**

**Multiple perforations**

**Pressure loss**

**Fatal ambient temperature levels**

**Fatal ambient radiation levels**

Jordan's eyebrows rose when he saw the statistics. The module had suffered catastrophic hull damage across multiple plates, as though they'd been hit with a shotgun blast. Rad counts varied, but it appeared as though the galley itself had been completely irradiated far beyond lethal levels.

Jordan activated one of the galley cameras and found himself staring into static. A quick check of the others confirmed what he already suspected—the personnel module was fried, and without a proper hazard or mining suit, he couldn't even think about inspecting the damage. For Til's sake, he hoped the man wasn't inside there.

*Don't write it off yet,* he told himself. *Could be just a single fragment in there.*

*Could be,* Jordan thought. But one fragment wouldn't explain why all the systems inside appeared offline or damaged. Dozens might but not just one. If there were dozens, the entire module would have been contaminated. Not good at all.

Jordan shut down the interface and headed for the cargo bay. If there was a properly functioning terminal left on the ship, it would be in the cargo bay or what remained of engineering. Failing that, he had to find Til and decide what to do next.

*Chu is next,* Jordan told himself. *Get Chu out of the tug and find Til, and then you can worry about everything else. Good plan.* Somehow Jordan didn't think it'd be that simple.

# CHAPTER TWENTY

When Jordan reached the railing looking out over the cargo bay, his breath caught in his throat. The aft end had a massive hole the size of a hover-car and a tear that ran through the decking leading into the ship's superstructure. He didn't want to know how fast whatever had hit them had been going, or how much mass it had had.

The thing that struck the ship had collided with them like a high-speed asteroid—a small one, to be sure, but still, Jordan hadn't seen this kind of damage outside of war footage. Not even reactor explosions created holes like that.

Orbital 2, their spare orbital lift, appeared undamaged and intact. Excellent. They still had a way to get down to MacReady as well as bring Aryana and the miners back up. It was something, at least. The only question was whether or not there was anything to bring them back up to.

Jordan headed to the lift, still unnerved by the thought of gliding over the railing, ignoring the debris floating above the refineries and mining equipment, and somehow landing in one piece. The field of metal and chaff didn't look that thick, but considering the other hazards Jordan had seen, he wasn't about to risk it.

The lift, gas powered and therefore immune to any kind of EMR, took him down without issue. When it reached the deck, Jordan mag-walked beyond its threshold and immediately headed starboard. Both tugs were gone, and most of the mining equipment had already been moved to MacReady, but there were still plenty of supplies lying around in secured, unopened crates.

As he walked to the line of supply cabinets and stacks of crates, he set up a new program to scan for all active frequencies on the network as well as the emergency comms. If Til so much as poked his head up to check on something, he'd get Jordan's hail. At least in theory. That, however, was something he couldn't afford to wait for.

Chu. He needed to find a way to get Chu out of the tug. Not many options if the tug's egress had been contaminated by the glittering, radioactive shards.

The suit station, large enough for two personnel to suit up at a time in safety, had its own airlocks for ingress and egress. Jordan stepped to the airlock and waved his hand across the sensor. The suit station's lights came to life, and the outer hatch cycled open.

His HUD flashed, and a message appeared.

**Chu: Made it a quarter midships. Still 200 meters from airlock.**

*Shit,* Jordan thought. That was a long hike to the tug, especially if he had to mind a minefield of radiation. Still, it was doable. Right now, that was about as good as he could hope for.

**Jordan: Haven't found Til. Gearing up for rads.**

**Chu: Ship status?**

Completely and totally fucked? he wanted to say but stopped himself.

**Jordan: Bridge power out. Unknown on engineering. Internal network down.**

**Chu: Can see damage to personnel module. Multiple impacts and perforations.**

*Well, that would explain a few things,* Jordan thought.

**Jordan: Will gear up. Out.**

Gear. He needed a mining suit, a grapple, and radiation shielding to help Chu. First things first.

The cargo bay had no atmosphere or pressure, and the temperature was far below what a human could withstand. Without the suit station, there'd be no way to get out of his suit and into a mining suit. Fortunately, the station had its own shielded, backup power supply.

He stepped inside the airlock and waited as it cycled, heated clouds of atmosphere flooding the enclosed space. A moment later, his suit announced he had breathable air, but the temperature was more than cold enough to instantly turn a human into an ice sculpture. Jordan stepped through the inner door and headed to the rack.

The deadly cold quickly departed as the station's furnace silently blasted superheated air into the locker room. He'd rarely used the station when the cargo bay had no life support. In fact, the only time he'd done so was when he'd suffered a suit failure. Jordan didn't want to revisit that memory.

His EVA suit announced the external temperature had reached 4.5°C, and Jordan inhaled deeply.

"Ready to freeze?" he asked himself. The answer, of course, was no.

Jordan stepped backward to the rack and waited while the suit disassembled around him. When it finished, he was left standing in the room, back nearly against the bulkhead, skin puckered and shivering beneath his jumpsuit. After tapping on the holodisplay, he waved his comms bracelet, and the system pulled his mining suit from storage.

The heaters were still working their asses off trying to get the room to a decent temperature, but by the time they managed that, he'd be wearing the mining suit. As if on cue, the rack moved, and the suit began assembling around him. First the legs and torso were fitted, followed by the chest-plate and helmet assembly. With the suit completely covering his body, the rack sprayed the seams with bonding material.

The HUD came to life, banishing the darkness he'd seen since the helmet assembled. Several messages appeared and faded away faster than he could read them. Finally, the darkness completely disappeared, and the room before him came into sharp focus.

Jordan flexed his hands and feet and felt the suit adjusting to his form. It would do that for the next few minutes, provided he moved around. The alloy fabric would flex and seat at the same time, eventually providing him with a second skin that could take punishing amounts of damage and augmented his innate strength.

**FITTING COMPLETE** flashed across the display.

He ran the diagnostic routine just for safe measure. While it processed, he thought over what he had to do to free Chu. A grapple tether could easily take the mass of a human, so no worries there. The only problem was that if the tug was irradiated, he wouldn't be able to simply pull Chu out of it.

The diagnostic finished by flashing a message on his HUD. No problems detected.

*We'll see how long that lasts,* Jordan thought.

He stepped away from the rack, the sound of his clomping boots thudding in his ears as he walked to the airlock. After turning off the suit's external mics, he activated the inner hatch and entered the airlock. As soon as it finished cycling, Jordan headed to the line of supply cabinets next to the station.

The first—a neatly luma-painted label glowing above its door—opened on an array of suit vests and belts. Jordan quickly donned a harness, checked its fit, and strapped on two belts of pouches.

The next cabinet? Emergency supplies. He grabbed two microprobes and a magnetic grappler. His belts were quickly filling up, but he had more to worry about, including two med-kits, an emergency radiation exposure (ERE) kit, four rolls of portable shielding, and a hatch buster in case he needed to fracture the tug's airlock collar.

After shutting the cabinet, he walked to the far end and opened another nearest the bulkhead. Ten handheld plasma torches hung upside down from the rack. Jordan pulled one of them, checked the charge, and slotted it into his belt. Apart from a rad blanket, he had everything he needed.

Jordan moved to the starboard personnel airlock and opened the large crate welded to the bulkhead, pulled one of the dozens of densely packed rolls, and clipped it to his belt. After double-checking his supplies and still feeling as though he had forgotten something, Jordan closed the crate and entered the airlock.

```
Jordan: In a mining suit. Going to bring a
grapple.
```

**Chu: Long walk. Be careful.**

"Long walk. Be careful," Jordan muttered as the airlock finished cycling and the outer hatch opened onto a view of darkest space above the shadowy MacReady. A chill started at the base of his spine, and he did his best to ignore it.

"Focus," he told himself and stepped off the ledge and onto the hull. He was now mag-walking on the starboard side of the ship as though it were the dorsal. A brief wave of nausea vied for control of his stomach, but he pushed it away.

The rectangular tug jutted off the hull like a tumor. It didn't look as though Chu had landed so much as crashed. *Must have run out of thruster fuel,* Jordan thought, *or really wanted to conserve it.* If that was the case, Chu had had the right idea.

Jordan's HUD flashed with radiation warnings, and he focused on finding the glittering shards of material embedded in the hull. It really wasn't all that difficult. Whatever the stuff was, particles of it appeared to be everywhere, but the only places that were radioactive enough to fry his suit were clumps rather than dots.

The more material, the higher the rads. The particles were enough to set off warnings, but the clumps? They tipped the scale a little too damned far in the red for Jordan's liking. Fortunately, the starboard hull seemed to be peppered with the material rather than covered in it.

**Chu: I can see you.**

**Jordan: Good landing?**

**Chu: I've had better. Til?**

Good question. Jordan didn't want to tell Chu about the bridge, the power loss, the emptiness, and the completely abandoned feel to the ship. How could you explain that in text anyway?

**Jordan: Not on bridge. Not in cargo.**

Seventy-five meters, Jordan thought to himself. Fortunately. All this thinking about Til and the situation had made him forget he was walking sideways on the hull of a ship that was floating in deadly debris. Shit.

He gritted his teeth and continued mag-walking, cutting a path slightly to his left or right depending on the radiation sensors. Apart from the occasional detour, he'd managed the trip fairly well. At least, that was what he wanted to think.

**Chu: Check engineering?**

**Jordan: Didn't have time. Explain soon.**

Hopefully that would satisfy the man. Jordan didn't feel like playing twenty questions when each one made him feel a little more guilty about rushing out of the cargo bay instead of performing a more thorough search. Training said to save the obvious, search for the hidden. It's what he had done and regardless of how things turned out for Til, it's the way he'd do it again.

A flash caught his eye and Jordan looked sideways in response. The light had come from MacReady's surface. Just a single, short lived pulse. Or a hallucination.

*No, you saw it,* he told himself. He continued staring at MacReady for a moment while he walked, his path completely unobstructed by the radiation. With each step, his mind conjured possible explanations for a flash like that.

Could be a reactor malfunction. Or maybe an electrical system exploding. Or maybe even–

A seemingly patternless, asynchronous group of flashes erupted, and Jordan's mind filled in the sounds of explosions, although they'd looked little like conflagrations. If he was right, the lights hadn't been around the camp, but around two of the mining sites. 3 and 4, to be specific.

Jordan's flesh prickled and despite the suit's comforting warmth, he felt as though someone had let space inside. Something had happened down on MacReady. It could have been caused by the orbital tether crashing into the gabbro. Could have been. Somehow Jordan knew it hadn't been that at all.

# CHAPTER TWENTY-ONE

When Jordan was less than ten meters away, he saw what he'd hoped not to—diamonds glittering back at him from the docking collar. No way could Chu leave the tug without being irradiated.

Jordan slowed his approach, mind already braced for the shrill radiation alert tone and the flash on his HUD. He made it another few meters before that finally happened, and he halted. He couldn't get any closer without either free floating out into space and approaching from underneath or launching himself above the tug. Either way would require him to leave the hull. That wasn't something he was ready to do.

**Jordan: Can't get closer. Using grapple.**

**Chu: Copy.**

He hadn't expected anything more from Chu. The man was notoriously succinct and had either achieved a calm Jordan would never understand or had far more control over his emotions than most anyone Jordan had ever met.

Jordan pulled the grapple from his belt and aimed it at the docking collar. A touch on the mechanism and the grapple gun pushed the tether at high speed toward the tug. The magnetic end hit the metal and stuck fast.

He attached the gun to his suit and touched the controls. Jordan forced himself to stare at the grapple point and not the surface of MacReady that he knew was a hundred kilometers below him. After taking a deep breath, he demagnetized from the hull and rose a few centimeters above it.

**Jordan: On my way. Make sure you're
depressurized.**

**Chu: I am. Good luck.**

Keeping his body oriented to the tug, he activated the suit's rear thrusters and loosed just enough gas to get moving. He continued to rise gently upward while heading toward the tug. His radiation sensors began chiming, and he pulled his legs up in response. The alerts quieted immediately.

He knew he was off course after a dozen or so meters.

*Off course, and if the grapple fails, do you have enough thrust to get back? What are you going to—*

*Shut up.*

He thumbed the grapple pistol, and a surge of electricity transformed the tether from a spool of cable to a stiff but flexible line, and his velocity decreased at the same as his altitude from the deck. In a moment, he more or less came to a halt, the line bending at a pivot joint a meter from the connection point to ensure it didn't break or rip.

Heart hammering, Jordan thumbed the pistol's wheel and slowly drew himself in. When he reached a meter from the docking collar, he came to a stop and pulled a roll of portable shielding from the ERE pouch. There in space, affixed to the stiff cable that now looked more like a pole, he pulled free a single, long sheet.

It took him several tries to find the seam and unfold the relatively thin material. In an EVA suit, it would have been a cinch. Not so much in a mining suit. He activated the magnetics on his left glove, and the sheet immediately stuck to it.

*Now for the fun part,* he thought, and unpowered the tether. Satisfied he was stable for the moment, he retracted the tether back into the pistol. He drifted slightly, but there was no help for it apart from getting this done as quickly as he could.

After blinking through a few menu options, the glove sent several sets of electronic pulses, each changing the orientation of the material's crystalline structures. The sheet unfolded practically by itself, transforming into a malleable 2x2 meter square.

With it held before him like a shield, he goosed his thrusters and approached the irradiated tug. When a slew of alerts didn't fly across his HUD, he knew the shield was at least working well enough to block most of the nastier radiation. It wouldn't be perfect, but it was the best he could do.

After another few blinks, the shield locked to the tug and over the docking collar, firmly attached but still malleable like a weighted blanket.

> **Jordan: I have shielding in place around the collar.**
>
> **Chu: Lovely. How are we doing this?**
>
> **Jordan: Can you force the collar door?**
>
> **Chu: Yes**

He'd written that last after a long pause.

> **Jordan: Then pop through the hatch, and we'll fold the shielding around you as you come out.**
>
> **Chu: This is a shit plan.**
>
> **Jordan: Got a better one?**
>
> **Chu: I didn't say it wasn't the best plan. I said it was a shit plan.**

Jordan grinned as he transferred the grapple from his belt to his hand. He was going to need it.

> **Chu: Ready. Now. Now. Now.**

As the last message appeared, bright white light slid through a widening crack in the tug's hull. Silhouetted against it, Chu looked like some kind of ethereal portent of doom or a Djinn Jordan had just loosed from a bottle. He floated a meter from the shield, his suit lights occasionally catching Jordan's visor.

A wave of static rolled over the comms for a moment.

"—there Jordan?" Chu's voice sounded tired and a little depressed.

"Here. Got me?"

"Loud and mostly clear," Chu said and waved at Jordan through the translucent rad shield.

"Okay. I've got the shield in place. Just move slowly into it."

"Right," Chu said. "I'm already getting rad warnings here, J."

*Fuck*, Jordan thought. He'd been afraid of that. The docking collar must have been drastically exposed. Between the more heavily armored mining suit and the shield, Jordan had much less to worry about. The EVA model, on the other hand, just wasn't rated for these kinds of rads.

"Okay," Jordan said. "Got a better idea?"

"Not really," Chu said. "If I had an extra shield in here, maybe. But even if you threw one in here, it'll get irradiated before it gets to me. Might not even help."

"Fuck," Jordan said. "Okay."

"On three?" Chu said.

"On three," Jordan agreed. He readjusted himself and his grip on the shield.

"One. Two. Three." Chu rose from the tug's cabin in a slow, smooth controlled motion. As he approached the collar, he put his arms at his sides and brought his knees to his chest. He tumbled upward in the fetal position and through the collar's open hatch.

Jordan rose with him, his hands letting the shield run through his fingers so as not to stop Chu's ascent. He touched his thrusters to try to match Chu but managed to get a little ahead of him.

The pair continued rising away from the radiation, Jordan doing his best to wrap Chu's body completely in the blanket. When they were twenty or so meters away from the tug, Chu said, "We planning on floating to MacReady?"

Jordan grinned. He'd been trying to reorient them to face the ship. He touched his jets multiple times, struggling. Finally, he managed to get it right.

"You maglocked to me?" Jordan asked.

"Yup."

"Then hang on." Jordan activated the suit's rear thrusters in multiple bursts to reverse their momentum. The tangled pair moved toward the *Kirkland* at a maddeningly slow speed, Jordan doing his best to save what thruster fuel he had.

When he felt he was close enough, Jordan pulled the grapple pistol, aimed in the direction of the ship, and fired. The grapple hit the hull and stuck fast. Jordan clipped the line to his suit and activated the retractor.

Their momentum increased significantly, and Jordan realized he'd thumbed the wheel a little too much. Instead of trying to reverse, he pivoted and hit the hull with both feet much harder than he'd intended, practically smashing Chu into the ship as a result.

"Shit," Chu said, "you rescuing me or killing me?"

Breathing hard and jittering with adrenaline, Jordan said, "Both?"

One of Chu's hands left Jordan's knee and stuck fast to the hull. "Okay. I'm letting go."

Jordan stepped away, his hands still grasping the shield and pulling it away from Chu. The smaller man unfurled himself and managed to stay connected to the ship. Jordan spread the irradiated blanket against the hull, where it stuck fast.

"Get walking," he said to Chu. "Personnel airlock."

"Aye, aye," Chu said.

"How many rads?"

Chu sighed heavily. "Too many."

"Great," Jordan said. "Need to get you into the medical bay."

"And where would that be?"

Jordan opened his mouth to reply and then remembered the personnel module had been virtually destroyed. Even engineering's backup bay had been annihilated or at the very least critically damaged. Plus? No power.

"Not on the ship," he said.

"Right. Meaning—"

"We have to abandon the *Kirkland*," Jordan said. "Get you in a mining suit and deploy the emergency orbital."

Chu said nothing but quickened his pace slightly. Jordan lengthened his own stride accordingly, his eyes still scanning for radioactive shards he might have overlooked.

Jordan glanced at MacReady, his eyes darting to where the orbital tether used to hang. The shadowy planet looked as dead as it had before the miners had descended.

*Only difference is you should be seeing lights down there now. And you aren't.*

If whatever had hit them had impacted the planet as well, there was no telling if any of the emergency gear worked. The only things that might work would be tools located inside the shielded modules. Maybe.

Chu's steps had slowed slightly, as though he were exhausted. Jordan imagined after all the stress of being locked in that tin can of a tug, not knowing if you could get out of it would make anyone stressed out. Or it could be the radiation.

"How you doing, Chu?"

"Need a nap," he said and stood beside the airlock as he waited for Jordan to catch up.

"Suit first," Jordan said. He tapped the stud, and the airlock's outer hatch opened. After gesturing Chu inside, Jordan joined him. Since they were leaving a depressurized area to enter another depressurized area, the process was fast.

After waiting for Chu to exit the airlock, Jordan led him to the front of the cargo bay. "You could have a blown engine array," the pilot said, head turned in the direction of the damage.

"I could," Jordan said darkly. "But then I'd have to look at it to know, wouldn't I?"

He could practically hear Chu shaking his head. "No, J. You know it's blown."

Ah, yes. Time to admit that to someone else. Someone who wouldn't panic.

"Yes, I do," he said as they made it to the suit station. Jordan carefully placed Chu back on the deck in front of the airlock. "Need help?"

"I can do this part," Chu said. "Just need to get out of this damned suit."

Jordan nodded, understanding all too well what he meant. God knew he was much happier with the knowledge the mining suit was protecting him. At least for now. Eventually the rads might break through, but that wouldn't happen for hours, maybe days. He hoped.

Chu entered the airlock and cycled the hatch. "See you in a few," he said and headed to the emergency shower. The station would tear apart his suit, recycle any nonradioactive damaged portions, and trash the rest as toxic waste.

Once Chu was naked, the station would spray him down with chemicals, inject anti-rad meds and the like, and tabulate the damage. Unfortunately for him, the suit station wasn't a medbay.

The suit station's meds were really just there to keep you from dying before receiving proper medical attention at the medbay. The only maybe functional medbay was the portable one on MacReady's surface.

The emergency orbital was their only chance down. Without a tug, it was going to be dicey. He looked down the cargo bay at the tremendous damage still glowing like the coals of a dying fire. It was also their only option.

# CHAPTER TWENTY-TWO

"Coming out," Chu said from inside the station.

Jordan nodded to himself without turning from what he was doing. "You going to announce everything you do now?"

"Didn't want to startle you. I know you can't hear."

He hadn't considered that. "Guess that's true."

Chu said nothing for a moment as Jordan continued typing on the virtual interface. Instead, he turned and headed to the cargo bay hatch controls. "You going to look for Til first? Inspect engineering?"

"No," Jordan said. "I'm getting this ready for us to descend. You're getting to the medbay down there if I have to drag you."

"Jordan, if we don't secure the ship—"

He snapped his head around and glared at Chu, the man recoiling slightly. "The ship is fucked. The personnel module has enough radiation to burn through a mining suit, and the engines are completely gone." He pointed at the emergency orbital interface. "All I can do is buy us time, and that means getting down to where supplies are."

Chu slowly nodded. "Okay. Thank you. Do you need my help?"

Jordan shook his head.

"Then I'll go take a peek and share the feed. We should at least know," Chu said.

Jordan sighed, his shoulders slumping inside the suit, the incredibly tough fabric flexing slightly. "Are you okay to do that?"

"Yes," Chu said and turned away, his steps cautious but stable.

*Fuck,* Jordan thought. He hadn't meant to lose his temper. Just too much stress and Chu was busy reminding him just how absolutely screwed they were. He could only handle one thing at a time. Plus, if he didn't keep Chu alive, he might find himself not only on the ship but alone on the moon as well. He didn't like his odds of maintaining his sanity very long before he decided to simply open his suit.

Chu's cam feed popped up on Jordan's HUD, but he barely glanced at it. The interface for the orbital was more important. Plus, he wasn't sure he really wanted to see the damage. The professional in him knew he should, but the sight of all the machines he'd taken care of over the years, the constant maintenance and love he'd poured into keeping the *Kirkland* in interstellar shape no matter what they were doing at the time—all of it was gone. At least he thought it was. He couldn't imagine it any other way.

Jordan finished programming the emergency orbital and watched the simulations on the interface. Frowning, he adjusted the attitude one more time as well as the tether deploy location, checked the sims once more, and called it good.

The emergency orbital, a slab of cubic alloy that was only 2x4x4 meters in dimensions with a massive goiter of a tether both above and beneath and a reusable but less than robust or spacious climber hanging below it, could fit a maximum of four suits at a time, but realistically, it could only hold three large ones. Too much mass and the climber wouldn't be able to do its job. Then the damned thing was useless.

"Chu?" Jordan glanced at the cam feed, and his mouth opened in a question he never asked.

Chu had reached the rear bulkhead connecting the engineering and cargo modules. The massive rent started halfway up one hull plate, cut through it in a jagged widthwise rip, and ended at the deck. The damaged hull plate had folded inward, revealing a shallow, half-meter-wide groove in the deck that didn't appear empty.

Beneath the overheads, it was easy to see the stuff glittering like diamonds, just as the radioactive material had done, but this was different—as Chu approached, it looked as though it was really glistening rather than glittering.

"Um, what the fuck is that?" Jordan asked.

"I don't know," Chu said. Through the cam feed, Jordan could see him pointing at the groove. "Don't know if you can see it, but it doesn't look smooth. In fact, it's about as far from uniform as you can get. The depth isn't even consistent."

Jordan had a bad feeling looking at the stuff. "What's your rad count?"

"Higher than ambient," Chu said. "That substance is radioactive."

"I, um, kind of figured," Jordan said dryly. He tried to sound casual, but butterflies swarmed in his stomach.

"That look like a burn to you? Not impact damage?"

Jordan rolled his eyes. "Can you zoom in further for me?"

"Oh, sorry," Chu said, and the feed focus narrowed considerably, showing him a 5cm rectangle on the edge of the groove. "See how it's not smooth? Like it was eaten away?"

"Nearly slagged, but you're right about the edges. Burned or something. Never seen metal do that," Jordan said. "Certainly not ship grade. What about the groove itself?"

The view shifted, and he found himself looking at a zoomed-in portion of the very bottom of the long gouge. The depth was inconsistent, as if whatever had caused it had come in at an angle. That tracked with the catastrophic damage between engineering and cargo. It also wasn't what had his attention.

The bottom of the gouge had a strange whitish, glistening substance that faded into near transparency. Now that he was looking for it, he realized that was what the jagged edges were—more of the gunk rather than serrated damage.

"The hell is that?" Jordan muttered.

"Got no idea," Chu said. "But I know I'm not going near it."

"Good plan," Jordan said.

Chu's cam view moved as he backtracked to the next aisle, presumably to take a peek into engineering. Jordan took another few seconds to watch before switching back to prepping the orbital.

The interface was ready. He'd already unfolded the propulsion mechanism, and the orbital would push itself away from the ship for 1.5 kilometers before dropping the tether. It would put them farther from camp than he liked, but he wasn't about to try to drop in the same place again. Without comms to the ground, it was impossible to know how much damage, if any, had been done by Orbital 1's falling tether. For all Jordan knew, the camp had been reduced to particles by a damaged reactor or something equally disastrous.

Something moved fast on the cam feed, and he switched his eyes to it. Chu stood before the rent in the bulkhead, his helmet lights piercing the gloom inside engineering.

Jordan saw the glow of flames and wondered just how much atmosphere was left in the tanks. One of the tanks had probably been perforated and was spewing out burning $O_2$. Lovely.

That was reason enough to abandon the ship, but it only got worse from there. The glare of the flickering blowtorches jetting out of broken pipes cast enough light for him to see a cracked micro-reactor and another that had been all but obliterated. The rest of the reactors and engine array were obscured from view, but he could also see space through multiple perforations in the hull. "Perforations" was actually an understatement. He'd been more correct about an aluminum can's bottom being blown out than he'd thought.

The *Kirkland* was dead in space and they had no way home now. Even if he had enough power and material to reprint shattered nuclear reactors and engine components, he wouldn't live long enough to fix them.

"What's that?" Chu asked. His camera view twitched slightly to the left and Jordan saw a tinge of orange-colored fabric, one edge glistening. "Um, Jordan?"

"Get back here. Now," Jordan said.

He didn't know if Chu had figured out that was a piece of mining suit, or that more of it was probably hidden by the remains of the bulkhead. Jordan didn't want to be the one to tell him. At least not until they were on the orbital. Jordan was fairly certain whose suit that was and that it had been occupied at the time it was smashed.

Chu didn't move.

"Chu? To me. Now."

Jordan had already shifted his focus back to the pressure gauges for the orbital's launch propulsion. "Check thrice, fuck up once," as the ancient, grizzled engineer he'd interned with had said. The old man had said it by rote and often enough that it became a phrase inseparable from his identity. Jordan sort of missed the cantankerous old fuck.

The cam-feed view swiveled slightly.

"Til?" Chu called out.

Jordan snapped his eyes to the cam-feed corner and blinked for it to zoom. Chu's helmet cam showed a shadow moving through the wrecked engineering bay, hints of orange visible in the flickering gloom. Jordan's mouth opened, but nothing came out.

"Til?" Chu called again and walked another meter closer to the hole in the bulkhead.

Jordan finally found his voice and shouted through the radio. "Chu! That's not Til! Move!"

The cam-feed bounced hard before receding as Chu stepped backward. The shadow, its form only slightly distinguishable as humanoid, leaned slightly, as though it were unstable. Chu was stepping backward a little faster now. The thing in the shadows stood ramrod straight and appeared to stare right at Chu, half a dozen bright green shapes glowing where the head should be. They seemed to blink, and then the shadow sprang toward Chu, its form gliding like a silent missile.

Screaming and stumbling, Chu turned and ran full tilt down the aisle. Jordan pressed the release on the orbital and grabbed the handle as Chu turned the corner and headed for the opening cargo bay door. Chu was mag-running, or trying to. He was still moving too slowly for Jordan's liking.

Chu cut his magnetics, breath coming in ragged gasps, and leaped from the deck much as the shadow had done. The cargo bay door was less than a quarter open, but that was enough as far as Jordan was concerned. He pulled the handle, and the orbital counted down on his HUD. 5-4-3—

Just as Chu reached Jordan, Jordan grabbed him by the shoulder and pulled him close while keeping his other hand in a death grip on the orbital. He released his magnetics just as the orbital's thrusters engaged.

Chu's momentum pushed him hard against the platform, but the suit handled the impact just fine. The fact that the orbital's thrusters had accelerated it away from the *Kirkland* made the collision much less dangerous than it could have been.

Jordan saw something move out of the corner of his eye and quickly glanced at the fully open cargo bay door. A figure stood at its edge, the bright overhead lights in the cargo bay backlighting it and making it once again appear like a shadow but not of something human.

For one thing the head was swollen, far too large to fit inside a helmet. For another, the figure was far too tall and the arms too long. It seemed to be watching Jordan, the green lights once again glowing from its face.

Jordan wanted to rub his eyes. That couldn't have been Til. Could it? Could it have once been Til?

He knew the answer. There had only been a single person aboard the *Kirkland* when the projectile hit. It could only be Til, yet Jordan absolutely knew it wasn't.

The *Kirkland* grew smaller and smaller as the orbital continued to its target coordinates. Chu, still panting said, "What the fuck was that?"

"I don't know," Jordan said.

"That…" Chu caught his breath, exhaled hard, and tried again. "Was that Til?"

"Couldn't have been anyone else," Jordan said softly. "No one else."

"Jesus." Jordan still couldn't see Chu's face, but the man sounded as though he were on the verge of a sob. "How? What?"

Jordan shook his head and readjusted his grip on the handle. They still had another five minutes before the orbital hit the proverbial brakes. Then they'd have another few minutes of deceleration. That seemed too long to him, but then if he had his way, they'd already be on MacReady and looking for Aryana.

"You injured?"

"No," Chu said. "Just—I don't know."

"Know what you mean," Jordan said. "You load up with any supplies?"

"No," Chu said dimly.

Now Jordan was sure the man had tears in his eyes.

"Thought I'd have time. Thought—" Chu sobbed once. "I don't understand what the fuck is going on!"

"I know," Jordan said, suddenly feeling more like a father than a coworker, and the fact that Chu was so much younger than Jordan made it that much more believable. "We just have to get down to MacReady. I have some supplies, and there's more at the base camp."

"If base camp still exists," Chu said. "You think it survived the tether falling?"

"Good chance," he lied. "You know how those things are when they fall."

He checked his HUD and found they were only two minutes away from the deceleration cycle. Ten more minutes and they'd probably be on their way down the climber. It wasn't soon enough for Jordan.

# CHAPTER TWENTY-THREE

The orbital decelerated, making Jordan clutch Chu even tighter. He could have let go of the handle, leaving him and Chu floating out in space while the orbital continued on to its final position, but he didn't want to waste thruster fuel, much less take a chance on missing the platform.

"Good thing I have all this armor," Chu said. "Otherwise, I'd be crushed into your sternum."

"And I'd have a hell of a bruise," Jordan said with a grin. "Speaking of, how's your suit integrity? And how are you feeling?"

He could practically hear the shrug in Chu's voice.

"Tired. I'd take a nap, but some asshole has me in a headlock."

"You know, Chu, you curse a lot when you're being held like a stubborn child."

"I curse a lot more in my head," Chu said. "Just because I'm not saying it doesn't mean I'm not thinking it."

"Fair enough," Jordan said. "How's your suit?"

"Good enough. Practically full on both atmo and power. No integrity warnings apart from radiation inside my suit."

Jordan had been afraid of that. The rads from the material must have seeped through the tug, slowly broiling the EVA suit even if the sensors didn't quite pick it up. Or maybe the moment the interior door opened, it was enough to eat through. Either way, the radiation poisoning was a little more severe than Jordan had hoped.

Chu needed another anti-radiation bath, one in a medbay followed by intravenous therapy and so many other steps that Jordan couldn't remember them all. He only knew from personal experience the year of taking tabs, getting your blood flushed twice a week, and the constant cancer monitoring. It wasn't fun, and he didn't wish it on anyone. Worst part? That was what it took to recover from a relatively minor reactor leak.

Chu had been hit much harder, and while his skin might not have broiled off the bone like overcooked rib meat, the chromosomal damage was the same. White blood cells die off and aren't replenished or go into overdrive. Cells with damaged DNA begin replicating into infinity, creating tumors and, well, so many other horrors Jordan didn't want to think about. Which was why he needed a real medbay and one equipped for severe radiation trauma.

The deceleration thrusters ceased as the orbital settled into place.

"In a minute, the weight will drop with the tether. We'll feel a jolt," Jordan said.

"Right. You know, now that we're not under thrust, you could let me out of this headlock and clamp me to the platform."

Yeah, he could.

"Um, right. Sorry."

When Chu finished maglocking himself to the massive chunk of metal, he turned to look at Jordan. With their visors up, it was easy to see the burst blood vessel in Chu's left eye and threads pulsing in the other.

"You know," Chu said and coughed, "you may have to walk alone."

Jordan shook his head. "One-third gravity. You'll be easy to carry."

"Like luggage," Chu said seriously.

"Like luggage but only if you can't walk." Jordan flashed a smile he didn't feel. "I'm not lugging your lazy ass without reason."

"I can accept that," Chu said. The man's adrenaline hangover had made him slaphappy, but the way his face faded, Jordan knew what the pilot was thinking about before he spoke. "Til."

"I know," Jordan said. What else was there to say? He wasn't one for sentimentality, never had been. He'd miss Til, of course, and he'd grieve when there was time. Until then, he'd shut those feelings down just as he'd done for Aryana.

*Aryana,* he thought. *Coming for you, too.*

The jolt he'd prepared himself for still managed to make him flinch. The rockets had come to life, blasting the counterweight to MacReady's surface, the tether spooling out behind it. While the standard orbital merely dropped its massive tether and allowed it to carry itself to the target's surface, an emergency orbital had been designed for rapid acceleration/deceleration drops from low orbit so personnel could either ascend or descend as quickly as possible. If you deployed an emergency orbital, things had already gone disastrously bad either on the ship or below. In either case, every second counted.

"Two minutes to surface," Jordan said calmly.

Chu looked past Jordan to the *Kirkland*, which seemed an aeon away and so close at the same time. "What is he? What is it?"

A nightmare, Jordan wanted to say. A group hallucination brought on by some strange alien radiation or previously undiscovered celestial phenomenon. The *Kirkland* wasn't damaged, and he and Chu weren't really strapped to an emergency orbital, getting ready to ride the rails to the surface at 10 Gs. Just a nightmare. Nothing too serious. Close your eyes and it will go away.

"I don't want to know," Jordan said flatly.

"I miss the tug."

Jordan laughed at that. "I don't. Now you know how I felt after I took shelter while you were safe and sound in your tin can."

"Not so safe after all," Chu said glumly. Jordan could hear phlegm in the man's voice.

"Guess not," Jordan said, feeling like a jackass. What else was there to say? Besides, now he was wondering when he'd begin feeling the first stabs of illness, notice that his aches and pains weren't going away, weakness taking over his strong muscles, leaving him—

"What's that?" Chu asked with a frown.

**COUNTERWEIGHT DROPPED. LOAD PLATFORM**

"Okay, time to move," Jordan said.

"But what's that?" Chu asked, his finger pointing back toward the *Kirkland*.

Jordan glanced in the direction, saw nothing immediate, and pulled on Chu's shoulder. "Nothing there. Come on."

Chu shook his head, reluctantly disengaging his magnetics, and allowed Jordan to pull him to the climber's cage. "There's something there. I'm telling you."

Jordan walked to the platform's ventral side, where the cage awaited them with an open hatch. After carefully maneuvering Chu inside and the pilot had clamped himself to the bulkhead, Jordan connected to the control panel and started the sequence.

"In thirty," Jordan said and checked Chu's safety harness.

"Only thirty? Then get fixed up. I'm good."

Jordan did have to hurry a bit, but he managed to clamp to the bulkhead and halfway into his harness before a red light flashed five times above the hatch.

"Here we… go," Jordan said.

His HUD flashed an alert from the orbital, causing him to pause between the words.

### INCOMING DEBRIS DETECTED

A number started at one kilometer and had already begun moving into the 900s of meters. Whatever it was, it wasn't moving all that fast relative to the orbital, but it was definitely coming faster than one meter per second.

**DEPLOYING** flashed on his HUD in bright red multiple times, and he felt the jolt of the climber's docking clamps opening. The lift jerked slightly, and through the transaluminum porthole, he saw the distant stars and the blue nebula appear to move as the cage accelerated toward MacReady.

Ten seconds later, the debris warning disappeared. They were out of the emergency orbital's mesh network, and he wouldn't pick up any kind of interface with the comms again until they practically reached the moon's surface. Even then, he'd only be on the emergency network, which spread in a 200-meter circle. Assuming the absence of interference and high obstacles, he could get all the alerts he wanted once they had that again.

"How long before that thing was to hit?" Chu asked after a single moist cough.

"Guessing four minutes. Maybe more," Jordan said. The cage had accelerated, the view moving a little more aggressively now.

"And how long before we reach MacReady?"

"Five," Jordan said. "Roughly, of course."

Chu sounded as though he were shivering, either from the cold or what he was thinking. "Any way we can make that faster?"

"Why?" Jordan asked. "Got somewhere to be?" He glanced at his HUD readings. "We're going to start feeling gravity soon."

"Lovely," Chu said. "Good thing neither of us has a bruised rib or anything like that."

Jordan winced, imagining a rib sticking through flesh like a broken, bloody split candy cane.

"More worried about the 'debris' warning," Chu said.

"Wouldn't worry too much about that. Whatever that thing is," Jordan said, "we'll have the climber on the ground in a couple of minutes, and even if the tether gets cut, we'll be safe." As he said all of this, he realized he believed none of it.

Even before the attack, things had felt off. The massive debris field, the state of MacReady's sisters, not to mention the radioactive material. Whatever that shit was. Nothing about this system added up. In a way, having an alien show up was just more of the same.

*Is it alien? What else could it be, though?*

"When we hit the ground," Jordan said, "we need to get moving as quickly as possible."

Chu snickered. "Still going to carry me?"

"Only if you need me to," Jordan said. "Seriously, though. I will."

"I know you will," Chu said.

They'd crossed through what little atmosphere MacReady had and were now shooting down from the sky toward a shadowy, amorphous landscape. Some distance away, he made out the pinprick of a light near the base camp. That meant something's battery was still functioning. Maybe a good sign.

The cage decelerated, and now gravity really went after him. If the planet had had more than 1 G, this might have been painful as hell. As it was, 1/3 G, it wasn't so bad. He'd been through a 4 G orbital drop to a gas giant's moon. Not fun.

The cage's strong lights finally found the surface as the cage neared the landing platform. The brightening circle of light cast from the cage as well as the platform itself proved Jordan had chosen well. The spot had no peaks or hills behind it for kilometers but was close enough to the mining camp that he and Chu could get there easily, if not quickly.

*If we'd had time,* Jordan thought, *we could have brought a scooter.*

**NETWORK ESTABLISHED** appeared on his HUD.

They'd finally come in range of the mesh network. Jordan blinked through a few menu items until he found the status he was looking for—connection with the base camp.

The surface computer complained the connection was intermittent and that engineer Jordan or Aryana should look into it immediately. Jordan mentally flipped off the surface computer.

The cage slowed and finally came to a lurching halt on the landing platform. If there had been enough atmosphere and if he'd had his external mics on, he'd have heard the hiss of air being forced from the landing platform's bladders that served as a cushion for the climber.

The light above the hatch turned green, and Jordan opened the cage. Chu undid his harness and acted as though he were moving to the hatch.

"Not yet," Jordan said. "Let me take a look before you go anywhere."

Chu sighed heavily through the radio. "You think—um—"

"I don't know what to think," Jordan said. "That's why you're staying here."

"Copy," Chu said, sounding a little relieved.

Jordan had removed his harness and brushed it aside, the restraints locking to the hull. Butterflies in his stomach, or maybe bees in a thunderstorm, Jordan stepped out of the cage and onto MacReady's surface for the first time.

# CHAPTER TWENTY-FOUR

Parasite flexed the host's fingers and toes, all now larger than they once were. The flimsy EVA suit had split beneath the pressure of growing bone and transformed, hardened flesh. A few tatters remained, but so long as they didn't hinder movement, Parasite ignored them.

The host body flared with pain from the ongoing transformation, and Parasite shut down the nerve centers. Connected to its host's spine, the creature's tendrils had flared out through the human nervous system as well as into the host's brain itself.

The "other" was conscious and screaming, its thoughts a collection of confused images and sounds that Parasite didn't understand. It didn't need to, for now. That would come later. Just as it had been designed to interface with multiple types of lifeforms, it had been designed to orient to their thoughts. Not read them, control them, or anticipate them but to understand them to an extent.

Stabs of pain erupted from its mutating chest, and Parasite felt fire soaring through the remains of the host's lungs. The tortured nerve endings died, new ones replacing them. Parasite continued absorbing the fluid pumped into the host as well as the host itself. Every secretion from every organ, analyzed, functionality cloned to handle vacuum and the lack of pressure.

Parasite activated its eye cluster, and five green slits came to life across half of its mutated face. Or was that faces? It no longer had a humanoid head but a partially bifurcated skull that connected Parasite's alien skeletal structure with that of the host's. The two were now one, although two different minds remained.

Once the last of the screaming nerves fell silent, replaced by a warm emptiness, Parasite sat up. The host's helmet lay on the damaged deck, broken and shattered. Its boots had ripped open, exposing long, thick toes with incredibly sharp nails.

Parasite got to its feet and shook off most of the lower portion of the suit, exposing more of its host's green and yellow mutated flesh. The reactors still burning inside the engine compartment made the shadows jump and writhe, Parasite's visual receptors slowly adapting to the low light conditions, transforming more and more with each passing beat.

The host's head, its flesh much paler than the rest of the body, moved its crooked jaw in silence, perhaps trying to say words. Maybe even pray.

Parasite's eye cluster received a series of ultraviolet flashes from the orb. There was movement on the ship. More beings like the host, presumably. Parasite crouch-walked to the nearest of the two massive modules in the bay. It peered around the edge using its eye cluster, the "other's" eyes stuck with the view of metal.

Two figures emerged from the airlock, one looking as though it was helping the other. One wore a much heavier suit than the other. Parasite looked down at the tatters around its waist and realized the smaller host had the same kind of suit. What was the difference?

It tried to forward the question to the "other," but the being was still nothing more than a screaming, insane clutter of images, sound, and bewildering thoughts. Parasite gave up immediately. For now.

Parasite watched in fascination as the flimsy-suited one entered an airlock, disappeared, and returned a few moments later wearing the same thick suit as its fellow host. One must be more powerful than the other. More protection, perhaps? More armor?

The smaller host paused a few beats before turning in the pod's direction. Parasite crouched low, the claws of one hand clicking silently against the metal. It didn't need this host. As long as the creature posed no threat, there was no reason to engage it. Besides, it was doomed regardless of whatever Parasite might do.

The potential host continued approaching, white lights shining from its new suit. Parasite moved forward slowly, melting into the shadows, its rough flesh breaking up any light the meltdowns in the engineering bay provided. When the host bent to examine the pod and the damage to the deck, Parasite stepped into the beam of white.

The suited creature backed away, nearly stumbling in its efforts to retreat. The other creature, the one who had helped its mate, was waving and leaning over something. Parasite asked the "other" what it was, but the intelligence was saying nothing, or rather, nothing of interest.

Parasite, more curious than intent on engaging the creatures, continued marching toward them. The slab of metal pushed away from the bay, and a moment later, the pair of creatures had jetted to it.

It watched the slab journey out over the planet, a tether finally uncoiling and plummeting to the planet's surface. Parasite knew what it was and also knew it would be perfect.

Parasite quickly made its way back to the pod and regarded the orb. The pair had a brief conversation in infrared that resulted in the robot descending until it hovered next to the host. Parasite moved forward and draped itself around the orb.

The orb struggled to rise a meter above the deck, but it was more than enough. Parasite held on as the orb moved through the smashed cargo bay out of the same hatch the creatures had used. Once beyond the ship, Parasite scanned the planet's surface, looking for telltale signs of anything that might have escaped the EMR blast. So far, it couldn't find anything. That was good.

When the orb reached within five meters of the orbital, Parasite pushed off, floated through space for a moment, and finally clutched the lift's superstructure with its free hand. The creature reoriented itself and used its clawed feet to grip the metal deck.

A holodisplay control panel floated in the air before it. Parasite didn't understand the words but thought it understood the diagrams. It queried the "other," asking for advice. The "other," somewhat calmer than before, either didn't want to help or didn't know, but a spurious image flicked through Parasite's consciousness. A little more confident, it pressed the "down" button.

A new message flashed across the display. Parasite couldn't read it but didn't need to. The "other" had begun gibbering again, fear mixed with curiosity and rage. Parasite didn't understand fear, but it understood the other two quite well.

The lift would return. When it did, Parasite could start its mission without riding the orb to the fragment's surface. The "other" gave no indication how long the process would take, but it would be soon enough. There was food somewhere below, and Parasite had all the time it needed.

# CHAPTER TWENTY-FIVE

The platform's bright white halo of light dispelled the shadows for a good fifty meters, exposing reddish-brown gabbro. Jordan idly thought the gabbro might be the most unremarkable he'd ever seen. Almost too normal.

The incongruity or weathering of the hills looked wrong to him somehow, as if portions had been more exposed to the elements than others. Considering the planet's lack of atmosphere, any so-called weathering was more likely caused by debris clouds, meteor showers, and collisions with who knew what.

If it had been from rain, glaciers, or even high winds, the gabbro would have slowly been pulverized into sand, and that sand would have further polished the sheer cliff he saw in the distance. With the planet permanently shrouded in deep shadow, it was impossible to know what it all looked like unless he was up close and with a powerful light. Then again, who the fuck cared?

Still, it just didn't seem right. Jordan walked a few steps on the surface, half expecting to feel it give. Instead, a little dust puffed up, and a few pebbles moved, but nothing more.

He pushed the creepy feeling away and focused on clearing the area, such as it was. Since the camp was some distance away, there weren't exactly any obstacles or equipment around. That also meant he had no way of determining their status. Unless...

Jordan blinked through his HUD and attempted a connection to the base camp. He immediately received a return ping. Smiling, he finished the connection and began looking through the available systems.

The mining camp drones were all offline, every single one of them dead to the world. The ones he'd re-tasked, on the other hand, were still up and running. That didn't much surprise Jordan—*Prospector's* drones were far more powerful and resilient than the mining crew's. A miner's drone could be repaired. If a Prospector-class drone malfunctioned, it was permanently lost and couldn't be replaced. As such, they were hardier, stuffed with sensors, and extremely expensive.

Jordan brought up the first of the drones after divining its location. It was some distance away from the cliff where they supposedly drilled the first cores. The drone's camera, more or less permanently stuck in night vision mode, provided a clear view of a sheer rock face, a supply cart and mining equipment at its base.

The drone, some 300 meters away, had been placed in static wide view mode. "Need something to watch our backs," Jihi or Aryana had said. That would explain why the drone hadn't been zoomed in.

Had the miners picked up on the feel of this place? How everything seemed, well, unreal? If Aryana had, she'd probably been too proud to say anything. Same with Jihi.

It wasn't as if they hadn't had plenty of reason to be wary. The strangeness of MacReady's two sisters, the debris field, the highly radioactive shards— all of it added up to a collection of unsettling oddities. That had been more than enough to put Jordan's guard up.

But the miners had been concerned about an actual threat. Or so he thought now.

Not that the answer would matter much. Jordan had just seen some fucking alien thing that used to be Til chasing them out of the ship. He didn't exactly need independent confirmation they were facing something both intelligent and inhuman. When you got right down to it, there wasn't much else you needed to know.

It didn't change the fact that he had to get Chu to the mining camp's medbay. Nor did it change the fact that they had to get their suits recharged and arm themselves. And then he could find Aryana.

He switched to another drone and the cam-feed made him blink. Instead of a view of MacReady's surface, he saw only shadow perforated by glints of steel. It took Jordan a moment to realize he was looking at a portion of Orbital One's tether. The drone had nearly been completely flattened by the falling object.

If Jordan wanted to see site 2, he'd have to pilot the drone far enough away from the tether to get an unblocked view. No time for that at the moment. He switched to the next drone, got no visual at all, and switched to the fourth. The view took his breath away.

While Jordan hadn't exactly studied the sites in great detail, it looked like the drone's camera pointed at site 4. He switched to the lowlight filters, and the world came to life in greens, blotchy whites, and gaps of pure black. He was looking at a portion of the mountain that appeared to have crumbled or fractured. Might explain why the image was so incredibly confusing. Was anyone at site 4 when that had happened?

The thought of a mountain collapsing on top of him left him cold. Inside the suit, he could probably survive a few dozen metric tons of rock sitting on top of him, but he couldn't imagine many worse fates than being trapped in your suit, unable to move, just waiting for the $O_2$ to run out.

He'd hoped to get a drone view of the actual camp, get a feel for any damage, but that was too much to hope for. He and Chu would just have to hope for the best. There really wasn't much else they could do.

"Chu," he said, "come on out."

Instead of turning to watch Chu, Jordan continued scanning the area using his lowlight filters. Some two-hundred meters away, he saw the crevasse he and Chu would have to traverse. It appeared as though the ground just fell away into nothing only to be picked up on the other side, the ground normal and unaffected.

*You mean that's what it looks like from here,* he corrected himself.

True. Once he and Chu were closer, he'd know for sure. Still, it was reason enough for him to turn and head to the platform's rear.

"What are you doing?" Chu asked.

"Emergency kit," Jordan said.

After hitting the stud, a panel opened on the back of the platform. Inside were spare $O_2$ cartridges, flares, and a backpack he could easily attach to his suit. He pulled open the pack and quickly checked the included supplies.

Tether, harness, rope, water, and nutrition cartridges. More or less everything he needed to get Chu to the base camp. In theory.

Jordan attached the pack and filled his pouches with as many supplies as he could carry. "Hey, Chu. Come here."

Chu coughed through the radio and shortly appeared next to Jordan. Jordan pointed at the remaining supplies, and Chu wordlessly gathered what he could. Jordan didn't like the way the man was breathing.

"You okay?" Jordan asked.

"Been better," Chu said and finished stowing the last of the $O_2$ cartridges he could fit. He turned to face Jordan and gestured to the open panel. "Anything else I can carry?"

"No," Jordan said. "You ready to be luggage?"

"Not yet," Chu said. With his visor up, it was easy to see the man's exhausted grin. "Think I'll let you have it easy for a while longer."

"Glad you're thinking of my welfare," Jordan said. "Come on."

The two men walked away from the platform and its welcoming circle of light. With each step, Jordan felt the shadows close in on them just a little bit more. By the time they'd made fifty meters, the ambient light had already started to fade, the gabbro and dust no longer looking normal but somehow less real.

"How far away is the camp?"

"1.2 kilometers," Jordan said. "We have plenty of $O_2$, so don't push yourself too hard."

"Don't worry about that," Chu said.

Jordan had slowed his own pace considerably, shortening his longer stride to keep Chu from having to walk fast. He didn't want the man out of his sight if he could help it. That feeling of everything being wrong, of malevolent eyes watching them, wouldn't leave him.

He set his suit to scan for radio traffic but received only static in return. The three main mining comm channels appeared to be completely offline. Add to that the fact that he didn't have access to any drones near the camp, and he thought it likely the entire mining team, including Aryana, had been lost or was injured.

*Until you know, you don't know,* he told himself.

"We're getting out of the range of the platform's mesh network," Chu said.

Jordan nodded. "I can still get to a few of *Prospector's* drones, so the base camp mesh must still be operational to some degree."

"Good news," Chu coughed. The phlegm in his chest seemed to be multiplying every few minutes. Pretty soon he'd probably start having the long coughing fits Jordan remembered all too well. "Well," Chu said, "nothing to do but walk, right?"

"Yup."

**ORBITAL LIFT ENGAGED** flashed across his HUD.

Jordan stopped in mid-step. "What?" he said and turned around to face the platform. The cage had begun climbing back toward the sky. "Oh, fuck me," he said softly.

Chu turned to follow his gaze. "What? How? Did you—"

Jordan shook his head. "No fucking way," he said. "No way did that just happen."

"How long?" Chu asked, sounding as though he were stifling another cough.

"Forty minutes to climb. Ten to fifteen to get back down, I guess." Jordan wanted to walk back to the platform and cut the tether. It wouldn't keep the cage from coming down, but it would certainly make for a rough landing. Did he have time for that, though? It would take them a while to get to the camp. Whatever was coming down for them might be able to move much faster than they could, especially if Jordan ended up having to carry Chu.

"Come on," he said to Chu and tapped his shoulder. "Have to keep moving."

"Yeah," Chu said. He turned and took several steps without waiting for Jordan. The sleepiness in his gait had dissipated, if not in his voice. "Get me to a medbay and put a mining hammer in my hands."

Mining hammer. Not a bad idea. With an augmented arm swinging it, it could seriously damage a mining suit. They were made for impacts from large objects and bludgeon-type damage. The sharp end of a tungsten carbide hammer could at least make a hell of a rent in a mining suit. It might take a couple of swings, but Jordan knew the tool could shatter armor.

Weapons. They needed handheld mining tools, mining explosives or incendiaries, zirconium powder, anything that could be used in self-defense. Whatever was coming down for them hadn't exactly looked friendly, but, even if it was, he didn't intend to give it the chance to make its intentions known.

They continued walking in silence until they reached a sheer crevasse that appeared to descend into an abyss. Jordan couldn't see the bottom even with lowlight filters. The surface looked torn and turned, as if the hole had been created from beneath rather than above. *Something in the crust settle?* He wondered.

Too many coincidences. This had to be artificial, and if so, what had caused it?

The gap, roughly five meters wide, appeared to run through the moon for kilometers, although with the shadows, it was difficult to know. He was somewhat surprised they hadn't seen it from space, but then again, no one was really looking for it.

But the drones hadn't seen it, proving it had to be new, relatively speaking. *Goddammit, what the hell was going on here?*

"How we going to cross that?" Chu asked.

"Well, I can launch a grapple to the other side and we can climb across, or we can do it the stupid way."

"The stupid way?" Chu said dumbly. "I'm afraid to ask."

Jordan grinned. "You should be. It's one-third gravity here. With you on my back, I can probably make that leap in this suit. If you use your suit jets while we're in the air, so to speak, we'll definitely make it."

Chu turned back to the crevasse. "You're right. That's the dumbest fucking thing I've heard all day." He paused a moment before looking back at the platform. "Then again, I'm game."

"Figured," Jordan said. "Lock your suit to mine. Put my pack on yours."

"Got it," Chu said.

Jordan dropped to one knee to give the shorter man access to the pack and other supplies attached to his back. For this to work, he needed Chu completely flush with his suit. Any gap between them or dangling limbs would create drag or, worse, an actual pull in the opposite direction, all but guaranteeing the pair a firsthand look at the bottom of the crevasse. That was a tour he could do without.

Once Chu finished removing and reattaching the pack and supplies, suffering two wet coughing fits while doing it, Jordan felt the man's mass clamp to his back. Jordan shifted him slightly, giving the magnetics a better seal and more natural balance for his weight. Last thing he wanted to deal with was one side being significantly heavier than the other. He needed all the help he could get.

"Okay," Jordan said after triple-checking the feel and weight. "I think we're good."

"Um, I'm having second thoughts about this," Chu said as Jordan took seven steps backward from the edge of the crevasse. "You sure"—Jordan leaned forward to run—"about this?"

The last words came out in a choked shriek of surprise as Jordan ran at the gap. At the last moment, he planted his feet and leaped with all the force he could. The pair shot three meters above the abyss, Chu's jets coming to life, pushing them farther upward and stalling the pair from descending too early.

Jordan raised his legs as they covered the gap to hit the other side. A meter from the edge, he stumbled to the ground, lost his balance, and tumbled to the gabbro. Chu's suit kept him from rolling all the way, but it was a close thing, leaving Chu gasping and cursing.

Seeing stars from the impact, Jordan rolled back onto his stomach and pushed with his augmented arms until he reached his knees. "You okay?" he asked.

"Sure," Chu said. "Brain slid in my skull, I can barely breathe, but yeah. That was fun. Let's do it again."

Every word had come out in a dull, exhausted tone that bordered on robotic. How many rads had the pilot been exposed to? He seemed to be deteriorating before Jordan's very eyes.

"Eight hundred meters and we'll be there," Jordan panted. He licked his lips, took a deep breath, and tried to get his breathing under control. Augmented suit didn't mean the operator had to do nothing. It amplified strength but didn't create it. His legs felt jittery and rubbery. He really needed to get more physical exercise. This was embarrassing. "I promise to go fast."

"Not too fast," Chu said. "I don't want my brain rattled any more than necessary."

Jordan took a sip of water from the nipple inside his helmet, the cool liquid exactly what his throat needed. He had a feeling he'd be drinking a lot more before he was done. "Ready?"

"Ready," Chu said.

With a groan of effort, Jordan stood without losing his balance. He took more than a dozen steps before falling into a fast walk that became a slow jog, Chu riding him like a child on a rescuing fireman's back.

# CHAPTER TWENTY-SIX

It had been a long damned shift, and there was still a long ways to go. Probably the rest of his life, in fact. Regardless of how tired he already was, he wasn't going to have the chance to sleep until he either found a way off this rock or simply decided to die.

Three hundred meters from the crevasse, Chu broke the silence, although his words had the edge of a growl from his sore throat and phlegmy chest. "Do you see it?"

Jordan slowed. "Where?"

"Up," Chu said. "Up and behind you."

He knew what Chu was trying to show him before he even turned around. It was expected, after all. Jordan did as he was told and saw the cage, its powerful running lights appearing as a single bright dot falling from space at a deceptively slow pace. He knew it was heading through the atmosphere now. Another ten minutes and it might be on the surface. That wasn't long enough.

"Fuck," Jordan said and turned. Instead of his slow trot, he pushed himself into a jog. The gabbro here was a little thinner, sparser, and flatter. It seemed nearly perfectly planar, but that had to be an illusion, his brain attempting to make sense out of what he couldn't make sense of. Or maybe he was just trying to occupy his mind before whatever had followed them showed up.

Til hadn't been a small man, but that thing had seemed so much larger, almost as if something had torn off his suit, eaten him, and dressed in the tatters.

*That's stupid,* he told himself. He didn't get a good look at the thing that he was certain used to be Til, but he had a feeling Til had become something alien. Would it destroy the orbital lift? Sabotage it?

A good question. Considering Jordan and Chu were only a few dozen meters from the bend leading to the camp, did it really matter? He wasn't going back to the platform unless it was to try to unfuck the *Kirkland,* which was permanently fucked, or pilfer the remaining supplies.

*If you're here that long,* he thought, *you might as well just call it a day. Open up your helmet and take in a deep breath of void.*

It had taken the *Kirkland* over a year to reach MacReady. A rescue mission, maybe even a company troubleshooting team, would take six months—maybe three if the company was interested in getting here in a hurry, but that was still a long, long time to spend in a mining camp without any support from a mining ship.

Still, if they were trapped here for six months to a year, he would have to go back to the ship to strip every possible component he could, or they'd have to go into stasis. He just hoped it didn't come to that.

He rounded the bend and slowed to a fast walk, eyes scanning everything and nothing all at once. The massive equipment containers and the various personnel modules stood on a slight rise like ugly skyscrapers amidst a post-apocalyptic landscape. With the modules unlit, his brain filled in the details he couldn't make out.

The three personnel modules had been connected together with a tunnel system but remained isolated from the other mining-related modules. To travel from personnel and back, you had to wear a pressure suit of some kind.

"Hey, Jordan?" Chu asked. "Can you take a knee so I can get off you?"

"Oh," Jordan said. "You sure?"

"Just do it, big guy."

An exhausted smile crossed his face, and he knelt as asked. Chu's mass shifted on his back and jolted against him, and then it was as if gravity had been lifted from his back. Jordan groaned in relief and stood. He leaned back slightly and enjoyed the sensation of his vertebrae realigning.

"Better?" Chu asked.

"Fuck, yes," Jordan said. He pointed at the personnel modules. "Can you make it up there?"

"Of course," Chu said.

Jordan walked up the rise with Chu close behind him, their suit lights banishing the darkness yet creating wide nests of shadows, not to mention their own personal ones that jerked and glided with their every step.

*Just shadows,* he told himself. *You know that. What's coming isn't here yet.*

Why had he thought that?

When Jordan reached the airlock, he touched the stud, and nothing happened. Sharing an uneasy glance with Chu, he activated the manual crank and spun it until the system had enough juice. Upon touching the stud again, the exterior hatch cycled and opened into a dimly lit airlock.

He and Chu stepped inside.

"Why are the lights out?" Chu asked.

"Don't know," Jordan said. "Might be a short, might be the result of something like an EMP, or maybe the reactor went down. Or Aryana shut it down."

"Why the hell would she do that?" Chu asked.

"She wouldn't," Jordan said. "Not without a damned good reason."

The inner door cycled after a moment, and his HUD flashed.

### ATMOSPHERE NOMINAL

"Surprising," Jordan said aloud and walked through the airlock and into personnel module 1's first floor, Chu on his heels. Four suit stations protruded from a silver wall with yellow status lights above each. An error message blinked in a bright, unhealthy yellow from a holo-sign near the ceiling.

### INSUFFICIENT POWER

"Yeah, I know," Jordan said to it.

Chu said, "Sounds as if you take that personally."

"I do," Jordan said. "Follow me."

During a normal mining tour, this entire module would slowly build up a layer of dust and other detritus left over from the suits clomping in and out, regardless of how well they were cleaned. Fortunately for everyone, the nasty stuff was filtered, but some of the annoying, harmless shit always survived.

The MacReady mining team had barely begun operations, so this corridor and the bulkhead had no sign of wear and tear, no stains, no marks or bludgeons from accidents.

He hooked a right and walked the short corridor before reaching the first ETS (emergency treatment station), Chu following close behind. Jordan cleared the rest of the corridor before opening the airlock hatch leading inside and clearing it.

Empty.

"Okay, get inside. Get undressed. Another shower."

"And another shot of emergency meds," Chu said with an exhausted sigh. "You going to stay out here?"

Jordan nodded. "Provide cover. Make sure you don't get caught naked."

"Least of my worries," Chu said. "You think the air in here is safe to breathe?"

"I'm staying in my suit for now." Jordan gestured to the airlock. "Get inside and get going. Sooner we get you triaged again, sooner we can get you to the actual MedBay."

"This is silly if the MedBay is in the next module," Chu said.

"It is, if the MedBay is working. If it's not working, then you'll be thankful we did this."

Chu snickered. "Prudence. I forgot about how you think, Jordan."

Jordan grinned. "In truth, I just fucking hate backtracking."

Laughing, Chu walked inside the airlock and began the process of stripping off his clothes. The whole cycle of cleaning up should take him about five minutes. That gave Jordan a little time to actually check on a few things.

He activated his connection to the network and flipped through devices. The mesh network connected to the emergency orbital's platform, and Jordan brought up its status. He took a deep breath and held it for a long moment as he tried to keep his heart from leaping out of his chest.

The cage had landed a mere moment ago, and the cam-feeds had captured what had walked out of it. The platform's lights made it undeniable.

When the cage opened, something a bit larger than a fully suited Til walked out onto the short ramp leading to the gabbro surface.

The thing's head was what really did Jordan's brain in. It might once have been Til, but it was nearly impossible to tell. The face had been stretched to the point of tearing as it tried to cover not one skull but two. The first skull, still looking mostly human, leaned to one side as if its neck were broken, while the other remained upright and alert. The alien skull had skin where there should be eye sockets and eyes where its cheeks and forehead should have been.

The alien eyes glowed a hellish, eldritch green that seemed to strike something in Jordan's soul, leaving his heart beatless and his mind thoughtless. The horror show seemed to peer down before following the trail he and Chu had left behind.

As it faded away into the distance, its back came into full view on another cam-feed. Thick, armored plates made of bone or hardened flesh covered the exposed area.

That thing was down here, and while part of its broken and mangled face might once have been Til's, it was clear he was dead. Wasn't he?

Jordan didn't want to consider the possibilities. He switched to the drone at site 1 to see if anything had changed, but nothing had. After setting motion alarms on the drones, he connected to the module's infrastructure systems.

Sure enough, the main reactor was down, and all nonessential systems had been powered off. Only the emergency systems were available. Fortunately, MedBay was an emergency system.

The camp's backup batteries had enough power for another twenty hours before they went into hibernation mode. Once they reached that point, the miners would either have to find a way into stasis or fire up another power source.

The cameras throughout the personnel module appeared offline, unless he manually brought them up, wasting a few more precious watts. The same with any other nonemergency equipment. Right now, there was no reason to do that. If needed, he'd leave Chu behind and check it out himself.

*Alone. In the gloom. And that thing is coming here. You know it is.*

Jordan shivered and pulled the portable welding torch from his belt. He knew it wasn't much of a weapon, but it made him feel better. For now, it was the best he had on hand.

"Jordan?" Chu called out.

"Here. Go."

"Got more anti-rads in my bloodstream. Getting back in my suit."

"Copy. All quiet."

Chu coughed once. "Can't decide if that's a good thing or a bad thing." The suit radio squawked and filled with static for a moment while Chu switched from the ERS's radio back to his own suit radio. "Any cameras working?"

"Not yet, no."

"What about the surface platform? That thing get down here yet?"

Jordan heard the edge of fear in the man's voice. Chu was just as unsettled as Jordan was. Fuck, why wouldn't he be?

"I don't know." He felt bad lying, but he didn't want Chu any more panicked than the man already was. If Jordan described what he'd seen, he was afraid Chu would completely freeze up or become hysterical. "We're locked up tight in here," Jordan said. "I'll perform a lockout on the personnel modules."

"You can do that?" Chu asked.

Jordan caught motion in his peripheral vision and turned slightly to see Chu step through the airlock. The man's suit looked just as it had before, only maybe a little cleaner.

"I can," Jordan said. "Give me a minute."

He hadn't wanted to lock down the personnel modules until he knew Aryana's status as well as that of the miners. He hadn't wanted to risk closing off any paths to safety they might have, but that was before the creature landed and Jordan had had a good look at it.

After connecting to the interface, he slipped through the emergency protocols and locked all external hatches and airlocks. Just to make sure, he set up proximity alarms as well as entry alarms. If anyone went in or out of the personnel modules, the system would alert him. If anyone, or anything, moved near the airlock, he'd get an alert as well.

"All taken care of," Jordan said. "Let's move."

# CHAPTER TWENTY-SEVEN

They left the suit stations behind and headed to the airlock leading to the tunnel connecting modules 1 and 2. Chu sounded a little less ragged, his phlegm rattles more muted. He needed a full blood replacement along with a lot of rest. He might get the former, but the latter might be all but impossible. Fortunately, Chu might not have long to live anyway.

The two men entered the airlock after Jordan brought up its power and waited while the system ran through its routine. Jordan's suit flashed a status message that the air was breathable.

*That's good*, Jordan thought. He still wasn't going to take off his helmet or let Chu do the same. Not yet. But at least he knew if they had a suit perforation, no one would die. Well, faster than they already were, that was.

"No lights," Chu said peering through the porthole into module 2.

"No lights, no people, no nothing," Jordan said. "Everything, including the heaters, is activated by motion detectors and via the entry systems."

Chu nodded. "Didn't know that. So people have to be in here for the main power to even function?"

"More or less," Jordan said. "Even life support goes into a low-power, low-$O_2$ mode. Can all be brought back online in seconds, but that's how it goes."

"Didn't know any of that," Chu said.

"Why would you?" Jordan chuckled. "You fly the ship. Your first time getting dirty on the ground?"

Chu nodded as the airlock finished cycling. "Never thought I'd touch down on one, to be honest."

"What? A moon?"

"No," Chu said, hand reaching for the stud. "An alien world."

The phrase sent a shiver down Jordan's spine, but he couldn't say why. Technically, anywhere that humankind hadn't settled was known as "alien," including MacReady. Unless colonists were running around, so to speak, it was just a camp or facility and nothing more.

Chu seemed to be waiting for Jordan to say something.

"I'm ready," he said to the shorter man.

Chu flinched as though a spell had been broken, his hand darting to the stud like a snake.

The exterior airlock opened on a short tunnel leading to module 2. The tunnel immediately came to life with warm, bright light that dispelled the shadows. Just as with module 1, it was mostly spotless and appeared barely used.

Jordan suddenly felt as though he had walked into an alternate reality, one in which he and Chu were the only human beings alive on MacReady. In fact, they were the only two that had ever been to the strange planet or moon or whatever the hell this thing really was. He half expected a holo monster to slither out of the support pipes and begin dissolving him and Chu.

"What about after MedBay?" Chu asked as they reached the second airlock.

"We'll figure that out once we figure you out."

Chu coughed as if on cue. "I appreciate that. But I know you have a plan. You always do."

The hatch cycled, and the two men climbed inside, the top of Jordan's helmet mere centimeters from the ceiling. When the air had been cleaned and exchanged, not to mention disinfected, the interior hatch opened, and a smattering of lights came to life. Room hatches lined a module-long corridor that ended in a lift. All the stateroom hatches had been closed and secured. Jordan grinned despite himself. First time he'd ever seen miners follow policy. Must be Aryana's influence.

Jordan turned to his right and saw what he was looking for—the MedBay. Unlike the tunnel, the sparse and flickering overheads cast a net of shadows that made his skin crawl. The MedBay's entrance, a wide hatchway made for lugging in heavily suited bodies, seemed to swallow the corridor's ambient light.

He knew what was inside the MedBay—two medical stasis pods, two airlock-encased autodocs, and a diagnostic/treatment bay, not to mention a bulkhead stuffed with medical supplies. Everything from a lozenge to a skull fracture kit. Standard company issue.

"Get behind me," Jordan said as he stepped to the MedBay entrance, his powerful suit lights cutting a wide swath through the nests of shadows. He was looking for movement, blood, anything that might give him a heads-up there was something in here that shouldn't be.

Nothing.

He walked into the MedBay, and the moment his foot crossed the threshold, three of the seven overhead lights came to life. Jordan flinched but quickly recovered, eyes darting to every corner and looking for an assailant or damage to the decking.

Nothing.

Jordan exhaled a breath he didn't know he'd been holding. "Okay, Chu," he said, "get into the autodoc."

"Oh, yes. My favorite place," the pilot said. Chu clomped to the nearest autodoc, cycled the airlock, and stepped inside.

Jordan turned back to the open MedBay hatch, thought for a moment, and finally closed it, effectively locking the room from the inside. He stepped back from the hatch and slowly turned in a circle, taking everything in.

The transparent aluminum encasing the autodoc was soundproof, so there was little to no point in Jordan turning on his external mics.

*Might help you hear something, though,* he thought.

The modules had pressure and atmosphere at the moment, and the ability to listen wasn't exactly something he should ignore. It was a rare gift, and he intended to make use of it while he could.

With the external mics on, he heard the nearly inaudible mosquito whine of his suit's servos, the ticking and clicking of settling metal, and the ever-present whoosh of air recycling. Apart from that, nothing.

"How goes it, Chu?" Jordan asked after connecting to the autodoc's comms.

Chu had removed his suit and stood naked next to the automated bed. Hands across his chest, he appeared to be shivering. "Just fucking lovely."

Jordan smirked. "You look cold."

"Yeah," Chu said, his teeth chattering. "Heater's not quite up yet." He lay down on the bed and hissed as his naked flesh touched the still-warming fabric-covered steel frame.

Chu growled something Jordan couldn't understand and finally stretched out his arms and laid them next to his sides. The autodoc had probably nagged him about keeping his arms on his chest. A moment later, a pair of waldos appeared and unrolled a layer of nano fabric across Chu's body.

He moaned in relief a moment later. "Oh, that's better."

"No longer frozen?" Jordan asked.

"Not anymore," Chu said and attempted to stifle a coughing fit. He failed.

The waldos disappeared from view, and a flat bar appeared. Light danced from it and bathed Chu's body as it slid less than a meter above him from toe to skull. When it finished, it repeated the process twice more, each time the light a different color.

Finally, the autodoc stopped moving, and a holodisplay appeared inside the device. Jordan couldn't read it and didn't want to—it was none of his business. It would give Chu the bad news, and the man could decide what to do about it.

"Okay," Chu said softly. "I'm pretty fucked, J."

"How fucked?" Jordan said, doing his best to keep his voice light and casual.

"Totally? I'll need blood replacement therapy and about ten hours of rest. Kidneys are already failing."

Not good. Not good at all. Ten hours. Ten hours without moving, without being in a suit, and being completely exposed.

"The good news," Jordan said, still trying to sound calm, "is that you're safe in here. I can lock you in and leave the key inside, so to speak. No one will be able to get in that you don't want to."

"Small favors," Chu muttered.

"And you have plenty of $O_2$ and nutrients here," Jordan continued. "Not a bad place to hold up, all things considered."

"Can think of worse," Chu agreed. "Do I have ten hours?"

Jordan didn't know what to say to that apart from the absolute truth. "I don't know. I'll do my best to give them to you."

Chu chuckled darkly. "And how the fuck are you going to do that?"

Now Jordan grinned. "I've no idea. I have to try to find Aryana. If I go out there and that thing sees me, I'll draw it away from you. If things get, well, you know, out of hand, crawl into a stasis pod. It'll be the only chance you'll have left."

"Short of the ones on the *Kirkland*."

"Right," Jordan said. "Not sure anyone wants to go back there."

"No one I know of," Chu said. "Can you bring me a weapon?"

He wanted to get the hell out of here, go arm himself, and head outside to find his charge, but he didn't even know if she or any of the others were still alive. At this point, protecting Chu meant protecting the last remaining crew member, which also made him the highest priority.

"I can do that," Jordan said. "Anything in particular?"

"I'd kill for an EET-style WRENCH," Chu said, a grin in his voice. "Mining hammer will work."

"Not without your suit, it won't," Jordan said. "You're going to be weak from the meds, half-asleep, and in no shape to swing anything."

"Oh. Right. Shit." Chu was silent for a moment. "Your torch. Give it to me."

"Um, you sure that's a good idea? If the autodoc decides to give you $O_2$ therapy, just turning that thing on could—"

"That's why," Chu said. "Put it in the airlock for me. Please."

Jordan pulled the remaining fuel canister from his pouch and put both it and the torch in the airlock. After cycling it closed, he stepped to the trans-aluminum viewport looking in on the autodoc.

Chu looked pale and had thin scarlet threads running through his skin. Shit, he might be much closer to death than Jordan had realized.

"You going to be okay here alone?" Jordan asked.

Chu slowly nodded after sitting up from the table. He removed the nano fabric, and Jordan could all but hear the autodoc scolding its patient. After taking a deep breath, he put a palm against the metal. "Take your time, J, but don't be too long." He said that last with a forced grin.

Jordan placed his own palm against the window, his augmented glove so much larger than Chu's frail-looking hand.

"Rest," he said to Chu. "I'll stay on comms and network as long as I have signal. Call out if something changes."

"Will do," Chu said. "Watch out for Til."

"Yeah," Jordan nodded. They stared at one another for an awkward moment before Jordan turned away and clomped to the MedBay entrance. After checking to ensure they were still alone, he stepped through the airlock, and after a moment, he was back in the corridor facing the staterooms down the hall.

He checked the airlock to the tunnel, made sure it was still locked down and locked out, and headed through the tunnel leading to module 3.

# CHAPTER TWENTY-EIGHT

The tunnel connecting the two modules was shorter than the first. Considering module 1 was both larger and served as the backup shelter in case something happened on site, it made sense for it to be farthest away. Although if something catastrophic did occur, it would likely take out more than just the mining modules. In the severe cases that had occurred sporadically over the years, the miners rarely survived.

That had led to superstitions regarding certain worlds, moons, or asteroids, and after an entire mining crew was wiped out, the mine usually closed forever, never to be traveled to again. If they weren't, they soon were because so few miners were willing to work them regardless of ridiculous pay and shares. When you knew you could die from a mere suit perforation every time you stepped out onto an alien world, or hell, even the settled ones, you tended toward caution, even if you didn't believe in spirits, hostile creatures, or haunted worlds.

*You can believe in aliens,* Jordan thought. *That one's safe. As for hostile creatures? I think that one's also a yes.*

Upon entering the airlock to module 3, he did another quick check, looking for anything out of the ordinary. Still nothing. The short tunnel had been just as clean as the first, and the airlock practically shined beneath his lights.

Lights. They had experienced flickering lights, meaning some were out. That, and the reactor being down, bore all the hallmarks of an EMP of some sort. Maybe not powerful enough to fry all the electronics through the significantly shielded bulkheads but certainly enough to damage some of the equipment. Jordan could only hope that if that was what had caused the malfunctions, it hadn't affected all the tools he hoped to use.

He once again found himself in a significantly shorter corridor than the barracks module. The hallway ended in a massive room that contained rows and rows of personal gear for the miners as well as emergency equipment. What he wanted was on the far bulkhead.

No matter how solid the shaft, no matter how skilled the operator, sooner or later, miners had an accident. At such inopportune times, it was important to have something to help wedge yourself out of a sinkhole, crevasse, or pile of rubble. Mining suits helped with that, sure, but what was to help if you couldn't get to the mining bays?

Three types of hammers hung on the bulkhead. The ubiquitous mining hammer, a piece of tungsten alloy with a pry hook on one end and a massive, blunt blob of depleted uranium melted into the bar, could smash through gabbro as though it were nothing. Unfortunately, it also weighed nearly 50 kg, so it was out of the question for an EVA suit or an unsuited human to handle. Fortunately, Jordan's strong, augmented arms could both easily lift and swing it. Chu might not be able to even in a mining suit.

Some of the miners were shorter than Jordan, but they were all built, including Jihi. Using mining hammers, shuffling drills about, having to brush away boulders and other stray debris that had shook loose—all those actions required strength. Flying a ship, on the other hand, only required a brain, an appendage of some sort, and common sense. That wasn't to make light of Chu. Far from it.

The other two hammers were much smaller, much lighter versions. They were primarily used for reshaping the habitat, minor repairs around the modules, and laying new construction material. The smaller hammers would make great weapons against another human but would glance off a suit. Useless but maybe not completely useless.

He put one of the smaller hammers into his belt, attached the heavy mining hammer to his back, and walked to the recharge station. One thing he hadn't had to do thus far was worry about the suit itself. He still had hours and hours of resources available, but it didn't hurt to top off. Never did.

After stepping into the station, he brought up his HUD and switched through the drones looking for movement of any kind or signs that someone—or something, he reminded himself—had moved through the cliffs and to the camp.

By now, the Til thing should have reached module 1. Actually, as fast as it had been moving, it probably got here five or ten minutes ago.

*And you're going to go outside?*

Jordan ignored the inner voice and walked to a bulkhead lined with shelves. An $O_2$ cartridge dispenser, full by the looks of it, glinted at him as though it had been polished. He tapped the release button five times, swiping each ejected canister and filling a pouch. When he was finished, his largest pouch bulged like a tumor, the fabric straining to contain the inflexible cylinders.

Jordan grabbed two emergency kits and attached each to his belt. Four zirconium powder flares went into a spare pouch. Next? Another torch and two refills.

He took stock, knew he was forgetting something, and headed for the airlock leading to MacReady's surface. When he reached the exterior hatch, he connected to Chu.

"How you doing?"

"Wonderful," Chu said, his voice sounding as though he were trapped inside a cracker box. In a way, he was. Autodocs weren't exactly marvels of acoustics, at least not in a good way. "Already fell asleep twice."

Jordan grinned. With any luck, Chu'd fall asleep again quite soon. "It happens. I'm getting ready to go outside."

Chu suddenly sounded alert. "You armed?"

"As well as I can be," Jordan said. "At least until I get to the mining supplies."

"Got any cam feeds there?"

"No," Jordan said. "We're blank except for three of *Prospector's* drones."

"Great," Chu sighed. "How am I supposed to know what's going on?"

"You probably don't want to know," Jordan said. "I don't know how badly the comms are damaged. If the network repeaters are out, I might lose you the moment I step outside."

Chu paused before responding. "Great. Don't suppose you have codes for this place?"

Jordan blinked. "Codes? What are you—"

"Admin access. Root. God. Whatever you call it."

"Oh," Jordan said. "Can you be trusted?"

"No," Chu admitted. "But I'd like to be able to open and close doors if I need to."

Good point, Jordan thought. He blinked his way through menus and added Chu to the list of admins. That would give him access to all the modules' remaining functional systems. Including the airlocks.

"Okay, done."

"Yup," Chu said. "Good. This autodoc is now my slave!" He mocked a villain's laugh, which quickly broke into a muffled and too-moist-sounding cough.

"Maybe you should rest before you start punishing machines."

Chu tried to laugh, but it sounded strangled and hoarse. "Maybe I will. I'll keep my ear to the ground."

"I set up alarms. If anything comes near an exterior airlock, you'll get notified."

"Even if it's you?" Chu asked.

"Even if it's me," Jordan said. "If I can keep network access, I might even be able to fix the external cams. Eventually. But first, I have—"

"Aryana. Got it," Chu said. "Be careful."

"I will," Jordan said.

Careful? If he wanted to be careful, he'd stay in the MedBay with Chu and forget about going outside altogether. Of course, doing that was a death sentence of a kind. Eventually, he and Chu would run out of supplies and out of power. Once that happened, they'd have to climb into the stasis pods. And then? Well, they might last three or four years, but would anyone ever find them?

*Maybe Til will find you all frozen up like a ready-to-eat meal.*

Oh, that was a cheery thought.

"Here goes nothing," he said to himself and opened the inner airlock hatch. A suited figure tumbled inside, making Jordan leap backward, his arm struggling to release the mining hammer.

The suit clunked to the floor face-first with a crash. Jordan, mining hammer finally in his hands, took another step back, knees slightly bent, balanced and ready to strike.

The suit didn't move, didn't so much as twitch. Swallowing hard, he tentatively stepped forward, hammer still ready to bludgeon. He blinked through the menus until he found the general mining channel.

"Hello? This is Jordan. Is anyone there?"

No response. He half expected the suit on the floor to raise itself using its balled-up fists, rising from the floor like some kind of dead thing come back to life to attack him out of jealousy and spite. No answer. No movement.

"Chu?" he said. "Sending you my feed."

There was a slight pause and then a sharp hiss of air.

"Who is it?" Chu asked.

"I don't know, but I guess I have to find out," he said.

"Use the hammer end," Chu suggested.

Rolling his eyes, Jordan walked forward until he was less than a meter away and used the tool to push the body. The suit half rolled over, exposing the helmet's visor.

The trans-aluminum face shield had partially shattered, the metal flecks all but tearing off the face of the unfortunate miner. Who wasn't, Jordan thanked the 'verse, Aryana.

"What did that?" Chu asked.

Jordan moved his eyes away from the pulverized flesh and bone and looked further down the suit. Now he saw what Chu had—the front calf armor plate had been completely shattered.

"The fuck did that?" Jordan asked.

"Is there an echo in here?" Chu snickered and coughed.

Sure the man was dead, Jordan pulled the supply pouch off the suit and quickly rifled through it. Sure enough, a mining charge. Excellent.

Whoever this was, they'd died in the airlock while waiting for it to cycle.

Unless they were hiding from something.

*Hiding in the airlock? Why? And from what?* He had to admit that an airlock was a good place to hide, so long as your suit functioned. If you crouched down, no one could see you even through the porthole. Unless they had camera access, it'd be impossible to know without opening either hatch.

"Sorry it didn't work out," he said to the body.

After pulling the suited corpse inside and pushing it up against the bulkhead, Jordan stepped inside the airlock, looking for damage, and found it immediately.

Several dimples marred the outer hatch as if someone had been pounding on it from the other side using something massive. Something like a mining hammer, maybe.

"Chu? There may have been something hostile here before Til."

"Oh, shit," Chu said. "You're right. That doesn't look good."

"Putting it mildly," Jordan agreed.

"Starting to rethink this plan?" Chu asked. "You said there were two stasis pods."

"I did," Jordan said. He couldn't help smiling. "But I'd rather figure something else out."

"So would I," Chu said. "You going out that way?"

Jordan touched the stud, and the inner airlock hatch closed.

"I'll take that as a yes," Chu said dryly.

Jordan's external mics filled with the hiss of air being sucked back in and vacuum replacing it. The sound quickly faded away to nothing, and he shut off the mics. When the light turned green above the exterior hatch, Jordan pressed the stud and returned to MacReady's shadows.

# CHAPTER TWENTY-NINE

The mining team had laid out the mining modules in a neat 2x2 formation. Jordan found himself looking at one of the four massive containers—the Shed.

Every mining camp had at least one Shed, the formal name used with both respect and miner joy. It was the place you took broken tools, printed new ones, and returned for resupplies. When you broke a tool, you or your runner ended up having to make a trip to the Shed, where they could dawdle and skive off while outside their suit and in a nice warm, oxygenated environment. With pay.

Jordan slowly turned to look for movement from the edge of module 3 to the Shed and the other mining modules. He couldn't see much apart from the massive structures, especially since most of them were more than five meters tall. Jordan saw a strange shape at the front of the Mule bay. Frowning, he zoomed in and used his lowlight filters.

Whatever it was appeared to be metal of some kind, although not much more than half a meter of it was exposed.

*Could be they left a Mule outside and the tether fall destroyed it somehow?*

Jordan ignored the voice. It didn't really matter what the shape was. If he crossed the aisle to the Shed, he'd be exposed to whatever it was. If he stayed here, on the other hand, he'd be left with only the mining hammer to defend himself. At least with the Shed, he had a chance of making it inside the armored interior and getting something a little more formidable in his hands.

He tried to move his legs, but it was almost as though they refused to do his bidding. Jordan gritted his teeth and forced himself into a run.

Without Chu's mass hanging off his back, he made surprisingly short work of the three hundred meters separating the personnel modules from the mining modules. He kept swinging his gaze from one side to the other while pumping his arms and legs, the servos whining loud enough for him to hear them inside the suit.

When he neared the Shed's airlock, he locked the servos and took a practiced slide over the mostly smooth gabbro. Instead of letting him stop on a dime, however, the one-third gravity made his maneuver sloppy, and he practically crashed into the open exterior airlock hatch.

Once he recovered, he quickly cleared the airlock before spinning to close the hatch, half expecting a disfigured, amorphous shape to come streaking at him from the shadows. Instead, there was nothing. He touched the stud, and the exterior hatch closed, the airlock cycling.

Lights flickered through the porthole as the module prepared for human company. When the inner hatch opened, the entire module came to life with strong, comforting white light.

The machine shop took up nearly a quarter of the module and had its own airlock to the outside. That hatch was large enough for an entire drilling rig to fit through. Tools and equipment hung from the ceiling on robotic arms and dispensers throughout the entire module. Wherever you were, you could be working on something. In theory, that was.

As expected, the racks of manual tools had multiple missing slots. There were three drill teams, meaning one driller and one runner for each team. Each drill team required multiple tools for both the driller and the runner. Considering they'd moved everything via Mule, a robotic vehicle built expressly for carrying and moving both personnel and equipment, the teams would have taken spares.

What Jordan really needed was a mining pack with all the accoutrements. He walked to the bulkhead, pulled off his EVA pack, and quickly removed all the items. Once it was empty, he tossed it to the deck and pulled a harness off the rack. After refilling it with his existing supplies, he fitted the rest of it with the standard mining toolkits, including plasma charges, and plenty of plasma fuel. He included another suit repair kit as well as a full medkit.

Once outfitted and much more comfortable with his mining hammer riding in the specially made harness, he walked to the bulkhead with the plasma hammer attachments. The massive, bulky thing connected to the mining suit at the left shoulder and was a bit longer than the distance to the elbow joint. Awkward to attach, awkward to detach, and awkward to run with, the tool could render gabbro and pockets of raw tungsten into slag. It also gobbled fuel like a starved hummingbird,

Unlike its narrow, focused twin, the plasma drill, the hammer bludgeoned the superheated substance rather than cutting it. It also required much less skill than the drill, something Jordan appreciated.

He pulled a plasma hammer from the rack, attached it to his shoulder, and brought it online. After connecting to its interface, he put it in standby mode. The tool vibrated slightly against his armor as it warmed up. In another twenty or thirty seconds, it would be ready to blast deadly pulses of plasma at whatever target Jordan aimed.

He peered around the warehouse, looking for other tools or devices that might come in handy and sighed. The truth was, damned near everything in the Shed could serve double duty. Whether it was protecting your suit or serving as a weapon, grapples, lines, charges, fuel, or nutrients, everything was something he needed and didn't need.

Jordan sent a frequency pulse into the warehouse-like building, hoping for a return ping from someone he didn't see. Nothing. Either no one was in range, or no one had a functioning radio. Speaking of.

"Chu? You read me?"

"Too well," Chu said sleepily. "You're a sentence, not a novel."

Jordan snickered and said, "I'm in the Shed. No sign of hostiles outside."

"Okay, good news, I guess. Didn't find anyone?"

"No," Jordan said and peered at the machine shop, facing a vacuum. The internal hatch was open, with the external closed. Odd. "I'm going to check the airlocks just in case, but it doesn't look like anyone has been here for a while."

"Afraid of that," Chu said through a loud yawn. "They would have been at the mines."

"Then who was in the airlock? And why were they there?"

"Don't know," Chu said. "Runner? On their way to the machine shop? Got, I don't know, interrupted?"

That was a casual way of saying "fled for their life." But fled from what?

"Tether fall," Jordan muttered. "Something worse?"

"What?" Chu said. "Didn't catch that?"

He sighed, not knowing whether Chu would think him insane. "We don't know what happened here when the attack occurred. No way of knowing if the radiation storm or similar sent the miners seeking shelter. Could have been the tether fall too."

Chu took a long moment before answering. "Something else could have come down."

"Meaning what, exactly?"

"A pod. Something like that. Maybe the same kind of thing that hit the *Kirkland*. Same kind of thing that got Til. Maybe there's another one down here," Chu said.

He knew where Chu was going with that thought, and it made his skin crawl. The idea of turning a corner and finding a misshapen Aryana with an extra head snapping its jaws at him was enough to make him want to head back to module 2. Fuck the survivors. Fuck everything and run.

*She might be hiding. And you're probably dead anyway. What do you have to lose?*

Jordan couldn't argue with that logic. In the end, death was death, something he'd known since his first mining tour. He'd seen it up close and personal multiple times and faced it every time he stepped out onto a hull or tinkered with a damaged reactor. It was just part of the job. You either got used to it, accepting the proverbial Grim Reaper standing over you, or you froze and quit the industry, never to willingly get near that kind of hazard again.

Unfortunately, there were few good jobs that didn't require you to risk life and limb. Fortunately, Jordan loved the actual job of repairing and maintaining, or else he'd have never even stepped foot aboard a mining ship.

He brought up the interface for the plasma hammer again and checked its status to ensure it was primed and ready. A pointed finger would be enough to trigger a deadly plasma blast. More immediate than using the mining hammer but definitely a ranged weapon unless you wanted super-heated plasma splashing back at you.

*You can take down Til or anything else with that,* he told himself. *Better than starving or suffocating to death.*

Jordan flexed his right hand before pulling the mining hammer. In his mind, he looked like some medieval knight carrying an oversized longsword with a jewel of eldritch fire glowing from its left shoulder. Humorous if he weren't about to step outside again, expecting something to jump him. Something that might once have been human.

"If there's another one down here," Jordan finally said, "I'll just have to take care of it too."

"Jordan," Chu said, "you don't even know if you can take care of one."

"You know, you're really pumping up my confidence."

"It's the meds," Chu yawned again. "Getting punchy. Seriously if you can't take it out, get back here. We'll take our chances in the stasis pods."

"That's the plan," Jordan said, knowing there was little chance of him returning if he met Til. That creature had looked as though it could tear him limb from limb, suit or no suit. Worse, it looked as though it could move much faster than he could. If he couldn't get some distance between him and it, he didn't think he could win a fight.

*Would be a slaughter,* he told himself. Apparently Chu wasn't the only one being pessimistic.

"Heading out," Jordan said. "Stay on comms with me."

"Until I fall asleep," Chu said sourly. "Can't help it."

"I know." Jordan cycled the airlock and left the shed behind, knowing quite soon, he'd be all alone again.

# CHAPTER THIRTY

The airlock's exterior hatch opened on MacReady's surface once again. The lights over the entrance flickered as though the emergency power for the module was shutting down. Jordan knew that was the case too.

He took a right and headed to the large module sitting at the edge of camp. The Stable, named for obvious reasons, held the Mules as well as interchangeable parts and tool attachments for the vehicles.

He kept his eyes moving and activated his rear cam, hoping to catch extreme motion before something could flank him. Jittery with adrenaline, he reached the Stable's oversized airlock and cycled the exterior hatch. After a quick look inside to ensure there wasn't another dead body waiting for him, or something a little more disgusting and dangerous, he quickly turned and expertly walked backward inside the airlock.

Once the exterior hatch closed, he exhaled hard, turned back to the interior hatch, and touched the stud. The airlock cycled for a moment before flashing an alert.

**ACCESS DENIED**

Eyebrow raised, Jordan tried again and received the same message. He connected to the interface and discovered why. Aryana or Jihi had performed a lockout. One of them had secured the Mules to make sure no one beyond those two could get back in.

*Or me,* Jordan thought.

He sent the admin codes, and the alert disappeared. This close to the internal mesh network, he should at least be able to connect to the module's interface, maybe get lucky and find an internal camera. Instead, he only found the Stable's airlock controls.

He'd have to get inside to have a chance at the rest, including the interfaces to the Mules, assuming they had survived the blast. Had the EMP, or whatever it was, scrambled their robotic brains to the point they weren't even operational?

The plasma hammer's pilot light cast a dim glare of sickly pale green over the shining metal control panel.

*Has to happen sometime,* he thought. *At least here, I know what the interior looks like. Know the places something human sized or damned near it could hide.*

*What if it's smaller?*

Jordan ignored the voice, took a deep breath, and tapped the stud. The interior hatch cycled open on the Mule bay. Three of them sat side by side, the vehicles all but stripped of their tools. Plasma hammer at the ready, he stepped across the threshold, cleared left and right, and cautiously made his way forward.

Here, too, the lights flickered and stuttered as though the module's power cells had been drained or perhaps damaged. His visor compensated for the shift between gloom and dusk, but it was still damned hard to make out what hid in the shadows.

He glanced in the direction of the southern airlock. The internal hatch appeared closed, although he thought he could see dimples in its surface, ones similar to what he'd seen in the personnel module 3's airlock. Did that mean something was still in there?

He'd much rather know where a threat was, even if it was only ten meters away from him—if it was still inside the airlock, that was. Jordan checked for atmosphere and found none. The module had been purged of $O_2$, which didn't surprise him much. Once the mining crew left for their daily shift, there would be little reason for the module to be heated or oxygenated. Life support was merely a waste of power.

Jordan hated the silence. If there was atmosphere in here, he'd be able to hear something moving around, metal settling, and anything touching the bulkheads. Silence was like having no peripheral vision, and it made Jordan skittish. Especially when his heart hammered so loud in his chest, he could barely hear his own breathing.

He turned his suit lights to full and scoured the shadows, but many were too far away to be affected much.

"Chu? Still there?"

"Yup, but I'm fading fast."

"Watch my cam? And rear cam?"

Chu sighed. "What else do you think I've been doing? Can only stare at my fucked vital signs so many times. It's boring."

"Thanks," Jordan said and blinked through the menus. The remaining Mules, 4, 5, and six, flashed on his HUD with their statuses. All three were fueled up and ready to roll, sans useful attachments. He could fix that.

Like Jordan's suit, Mules supported and powered multiple attachments. From performing towing duties to acting as a massive, portable drill, the Mule was incredibly versatile. The only thing better would be to use an actual construction mech.

But the vehicles did have limitations. For instance, fully loaded, there wasn't much room for more than two personnel. Instead of seats, extra passengers had to mag-lock themselves to the Mule's side and do their best to avoid obstacles.

With just him, he could ride in the front jump seat, and while the Mule's manual controls were clunky as hell, he could use them. Still, something felt off about this—he just didn't know what.

He pulled an oversized plasma drill from its place on the wall and carried it to the vehicle, his breath puffing. Again, the augmentation didn't mean there was no strain against the muscles and tendons of his arm. He could hear the servos whining inside his suit as they locked to help hold the massive piece of equipment.

After carefully moving it into its slot and waiting for the interface to come up on his HUD, he breathed a huge sigh of relief. If he'd had to carry one of those drills, he wouldn't have made it a kilometer before his arms turned to overcooked pasta. Not to mention his back and legs.

The Mule sat noticeably lower now, which, in one-third gravity, might be a good thing. Jordan didn't exactly want to hit a bump and go flying through the air before slamming back into the ground. One more attachment and he'd be good to go.

He pulled the grapple assembly from the bulkhead and quickly fitted it to the second attachment slot. Next, he loaded a fresh clip of harpoons. The projectiles, encased in a roll belt, destroyed the roll as they fired. Six harpoons per clip. He dropped two spares in the vehicle's rear after topping off the Mule's plasma reservoir.

It wouldn't be the most graceful of mobile weapons. Mules turned like shit when loaded up, were unstable with their short wheelbase, and tended to be stubborn at times. Still, they were the most tenacious, functional vehicles in the galaxy. Just not so much in a combat setting.

Potential combat setting, he corrected himself. So far, apart from the Til thing, he'd seen no sign of life, hostile or otherwise. The mining modules appeared deserted.

*Won't know that until you check them all.*

True. And maybe that was where Aryana was—hiding in the ore packaging module or the slag recycler. He imagined her crouched behind an exchanger, doing her best to remain in the shadows while waiting for someone or something to leave. Or maybe she was simply waiting to die.

Jordan activated the comms scanner again and searched for any active pings. Nothing. No one listening, apart from Chu.

Either she couldn't respond or wouldn't. In either case, he'd no idea where she was or of her condition.

*Did you really expect to get an answer from her?*

*Yeah,* he thought. *I kind of did.*

He climbed atop the Mule, maglocked himself to the jump seat, and sent the command to open the Stable's vehicle airlock. The four-meter-wide slab of alloy rose almost immediately. Jordan held his breath, his arm thrust forward, fingers curled and ready to point his index finger in a heartbeat.

The flickering room's lights cast an unsteady ambient glow out into the perpetual twilight. As Jordan was about to move forward, he saw something in the gabbro just beyond the hatch. A track of deep indentations, as if they had been made by something far more massive than a human being, led off into the shadows.

No machine he knew of made those marks. And had that been there before he walked inside? Did he simply not see it?

The marks implied MacReady wasn't uninhabited. It implied

something as potentially dangerous as Til, if not drastically more so, wandered the landscape around him. The only question was if it would find him before he found Aryana.

Electric stress tingled his skin, but he sent the command for the Mule, and it slowly maneuvered its way to the airlock exit without him having to actively control it. He could sit up here and send the Mule commands and have its brain figure out where to go—so long as he trusted it, that was.

# CHAPTER THIRTY-ONE

The Stable's airlock closed behind Jordan like the sealing of a tomb. "Where to now?" Chu asked. He sounded barely awake.

"Slag," Jordan said. He'd already programmed the Mule to make its way to the module that lay some two hundred meters away, and while the computer did little to keep the ride from being bumpy, it at least left him free to scan the area for threats.

As the vehicle continued away from the Stable, Jordan turned and looked for the dreaded airlock and groaned. The exterior hatch was wide open, and the hatch itself looked as though it had been practically torn off its hinges.

*Jesus,* he thought. *No mining suit could do that on its own. What the hell had been trapped inside the airlock?*

The vehicle's wheels ground into the loose gabbro and made puffs of dust that slowly settled behind, creating a floating rooster tail any fool could follow. Jordan was leaving a trail and maybe even ringing the dinner bell. He shivered again at the thought of a Til thing, only larger and more horrifying.

The Mule continued moving at a healthy pace, but it was too slow for Jordan. Out here, there were no natural obstacles to give him cover. The good news about that was that nothing could sneak up on him, in theory. The bad news? It didn't have to.

If it was already in front of him, it could be anywhere around the large module, lying in wait for a morsel. Without sound, it'd be impossible to know if something was creeping up on him unless he saw it directly.

"Chu, still with me?"

No response.

Jordan sent a ping to the mesh network and got back nothing but lost packets; he was out of range of the mining camp's main mesh. Must be something interfering with the signal, Jordan thought. Although it might be weak, he should still get reception this far out.

*Probably more damage from the EMP,* he thought, *maybe some kind of lingering effect?* That didn't make sense, though, unless there was something on the planet occasionally sending out pulses. And why were some electronics affected but not others?

He shook his head in frustration. The chances of him ever figuring out what happened here were close to nil unless he found someone alive.

*Please be alive, Aryana,* Jordan thought.

Although it only took a few minutes for the Mule to cross the terrain to the slag module, it felt like an eternity. The tingle of spent adrenaline had left him feeling exhausted and wanting to crawl into a coffin for a good off-shift's rest. He could have missed something while being dopey and lost in his thoughts.

The Mule arrived at the Slag module, which hadn't been fully set up. The structure measured five meters high and had a mass he didn't want to think about. With a fully operational mine, slag lines would run from the mine to the module, depositing melted ore and gabbro. The Slag's separators would then filter precious and so-called rare earth metals into their own collections while the gabbro filled up a trench.

Since it wasn't set up, packing material still covered the meter-diameter pipe fittings. The module looked as though it hadn't been touched since it was first offloaded from the orbital, which didn't much surprise him.

Until the mining team determined the first locations, they wouldn't know where to put the damned thing. That was why the miners had been drilling the cores to begin with.

Jordan brought the Mule to a halt in front of the southern airlock and frowned. Grooves in the dirt led from the airlock out into the wastes. He brought up the terrain map, and his frown deepened. A fairly large crater lay only two hundred meters away from the Slag module.

Unsure of what to do next, he peered around the area, making sure nothing had followed him or appeared while he'd been staring at the tracks. Nothing except the dim glow of the airlock's single, flickering overhead. Beyond that were crowded shadows and limited visibility that made discerning between terrain and metal difficult, even with low-light filters. He just had to hope a life-form would show up in glowing detail.

A life-form. What kind of life-form was the question. Or had there been some automated system down here buried beneath the ground? Perhaps inside the peak?

Jihi had said the peak was practically stuffed with metal. Jordan's mouth opened slightly. Tungsten alloy. Titanium alloy. Iridium. All common components of human ships, all fairly plentiful metals if you were willing to do the work to find them.

What the fuck was this moon, or planet, or whatever the hell it was?

*It's a ship, you idiot,* Jordan thought. A ship. Surrounded in rock and made to look like just another piece of big bang accretion. Hidden from remote passersby and even less curious explorers, the ship, if that was what MacReady was, might be almost undetectable.

Except something happened. A collision or another event damaged the outer gabbro layer and made the hull visible to *Prospector.* Detectable. Who else had been looking for it?

*You mean* what *else.*

Whatever had been looking for it had obviously found humans instead and—

Taken over Til. And then it came down the orbital. Why? Why not just blow up MacReady if you wanted to, or maybe send whatever had infected Til to the surface and let it cause havoc and mayhem instead of killing the innocents aboard the ship?

Unless there was a reason. Unless the aliens needed a body of some kind, or biological material.

Oh, he didn't like that idea. He, Chu, and the miners were all the biological material he knew of.

But that wasn't exactly true, was it? Miners pulled a two-week shift on the surface, which meant the camp had more than enough supplies for that two weeks. In fact, the camp normally carried a six-week reserve, which could last even longer with rationing. That was a lot of biological material.

*You're guessing,* he told himself. *No way to know if you're right.*

*Unless I go back to the camp or get Chu to check.*

But he couldn't contact the man. So how the hell would Chu know to look?

Another shiver wracked his spine. The Til thing had been heading toward the camp, hadn't it?

*No, I would have gotten an alert. Unless...*

He was out of range of Chu. Meaning he'd also be out of range of the airlocks. Fuck.

Jordan caught movement out of the corner of his eye and turned in the direction of the crater. He saw nothing but shadows clothing a small rise cluttered with rock.

*Stare at everything and nothing,* he told himself.

A moment passed. Then another. Finally, something shifted just behind the outcrop. He'd seen it. He knew he had.

He blinked through the interface commands and found what he was looking for. The Mule's directional lights blasted the area fifty meters away, banishing the shadows, and glinting off something that might have been metal in the rock.

The glint disappeared as if whatever had cast it had moved behind the rock again. Jordan raised his arm and pointed it in that direction, the plasma hammer following his movements. He waited a moment, his heart beating fast in his chest, breathing deeply to keep his arm steady.

"Move," he said aloud. "I fucking dare you."

Nothing happened, although he felt a slight vibration in his boots.

**SEISMIC ANOMALY DETECTED** glowed in red translucent letters across his HUD.

The vibration increased in intensity, and the Mule actually started to shake. Jordan jumped out of the vehicle, his leap taking him several meters away, and hit MacReady's surface with an inaudible crunch that kicked up loose rock and dust.

The Mule shook harder, and he could actually see the wheels marking the dirt. A moment later, something bright metallic flashed up from the ground and smashed into the back of the Mule. The appendage, or whatever it was, seemed alive, its surface writhing and rippling. The segmented limb or weapon rose high before crashing down into the Mule once more.

Jordan, finally catching his wits, raised his arm in the direction of the thing, pointed his index finger, and tapped down his thumb. The hammer loosed a blast of plasma that obliterated the limb in a splash of superheated steam that quickly fell back to the surface like metal rain.

The blast, too damned close to the Mule, had also removed the rear portion of the vehicle and flipped the remaining half into the ground, burying the very front of the massive machine.

Jordan stumbled backward into the airlock housing and caught his balance just as the ground moved like liquid beneath him. He magnetized one of his gloves just in time to keep himself locked to the bulkhead. The front of the Mule flipped through the air and out onto the surface toward the crater while a hole swallowed the gabbro where it had stood.

Another metal appendage, nearly identical to the first, rose upward from the newly formed crater and reached for Jordan. He aimed the plasma hammer, braced himself, and activated it.

The half-meter spherical ball of plasma darted from the hammer's end and hit the metal thing at the second joint. The blast vaporized the metal and sent one end flying into the module's wall, where it crunched into the alloy like a knife through stubborn bone.

*Three more shots,* he told himself, and aimed the tool at the crater. He didn't wait for another limb to appear, opting instead to make a bigger hole. The tool belched another wide ball of plasma that met a limb just as it tried to rise.

A geyser of light silently exploded from the hole, the ground beneath Jordan turning to liquid once again. He recovered and connected to the airlock interface. It was time to get some cover, and the Slag module would do nicely, thank you very much.

The external hatch cycled and opened far too slowly for Jordan's liking. The ground quaked again, this time much farther away. Without the Mule's more powerful lights, he couldn't make out much detail of the outcrop, but he had a feeling another one was back there. Maybe more of them.

He stepped backward into the airlock and quickly closed the hatch, which cycled, but no atmosphere filtered inside. Malfunction? Maybe the tanks had been damaged?

Jordan turned to face the inside of the module when the interior hatch finished cycling. A few lights flickered here and there, making Jordan want to curse. Unlike on MacReady's surface, however, he could make out details just fine even in the thickest of the shadows. The strobing was merely annoying.

The module's feed slots remained closed, and the pumps hadn't even been hooked up. Jordan was sure that had been on Aryana's list of chores in the next several days. Exhaust piping led to a port high in the module's ductwork before ending in a closed cap leading to the planet's atmosphere.

Piping and ductwork filled the large module, with the exception of crawlspaces and aisles just large enough for someone like Jordan to traverse. In a mining suit, the chances of getting stuck were high, but he'd learned over the years how to handle it. It also meant that if whatever that thing had been in the ground came for him, he could wind up more or less trapped or only able to move at a snail's pace. How would he escape then?

The deck beneath him rumbled, and Jordan froze. Could it detect vibrations? If so, he was incredibly screwed. Attempts at stealth in a mining suit were comical to imagine. Unless you were in vacuum and on a stone like gabbro, you could kiss that dream goodbye. And if you weren't in vacuum, the mosquito whine of the servos was more than enough to give you away.

Jordan waited for the vibration to continue, but it didn't. When he got his heartbeat and breathing under control, he moved his right foot to take a step before stopping in mid-motion. Vibration.

Whatever the thing was, it had somehow known how to track him. It had either seen the lights, noticed the motion, or sensed the vibration of the Mule traveling over the gabbro. Which was it? Sight? Or the ephemeral sense that something had moved? Or was it both?

Would be nice to know which, he thought. How could he know if—

Jordan blinked, cursed, and pulled the grapple from the pouch. Instead of loading it into the gun, he palmed it, tested its mass, and decided it would do nicely. Reminding himself he was in one-third gravity, he aimed for an opening through the piping and launched the grapple.

It flew from his augmented suit like a baseball, although it had more than ten kilograms of mass. He'd flung it hard enough for it to sail through the opening, but his aim had been slightly off. Instead of continuing to the other end of the module, it smacked into the side of a heat exchanger and bounced into the shadows.

A moment later, he felt a slight tremor though the deck. Whatever was beneath him could definitely sense vibration. What was more, it was actively tracking, meaning if he moved, it would know where he was.

*Great,* Jordan thought. *Now I'm trapped.*

# CHAPTER THIRTY-TWO

Jordan pinged the module's local network, and it came up immediately. He blinked through the menus until he found the cameras. Three of them were dead, although one still functioned on the module's northern side. He brought it up on his HUD and blinked at it.

What he hadn't seen as he approached from the south was the massive collection of craters spreading out behind the module. It looked as though a dozen or more had appeared—he knew they hadn't been on the original survey. What was more, he could see the remains of a Mule, its equipment trailer smashed into bits with the battered and bent frame cast to the side like a broken toy.

The vibration started up again, but its epicenter was definitely closer to the middle of the module, the area where the grapple had landed. Jordan waited, his breathing still too loud in his own ears. Finally, he heard it—a thump from beneath the module.

*They travel beneath the rock,* Jordan thought. *Like a worm or something.* Spider.

He didn't consider himself arachnophobic by any means, but the word made his flesh prickle. Spiders. The limbs that had popped up from the ground could have been arachnid had they not been made out of metal. The fact that the things might look like spiders didn't terrify him as much as the thought that any step he took might bring one right to him.

MacReady had no wind to shuffle around loose rock and sand. There was no weather to hide the sound of your footsteps on the surface. The things might be able to sense you from kilometers away.

*I'm so fucked,* he thought.

Jordan flipped from the surveillance interface to the module's statuses and scrolled through the list, finding reds, yellows, and greens. Aryana had set up the reactor but hadn't yet started it. As such, the structure's backup batteries provided what little power was available. In short, the lights, the computers, and not much else.

A grin lit Jordan's face. *Let's see if we can fix that,* he thought.

After a few blinks, the nuclear reactor in the module's northeast corner came to life. He'd set it in diagnostic mode for a warmup, which would keep it from reaching detectable power levels as well as prevent him from annihilating himself if the reactor had an issue.

It was impossible to know by looking at the thing that it was even operational. "Can you feel it?" he asked no one.

The vibration's epicenter seemed to have moved again, farther toward the reactor.

"Yes, you can," Jordan said.

Ready to increase power to the reactor, Jordan took a cautious step backward. He wasn't really sure he wanted to go back outside, especially if there were more of these things, but he needed to know if it was even possible. When his boot touched the decking, his mind provided the sound of a heavy clomp.

Heart racing, breathing a little more shallowly, he waited. The vibrations from the deck didn't move closer but farther away. Was it going for the bulkhead nearest the reactor? Would it try to tear through?

It hadn't tried to come through the airlock behind him. Why not? Had his distraction and wounding of the thing made it cautious, or merely pissed it off?

When the source of the thumping beneath the deck didn't change— in fact, he could barely detect it now—he took another step, paused a few beats, and took another a little faster this time. He reached the airlock without issue.

The reactor was the distraction he needed. The only question now was when and how to set it off. Jordan went over the items in the Slag module, desperately trying to remember the common tools it might contain. He couldn't think of a single useful one. Shit.

Aryana had properly installed and set up the reactor, but since the module wasn't fully operational, he didn't even have exterior piping or conveyors to work with. Just a ridiculous amount of metal alloys, nano-ceramics, and a reactor he was about to sabotage.

He glanced toward the airlock on the other side of the module. What was out there? And how long before it tried to come in here?

Jordan brought up the reactor's interface. The diagnostics had all passed, and it was ready for a full power cycle. The only problem? He had to get a bit closer to it. Well, much closer. But first things first.

He increased the power to ten percent and waited to feel vibrations through the floor, but nothing happened. After waiting a few beats, he increased the reactor's power to twenty percent. This time, he did feel something through his feet, or thought he did, but it lasted less than a couple of seconds before fading away. The things beneath the gabbro might be gathering near the reactor. They could be preparing to try to pop up through the deck.

*Welcome to try*, he thought. *You might be able to slice a Mule in half, but good luck getting through the hull.*

Jordan increased the power another ten percent and waited. Nothing happened. No vibration, no tingle in his toes, nothing.

Teeth clenched tightly, he upped the power again. The deck vibration sent barely detectable tingles through his toes, which made him sigh inwardly with relief. He hadn't been sure the reactor would shake enough to matter. In truth, he'd never paid attention to the slag module much before it was prepped and running. He'd never needed to.

What he didn't feel, however, was an answering group of vibrations beneath the deck. If the creatures were all waiting for a sign to attack, he wasn't sure what it might be.

*You really want them to attack?*

In a way, he did. If they were busy destroying the other side of the module, he should have no difficulty in getting out of here alive. Whatever tremors he caused by moving around wouldn't be noticed while they were smashing and crashing through steel. At least he didn't think they would.

He could spend the next hour testing theory after theory, gathering more and more information about how to proceed, all while he continued depleting his oxygen supply as well as power, not to mention his own energy and focus. And Chu? How long could he hold out if the Til thing returned to the personnel module?

Jordan raised the reactor's power levels to seventy percent and once again concentrated on his toes, desperate to feel the slightest tingle. Instead of a tingle, it felt as though thunder boomed beneath his boots, the powerful vibrations lasting a few beats before fading away.

*Jesus, how many of them was that? And where were they coming from?*

He slowly walked inside the airlock interior. Several moments passed before he was relatively sure the things hadn't realized where he was. With any luck, they were a little more interested in the reactor itself.

As Jordan reached for the stud to cycle the airlock, a tremor rose through his toes. He flipped his HUD to display the module's external cam, and his mouth dropped open. Multiple thick, multi-segmented metal legs had broken through the gabbro and smashed into the corner near the reactor. The planet's surface surrounding that corner of the module moved like ocean water beneath an aircraft's rotors.

*Is that enough of an attack for you?*

Jordan touched the stud, and the interior hatch cycled closed. Since there was no pressure to equalize, the outer hatch opened almost at once, and he found himself staring at something standing amidst the shadows at the outcrop. It was too far away to make out much detail, but he could see enough as it was. Five points of eldritch light burned from its wide, misshapen features.

Jordan didn't move. He didn't breathe, and he would later swear his heart had stopped beating. The thing in the shadows didn't move, its glowing eyes remaining steady as if the thing was studying him. Maybe he had surprised it as much as it had surprised him.

Jordan slowly extended his hand toward the exterior hatch stud. The moment his hand neared it, those five bright green distant lights blinked. A heartbeat later, he knew the Til thing no longer stood in the shadows—it was running toward him faster than he thought possible.

His finger tapped the stud, and the hatch cycled shut. Jordan stepped backward until his back was nearly up against the interior hatch. He was trapped. The Til thing was probably nearing the hatch, its arms no doubt rearing back and ready to pound at the steel. Or do something worse, like opening the airlock by simply touching it.

No choice, Jordan thought. He tapped the hatch stud and turned as the airlock cycled. A moment later, the interior hatch opened, and Jordan took a tentative step inside the module, impact tremors from the attack tingling his toes. He didn't know how many creatures were now trying to get at the reactor, but it seemed as though a near-constant earthquake bit and chomped at the module's northeast corner.

With all the piping and other equipment blocking his view of the reactor, it was impossible to know if the module's bulkheads flexed and jittered from the assault. It also made it impossible for him to know just how much time he had before the damned things came through.

Jordan caught movement in his peripheral vision—the interior airlock hatch was attempting to close, and he shot out a boot before the steel completely sealed. A yellow light flashed above the hatch, and he knew that if the module had had oxygen, an alarm would be splitting the ears of anyone unlucky enough to be inside without a suit.

He had the Til thing trapped outside, provided he kept the airlock hatch from closing. But the moment he moved from his position and the hatch closed, the creature could easily enter.

*Yeah*, Jordan thought. *Smart enough to use the orbital? Opening an airlock is nothing.*

"Shit," he said loudly enough to hurt his own ears.

*Now what?*

He flipped to the cam view and realized the bulkhead the spider things had been bashing against had blistered, their segmented metal arms battering the hull to the breaking point. Before too much longer, those sharp ends would perforate the alloy. After that, the creatures could tear through it like an aluminum can. Jordan was fairly sure he didn't want to be here for that.

The Til thing was on the other side of the airlock. The creatures were coming in from the northeast corner. Jordan cast his eyes west and blinked. Another airlock. Each side had one. If he could trick the Til thing into coming inside, he could escape through the other airlock before it had a chance to see him. In theory.

Jordan walked as carefully as he could to the western airlock, pulling the small mining hammer from his toolbelt and holding it firmly in his left hand. The vibrations through the deck continued making their way up his toes, but they hadn't changed in intensity. Maybe he was right and the things couldn't detect his movements over the metal thrumming like a tuning fork.

He caught a flicker out of his peripheral vision and turned. The airlock indicator had turned bright red from its normal green. Someone had opened the outer hatch. Fighting a surge of panic, he blinked through the module menus, found the south airlock and shut it down.

The airlock computer complained that a life-form was inside and it would be unable to enter the module. Jordan told it to politely fuck off and mind its own business. The airlock's indicator flashed red like a digital heartbeat.

Jordan sighed and relaxed. Slightly. Step 1, complete.

As quickly as he dared, he made his way to the west airlock, reactivating the south airlock as soon as he reached the threshold. The flashing red heartbeat disappeared, replaced by solid crimson. The south airlock's external hatch was still open. Good. He tapped the stud to cycle the west airlock and waited for it to slide aside.

Jordan entered the airlock and tapped the cycle stud. The inner hatch closed, leaving him in darkness. After reconnecting to the module interface, he locked out the west airlock. Til, even if he were still Til, wouldn't even be able to break the codes. In essence, Jordan was safe here inside the airlock. The Til thing couldn't get in from outside or inside the module.

Unless it wanted in real bad.

Jordan sighed and watched the south airlock's status. It had just turned green.

# CHAPTER THIRTY-THREE

The south airlock opened, but Jordan had no cameras to see what was going on. He could, however, feel a change in the deck's vibrations. Curious, he brought up the last remaining camera covering the module's northern side. The metal arms had finally punched through the bulkhead and were widening the rip while pulling themselves up from the ground at the same time.

Spider had been an appropriate description, except the things had five legs connected to a single glowing green orb. Jordan shivered at the sight of three of the creatures leaving the ground and working in concert to destroy the bulkhead.

Modern mining automatons were more than capable of coordinating their movements, but he'd never seen anything like this. The three creatures, or robots, or whatever they were, moved with an elegance he'd never imagined possible. Even the leg segments moved in a rhythm he could hear in his mind.

The three creatures suddenly stopped, their legs poised as if all three had been frozen in time. The orbs flashed so rapidly that he could barely tell the lights had changed at all.

\* \* \* \* \*

Parasite watched the strange creature as it stood in the airlock, frozen as if in fear. Rather than rushing the suited thing, Parasite chose to remain still and observe. Was this one armed? Could it harm Parasite and the body it now inhabited? What about the remains of the suit Parasite's host wore?

The suited thing reached out its hand, and the parasite responded by moving forward. As expected, the creature pushed something, and the thick, massive hatch closed. Parasite continued walking to it, wary of an unseen trap.

The once-human feet had widened, alien flesh stretching between the toes, giving them a webbed appearance. Its taloned toes easily gripped the gabbro just as they had the ship's deck.

Parasite walked to the airlock, its feet changing color slightly beneath the nearly translucent flesh. The extreme cold and near vacuum did nothing to damage its new, hardened skin or the lungs it no longer had. Physiologically speaking, the host body's organs no longer resembled a human's. Instead, they had been twisted and morphed, the DNA rewritten, leaving in its wake a humanoid form, the tatters of an EVA suit, and the screaming, clawing, terrified mind that used to control this body.

Parasite could sometimes hear the "other's" unintelligible thoughts. They held only the barest remains of sentience and were a constant clatter beneath Parasite's own musings, of which there were few. Few, but it had a mission to complete, and all excess power of consciousness remained focused on its goal.

It pressed a wide three-fingered, one-thumbed hand against the frigid metal, its alien flesh incapable of feeling the cold. It found the same stud the creature had pushed and touched it. A light above the hatch changed color, startling Parasite. It took a step backward, suddenly unsure of what to do.

Tool. What it really needed was a tool it could use to pry open the hatch. The Parasite turned and stared at the remains of a metallic limb. Parasite's horror show of a face, or rather two faces, sucked in its cheeks in revulsion. If Parasite had had the capacity for amusement, the thought of using Enemy's very own tools against it would have generated an ironic smile.

Instead, Parasite bent down and lifted a two-meter portion of the spiderlike metal leg. It examined the joint for a moment before bringing its massive arm down in a single chop.

The joint, already damaged, easily gave way, leaving the creature with a 1.5-meter-long pike with a broken, sharp end. It would be perfect for prying or using as a spear. Parasite, now armed, turned back to the airlock.

On some primitive level, Parasite admired the creature that had destroyed the foraging drone. The creature, identical to the host Parasite had transformed, had fought and critically damaged one of the drones, which was hardly an easy task, considering the creature's fragility.

Parasite pressed the stud it had seen the creature touch, and the light above the airlock turned green. Parasite's multiple eyes, each tuned to a different aspect of the visible spectrum, saw the change in color more as a rainbow than a single hue, but it innately knew what that meant.

The hatch, opened and Parasite knelt slightly to fit through the personnel airlock. At two and a half meters tall, it would graze nearly every airlock or personnel hatchway, although it didn't know that yet.

Once inside, it pressed a similar stud on the inner wall. The outer hatch closed, and the inner cycled. A moment later, the hatchway opened.

The moment Parasite stepped through the inner hatch, its eyes caught the glow of green lights from the far bulkhead. Although machinery hid their causes from sight, Parasite knew what they were—it could sense them. More foraging drones.

The continuous glow became a rapid strobe. Silently snarling through the maw it controlled, Parasite crouched as low as it could and walked past the machinery, knowing full well the things had sensed Parasite in the same manner it had detected the drones—a programmed fear and hatred. Thousands upon thousands of years of knowing your enemy, or its creations, had that effect.

The drones knew what Parasite was, just as it knew what they were. They also knew what Parasite was here to do.

When Parasite reached the far edge of the machinery, it stopped and waited for the colors to cease strobing. They didn't. The drones were too busy scanning, or maybe something else had distracted them. Either way, they were still mostly on the other side of the bulkhead, although they'd done a tremendous amount of damage.

Parasite detected radiation. Contained. Shielded. Power. Good.

It pulled a strip from the tattered remains of Til's suit and laid it across one palm. It opened its mouth and drizzled viscous fluid on the alloy-threaded fabric, crumpled the material into a rough ball, and tested the mass. It would be enough. For good measure, it created a second, smaller ball.

Holding the massive leg in one three-fingered claw, it clutched the other two tightly, spearing the smaller one on the talon protruding from its misshapen thumb. Parasite, as satisfied as it was going to be with its arsenal, peered around the far corner to the strobing lights. It saw through a jagged tear in the northern bulkhead and counted three of the drones. That didn't mean there weren't more in the area, much less beneath the very deck Parasite stood upon.

Parasite threw the larger of the two fabric balls at the northern bulkhead but to the other side from the drones. The strobing immediately became a solid glow. Parasite waited to feel them moving, not through its toes but through that sense no human could understand—the sense of presence, digital or living.

Parasite had been designed to be the ultimate scout, a weapon that could find its target and destroy it with haste and take as many enemies with it as possible. The blood running through its veins, moving nourishment through its circulatory system, was composed of one of the deadliest acids in nature. For non-$H_2S$-based lifeforms, the substance melted their flesh and typically extinguished their lives. Combined with the other chemicals making up its blood, it could also melt most metals.

It finally sensed the movement in its mind, but even if it hadn't, it felt the massive drones moving across the alloy deck. Parasite clutched its makeshift club tightly. The glowing lights flickered into strobes again before another tremor quivered through its feet.

One. More tremors. Two. The tremors doubled in number and then tripled as the drones moved inside the structure. Parasite couldn't see them yet, not all of them, but had more than a good enough view to know the drones had caught on to the ruse. Their scans were coming up empty, and they'd likely stand sentinel until something else called them away.

Parasite pulled the remaining ball from its talon and hurled it over the top of the machinery and to the other side. It had been too strong of a throw, and the ball hit the module's roof before its trajectory carried it into another piece of machinery, where it bounced toward the deck.

The moment it saw the glows turn to strobing flashes, Parasite rounded the corner and ran in long, loping steps, the makeshift club brandished before it. The first of the three drones had no chance to recognize the danger before the sharp end of the club plunged into the center of the orb. Colorful liquid and sparks exploded in a lazy cloud. Parasite smashed its dying legs aside just as the second of the trio advanced.

No ruse now. The pair would start to choreograph their attacks, transmit the dance to one another, and slowly nip away at Parasite's host until there was nothing left. It knew from its innate training how to fight them.

Parasite bent its legs and uncoiled like a spring. As the drones sliced their forelegs at the place where Parasite had just stood, it flipped over the first of the pair and launched the club-like spear. The sharp metal fragment flew true in the one-third gravity and easily penetrated halfway through the orb. More gunk and short-lived arcs of electricity spewed out.

The moment Parasite hit the deck, it rolled to the damaged and split orb, pulled the weapon, and launched it just as the last drone attempted to close the distance. The automaton danced aside, and the massive piece of metal clipped a leg and embedded itself in the deck.

Before Parasite had time to react, the drone had already snapped two of its remaining legs out like rapiers. The first attempted to slice Parasite's oversized neck, but the bladelike end glanced off the remains of the host's suit, perforating it and nicking the rugose, mutated flesh beneath.

Sulfuric acid sprayed in fine, viscous droplets, the wound coagulating nearly instantly. The droplets arced out and spattered against one of the drone's pincers, the metal discoloring and bubbling. Parasite leaped over the drone as it lunged forward. The drone got more than a hunk from a foreleg this time, and another spray of sulfuric acid pattered down as a reward.

Parasite tumbled and grabbed the club on its way to its feet. In a smooth, graceful turn, it flung the club at the orb and ran forward at the same time. The drone raised three of its many legs to block or catch the spear. The club glanced off the metal legs and to the side, but the distraction had worked.

Without hesitation, Parasite continued forward, taloned fists clasped together like a battering ram. It reared them back before launching them downward in a savage arc. The thickened, practically armored knuckles crashed into the metal like a sledgehammer through glass.

The orb's colors crackled twice before going dark.

Parasite stepped away from the dead drone and peered at its hands. Pain was not a sensation that ruled its existence, and pain would never keep it from doing its job. Pain was there to tell it when it was being damaged, nothing more than that. One of its fingers had broken at the second joint, and its host had a fracture in one palm.

It made the alien equivalent of a mental grunt and lifted its club. The metal had been damaged by both the impacts as well as the drone's ministrations. The middle had warped slightly, giving the makeshift weapon a more scythe-like appearance. Parasite stared at its end for a moment before he began disassembling the nearest drone.

* * * * *

Jordan had watched the metal things crawl inside the module, the strobe of their lights easily visible against the dark beyond. Without any of the module's internal cams functioning and no other external cams, it was impossible to know what was happening. Whatever was going on, though, made a hell of a lot of vibrations.

*Maybe they're wiping each other out,* he thought. The vibratory racket lasted no more than a few moments and then? Nothing.

He should have gotten out while the getting was good, but fear had overridden common sense, and he was afraid of going back outside. He was also afraid of returning inside the module. No matter which way he went, something could easily kill him. Staying here, staying silent, seemed like the best option.

Besides, whatever made vibrations inside the module masked whatever might be happening just beyond the airlock hatch. He could open that airlock to flee and, instead of open space, find himself staring at the Til thing's misshapen faces or one of those robots. He was pretty sure the spiders would kill him fairly quickly, but that was better than ending up like Til. Anything had to be better than that.

Jordan wanted to smash his fists against the bulkhead, or maybe his skull. Anything to release the desperate anxiety threatening to suffocate him. But there was nowhere he could pull off his helmet and shriek to the nebula in impotent rage. Nothing to do but lean his helmet against the bulkhead, close his eyes, and wish he was anywhere but here.

Chu. Chu was alone in the medbay. Jordan clenched his teeth. Finding Aryana alive at this point might be a long shot, but he could still keep these things away from Chu. Maybe lead them away. If the pilot was smart, he'd already be inside one of the stasis pods, awaiting rescue.

Did it really matter, though? Dead out there, dead in here—there was no redoubt other than the ship, and it was never going to travel again. They were trapped on MacReady one way or another.

*So, does it really matter what you do?*

*No. No, it doesn't.*

Jordan pushed himself away from the bulkhead and faced the exterior hatch. "Do it for Chu," he told himself as his shaking hand reached for the stud.

# CHAPTER THIRTY-FOUR

After tapping the stud, Jordan waited the five excruciatingly long seconds for it to finish opening. The gloom seemed to roll in like fog, his suit lights cutting through it easily, yet appearing no brighter than a spark against the eternal evening. He cleared left to right and even took a peek above him before fully exiting the airlock. Once he did, the feeling of being watched made his spine tingle, and the sensation made him want to crawl back inside.

Jordan walked away from the airlock as fast as he dared. Every step risked attracting the spider-looking robots, if that was what they were, but he couldn't help it. Vibration or no vibration, he had to get away from the module quickly.

He saw a light glowing at the edge of a ring of absolute darkness. It was site 2, a crater deep enough that it never received light at all. If the same EMP effect that occurred in space had radiated down here, then any lights Aryana had set up were more than likely inoperable or scrambled. Without shielding to protect them, the circuits were probably fried.

Jordan continued moving, his head cocked to one side as if he could hear a threat coming from beneath the ground. The feeling of being watched, of something chasing him, was palpable, a cloying scent of fear that wafted into his nostrils with every exhale.

*Don't turn. You'll slow. It will catch you.*

One-third gravity allowed him to move in long, loping strides, and he made quick work of the two hundred meters separating him from the crater's lip. He slowed as he reached the edge, turned slightly, and looked behind him.

The Slag module appeared as a hulking shadow against the landscape, its angles all wrong compared to the rock and accreted gabbro that littered the planet's surface.

Not a planet, he reminded himself. Not a fucking planet.

Something caught his attention, and he moved his eyes slightly north. A green dot, so small it was barely visible, bumped up and down in a smooth, rapid motion. Jordan blinked at it twice before realizing two things—it was more than one green light, and it was getting closer.

He turned and shuffled over the crater's lip and onto its gentle slope. The crater's bottom curved as though hollowed out, and his lights found what looked like a tunnel, a shard of metal twinkling beneath his lights.

*Holy shit*, he thought. *If you weren't sure it was a ship before, there's your proof.*

Jordan continued forward until he stood a mere meter from the tunnel. The shard of metal lying at its opening was a little too familiar—a fragment of a mining hammer. A deep groove in the gabbro showed signs of something having been dragged.

*The bots*, he thought. *Did they attack and drag the miners inside the tunnel? Was Aryana in there?*

Jordan turned and scanned the lip of the crater. He saw no green lights but knew it was just a matter of time before the Til thing arrived. If he stayed in the crater, he'd either have to fight or flee into the tunnel. Inside the ship. Or whatever it was.

*Wait any longer and it'll be on your ass.*

He turned back to the tunnel and took a deep breath as his suit lights illuminated the three-meter-tall circular crevice in the rock. Two meters inside, the rocky outcrop facade gave way to scarred and weather metal, perhaps an alloy like tungsten carbide. The ground, or deck, as he was beginning to think of it, had thousands, perhaps millions of microscopic dents.

*The spider things*, Jordan thought. *Was this where they had all come from?*

No. They had come from beneath the module. This was something else. Meaning there was something he hadn't seen. Jordan shivered at the possibilities and continued walking as quickly as he dared.

Another thirty meters and he came to a junction, only instead of leading through the rock in branches, it led down a curving, gentle incline. If he had his geography right, it could wind around to the base of the peak.

*What is this?*

Fighting the urge to turn around and find the Til thing behind him, he quickened his pace, somewhat certain Til was the only threat at his back. If there was something up ahead he had to worry about, he wouldn't have to worry about it for long.

The Til thing had survived the three spiders, he assumed, and if that was the case, the Til thing might be scarier than anything else Jordan could run into down here. He hoped.

The tunnel continued downward, only his calves told him the incline had steepened slightly. Up ahead some twenty meters, the tunnel ended in a sharp turn. The farther in he'd traveled, the more dilapidated and aged the metal appeared, as though something had happened inside the tunnel. Some kind of solvent or acid damage, perhaps.

Jordan slowed his pace as he approached the turn, the mining hammer in his hands and ready to smash into anything around the bend. He needn't have bothered. The sharp curve led to a long corridor nearly identical to the tunnel itself but even more fatigued than the other had been.

His suit lights pierced the darkness but touched nothing. Another shiver wracked him. At some point, the corridor might simply fall off into an abyss, or maybe it was the maw of some creature his mind couldn't comprehend.

He turned, half expecting to see the shape of five eldritch lights burning from a horror show of a face, but as far as he could tell, he was still alone.

After psyching himself up, Jordan walked cautiously forward until the corridor opened into a wide space where there was plenty for his lights to reflect off.

Large metal cylinders rose from the decking and toward the sky. Jordan raised his head to try to see the top but couldn't. He was inside the peak and probably two or three hundred meters below MacReady's surface, the interior of a mountain that wasn't a mountain but the top of a tall, wide cylinder seeming to stretch to infinity in either direction.

A nest of smaller cylinders protruded through the deck and below. The deck was made of solid alloy, although it looked as weathered as everything else inside. However, he saw two openings in the floor that appeared to be wide enough for one of the spider things to fit through. That made him shiver.

He wondered if he'd hear anything if he were able to take off his suit helmet. Did the cylinders make noise?

*You could always touch them.*

Jordan considered that and decided it was a bad idea. Right now, the Til thing was either in the tunnel or heading this way. Before it showed up, he needed to either not be here or be hidden.

Apart from crawling between the smaller cylinders, the wide space held no cover. In a mining suit, he'd not only stand out but find himself fighting to escape before the Til thing easily closed in on him.

No, he needed a place he could defend as well as hide, but there was nothing here.

There had to be a tunnel on the other side of the cylinder, didn't there? This couldn't be the only entrance to the ship. Had to be another one.

He ran parallel to the tunnel he'd come from for nearly a hundred meters before slowing down and coming to a halt. The tunnel that should have been there had collapsed. A large portion of the bulkhead had either been blown apart from the rest of the ship or uncurled due to stress. Either way, layers of twisted or dried molten alloy clumped around tons of gabbro made it impossible to get through.

Jordan grinned. Unless you have a plasma hammer.

He pointed and activated the tool and hundreds of balls of superheated plasma spread out in a cone. The gabbro instantly melted to steam while the metal took a little longer to vaporize. Using the tool like an old-timey leaf blower, he fired shot after shot at diagonals to vaporize and push the slag to the side.

He ran out of plasma fuel before he put much of a dent in the debris. Not even big enough for him to hide in. Whole fucking thing must have come apart. So much for that egress.

Jordan turned and froze. At the far end of the cylinder, five eldritch lights stared at him with curious indifference. He shivered, his mind adding details he couldn't possibly see from this distance and in the gloom. The Til thing had found him.

Jordan ejected the magazine and reloaded the plasma hammer. If the creature came within range, one hit would be enough to blow it in half. He hoped.

That in mind, he stood his ground and waited for the creature to do something. Instead, the pattern of glowing dots remained fixed and unblinking.

"How do you breathe?" Jordan asked. "And how are you not frozen?"

It didn't move.

*Standoff, eh? Guess you saw me using the hammer. Don't like the possibility of it being aimed at you. I bet you don't know the range either.*

Jordan thought that was a pretty good bet. Otherwise, the creature probably would have fled or rushed him, or at least attempted to hide. Instead, it stood there like a statue as if it were making sure he'd seen it. Did it want him to see it? And why?

Considering Jordan had a finite amount of life support, it was a standoff only one of them could win, and it wouldn't be him. He had a feeling the thing would stand there forever.

Jordan felt the deck tremble beneath his feet. The glowing eyes seemed to look downward, the orbs or dots briefly disappearing from the two-headed thing craning its neck. It had felt the vibration too.

Now, it was a wave of vibrations, and Jordan realized where they were coming from—the spider things were clinging to the deck beneath him and heading for the ingress. Probably on both sides.

The Til thing seemed to have the same thoughts. The glowing dots moved, disappeared, then reappeared several meters away, almost as if it was checking the shaft on its side. Between the two beings? The copse of cylinders and the gaping holes that led who knew where.

Except that was where the things were coming from. Jordan walked backward and away from the vertical shaft, the mining hammer held before him like a holy relic. He glanced to the side to see where the Til thing had gone but saw nothing.

Clomp. Clomp. Jordan's mind once again filled in the sounds of his heavy boots against the dilapidated and partially corroded metal. As if in response, the vibrations through his feet increased for a moment before decreasing. He knew, however, exactly where the spider things were headed.

He aimed the plasma hammer and waited while doing his best to slow his heart rate and steady his shaking hand. A pale glow crept across the darkness shrouding the shaft. In mere heartbeats, it doubled and tripled in brightness. The lights started strobing.

The pulses cast strange shadows that seemed to dance and increased in frequency until they became nearly solid beams. He'd seen that strange behavior before, just before the Til thing entered the module. What did it mean?

Jordan held his breath and waited to find out.

# CHAPTER THIRTY-FIVE

He didn't have to wait long. The strobes brightened like starlight, and a moment later, he saw the first of the glowing orbs climb over the top of the shaft, the spider's metallic legs looking freshly minted. The orb swiveled in his direction as though it had instantly spotted him.

The spider's legs moved in elegant, rapid motion as it darted toward him faster than he believed possible. When it was a mere five meters away, the outside range of the plasma hammer, two grasping arms popped out and reached for him.

The plasma hammer came to life and blasted the orb just as the spider's graspers snapped together mere centimeters from his faceplate. The shotgun-like blast of tiny balls of superheated gas obliterated the left side of the orb and sent the thing sideways, one of its legs smashing into Jordan's hip.

The robot's greater mass sent him sprawling to the deck. Something heavy landed on his left leg, pinning it. Slightly concussed, hip screaming in pain, and suit alerts flashing across his visor, Jordan struggled to pull himself free.

The flashes against the bulkhead increased in intensity. More were coming. Maybe they were already over the edge of the shaft and scuttling toward him even now.

Groaning with effort, he pulled himself forward, kicking with his other leg to try to get free, but his boot was caught on something. He twisted his body and managed to flip mostly to his side. No longer looking at the deck, he shined his helmet light at his torso and legs. The spider thing he'd destroyed had damned near parted in two, its remaining, multi-jointed leg folded across Jordan's like a restraining band.

The lights were getting brighter. Jordan flicked his eyes to the shaft, and his heart stopped. Two of the things had crawled up onto the deck and slowly trundled toward him. He maglocked his gloves to the deck and pulled, the servos whining through his suit as they did their best to help his tired, strained muscles.

He moved a few centimeters closer. Another grunting pull and he moved a little farther this time. The lights were so bright now they had all but dispelled the shadows around him.

The deck vibrated hard as the things approached. He wasn't going to get free in time. Desperate, he pulled the mining hammer from its sheath and turned just as the nearest spider thing reached him, one of its legs nearly piercing his hand. A pair of graspers extruded from the orb.

Jordan swung the hammer at the leg, but without leverage, the heavy metal tool bounced off the appendage without much force. He was done. Jordan closed his eyes.

He felt the impact tremor through his body before he realized something had fallen from above him. The bright lights of the orbs flickered and dimmed slightly. The graspers reaching for him disappeared as the orb swiveled in the other direction and moved away from him.

Confused, Jordan tried to see past the spider and to what had captivated its attention. When he saw the flash of a spider leg being used like a club, he had a pretty good idea.

The Til thing had leaped from the cylinder nest, he assumed, and dropped onto one of the spiders, the makeshift weapon coming down upon it like a real sledgehammer. The orb had shattered, the legs twitching uselessly. The two remaining spiders danced around the Til thing, doing their best to stay out of reach.

Jordan bent at the torso toward his toes, not exactly an easy maneuver while wearing a mining suit, and locked one hand to the metal. He turned and pulled at the same time while lifting with his knees. The leg pinning him to the deck moved upward a few centimeters, and he pulled himself with his free hand. One more attempt and he had the remains of the spider thing off his legs.

The Til thing stared at Jordan, its eyes glowing intensely. It wasn't watching the spiders at all. It was watching him.

He scrambled to his feet but wasn't sure what to do. One of the spiders darted, and the Til thing immediately responded with a whirling turn, its metal club, looking more like a scythe, flashing out and sparking against the spider's nearest leg.

The spider's leg cracked at the joint and folded uselessly beneath it. The robot, or whatever it was, danced backward again and out of reach. The Til thing returned its stare to Jordan.

Then he felt it. The rattling vibration of impacts beneath him. More spiders were coming. Shit.

Jordan took a step backward and another, the Til thing's head moving to follow his progress. What was it waiting for? What did it expect him to do?

Without warning, the Til thing swung its scythe in a wide circle, the end not touching the spiders but making them wary enough to give the creature a little more room. It returned its stare to Jordan, but it also seemed to be looking past him.

Jordan blinked and quickly whirled. Three spiders had come up from the far shaft and were making their way toward him. Jordan instantly realized two things—the Til thing had been trying to warn him, and he'd understood the warning far too late.

The devil you know or the devil you don't?

Jordan didn't know about either devil, but he was more terrified of the spiders than he was of the Til thing. He turned back and ran at the spiders surrounding the creature. The nearest paused in its dance, the orb swiveling again and a pair of graspers appearing. He came to a stop, aimed, and was about to activate the tool when the scythe flashed out and smashed the orb like a hammer on a lightbulb.

Before Jordan had time to react, the Til thing leaped from the deck, somersaulted over the remaining spider, and landed just behind the orb and between its robotic legs. Instead of using the scythe, the creature whirled in place and smashed its misshapen fist through the orb.

The light immediately went out, and the spider's legs sagged. The Til thing looked up at Jordan, its eyes flashing in either rage or urgency. Urgency. He turned around and saw the new arrivals were only twenty meters away and closing.

Jordan looked back uneasily.

The Til thing headed to the nearest shaft.

"Are you fucking crazy?" he said to the thing, knowing it couldn't hear him, much less understand him. It looked back at him one last time before dropping through the shaft.

The spiders noticed, and one of them sped away to the shaft it had come from, moving faster than Jordan thought possible.

The remaining two, their orbs strobing like chain lightning, quickened their pace. He had to take two of them out. Two. Fuck.

No way could he take out one while the other disarmed him or did far worse, like grabbing him with its pincers and shredding him to pieces.

He yelled unintelligible syllables as he ran for the shaft. The moment he touched the lip, he knew he'd made a mistake. The shaft appeared to drop into infinity, and for an instant, he was certain it did. Then he saw five glowing dots several meters below him.

Knowing what was about to happen, he reached out his free hand, turned the magnetics to full, and dropped. The suit slowed his descent, but even in one-third gravity, he was going to hit hard.

Readying himself for a jolt up his spine, eyes shut against the oncoming pain and shock, an increasing pressure started against his ass, and he came to rest gently on the deck. The Til thing let go of him and took a step backward.

Jordan, not a small man, felt like an adolescent standing in the shadow of a giant. The Til thing's misshapen face, well illuminated and still for the first time, made him want to retch.

The creature's thick neck supported not two heads but a bifurcated skull somehow connected at the base. The two halves jutted out like overripe melons grown from ill vines. The left had been Til, his cheeks now melted, lips all but disappeared, and flesh pulled tight against his mutated body. One eye stared balefully, pleadingly at Jordan. The lipless mouth writhed in silent syllables, brows scrunched together above its stretched eye sockets.

Til's fine, luxurious blond hair had disappeared, offering a horrorscape of bony growths and a jutting forehead. The nose, little more than a twisted knot, flared in spasms.

The creature's right head was the true horror. The mash of features canted to one side, its glowing eye cluster off-center from the ragged oval skull. It had no nose, and its sphincter-like mouth sported sharpened diamond-shaped teeth. The sphincter pulsed in its own rhythmless spasms.

Jordan stepped backward and raised the mining hammer slightly. The creature immediately responded by lashing out and knocking it out of his hands, where it bounced impotently to the deck.

The Til thing advanced on him and leaned in, Til's mangled face practically filling Jordan's visor. The lips moved in silence, only this time, they weren't spasms. Instead, Jordan thought they were words.

Til's expression had been one of terror and pain, but now it had cleared. Even with its deformities, the Til face looked less plaintive and more commanding. Jordan didn't understand what Til was trying to tell him. Then it swerved its remaining eye to the right, as if gesturing to the other being that had somehow taken over his body. The eye returned to stare at Jordan.

He felt a tremor in his boots, and the Til thing jerked backward before slamming against Jordan and being jerked again. Only the creature didn't come forward again—it flew through the wide gap leading to the shaft.

Jordan saw two spider limbs jutting from the Til thing's shoulder, thick vapor rising from the metal like steam from ice. The Til thing pulled up its legs and pushed against the orb, ripping itself off the tines.

Another spider appeared behind the first, its legs poised to skewer the Til thing. Jordan moved to get a clear shot. The plasma hammer wouldn't do much damage at this range, but that wasn't the intent. He activated the tool in a single blast, and plasma balls spread out just far enough to superheat the deckplate beneath the second spider. It turned its graspers in Jordan's direction in time to see him running forward.

Recognizing the threat, the spider lowered its raised legs and skittered to Jordan. He waited until he could see every detail of its graspers and fired again.

This time, the plasma blast caught the thing directly in the orb. Jordan's suit flashed alerts about overheating before they quickly disappeared. The orb had been blown in half, the metal surrounding it melted into slag.

The spider had hit Til again with another leg, this one puncturing the creature's thigh. The Til thing attempted to turn and face its attacker, but another metal leg stabbed downward, puncturing one hand. The spider legs smoked where they made contact with the mottled, speckled fluid rushing from the creature's wounds.

Jordan strode forward, mindful of another spider appearing. The one holding Til in place swiveled its grabbers in his direction. The spider, while securing Til, couldn't move. Jordan had counted on that as he stepped within three meters and shot one of his last plasma blasts.

The orb melted along with the metal, and the massive robot slumped. Jordan carefully probed the level with his suit lights, but it appeared even larger than the one above. The cylinders jutting through the ceiling and through the deck seemed to be the only similarity, other than how empty it was and the dozen or so shafts across from him. The sight made him want to hide.

He knelt down and lifted the spider leg that had perforated the Til thing's hand. Its end popped out far more easily than he'd expected, and he briefly examined it before tossing it aside. Wherever it had touched the creature's blood, the metal had corroded to the point of near disintegration.

*Don't want that on me,* he thought.

For the thigh, he was much more cautious, making sure he was well away from the Til thing when he pulled it out. A short-lived stream erupted from the wound, dissolving the remaining tatters of the EVA suit material around the leg. The Til thing rolled over, its human eye regarding Jordan with something akin to thanks.

He backed away from the creature, nearly stumbling over the remains of the spider. The Til thing slowly raised itself and retrieved its scythe with the club-like handle. It stood there for a moment, its sphincter-like mouth pulsating in a steady rhythm, eyes burning brightly.

*What are you thinking?* Jordan wondered.

The Til thing finally turned its heads and stared at Jordan, the partially human head's mouth spasming in inhuman contortions. It seemed to be asking a question, or maybe expressing gratitude. Maybe it was planning to eat him.

The perforations in its flesh appeared to have healed, the wounds sealed by a coagulant in its blood, or maybe by ice. The fluid the creature had leaked had burned the deck like acid and shortly after frozen against the metal. What the hell was this thing?

The creature turned away from him and walked to the chutes lining the cylinder's far edge. After reaching the bank of chutes, it turned once again to face Jordan. Did it want him to follow?

*Do you dare?*

After making sure no other spiders had gotten onto the level without him seeing them, he walked to join the Til thing.

# CHAPTER THIRTY-SIX

The chutes looked nearly as scary as the shafts had. Without the spider orbs' glow, the large, open level had once again plunged into darkness apart from Jordan's suit lights and the creature's burning eyes. The shaft had looked like hungry mouths. The chutes looked like something made for livestock.

The Til thing walked to the edge of one of the chutes and peered down and back at Jordan. It seemed to be asking what he was waiting for, or perhaps it was a "follow me" pause. Either way, the creature, still looking at him, stepped forward and dropped into the chute.

Jordan stood there for a moment, unsure what to do. Again, he'd had a pretty good idea the creature wanted to go below, but why the chutes when there were other shafts? The shafts were larger, provided more width for his oversized suit. In the chute, he'd be relatively cramped but not as cramped as the Til thing had been.

Trembling with fear and adrenaline, Jordan stepped forward into an adjoining chute and fell through. He bounced gently on what he assumed was coated alloy and slid on a rapid incline into a dry, recessed crescent-shaped pool, its edges over a meter high.

The Til thing stood in the center, its head regarding the ceiling before dropping to stare at the nest of cylinders. How many levels did the damned things descend? he wondered. The whole planet? Were they supports or something else?

Jordan walked forward, although he kept several meters between him and the Til thing. As he approached the lip, his suit lights chased away the gloom, and he made out what appeared to be a large rectangular structure. Unlike the upper levels, the metal here appeared less aged, as though this level hadn't been exposed to the same atmosphere as the ones above.

The creature stared at the structure before climbing out of the empty pool and onto the shining matte-gray deck. Jordan, not sure what to do apart from following its lead, climbed out as carefully as he could and stood facing the same direction as the Til thing.

A strange shadow caught Jordan's eye, and he turned slightly, his light moving over an area he hadn't cleared. He swallowed hard at the mining hammer lying on the deck. It would be impossible to know whose it had been, and he saw no other signs of the miner.

Or Aryana, for that matter.

He traded a glance with the creature before cautiously stepping toward the hammer. The center of the cylinder was larger than the other levels, although the strange nest remained in the same place. Several pyramid-shaped pylons grew out of the base of the cylinders, each several meters in both height and width.

*What the fuck are those?* he wondered.

The Til thing had made its way behind the cylinders and stood like a statue, following Jordan's gaze. Its eyes burned a little darker for a moment before returning to their normal brightness. It raised its massive skull slightly, cocking it to one side as if listening. Then Jordan felt it.

The vibration was more like a chainsaw slashing impotently against steel than the skittering of metallic legs across metal. A second later, Jordan saw the telltale flicker of yellow emanating from the rectangular structure.

The Til thing leaped upward into the piping and supports surrounding the cylinders. Jordan opened his mouth to ask the thing what it was doing, but he had a pretty good idea.

Jordan turned and ran to the far side and hid behind one of the pyramid-shaped housings. He crouched low, mindful the spiders could probably see him if he so much as twitched beyond the cover of metal. Watching the far bulkhead, he counted the sets of strobes, and his heart sank. He couldn't be certain, but he thought there were at least four and maybe as many as six trundling out of the machine and onto the deck. The level was going to be packed with the damned things.

How many charges did he have left in the plasma hammer?

The deck trembled beneath him, the impact from dozens and dozens of legs smacking the deck as they moved away from their spawning area and fanned out.

Although he couldn't see them, he could feel their movements. The spider things had no doubt been warned there were enemies to attack, or maybe food, and he imagined they were out for blood. With the massive nest of cylinders crowding the center of the level along with the pyramids spread out around it, the spiders would have no choice but to scurry around the edges, probing to find the trespassers.

*I'll show you trespass,* Jordan thought as the vibrations strengthened.

The Til thing was somewhere above him, but Jordan didn't think it had fled. Instead, it was trying to find an opportunity to fall upon the spiders, no doubt planning on cutting another one to pieces. Jordan hoped the thing could take out more than one, because he didn't think he had enough fuel to take two, let alone three.

The tremors continued growing in strength and number. The spiders were probably rounding the first pyramid, their orbs flickering and flashing as they scanned for movement. The shadows danced with the strobes, and Jordan breathed too shallowly, too rapidly.

How many seconds did he have? Ten? Fifteen? The lights grew brighter, their flashes more sporadic, less rhythmic. How many meters away now?

The first of the spiders moved into view, traveling fairly quickly. Scrunched up against the side of the pyramidal housing, he hoped it would take the thing more than a single glance to find him. For a moment, he thought he'd managed to escape its notice until the orb swiveled and a pair of graspers appeared. It changed direction and went straight for him.

Jordan barely had time to raise himself to his feet, aim, and fire before it was on him. The robot's left side disappeared into slag, the orb crashing into the deck, its remaining legs twitching spasmodically. He caught movement out of the corner of his eye and pivoted. Another spider was coming for him, but this one appeared smarter than the first. Rather than charging him, it danced several meters out of range, the orb flashing in a stuttering, stumbling rhythm.

Jordan felt more impact tremors on the deck and suddenly knew where the third one was. It was hiding on the other side of the housing, probably trying to figure out how to sneak around without getting blasted.

"Okay, not good," he said aloud and carefully crouch-walked a meter away from the housing, the hammer pointed in the dancing spider's direction. He continued walking backward with slow, cautious steps, taking the time to make sure he didn't trip over anything. Once he had an angle that allowed him to see both the spider in front of him and the edge of the housing, he came to a halt.

The dancing spider stopped its jittery movements, the orb's glow suddenly steady. Jordan felt a chill. The strobing from the other side of the housing ceased as well.

A new set of impact tremors vibrated his boots. They were coming from behind him. His hands dropped slightly, his aim faltering. The things were behind him. If he managed to destroy the two in front of him, he'd still have to deal with the others.

\* \* \* \* \*

Parasite clung to the piping five meters above the deck. It watched the spiders move away from their factory and split their numbers three to a side. Their strobing lights went active the moment they were spawned meaning the drones were on alert and searching for hostiles.

The suited thing, the one Parasite had used as bait, saved, and now wanted to protect, had hidden next to a power conduit, its energy weapon ready to attack the nearest drone. Parasite carefully maneuvered around the stack until it faced the drone factory. It peered past the corner just as the suited thing blasted the nearest drone.

Parasite watched how the others reacted, making note that the three on the opposite side were already moving into flanking position. Good. That meant they were far enough away. The two-headed thing coiled like a spring before launching itself. In the one-third gravity, Parasite practically glided to the top of the rectangular structure.

Without missing a beat, it ran to the edge of the factory and somersaulted to the deck. If Parasite were capable of grinning, it would have. The factory's internals moved and knitted another drone. Or would have if Parasite hadn't walked inside, its makeshift scythe cutting through and destroying machinery. Several lights blinked, and a powerful pulse made the deck vibrate. The Factory was calling for help.

* * * * *

The spider that had danced nearest him hesitated, its steps unsure for a moment. The orb swiveled, and the grabbers moved back to face the other side of the level, the place where the structure had been. A beat later, the three spiders that had flanked him ran past as though the world were ending.

The one that had trapped Jordan continued tapping its legs with uncertainty. Instead of waiting for it to make up its mind what to do, Jordan stepped forward and blasted the thing practically point-blank.

The creature fell in two, the orb nothing more than vapor while its base remained. The useless legs sagged and remained lifeless. Jordan walked past the pyramid housings and followed the strobing glowing lights.

The spiders had headed to the structure, each of them mere meters away from it, surrounding it. Strange hues erupted from the end of the building, making Jordan wonder what the hell was going on. One of the building's bulkheads pimpled, followed by another. Jordan had an idea of what was about to happen as one of the spiders entered the structure.

A heartbeat later, a piece of spider leg came flying out of the building and crashed against the ship's far bulkhead. Jordan stared in disbelief as the Til thing smashed through the side of the structure with its metal scythe, the building quaking from the impact.

The spiders, unsure of what to do, took a few steps backward as the Til thing ripped the metal and stepped confidently through the wide tear, its makeshift weapon bared and already swinging.

The nearest spider hadn't moved far enough away, apparently not counting on the Til thing's swing or the fact that it was going to pop out of the building like a jack-in-the-box. The leg facing the scythe immediately shattered from the impact of the heavy weapon. This time, however, the weapon itself broke in half, the scythe end spinning away and whizzing by Jordan's shoulder.

Without so much as a pause, the creature flipped the broken end of the tool and crunched the metal base into the orb. Even from this far away, Jordan could see the orb crack, the color bleeding out as though bleached by the flip of a contrast setting.

Before the spiders could recover, the creature leaped in the air, a pair of spider legs slicing through the space where it had just been. It came down atop the second spider and plunged its short club toward the orb. This robot, apparently better prepared than the last, slid sideways, and the Til thing crashed to the deck, immediately rolling in Jordan's direction.

The remaining spiders quickly advanced, their graspers seeming sharper, more like terrifyingly sharp pincers. The Til thing flipped over and to its feet, but it was going to get massacred by the spiders. Before he knew he was going to do it, Jordan rushed the robots, plasma hammer aimed before him. The spiders, upon seeing the suited madman heading toward them, hesitated just a beat. It was more than long enough.

The Til thing jumped away from the spiders and leaped atop the robot factory, and one of the spiders turned in that direction. The one that hadn't turned made a crucial mistake—it rushed Jordan.

Jordan waited until its legs had practically touched him before activating the tool and blasting the orb to vapor. The spider continued moving forward from momentum and knocked Jordan to the deck. Stars speckled his vision, and he kicked upward while wriggling out from beneath the dead robot.

He got to his feet just in time to see the Til thing leap from the scaffolding face-first and fall on the remaining spider, a new piece of metal in its massive hands. It plunged the weapon into the orb, the material shattering, and the robot stopped moving.

Jordan turned around to look for another threat, but his lights found nothing but shattered metal and iridescent shards of orb. Unsure of what to do, he faced the Til thing. It had regained its feet, reclaimed its blunt edged segment of spider leg, and held it over its shoulder like a lumberjack holding an axe.

Its green eyes glowed with a ferocity that made Jordan want to run and run away fast. The thing stared at Jordan as if waiting for him to do something. The problem was, he wasn't sure what to do. The chutes he and the alien had descended ended in troughs, which, now that Jordan thought about it, seemed more than a little suspicious. Troughs. What would robots need troughs for?

The Til thing stepped away from the robot and lowered its weapon to the deck. It stood there, patient as eternity, waiting.

"What the fuck do you want?" Jordan asked it, knowing it couldn't hear him. "What are you waiting for?"

It didn't move.

Finally, Jordan stepped toward the troughs, thinking maybe he could climb them to the previous level. The alien picked up its weapon and held it over its shoulder again before following. He wasn't sure, but he thought the heads were… shaking? As in "no"?

"The fuck?"

The alien took another few steps, and Jordan, although every portion of his brain screamed at him to flee, held his ground. Just as the alien held its weapon in a resting position, he did the same with his own. The last thing Jordan wanted right now was to have to face off with this thing. He had a feeling that was a fight he'd lose.

It continued walking until it was fewer than two meters away from him. Jordan realized that meant he was in range of the creature's massive weapon. If it wanted to kill him, all it had to do was swing the hunk of metal from its shoulder and cut him in half or take off his head. Adrenaline born of fear made Jordan's veins tingle with flight or fight.

The creature pointed into the trough directly behind Jordan. He didn't want to break eye contact with the creature and so ignored it. The Til thing moved slightly and bent its knees, its misshapen pair of heads purposely catching Jordan's suit lights.

The head that still looked human, still looked like Til, mouthed something. Jordan blinked as he tried to determine if they were words or just gibberish. The fact that the face staring at him, if not the entire body, used to be that of his captain and someone he considered a friend made it difficult to focus.

Food.

Was that what the Til thing was trying to say?

Food. Bad.

Jordan cocked his head as he tried to make sense of the words. The creature cocked its head as if mimicking him. He could have told the thing it didn't make it more human, only creepier.

Once certain the creature wasn't going to kill him, he half turned and stared into the trough. What he hadn't noticed on his way down the sluice were the stains on the metal. The one he'd come down was stained with splatters of rust-colored liquid that had frozen or dried or maybe both.

He caught movement and turned again. The creature pointed at the sluice next to Jordan's. The metal was more than stained—it might as well have been painted by an expressionist. Yellow, green, and purple spattered the outer edges while the center of the sluice was nearly black from the mixture of the three.

"Food. Bad," Til had tried to say.

Jordan paused for a moment as he examined the colors. Something in his brain was screaming at him to figure this out. It was important, dammit. The colors were almost like—

The colors were much the same as the Til thing itself. The greens, the yellows, the fluid he'd seen the creature bleed. Food. Bad.

"Fuck me," Jordan said. "They ate your people?"

The creature, unable to hear him, had no idea what he'd said and pointed at the trough behind Jordan again. Jordan turned fully around this time and peered into the trough. Red. Rust.

"Blood," Jordan said with a sickening feeling. He whirled and faced the Til thing, but it had already begun walking away toward the far side of the massive room. Jordan made out another rectangular structure, but this one appeared far more complex than the robot factory.

Curious, and because he had nothing better to do, Jordan followed and took up position three meters to the creature's side. Although the alien had saved his life and certainly seemed to be an ally for the moment, Jordan didn't want to give it any reason to get hostile or feel threatened. He'd seen what it could do, and his mining suit wouldn't stand a chance in a fight against it.

The creature stared at the large collection of cubes and spheroids. Several empty containers sat in a row on a conveyor belt to the strange-looking machine's side. There was no conveyer leading out, merely an exit for the container itself, which popped it back on the conveyor.

"What the hell is this?" Jordan asked.

The alien moved to the conveyor, and before Jordan knew what was happening, the creature's weapon whirled off its shoulder and began destroying the machine. It bashed the conveyer into twisted metal before shoving the weapon inside the conveyer entrance and pushing upward with the tool.

Green and yellow sparks of color illuminated the inside for a few beats before they went dark again. The creature removed its weapon and put it back on its shoulder, glancing at Jordan as if to say, "Well, that's done."

It moved through the wreckage to one of the containers, examined it, and then tossed it to Jordan's feet, where it silently clunked to the deck, giving Jordan's toes a tingle. He flinched and took a step backward, the mining hammer held before him in a defensive posture.

The creature merely stared at him, its green eyes peering with curiosity.

Jordan, feeling foolish, put his hammer back into a resting position and peered down into the container. It was stained with dried rust. Human blood.

# CHAPTER THIRTY-SEVEN

Jordan kicked the container aside and looked up at the creature. The head that still appeared partially human bobbed forward the slightest bit before returning to its original position. A beat later, it did it again.

Was that a "yes"? Jordan wondered. "Yes to what?"

The creature repeated the movement, only this time, it doubled over, and a spray of vomit erupted from the human head onto the deck. A short-lived cloud of vapor rose before falling back to the floor, frozen. The metal, however, appeared significantly corroded from exposure.

After a beat, the creature stood to its full height and regarded Jordan with its blazing green eyes. The human head was mouthing words, but a portion of its lower lip had disintegrated, burned through by the liquid. *Acid,* Jordan thought.

"What the fuck are you?" he asked the thing again.

Without warning, it strode to the damaged machine's housing, leaned forward, and sprayed a stream of vomit across the metal. The liquid bubbled and quickly turned to vapor as it had before. After a second or two, the creature lifted a massive foot and kicked out at the damaged metal.

The oversized, mutated heel that looked like a wide oblong chunk of bone punched through the housing, leaving shards of metal dancing in the air that slowly rained on the deck. The alien kicked again and widened the damage. It continued kicking and bashing with its hands until the rip was more than large enough for it to crawl into. The creature considered its work for a moment before returning its gaze to Jordan.

Til's head, the one that had once been human, mouthed words, but even with Jordan's lights playing across its features, Jordan couldn't tell what it was trying to say. The damage from the liquid had eaten through almost the entire lip portion of the face, leaving behind a dull red-and-green sheen that didn't line up with the upper lip.

Jordan shook his head in frustration before raising his hands. "I don't understand," he said.

Til's mouth continued moving, its eyes wild and insistent.

"I don't understand!" Jordan yelled.

The creature might be unable to hear him, but it somehow understood. Or maybe it had just lost patience. Either way, it shuffled forward into the gloom of the machine, its left hand darting out for Jordan's shoulder and pulling him. He activated his mag-boots and set them to full. The creature continued pulling, but Jordan remained affixed to the deck, bending forward from the pressure. The creature paused, shuffled back out of the housing, and glared at Jordan, its eye cluster blazing with either anger or frustration.

It released Jordan's shoulder, and he popped back upright, swaying slightly. For a moment, the two entities merely stared at one another, one in anger, the other in confusion and fear.

Finally, the alien thing took a step away from Jordan and pointed at the housing. It then pointed down as if at the deck.

"Okay," Jordan said to himself, "so that's how you want to go down?"

The creature pointed at the housing again and once more at the deck. It paused for a few beats, shuffled forward, and crawled inside the machine. Jordan waited until the creature disappeared, took another look around the stained and debris-strewn deck, and followed.

The rip was more than wide enough for the creature, so it was no problem for Jordan. The mining suit was hardy enough to shrug off the odd sharp piece of rock or metal debris that would instantly perforate an EVA suit. Even so, he took great pains to stay as far away from the damaged metal as possible.

The machine's innards consisted of shattered electronics—at least, he assumed they were electrical or energy related—components that defied description, and globs of green and gold liquid. Jordan couldn't see past the creature's hulking form, but from the vibrations, he was fairly sure the Til thing was continuing to bash its way farther inside. How large was this? The other appeared to have been adjoined to the cylinder's inner ring, whereas this machinery seemed to go through the cylinder's walls.

*Then where the fuck are we?* Jordan wondered.

He'd assumed the "ship," as he was beginning to think of this place, was a single cylinder that ran all the way through the planet. The gabbro on the planet's surface had been placed around the cylinder to provide protection and...

"Disguise," Jordan said aloud as he continued following the creature. "For what?"

MacReady's whirling dervish of a triplet, the other so radioactive, it could destroy an EVA suit from 5,000 km away, and MacReady herself, a false planet hiding a massive ship with who knew how many levels and how many cubic kilometers of space.

*Put the pieces together,* Jordan told himself. *Think!*

The debris. The radioactive shards on the *Kirkland*'s hull. Metal. Debris.

Shit, unless you counted the ice giants *Prospector* had found on its way in, the gas giant and MacReady's star, the entire damned system appeared to be littered with debris and the mere memory of its planets. Assuming it ever had any apart from the gas giant and ice—

He stopped in mid-shuffle.

Who was to say the ice giants were ice giants? Did Til and Chu ever confirm that? Shit, did anyone? And just how damned big were they?

If this was a ship, none of it made sense. But if this planet, this MacReady thing, was only part of a ship, then...

The deck trembled, and Jordan looked up. The creature had turned, its eyes glaring into his, but the human head's eye seemed raised in a question.

*Fuck,* he thought, *what I wouldn't give to speak your language. Whatever that might be.*

He continued forward along the path the creature had made through the wreckage. At this point, they had to be nearly twenty-five meters inside the machine. How far did it go?

Not much farther, as it turned out.

The Til thing stopped for a moment in front of a large pipe or tube that descended through the deck. The creature clutched it with both hands and shoved forward. The piping, or whatever it was, came apart, and the creature continued bending struts and supports.

The entity moved to where the pipe had been and appeared to perform a push-up, and then Jordan saw more vomit fly. He simply stared, mouth open, while the creature got to one knee, its heads still staring down at the deck. After a few more beats, it raised one of its arms and smashed it into the decking.

Jordan felt the tremor and shuddered to think just how powerful the creature was.

It leaned down and punched the area with both hands, shards of metal and debris flying upward.

Jordan merely blinked, unable to process what he was seeing.

It was widening the hole, or maybe destroying whatever the large-diameter pipe had been attached to. Either way, it dug like a dog looking for a bone, while intermittently vomiting into the widening hole.

After a minute or two, the creature stopped and turned its heads to look at Jordan. The human head's lower jaw had completely disappeared. The mess of burned and dripping flesh of where it had once been attached made Jordan's stomach squirm.

Its eyes, however, were more expressive than ever and seemed to blink in a recognizable pattern.

"You're fucking shitting me," Jordan whispered.

Morse code. Til, whatever might remain of him inside that deformed and mutated body, was sending a message.

Wait. Wait. Wait.

Jordan turned on his interior helmet light, making his face visible to the thing.

*This is stupid,* he thought.

"Wait for what?" he said aloud, each word slow and exaggerated.

The alien-looking, bloated skull's five eyes flashed at him like beacons, although they didn't have a pattern he understood. The human head's eyes, however, slid to the side and down.

Jordan followed its gaze. It was looking at the hole that it had made, but now that Jordan focused, he saw a hint of gas rising from the perforation in the deck. The creature's eye cluster burned low before rising to a brightness that cast ambient light. They held that intensity for a few beats before the creature leaned its head into the hole and vomited again. More gas rose, the particles clinging together in the thin atmosphere before tearing apart into nothing.

Wait. Otherwise, you'll burn like the metal, it seemed to mean.

When it raised its heads, the mostly human portion was missing its upper left cheek, the flesh seemingly vaporized, the edges still sizzling. Jordan shut his eyes to wait, but that wasn't enough to blot out the image of what was happening a few meters from him.

Think. Think. Think about something else. Think about MacReady.

If this was a portion of a ship, what portion was it? MacReady's radioactive sister might be some kind of propulsion system that melted down, or had maybe been partially destroyed. The spinning sister? Still no clue on that one, but it pointed more and more at the idea that whatever the massive craft might have been, it had been attacked by some powerful weapon.

But instead of being blown to bits, the damage had only partially destroyed the craft and deconstructed it into its constituent parts. The debris field might be the remains of what had once connected the three planet-sized objects.

*You're guessing,* he told himself. Of course, he was, but it felt right. He knew he didn't have all the details or any concept of what the ship might have looked like, but it had the ring of truth. The ice field was their water. The ice giants, if that was what they were, had maybe served as shields from cosmic rays or other radiation. Or maybe against some other kind of weapon they feared.

Shit, he didn't even know if the goddamned gas giant they orbited was really a planet. It was impossible to know. *Prospector* had mistaken all of this for a star system. It hadn't had a clue what it had wandered into.

*And neither did we,* Jordan thought.

He felt a tremor through his hands and looked up. The creature stared at him, the human head's eyes glancing downward at the hole. It paused a beat and descended face-first.

Not quite knowing what to do, Jordan watched as its feet disappeared. The thing had made him wait until it was safe for him to follow. Did that mean it needed him for something? Was he just a convenient ally or some kind of snack in waiting?

A hand rose from the hole, the thick, alien fingers giving him an awkward, stiff come-hither gesture.

Jordan shivered. It was a gesture he'd seen Til make many times.

# CHAPTER THIRTY-EIGHT

The creature had not only ripped open the decking but through the deck below. The next level, unlike the previous ones, was not completely dark.

The machine had connected to some kind of delivery chute, but any remains had been swept away. The creature stood two meters below the deck upon a strut molded into the bulkhead. Jordan stared at the relatively narrow support, activated his magnetics, and climbed down.

The creature must have incredible balance, or else its claws had perforated the metal. Jordan wasn't sure he could stand on it in the bulky suit without magnetics, and the creature was larger than he was.

By the time Jordan reached the narrow lip, he realized it was too late to move farther away from the Til thing, and really, there was nowhere to go. He ended up facing the bulkhead, the creature's flank exposed to his peripheral vision. This close and without something trying to kill him, Jordan had time to take a good look at it. He just wasn't sure he wanted to.

Heart racing, he awkwardly repositioned himself to face away from the bulkhead and the creature at the same time. He wasn't ready to see it for what it was. He didn't want to know how much of Til it had consumed or how much of his former human body remained. Jordan was afraid he'd freeze up and never be able to move from this wall.

Standing this close also meant it could touch him, easily perforate his suit with one of those dangerously sharp and thick clawed fingers and the feet that could shred him with a well-balanced kangaroo kick. It also meant it could do to him whatever it had done to Til.

The creature moved in his peripheral vision, but Jordan was afraid to turn to see what it was doing. He saw a shoulder and then realized it was climbing down to the next lip. Or rather, it was sliding.

Jordan, unable to resist, leaned over the lip, one hand still connected to the bulkhead, and watched the creature descend as though it were rappelling, its clawed fingers and feet leaving nearly imperceptible grooves in the metal. It reached the next lip and looked up at him, the human eye darting back and forth.

He ignored the shudder of horror he felt every time he looked at the creature and climbed down next to it. It was then he realized the bulkhead wasn't completely dark. Confused, he killed his headlamp and was surprised to see a dim light blue glow.

Jordan repeated his shuffling technique but this time leaned out over the edge of the lip and stared into what had been darkness. For what seemed to be kilometers, arrays of dim blue shapes appeared below him. Hundreds of thousands. Maybe millions.

"Holy shit," he whispered. "Where the fuck are we?"

A massive conglomeration of rails, supports, and machinery hung from the ceiling and stretched far into the distance in all directions.

The creature descended to the next support, Jordan following. After five more lips, with the blue glow nearly bright enough to chase away the shadows, he finally realized what he was looking at. The orbs weren't orbs at all. At first, he thought they were tubes, but then he realized each was a squat cylinder, its width maybe as large as four meters and three or so meters high.

The top of each cylinder seemed different but similar. Almost as though whatever they contained was visible.

Jordan thought The level must run through MacReady's entire core and a significant portion of it. If each of the orbs represented a cylinder, with an aisle of a half meter between them, a single row must represent dozens of kilometers. He and the creature were at its edges.

After they descended another two lips, he saw that each cylinder was translucent. After another, his brain realized they were transparent but filled with a cloudy liquid that mostly hid whatever they contained.

One more lip, and he didn't have to wonder what was inside them. The nearest cylinder, the liquid itself seeming to be the origin of the color, contained a creature whose form made his mind hurt. It had too many legs, too many tentacles, and too many eyes for his brain to make sense of. What you could call its trunk, or base, appeared amorphous, almost as if the thing was part liquid itself. It also appeared incredibly black.

The Til thing dropped to the deck, and a puff of something rose in response. Ice crystals, perhaps? Or something biological? Maybe just dust?

Jordan climbed down, feeling relieved with his feet finally on the deck. The Til thing stood next to the cylinder for a moment before walking to the next. He followed, but Jordan's eyes continued to linger over the strange-looking thing until it was out of sight.

The next wasn't nearly as strange but almost as unnerving. A four-armed humanoid, its skin, or flesh, or carapace, a patchwork of dozens of indeterminate colors, floated in the liquid, its form collapsed into the fetal position. It had no claws, but its fingers and toes ended in tapered points with flowing tendrils. It was as beautiful as it was unsettling.

The Til thing's hand brushed almost lovingly against the cylinder as they passed. They walked several more rows before Jordan realized the light had changed slightly. The blue glow, now much more powerful from all the ambient sources, seemed to pulse farther up ahead. The creature, appearing relaxed before now, slowed its pace, and leaned forward slightly.

Jordan checked the plasma hammer's charges. He had maybe one burst left. After that, he could ditch the harness and use his mining hammer as a melee weapon until it broke. Then he'd be down to swinging what was essentially a corundum caveman club.

He still had enough energy and oxygen for ten hours even if he ran full bore, so that wasn't an issue. Keeping his suit intact and fighting off mechanical spiders, on the other hand, was kind of difficult without weapons.

The Til thing continued creeping in the direction of the pulses, and Jordan found himself matching the creature's posture. He left two meters of space between the Til thing and himself, making sure he had a clear line of sight around the creature's hulking form.

Each cylinder Jordan peered into had a different type of creature in it, although, with the exception of the black thing he'd seen, each row appeared consistent. Kilometers of one type of creature or another. How many were here? Shit, how many different types were here?

Jordan's tactile sensors picked up a tremor from the deck. More like a vibration, really. Machinery of some kind, he was sure. Til slowed its approach, and Jordan followed suit, the mining hammer raised slightly in his hands.

The pulses were coming from a far row, where most of the cylinders appeared dark and unused. Two cylinders on its end remained steadily blue while the three next to them flashed in a heartbeat-like rhythm. The closer they got, the more Jordan was sure of what the cylinders contained.

As he reached the pulsing row, the last row of cylinders, his eyes caught something familiar. A quick glance and he knew where he was and what they were doing. He forgot about everything because the creature floating inside the cylinder was Aryana.

She stared at him with vacant open eyes, her body curled in the fetal position, yet her head faced toward him. She wore no expression and no clothes, the vibrant woman he knew now no more than a statue frozen in time.

Was she dead or merely asleep?

Jordan saw something move in his peripheral vision, and suddenly he was knocked to his side. His boot magnetics, still on and holding him fast to the deck, forced him to lean sideways before one broke its connection with the metal.

He stumbled into the bulkhead as something smashed into his back, suit integrity warnings flashing across his HUD, a klaxon in his ears. A lightning bolt of pain rose from the base of his spine, rattling his teeth, and making him see stars. He pushed himself sideways, caught his balance, and turned, the hammer coming up to meet whatever had hit him.

It wasn't a spider, but it was mechanical. The thing stood nearly three meters tall, its body made of metal and what looked like rotted, rugose flesh. Instead of a head, it had a sprout of tentacles that waved menacingly, a quartet of dangerous-looking limbs slicing toward him.

What froze him, however, was the thing at its center. A transparent, glowing blue cube contained a mess of strange-looking organs and greenish veins running with dozens of colors. Jordan thought he noticed what looked like a mutilated human brain squashed to the side.

It reared back a pair of its arms and punched forward. Jordan dove to the side, and they slammed into the metal, making the deck tremble. It followed him, the liquid glowing with a malevolent intensity.

A spray of liquid erupted from the top of the nearest cylinder and splashed across the mechanical suit's shoulders. Tendrils of gas rose from the surface, and the massive thing pivoted, its arms rising upward. Til, standing atop the cylinder, leaped just as the creature's metal hands swiped where it had been.

Jordan raised the plasma hammer, aimed at the transparent cube, and activated the tool. The blast knocked the thing backward and to the side, runnels of molten metal streaming down its legs. It swiveled at the hips to regard Jordan, its upper arms already swinging for him.

It struck the end of his mining hammer, the tool tearing out of Jordan's hands and breaking into pieces against the nearest cylinder. Jordan spun from the impact, lost his balance, and fell to one knee.

He saw the shadow of one of the arms moving behind him and realized he was dead. The thing was going to crush him or tear him limb from limb. He rolled away, doing his best to tumble into the aisle. If he could get between the cylinders, he might be able to get out of reach, or at least find some cover.

The Til thing leaped from atop the nearest cylinder, the thick metal spider leg thrust downward like a pike. The slab of metal plunged into the center of where the head would be, the fleshy tentacles all straightening either from pain or in alarm. Iridescent liquid splashed and stained the transparent cylinders as well as the deck.

The robot's arms rose and reached to slam against its shoulders, but Til had already pulled the weapon loose and leaped away. The metal hands smashed into the robot's own tentacles, more liquid splashing from its wounded shoulders.

The massive robot shuddered in place for a beat before turning away from Jordan, presumably searching for Til. It didn't have much of a chance. Til appeared from the side of a cylinder, its free hand slashing out and cutting across the transparent cube, leaving thick white grooves in its surface.

By the time the robot could swipe at it, Til had disappeared around the corner. While the massive thing was distracted, Jordan quickly moved around the cylinder. Here he was worried about his plasma hammer, and the Til thing was kicking the robot's ass using nothing more than a slab of metal.

The deck trembled, and Jordan's ironic grin disappeared in a flash. He turned and ran down the row even as the impact tremors continued. He didn't have to look back to know the robot had turned the corner. Hadn't forgotten about him after all.

He couldn't take the thing toe-to-toe, and he sure as shit didn't want to be bait again, so he moved to the next full aisle and forward once more before pivoting and running down the row.

The tremors moved farther and farther away, and he thought maybe he'd lost the thing. Jordan ducked behind a cylinder, doing his best to peer through the murky blue liquid at the same time as around the creature it contained.

This one had six legs and an abdomen that rose a meter from its base. A strange insect-like thing whose head appeared to have room for a large brain case. Maybe it had been sentient before being trapped inside the liquid. Maybe it had been intelligent enough to know what had been happening. Maybe it had been afraid.

He pushed the thoughts away when he saw something move. Jordan watched, ignoring the strange limbs in the liquid and the way the imprisoned thing's mandibles appeared to flutter from an unconscious dream.

It was the robot. He could see the transparent cube in its center, the strange conglomeration of living tissue appearing undamaged from Til's attacks.

Til had chopped it at the top, but whether the creature had done it as a distraction to save Jordan or if it was a genuine vulnerability, he'd no idea. But the second attack had targeted the cube and nothing but the cube.

Jordan held his position, his reclaimed mining hammer feeling too light in his hands. If the Til thing hadn't been able to destroy the robot with those claws, what exactly made him think he could do any damage with a hunk of corundum?

He looked away from the cylinder and scanned the tops of the others, hoping to see Til somewhere up there in the machinery or stalking the robot. Instead, he saw nothing moving except for the cylinder extractor gliding from its station.

If he could somehow coordinate his attack with Til, they might have a shot at disabling it, although there was no way of knowing if that was even possible. But if he didn't do something, there was no way of freeing Aryana, or the others he might not have seen.

The robot moved to the next aisle. It was coming this way, doing its best to maneuver between the cylinders. Every few steps, it bumped one, but the containers didn't so much as vibrate in response. The engineer in him wondered what they were made of. The fighter in him, desperate, terrified, and completely unskilled, sighed in relief. Less collateral damage to worry about, he hoped.

A cylinder near Aryana's began pulsing more quickly. He glanced overhead again and noticed the glider approaching their side. More specifically, the flashing container.

The strange-looking glider hovered over the cylinder for a moment before descending atop it. The liquid inside the container became a deep blue that pulsed in the rhythm of a human heartbeat.

*Shit,* Jordan thought. *What the fuck?*

The automaton rose with the interior of the cylinder, leaving the armored shell behind, and returned to its original height. Jordan realized the robot had moved into position to give it cover.

Protections for the machines up here. But what the fuck was this place? Some kind of capture area? A storage area for beings from who knew how many alien worlds, almost like an intergalactic ark, or a collection?

It didn't sound right, didn't feel right in his head. There had to be something he was missing. If it was a collection, why had he just seen someone removed from storage?

The hair on the back of his neck tickled, and he felt an impact tremor in his heels. He whirled around, hammer ready to smash, but there was no one there. One of the cylinder lights twenty or so meters away dimmed and all but disappeared before returning to its former brightness.

Either that was Til, or another robot was coming.

*Or something you haven't seen.*

*If only I could fucking hear,* he thought. The atmosphere was far too thin for him to hear anything useful unless it was right on top of him.

He turned his attention back to where he'd last seen the robot. It had moved into position by Aryana's row. The mechanical suit, or whatever you wanted to call it, turned slightly every few seconds.

*Either you only have cams in front, or you're afraid you can't turn in time to counter a flank,* Jordan thought. *Which is it?*

A cylinder in the distance flashed deep yellow before its light went out altogether. A few beats later, another met the same fate. They were all on a row much farther back.

The robot stopped turning and walked to the aisle, facing the now-lightless cylinders. It seemed to be waiting for something, or merely watching to see if it could catch sight of the saboteur.

If he moved, the robot would see him. No way it couldn't with all the transparent cylinders. The murky liquid wasn't going to provide much camouflage. At least he didn't think it would.

Then again, he'd no idea what color range the thing saw. Shit, he didn't even know how Til's senses functioned. All bets were off.

Except infrared. The bot's sensors obviously couldn't detect his suit or wasn't equipped to.

*Can't see heat,* he thought. *Or don't want to.* Either way, that might be something he could use. If, that was, he found a way to set anything ablaze in such a thin atmosphere.

Another cylinder went out, followed by another. If that was Til, it had moved to another row and aisle. Jordan frowned. Til wasn't moving farther away from the robot but moving closer and heading directly toward Jordan.

# CHAPTER THIRTY-NINE

The robot had moved an aisle farther toward Jordan and the Til thing's advance. Now Jordan really couldn't move. If he so much as twitched, the robot would see him for sure.

*Shit. Maybe that's Til's plan.*

Then the question became, did Jordan move now, or when the metal monster got a little closer? A moment later, he didn't have to wonder.

Til rounded the corner on the robot's blindside, the piece of metal raised at shoulder height like a hitter about to swing, but it was practically bouncing in the one-third gravity. The robot started to turn, one arm rising to block, the other presumably to smash or grab Til.

Jordan scampered out of hiding and sprinted at the robot, mining hammer raised similarly to Til's. The robot's sensors obviously saw Jordan coming at it, but rather than turning to face him, it remained fixed on Til. As Jordan closed, he swung as hard as he could at the cube.

The sharpened end of the hammer smashed into it, and Jordan felt as though he'd just hit a wall. The mining hammer punched a crack through the metal holding the container in place but did no more damage than that. He banged his shoulder off the robot's waist and stumbled into a cylinder.

*I'm dead,* he thought. *I'm so dead.*

He turned, and one of the robot's four arms punched the deck next to his boots. He leaped backward but hit the cylinder. He had nowhere to go.

The Til thing leaped in the air, and its club impacted the shoulder joint holding the top left arm in place. A spark flew, and a shower of metal flakes puffed into the air. The arm went limp and fell to the robot's side.

Instead of swinging where Til had been, the robot swiveled at the waist, bringing up its remaining upper arm in a vicious backhand. The armored fist struck Til as he was leaping past. Jordan saw Til framed in the blue glow for a moment, a spray of some liquid fanning out in all directions. And then Til flew off into the darkness.

The robot, rather than pursuing, turned to face Jordan. His arm still felt numb from striking the cube and hitting its supports instead, and his wobbling legs made it difficult to stand up straight.

Vapor briefly rose from where Til's acidic, toxic blood had struck, droplet-sized blemishes peppering the robot's left side, almost as if Til had vomited during his leap and before the robot had hit him.

Jordan sidestepped just in time to avoid the creature's long upper arm. The limb struck the containment cylinder behind him with a vibration that rocked his feet. This time, the cylinder definitely budged, but Jordan barely noticed.

Realizing another arm was swinging for him, he moved forward in a mostly controlled stumble until he was beneath the thing's oversized torso. It either lost sight of him for a moment or couldn't reach him. Regardless, he stabbed the tool upward as hard as he could and into the metal above him.

The robot shuddered, probably more in shock than from any damage, and began bending at the waist. Jordan ducked again and ran the other direction and into the darkness, where it had flung Til.

He knew the robot was behind him, probably doing its version of a fast walk. His suit lights panned over what appeared to be an endless expanse of metal deck, no containment cylinders, no lights, and no cover. It wasn't going to lose him this time unless he simply outran it.

Without knowing how close it was, he pushed off hard with his left foot and to the side. In the one-third gravity, he bounded more than leaped, his body moving faster than it should have and hanging above the deck far longer. The moment he landed, he bounded forward with another exaggerated step. He continued the pattern, his legs burning from the effort and a stitch forming in his side.

He couldn't keep this up forever. Instead of running forward into the darkness, he changed direction, heading perpendicular to where he and Til had originally dropped. They had come down a wall, and he just needed to find it again.

A glint reflected from his suit lights. Two steps later, he saw the bulkhead rising upward into darkness and seemingly as wide as infinity. Every breath hurt, every step another stitch in his side and a firebolt through his thighs.

Huffing and puffing, he put everything he had into one last bound and switched his glove magnetics to full. He rose five meters into the air before his gloves caught. Shouting with the effort, throat raw and burning, he lifted his legs as high as he could and locked them in place.

A cautious look down and he realized just how close he'd come. The robot's massive hand was lodged into the steel a mere meter from his feet. The thing moved forward and looked as though it would leap at him.

Yelping in surprise, Jordan climbed as fast as he could, his legs still shuddering with effort from sprinting that far in the bulky suit. He managed a few more meters before he felt impact tremors against the bulkhead.

He didn't dare look down, instead redoubling his efforts toward the ceiling and the nest of pipes and machinery strung somewhere far above. When he counted another six body lengths, he looked down again.

The robot stood looking across the dark expanse, its three functional arms in ready positions to either block or cut. He guessed it had given up on him and instead waited for Til.

*This could be your chance. Just skin that hammer and drop atop it. From this height, you'll probably cleave it in half.*

*And die in the process.*

There wasn't much else he could do, though. He could try to shimmy across the bulkhead back to where they'd come through, but what would that accomplish?

*Aryana and the others,* he thought. It would get him closer to them.

But how far had he run? How far was he from them now? The blue lights of the occupied rows of cylinders seemed like a lifetime away, an orderly constellation of stars steadily burning in some alternate universe. Some place where things made sense and fucking aliens weren't trying to kill you or turn you into a horror show.

The robot thing remained bent upward, its headless shoulders seeming to peer at him. It stood that way for a moment, maybe unsure of what to do. When another bank of cylinder lights flickered out, it turned and lumbered in that direction.

Jordan waited until it was several bounding steps away before he even considered dropping. Just as he started to move sideways and down, he felt an impact tremor through his gloves. Then another. Then several more.

He looked up, he looked down, and then he looked in the direction of the gloom rather than the cylinders. His helmet light glinted off something shiny that moved toward him a little faster than he liked.

Jordan partially demagged his boots and gloves and slid down the bulkhead in much the same way the Til thing had. By the time he touched the deck, the bulkhead crawled with the large spider things. Either there were more of them in the facility, or there was another automated factory somewhere else. Either way, he had company.

He saw the outline of the robot moving across the rows and heading inward, desperately trying to find Til. That left Aryana's row unprotected. Without hesitation, he started running, pulling the mining hammer from its slot. He didn't know if he could break her or the others out, but he was sure going to try.

The spiders had no doubt dropped from the bulkhead and were probably mere meters behind him and gaining. Any second, he was going to feel one of those legs smacking against his armor before it knocked his feet out from under him.

He could see the individual cylinders now, make out the shapes inside them. A glider appeared over the row and descended.

"No," Jordan said between huffs, his body sizzling with adrenaline and rage. "No!"

The glider attached itself to Aryana's cylinder.

"Let her go!"

It rose into the gloom and disappeared from sight.

"No!" Jordan screamed and bounded as high as he could, as though it would help him catch what was already long gone.

He landed a good ten meters from the row, stumbled, and turned. His lights showed him two spiders bearing down on him, the pair staggered a few meters apart. Jordan raised the mining hammer and ran at them.

The spiders, preparing to leap, stuttered for an instant as if confused by the suited lunatic running at them. By the time the first managed to raise a leg in his direction, Jordan had ducked under and jabbed the sharpened end directly into the spider's yellow orb. The light exploded, and the thing collapsed with him in the center.

The other spider jumped and landed atop its dead brethren, its legs raised to stomp him. Jordan allowed himself to fall back as the leg came down, impacting the edges where the orb had once been but missing him completely. He scrambled away from the dead spider as the other crept forward.

It prepared to leap again, and Jordan flung himself into the aisle. The spider legs came down where he'd been, the robot turning and looking for him. Considering the cylinders were translucent and not opaque, he didn't think it would take long.

Through his peripheral vision, he saw another bank of cylinders go dark, followed by a shape flitting across another lit aisle. A moment later, a much larger shape blotted out the endless rows of blue lights.

Jordan held still. In lieu of cover, being a motionless target was the next best thing. He still didn't know how these things saw, if their vision was based on movement or something else. Shit, maybe they couldn't see him through this suit for whatever reason unless he moved. Was that possible?

The spider thing moved farther into the aisle. One of its legs punched down into the metal less than a meter away from his booted foot.

He held the mining hammer at his side while doing his best to calm his heart and mute the sizzle of adrenaline pumping through his veins.

The spider was partially in the aisle now but going the opposite direction. It had to fold its legs inward in order to fit, drastically affecting its mobility. He hoped.

Once somewhat certain it didn't know he was behind it, Jordan took a deep breath and leaped into the air. The orb flashed at once, and a leg flipped upward and swung toward him. The moment his hammer cracked the orb, the leg slammed into Jordan's hip, sending him cartwheeling into one of the cylinders.

Something in his side screamed with pain, and a new suit alert popped up. Internal damage detected. Armor cracked, atmosphere holding after auto sealant. *Fuck.*

Another hit like that and he wouldn't have to worry about ending up like Til. He'd be dead long before that had a chance to happen. Jordan rolled over, gritting his teeth against the pain roaring up his side.

He rose to one knee, the hammer dangling from one hand. Still seeing dots of color against his vision, he scanned for other nearby threats but didn't find any. Another flash in his peripheral vision got his attention and he turned.

While he couldn't see either of the combatants clearly, their silhouettes danced in a clumsy game and of advance and retreat, the Til thing leaping atop cylinders, one to another, across aisles and rows, dropping down every now and then to inflict damage. Jordan hoped.

Ayrana.

He stumbled back to the row that had had her cylinder. The other two had miners in them. No Jihi.

Had they already taken her wherever they'd taken Aryana?

Jordan doubled his grip on the mining hammer and walked slowly to the row where Til and the robot battled. After a few meters, he started moving much faster.

# CHAPTER FORTY

Parasite's weapon had broken on the last swing. It had leaped from atop a cylinder and swung, using its twirling body to put momentum behind the strike. The savage club and scythe it had made out of the spider leg fractured near the handle, leaving Parasite with little more than a half-meter-long hunk of alloy.

The moment Parasite touched the deck, it leaped away to the nearest cylinder just as the still-functioning robot arm swung through empty air. Parasite ducked between a pair of cylinders and wound its way to the next aisle. While passing one of the cylinders, it slapped its wounded, bloody yellow-and-green hand against the container's translucent surface. A thin trail of vapor immediately rose from the exposed material. By the time Parasite reached the new row, the blood had eaten through, and the cylinder went dark, the bluish liquid leaking out, the specimen inside dying instantly.

Parasite knew that with every cylinder it took out, the hive would send more sentries and more scouts. The factories on the lower levels would no doubt be spitting out as many as they could. Luckily, the initial radiation attack eons ago made most of them nonfunctional. Parasite didn't know that, didn't care about that. It only knew it had to hurry. Time was running short in more ways than one.

The Sentry moved into the aisle, but Parasite had already flanked. Rather than leap, this time it ran directly across the aisle and vomited on the brain cube. It didn't pause to see the effects, knowing that the metal and connections holding the interface would ultimately melt. If

Parasite could keep from getting hit, time itself would do the damage.

But it didn't have time. It needed to end this. It had seen one of the host's species chosen and gathered. All too soon, that would become a problem. It needed to finish this as quickly as possible.

It hadn't seen Ally since it ran off into the darkness. Parasite had used the time to sabotage as many likely species as it could, knowing that with hundreds of them to choose from and hundreds of thousands of individuals of each species, it was a wasted effort. But that wasn't the point.

The point was to cause mayhem. To cause panic, inflict catastrophic damage, and end it once and for all. Parasite didn't exactly know the history of the Enemy, hadn't been bred with that innate knowledge. It only knew how to move, how to use, and how to destroy.

The Sentry whirled where Parasite had crossed, its shorter arms snapping at the empty air. Rather than swing around and tempt fate, Parasite ran down the next aisle and quickly accelerated away from the robot. It sabotaged another two cylinders on its way by, instinctively keeping the wound from completely coagulating.

The cylinders went dark, and Parasite could practically feel the hive's frustration. Parasite looked back to make sure the sentry had seen where it was headed and crossed two more aisles and moved farther down the next row. The sentry lumbered after it.

Parasite needed another weapon. It needed a spider to come for it but no such luck. It could climb the wall and tear out some of the machinery, but by that time, there might be four more sentries to deal with. No, it needed to finish this fast.

It doubled back to attempt another flank, its eyes quickly finding the robot's silhouette against the glowing containers, and a dot of yellow appeared on the cylinder next to Parasite. The creature looked upward for half a beat before leaping. A projectile slammed into the deck and shattered into harmless chaff.

Parasite knew the slug was far from harmless. Its implanted knowledge had prepared it for all the tricks, all the traps, and all the known weapons cataloged for millennia after millennia. This one had been a favorite of its enemy. Purely biological in nature, incapable of harming their technology, but utterly deadly to $H_2S$-based organisms, let alone Parasite.

Another hit the deck in front of the creature, and it dove away toward the darkness that used to have working cylinders. Or filled ones.

The sentry was now the least of its concerns. Somewhere above, a glider shadowed the Parasite's movements, preparing an array of weapons to use against it. If Parasite took too much more damage and functioned at this rate for too long, Parasite would be forced to consume its host body. Once that was exhausted, it would have to find a new host. Or food.

Although sentient, the Parasite knew nothing of a future, only a muddied, violent past that included multiple extinctions of multiple species, a gathering of all biological creatures to enslave them, use them for both power and biological material to spread. Consume. Grow.

As another round streaked into the darkness, less than two meters away from its foot, Parasite rolled farther toward the massive room's edge. The wall wouldn't protect it, though. Not with an armed glider as well as a ground unit.

The Til thing felt the deck tremble beneath its gnarled and rugose, clawed toes and whirled in time to catch sight of the robot moving faster than the creature had imagined possible. Parasite stood its ground until it saw the yellow dot and leaped sideways. Another canister of the deadly chemical base slammed into the deck and detonated.

A burning sensation started on the creature's left side, and it knew it had been touched. It ignored the pain, instead choosing to focus on the oncoming robot. Parasite jumped as the sentry reached it, fully expecting to leap over its left shoulder as the robot continued forward, but the sentry came to a dead stop, its good arm rising upward.

Parasite saw the move too late, and its right side scored across the sharpened fingers. Liquid sloshed out of the wound, but it immediately mended, scarring and burning the cut into a smooth patch of angry alien flesh. Parasite landed in an awkward, rolling heap, the cheekbone of its host fracturing like a pulverized candy cane, the skull crunching and barely holding its form.

The sentry's waist swiveled, and it brought its arm low, the fingers ready to impale the host. Parasite twitched to move left and rolled right instead. The sentry's oversized fingers skated across the creature's hide, before scraping against the deck.

A light panned over the sentry, and it looked up just in time for Ally to smash his steel against the sentry's brain case. The metal, already distressed and melted in places from the highly concentrated acid Parasite had been spitting, fractured into flakes. The cube shifted slightly, and the case flickered.

Ally didn't wait for a reaction. Instead, it planted both feet firmly and swung its corundum club. It impacted with the transparent metal, and a large crack appeared.

Parasite got to its feet and jumped atop the sentry, its arms locked on the joint and preventing the robot from reaching Ally. Parasite felt a sense of grim satisfaction when it saw Ally flip the tool in the opposite direction, tilt back, and put all its force into a stab.

The club's sharpened end crashed through the casing and into the tangle of ganglia and connective nervous tissue. The robot stuttered, its servos locking and unlocking at random, the arm quivering and shaking beneath Parasite's tight embrace. Ally took one last swing, the club smashing completely through the cube, liquid splashing over the sentry's feet.

Parasite dropped to the ground next to the sentry's hip. Ally, quivering with excitement, exhaustion, or maybe even rage, held its club in the ready position, fingers changing their grip as if to reassure itself. Parasite didn't want to move, lest it spook Ally. It didn't know how to communicate what it wanted, what it needed. It would have to convince Ally to come. It hoped it wouldn't have to kill Ally instead.

* * * * *

Jordan had watched the robot corner the Til thing, as well as the projectiles a glider fired at it. Instead of immediately joining the fray, he did his best to circle around through the darkened areas, the cylinders he now saw had been damaged, their liquid spilled out, and their prisoners appearing actually dead rather than simply in stasis.

Where had they taken Aryana? And who was the other missing human?

He'd watched from the shadows as the creature and the machine tussled until it was pretty damned clear Jordan had no choice but to engage. He ran from the shadows and attacked. His suited body, even as large as it was, was much smaller than that of the creature or the massive machine.

He slid easily forward and smashed the mining hammer into the cube.

The moment he saw a crack appear, he flipped the hammer and stabbed the cube as hard as he could, a rush of victory spreading over him. Another flip and this time when he swung, he could practically hear the crunch of metal and the sloshing of liquid. The point stirred the tangle of nerves, brain cells, and who knew what else.

The robot thing went limp after shuddering and shivering. The adrenaline surge that had powered Jordan for the last half hour was finally fading, or maybe his nervous system was just too strained. Regardless, he had trouble catching his breath, and the hammer felt too heavy in his hands.

He finally noticed the creature standing beside the dead machine, almost as if it were using it as cover. It took Jordan a minute to realize that was exactly what it was doing. A projectile hit the deck near the creature, and Jordan saw a puff of blue-and-white powder. The creature reacted by tumbling away, one hand clutching its side. He wasn't sure, but Jordan thought he saw vapor.

His dulled and exhausted mind finally made sense of what he was seeing. The glider was using chemical rounds or something that burned the creature's alien hide. The Til thing ran off into the darkness, and Jordan followed in its wake.

\* \* \* \* \*

Parasite's flank burned and burned, requiring it to disconnect the pain receptors, effectively muting them while keeping the other nervous system messages intact. That did not, however, reduce its concern. It had bled far too much, and running was only worsening the issue. It needed rest. It needed food. But if it found its target, accomplished its mission, rest and food would be immaterial. Being immaterial was Parasite's real desire. For what was left after one fulfilled one's purpose?

These were not thoughts Parasite had, but it did know its purpose. That was burned into every strand of its being, every chemical message traveling through its circulatory system, and the combination of human and its own version of DNA. Recombinant. Reformative. Transmutative.

It looked over its shoulder to see if Ally was following and was pleased to see its white lights. Good. Another canister landed a meter to Parasite's right, and it wove to the left before beginning a random zigzag, breaking the rhythm of its steps, and making sure the glider couldn't anticipate.

Parasite knew how much ammunition a glider carried but didn't know that there was only one above it. In a few minutes, there might be dozens or hundreds. All the more reason to find what it was looking for.

It found the seam in the deck, which led to a space without light. The ambient blue of the other thousands or hundreds of thousands of light sources did little to illuminate the area. Another reason Parasite was able to rest next to an empty cylinder, its eye cluster switching frequencies of light, looking for sources of heat or vapor disturbance.

The glider appeared to have lost Parasite, or it was following Ally. Parasite raised its eyes to look and found it. The glider had stayed near the pipes and ceiling machinery, no doubt trying to lose itself in the glare of Jordan's approaching lights.

Parasite reached for the amorphous space in what served as its mind, the place where its connective tissue met that of its host. Parasite sent the "other" the image of what it wanted. The "other," a thing that had once had a name, sent back an image of what it should do.

Parasite raised its hand and waited for Ally's lights to find it in the gloom.

\* \* \* \* \*

The creature moved faster than Jordan, not that that was difficult. Even bounding, he'd lost the Til thing in the darkness. The glider had still been firing at it. Jordan wanted to help, but what the hell was he supposed to do?

The mining hammer still felt too heavy, and his legs burned with the effort to keep bounding. He didn't know if he'd damaged a few servos or not, but it seemed to take more energy to keep moving than it should.

Despite wanting to maintain the pace, he took shorter leaps, doing his best to slow his heart and breathing. If he kept going flat out, he'd have nothing left to try to find Aryana. Or the others.

But the Til thing might. Probably did. Whatever the creature was, it somehow knew this place, what things were, and where to find them. It had to know. Jordan just needed to find it.

That was enough to get him moving again. He bounded in longer leaps, putting more force into each stride while ignoring the burn in his legs and lungs. His lights bounced and caught sight of something in the distance. It took Jordan three more five-meter leaps before he realized it was the Til thing. It was holding up one hand.

Jordan came down from his leap and stumbled a few steps before halting. The creature, fully illuminated by his helmet lights, looked much worse for wear. One side appeared blackened and pitted, and streaks of alien gore had dripped down its side and frozen in runnels.

The head that still looked part human sagged on its outer edge, as though the skull had lost its shape. The upper bones of its face appeared fractured, a pinkish-white nub of bone poking through the tortured flesh. For a moment, Jordan simply stood there, catching his breath and waiting for the creature to do something.

The Til thing then bent its knees and flung its arm like a pitcher. Something streaked from its hand and into the darkness. A second or two later, Jordan felt an impact tremor behind him. He turned and saw a broken machine, its innards spread across the deck.

When he peered back at the Til thing, it had already moved to the remains of the glider, which was much larger than Jordan had thought, nearly two meters wide and three long.

"Jesus," Jordan muttered.

The Til thing bent over the machine, ripped off part of its wing, and held it at the joint. With the creature clutching it, it looked more like a shield than a hunk of debris.

"Um, okay," Jordan said to no one. "What now?"

The Til thing couldn't possibly have heard him, and he wasn't even certain the human portion of Til could see well enough to make out his lip movements, but the creature gestured to the base of the machinery in the far distance.

"There? We're going all the way there?"

The creature thrust the shield at Jordan.

Confused, Jordan stepped forward until he could take it. He reached for it, realized he had to put away the mining hammer first, and finally took the mass of metal.

The creature bent down in front of the shield and began rummaging across the deck with its claws.

"Digging for bones?" Jordan asked.

He felt something beneath his boots like metal hitting metal. A second later, the creature stepped away and gestured for Jordan to follow. Once they had moved several meters away, the creature still doing its best to stay next to the shield, the deck vibrated again. This time, however, it felt more like an earthquake.

Jordan watched in silent fascination as a panel recessed for as much as a meter before sliding aside and leaving a giant open space in its place. The creature immediately stepped down into the slat of darkness. After landing, its head was barely visible.

"Please take me to Aryana," Jordan said and jumped down to join the creature.

# CHAPTER FORTY-ONE

The open panel led downward into a generously sized crawlspace. Jordan barely had to crouch, but the Til thing had to go low on its knees to fit. There was no light here except for Jordan's helmet, but in the relatively tight space, it was more than enough.

The tunnel had to be used for maintenance, and Jordan saw blemishes in the metal that spoke of a well-traveled path. Automated robots, Jordan assumed, used this for transit. Or maybe there was cleaning machinery that performed a regular sweep. But after a few meters inward, he realized this was part of the conveyer system. In other words, the cylindrical prisons-for-one traveled through here to get to wherever they were going.

Jordan gave an exhausted grin. Maybe the creature had read his damned mind. Either that or Til, whatever might remain of him, knew where he wanted to go, or maybe it was where the creature had been headed all along.

The crawlspace, or tube, as Jordan was beginning to think of it, met a junction that led downward. When the creature reached the edge, it handed the shield to Jordan. Confused, Jordan took the slab of metal and waited. Without a beat, the creature dropped into space, whirling around at the same to grasp the edge with its fingers. A moment later, the claws disappeared, and so did the Til thing.

Jordan remained crouched, the oblong makeshift shield making him feel all the clumsier. He wasn't sure how long they could stay here before the machinery activated or until some new robotic horror stumbled its way down here. Every second that ticked off was another eternity. He fought the urge to peer over the edge. If the creature had to retreat in a hurry, he'd have a hell of a time getting out of its way. So he waited.

* * * * *

Parasite dropped into the transit system, its host body sliding easily through the vertical shaft, claws raking the sides to control its speed. When it saw the hint of a blue glow, it dug its claws in deeper, mere scores becoming gashes in the hardened metal. It slowed to a crawl until it saw the retrieval mechanism below. A cylinder would travel the transit until it reached here. Once here, the automated system would grab the cylinder and load its contents. Not for food, however. Something worse.

The creature didn't know the details for the process or its point. It only knew that this process was what must be interrupted. The reason to exterminate, commit genocide, make extinct. It also knew what would happen if the machinery started in earnest. The radiation weapon used millennia ago had damaged the energy sources and all but destroyed the ship, but that didn't mean it hadn't been repairing itself all this time.

From power sources to hull integrity to preparing for a renewed radiation assault, the robots had been busy. Parasite had expected sentries but hadn't thought the automated systems would figure out its chemistry so quickly. Adaptation was something Parasite's creators revered but also greatly feared, both with good reason.

Parasite, weaponless, awaited an attack, but one did not come. Either the systems hadn't figured out the creature was down here, or this was considered a sacred area, too delicate for unsupervised drones or mere sentries. The open area was certainly large enough for a sentry, but the risk of damage was likely too great. Good.

It dropped from the transit system and tumbled forward once it hit the deck. The space before it had several panels that glowed a soft, nearly imperceptible blue. It swung its head to the left and saw exactly what it wanted, but first, it had to make sure it wasn't interrupted.

Parasite found the only hatch leading farther inside the level, probably to another set of labs exactly like this one. It walked to the entryway, scratched against the column until its claws found the seam, and ripped hard. It had just disconnected the hatch from all the backup systems. If the primaries hadn't been damaged by the radiation weapon Parasite's creators had used, Parasite would never have been able to enter the ship, let alone find its way into the vulnerable interior. Somewhat assured of its safety, Parasite turned and regarded its prize.

The cubicle had once held blue liquid, the kind Enemy used to keep specimens in stasis, but now held nothing of the kind. Instead, the transparent aluminum chassis showed a suspension harness, a nest of tools hanging above, and spatters of gore and blood. One of the host's "crew." Parasite felt the "other's" horror, which matched that of Parasite's creators'.

The body had been flayed open, its dermis strategically cut and folded outward, exposing bone and organ alike. Or where intact organs should have been. Each of the internals had been dissected, scarred by different chemical agents and nano-scalpels. The body's skull had been sliced cleanly open just above the brain case and the brain removed, flaps of flesh folded over to expose the facial bones.

Parasite smashed the transparent metal with its fist. The relatively thin partition shattered, shards silently tinkling to the deck. The Til thing walked forward until it could hold the dead vivisected creature's wrist and pulled hard, and the fleshless bone slipped through the metal restraints.

Parasite slowly released the body and laid it upon the cubicle's floor. It stared at the eyeless, brainless corpse, felt the "other" think a "prayer," knelt, and began to feed.

When it finished consuming the body, there was little left apart from a thin scum of dissolved bone and a slurry of half-digested flesh. Parasite slowly stood while its body metabolized the meal. The wounds began to heal, although the pain centers were permanently damaged. Its host, however, fared better. The host's skull knitted together enough to protect the already damaged brain as well as the precious ganglia connecting the two separate beings.

Parasite waited for its pain centers to reset while it stared upward at the cubicle's nest of tools. Most of them were laser or plasma fueled and wouldn't work without a power source. There were, however, heartier manual tools to handle certain life-forms whose very physiology required shattering their crystalline structures to get at the intelligence inside.

Parasite leaped upward, grabbing the nest with both hands and yanking at the same time. The strong metal components hadn't been made for the stress, and their relatively fragile joints cracked and fractured. Holding the massive collection of tools, heavy even in the one-third gravity, it quickly broke away the delicate or powered ones. The cubicle floor quickly became a miasma of broken and warped metal.

The creature picked up two of the tools and snapped off their ends. Each had a long, thick blade, one smooth, one serrated, both especially made to cut through silicon lifeforms. Neither blade would serve its purposes. Their handles, on the other hand, were perfect for what it needed. Each would stick out roughly a meter and a half above its fingers.

The handles might not work well as ranged weapons, but that didn't matter. Parasite knew it would have to use stealth as much as possible to attack. It couldn't handle a straight-up fight with another sentry or a horde of gliders. It just hoped Ally had realized that too.

\* \* \* \* \*

Jordan crouched in the dark much longer than he wanted. He hadn't noticed the time on the chronometer when the creature dropped, so he had no way of knowing how much time had actually passed. Once he did pay attention, however, more than fifteen minutes had elapsed.

He felt a tremble through the tunnel and turned, expecting a cylinder to come flying at him or maybe a spiderlike robot looking to feast on an intruder. Breath caught in his throat, it took him a moment to realize the vibration had come from beneath him, not behind him.

The vibrations increased for a moment, and then he saw one clawed hand rise over the side. The creature held a hunk of metal and used it to help pull itself back into the tube. Jordan stepped back to make room for it, and the creature filled the space, its two new weapons looking like monstrous metal billy clubs.

"Rearmed?" Jordan asked it.

The creature's only answer was to point in the other direction. Without waiting for Jordan, the creature turned and easily hopped over the opening and to the other side. He hadn't gotten a good look, but Jordan thought he'd seen streaks of red lining the alien face.

Not knowing what else to do, Jordan activated his magnetics to get over the opening and followed the creature farther and farther through the tunnel. They passed four creases in the passage, each corresponding to a rise in the ceiling. Just like at the other spot, only these were closed.

The creature didn't pause at any of them, merely kept moving. Jordan's back began to ache from the crouch, and he couldn't imagine what the creature must feel like. Maybe it didn't feel much of anything? Did Til? Whatever remained of him?

*Don't really know that anything remains of him, do you?*

*No*, he thought. *I really don't. And if anything does, it's probably not a good thing.*

At the fifth junction, the creature stopped at its edge. Jordan shined his lights on it and frowned. This was different. Instead of being the size of a stasis cylinder, it was much smaller.

"Access hatch?" Jordan asked.

The creature, unable to hear him, much less understand him, smashed its foot into the rectangle. The metal held for a moment until it stamped again. The front lip bent and warped, and suddenly the hatch door fell to the deck beyond. The Til thing immediately dropped down.

Jordan peered over the edge and saw the creature standing in pale blue light, its makeshift weapons held at the ready, heads and eyes moving as if on alert. Jordan dropped through the tube, landed awkwardly, and pulled his mining hammer. When he looked back at the creature, it looked as though it was nodding to him.

The corridor, if that was what it was, appeared to be circular, although it was much too long to know for sure. Soft ambient blue light filled the area, although Jordan couldn't find its source. It was as if whatever material the ship was made of naturally glowed.

Not for the first time, Jordan wondered exactly what kind of exotic radiation his suit had been subjected to. Not that it mattered much, since he didn't see a way of getting home. Oh, well, the scientists, if they ever found him, would have an interesting specimen to study, to say the least.

The creature turned from him and walked forward to what appeared to be the inner bulkhead. It touched the wall, and the material turned translucent. Jordan walked forward and realized his helmet lights reflected off the bulkhead. He killed his lights, allowed his eyes to adjust, and stared into hell.

It was impossible to know the exact size of the chamber, but it had to be at least four kilometers in diameter. What it contained was a forest of organic-looking matter, striations of multiple metals, or perhaps minerals, running through the blue-colored fleshlike veins. A liquid of multiple colors circulated through the gnarled and twisted growth.

*What the fuck am I looking at?*

He let his eyes unfocus and scanned for movement. Movement. The whole fucking thing was moving as though breathing. Also, it was even larger than he thought. A look down showed him they were at the top of this chamber, not its base. The standing tower of alien flesh and metal stretched downward as far as he could see. But something else moved as well.

What he'd first mistaken to be a pattern on skin or something similar was an open, hexagonal eye. Its colors changed slightly, although it wasn't peering at him or Til. Instead, it appeared dead and sightless. Looking at it made Jordan want to retch.

Not all of the flesh writhed and pulsed, however. In fact, much of it looked diseased or altogether dead. The branches of these areas looked gray in the blue light, lifeless and disconnected. The colors here at the top all but faded the lower he looked.

The creature tapped the panel, and it flicked back to opaque, hiding the horror from view. It stared at Jordan, the soft blue light hiding most of its revolting features while bringing out a brightness in Til's remaining human eye. It wasn't brightness, though. Jordan saw the creature flexing its fingers and understood all too well that it was as disgusted and as horrified as he was. The difference was the rage lying beneath that look, the tremors rippling across the thing's musculature. It wanted to fight. It wanted to destroy.

Jordan couldn't disagree.

# CHAPTER FORTY-TWO

The creature pointed down the corridor and began moving in long, powerful strides. Jordan took a deep breath before following, the images of that thing in the chamber still playing through his mind.

Had it been half-dead? More than that, maybe. "Diseased" was a good word. Had whatever happened here permanently damaged it? Or was it even now regrowing?

Regrowing. That somehow sounded right. Most of what he'd seen thus far appeared to be barely functional, or woefully maintained. Maybe the power plants feeding the machinery had broken down or had been destroyed.

*MacReady's sister,* he thought. *Irradiated maybe?*

His suit hadn't picked up any radiation warnings in a long time. Maybe whatever had been done to MacReady's radioactive triplet hadn't damaged this portion as much. Maybe MacReady was all that remained intact of the larger ship, if he was right about that.

What kind of weapon made a planet-sized object that radioactive? He wondered if the Til thing knew. More and more, Jordan was certain the creature had been sent here to do something very specific. It knew about the ship, it knew where to find what it was looking for, and its physiology seemed to have been engineered to survive harsh environments, including vacuum.

How the hell had it transformed a human being into that? And how did an alien species know it would come across a human to begin with?

Did it matter? Not really. Just seemed too big of a coincidence to ignore.

If only he could communicate with the creature, ask it questions, and have it respond with answers he could understand. The creature might have access to some of Til's memories, or maybe he really was still in there somewhere.

The creature came to a stop at a junction that Jordan hadn't noticed until they were on top of it. With the constant blue glow, it was nearly impossible to tell the corridor was anything but an unbroken circle.

Til pointed down the adjoining corridor then at the mining hammer. Be ready, it seemed to be saying.

Jordan gave a curt nod and gripped the hammer with both hands.

The creature moved into the corridor, no longer bounding but carefully choosing its steps.

He got the hint and followed as closely as he could to where the creature put its feet.

The pair walked like that for nearly ten meters before the creature held up one hand and came to a halt. Jordan practically stumbled. The gesture was so human, so much like something he'd seen military leaders do in war holos. The kinds Til enjoyed.

Jordan held his breath and tried to ignore the beating of his heart, sure that the creature sensed something. Then he felt it. A nearly undetectable tremor that seemed to be growing beneath his feet. His toes tingled first, and he frowned. Whatever it was, it was headed right for them.

He expected the Til thing to move or wave him back. Instead, it stood still as a statue, arm still held in a stiff right angle, the fingers pointing directly at the ceiling. The tremor increased enough that Jordan's visor shook slightly. Whatever it was, it was directly below them now.

Til looked back at him, its hand still held high. Don't make a sound, it seemed to be saying, although he imagined the creature meant "vibration." In other words, don't step.

Jordan stood there with just the sound of his breathing and the slow, strong beat of his heart. If nothing else, the pause gave him a chance to catch his breath and find another, well, maybe his last, reserve of energy. From the way the Til thing stood, it was expecting a fight. Only question was from where.

He got his answer when a panel in the deck behind him slid aside. Before he felt the tremble of the metal moving, Til had reached out and grabbed his waist, pulling him away and tossing him to the bulkhead like luggage.

Four hands appeared at the opening's lip, each covered in scales with long, tapered fingers. The grossly enlarged knuckles and wrist told Jordan what was coming was big. He wasn't wrong.

The new creature lifted itself from the opening and crowded the hallway.

Jordan, half-stunned from being thrown, stood on barely stable feet, wielding the mining hammer like a sword. The thing in the hallway took his breath away.

Three and a half meters tall, a meter and a half wide, the new horror had four arms similar to those of the robot they'd fought on the upper level, but these were biological in nature, although its skin looked more like well-tanned hide.

A strange patchwork of colors covered its chest and back, and Jordan thought he saw evidence of micro abrasions. It lifted its head, the massive bony hood protruding from its brow finally showing off what lay beneath—burning blue eyes affixed to something that looked like an alien version of a brain.

Loose tendrils of ganglia drifted through the blue liquid and behind the thing's haunting, glaring eyes.

"Fuck me," Jordan said.

The thing moved forward, its first step causing a tremor beneath Jordan's feet, and swung an upper arm at Til. Til responded by ducking beneath it just in time to catch the lower arm swinging the same direction.

The first arm bashed into the wall while the second clipped Til at the hip, spinning it into the bulkhead and leaving a small smear of smoking color on the bluish metal. Til rolled away from the four-armed thing and rose to its feet with a leap forward.

The thing's eyes remained fixed on Til, and it seemed to have lost interest in Jordan. Maybe it didn't consider him a threat. With that in mind, he felt both offended and reassured at the same time. Before he even knew he was going to do it, he charged.

A half beat afterward, Til was up and crouching backward, its weapons still held before it. The giant swung an arm at Jordan, although he was out of reach, but close enough to make him stop his advance and hold up the hammer in retreat.

The giant moved forward and swiveled at the hips, its other arm coming in to crush Jordan against the bulkhead. Something flashed by, and Jordan's foot went out from under him, and he fell backward. The giant hand hit the suit's chest plate, and he heard it crunch like thin ice beneath a boot.

Momentum carried him into the bulkhead, his HUD fuzzing out for a second before reappearing with the sound of muted klaxons and a slew of warning and error alerts. The suit's chest plate was gone, shattered. The only thing protecting him from the frigid temperature and the noxious, thin atmosphere, was the thin layer of alloy fibers. If he got hit there again, he didn't have to worry about broken ribs or even being cut in half. He'd be dead in less than a minute.

His legs sagged, and he slid down the wall to his ass, feet curled beneath him. He couldn't catch his breath and sat in a daze, the mining hammer all but forgotten.

*  *  *  *  *

The moment the chimera dragged itself up, Parasite knew two things—Enemy was desperate, and Parasite was in big trouble. The corridor was wide but too close to allow it to move freely, to flank, circle, and exploit weaknesses. The chimera had enormous strength, far greater than Parasite's, but the abomination wasn't nearly as agile, which was why it chose to attack them in a tight space and block their only escape.

Parasite knew that retreat would only bring them to a pair of hatches—one heading down and one heading up. It wouldn't have time to open either hatch unless it was willing to sacrifice Ally, and that assumed the chimera didn't simply ignore Ally and chase Parasite down instead. More importantly, though, it didn't want to sacrifice Ally. The "other" had continued feeding fragments of thought and memory, Parasite unable to stop the bidirectional flow. It was the nature of the connection. A blessing and a curse.

Parasite tossed Ally aside and took a few steps back, weapons at the ready. The chimera swung its upper arm, and Parasite ducked just in time to catch the lower arm in the hip. Parasite spun and hit the bulkhead, a new fresh jag of pain running up its spine.

Before the chimera could take another swing, Parasite rolled out of reach, got to its feet, and crouched in the combat position. The chimera, its stolen eyes glaring at Parasite, lumbered forward.

Before Parasite quite knew what was happening, Ally rushed the giant. Parasite instantly ran to follow, quickening its pace when it realized what was about to happen.

The chimera planted its feet, its muscles tensing and rippling in anticipation of a swing. Parasite leaped forward and kicked Ally in the hip as it bounded at the chimera. With its attention focused on Ally, Parasite hit the chimera twice just below the hood of bone, cracking the creature's armor.

Surprised, the chimera swung both its arms in Parasite's direction, but it had already leaped backward in a crouch, just out of reach. The chimera stepped toward Ally, but Parasite did nothing. The giant thing paused for a moment, considering what to do.

Parasite took a step toward it, the chimera's eyes immediately swiveling back to Jordan. Parasite took another step, its weapons moving through the air in tiny circles, prepared to strike or block. The chimera turned fully to face Parasite, seeming somewhat satisfied Ally was no longer a threat. Considering Ally's weapon lay more than a meter away, it was a good bet.

Parasite feinted a swing, and the chimera twitched in that direction but didn't commit. Keeping its feet moving, never staying in one position for more than a beat, Parasite crouched low, tensing muscles it had no intention of using.

Chimera followed the movements, eyes focused, its own muscles rippling and twitching in anticipation. The shorter, upper arms were designed to pierce while the lower arms were for grabbing and punching. Both sets were heavily armored, the hide tough and resistant to bludgeons and blades. The creatures served as shock troops, breaking and cracking carapaces, bones, shells, crystalline shields, and any other manner of alien physiology. Their jobs were to pacify and collect, not to kill. But Enemy didn't mind that, either—even the dead provided food and fuel.

Parasite closed within reach of the lower arms, its eye cluster splitting focus between the overly tall upper shoulders and the lower musculature supporting the massive arms. The creature tensed as though it were going to swing to the left, but Parasite was ready. It danced backward as the monstrous thing's heavy arm flashed through empty space. It had overcommitted, as Parasite hoped it would.

The host's mouth erupted a stream of vomit that covered the entire upper shoulder joint. Parasite smashed one of its makeshift weapons against the other before sliding beneath the chimera. Rather than waiting for a reaction, Parasite whirled and slashed twice with the metal bars. It leaped away beyond the panel before the chimera could turn.

Vapor rose from the creature's joint, the hide all but eaten through by Parasite's bile. Chimera's eyes glared with both pain and hate. If Parasite could have sneered, it would have. Instead, it crept backward another step away from the panel.

Chimera responded by leaping over the opening to land safely on the other side. While it was in the air, Parasite leaped to the bulkhead and scissored by, a single baton contacting the joint it had hit before. One of the chimera's upper arms slashed against Parasite's flank on its way by, and Parasite spurted more blood across the giant.

Parasite landed on the other side, its nerves screaming with pain. One of its mutated, armored ribs had cracked and sent a jolt through its spine. Pushing away the discomfort, Parasite rolled backward, got to its feet, and held its weapons ready.

The chimera turned in an awkward circle, one arm hanging at an odd angle. The ball and socket joint had eroded, the arm practically dislocated. The giant reached for it with the other arm and crunched it back into place. Parasite waited, knowing the chimera would attack as soon as it could. As the creature turned, Parasite saw the muscles move on its oversized calves, the anticipation of the ball joints of its monstrous heels. It was going to leap.

Parasite tumbled backward before the creature had even left the deck. By the time it landed, making the deck tremble, Parasite was once again between it and Ally. The only problem was the giant wasn't going to wait this time.

Chimera jumped over the panel and charged with its eyes barely visible beneath the bony hood, its damaged upper arm curled like a battering ram with the other raised slightly above its shoulders to pummel or grab. Rather than tumble backward, Parasite launched itself forward beneath the battering ram and well below the grabbing arm's range. As it slid between the chimera's thick legs, it sprayed vomit in a stream, the substance geysering upward, splashing against the hood and directly on the brain case.

In a fluid motion, Parasite rose to its feet and turned. The chimera, realizing it had been duped, had its smaller arms wiping away the bile, vapor rising from the ministrations. Without hesitation, Parasite leaped back over the panel, weapons already in mid-swing. At the last possible moment, the chimera swung its undamaged upper arm and connected with Parasite just before one of its batons made contract.

Parasite flew into the bulkhead and crumpled to the deck, its vision blurred and mind reeling. An image of the chimera advancing fluttered into Parasite's mind. It had been from the "other," its eyes still functioning and staring at the oncoming threat while Parasite's own remained confused and jittery. The "other" didn't want to die just yet.

When the chimera reared back for its killing blow, Parasite rolled beneath the creature's raised leg, put a baton across the chimera's knee, and pulled its feet using the bulkhead as a fulcrum. The chimera immediately lost its footing and stumbled forward.

Parasite, at least two of its thick, alien ribs fractured and its mutated organs leaking fluid, forced itself into a tumble, nerve clusters screaming with pain, its left shoulder feeling stiff and unstable. Two of its eyes no longer glowed green but had gone completely dark. Its remaining eyes remained blurred and fuzzed, its analog of an optic nerve severely damaged.

It rolled again until it faced the ceiling, its single functioning human eye darting in all directions to provide a clear picture. The chimera had recovered, although its shoulder had taken another hard hit on the bulkhead. It turned around a little more slowly this time, one leg dragging slightly.

The piercing blue eyes stared at Parasite through a film of pitted and scorched transparent metal. The bony hood that had provided cover from overhead attacks had partially dissolved, ichor bubbling away into vapor. A dribble of turgid goo dripped from its damaged shoulder joint.

Parasite got to its feet, firmed its grip on the batons, and stepped backward with slow, measured strides. The chimera stomped with its good leg as if in challenge and took a step forward.

* * * * *

Jordan came back to himself when the massive thing leaped over the open panel and charged Til. It took him only a few beats to realize two things—that Til was seriously injured and that the giant was going to kill it. Til slowly crept backward from the creature, but Jordan could see by the way it favored one side and the dribbles of liquid crawling over its skin that if it wasn't already dying, it soon would be.

The giant didn't exactly look in good shape, either, one shoulder much lower than the other, the limb hanging at an awkward angle as though it would slip out of joint at any moment. Jordan reached for his hammer, but it wasn't there—it was more than a meter away.

Groaning, he got to his feet and stumbled to the hunk of metal. Once in his hands, he felt a little better, a little more there. He turned in time to watch Til duck a swing and kick itself up to the wall and over the giant before the monster could react. While in the air, Til hit the creature twice in its damaged shoulder. Til landed in time to catch a vicious backswing to its waist.

The thing that had once been his captain spun sideways and crashed shoulder first into the deck. The giant swiveled slowly, its damaged arm dragging against the metal deck. Til rolled over and held up its batons in an X to fend off an unexpected blow. It needn't have bothered—the giant wasn't in a hurry.

Jordan flattened himself against the bulkhead, feeling exposed and foolish at the same time. The giant hadn't shown any interest in him until he'd tried to attack it. Maybe if he stayed close to the metal, he'd just fade into the background. If he didn't? Well, his suit would do little to protect him now. One more smack from that thing and he was going to be either pulverized or asphyxiated.

# CHAPTER FORTY-THREE

Parasite couldn't lift its left arm. The baton remained vice gripped in its hand, but the arm refused to rise. Despite its powerful, hardened, mutated body, muscle damage, ligaments, and torn tendons had finally taken their toll.

It rolled over on its broken ribs, the "other" shrieking at it to get up. Parasite got to one knee and looked ahead with its remaining human eye. Its last few attacks had been successful at disabling one of the chimera's arms, maybe damaging the upper breastplate of bone. Its hood had all but disintegrated on one side, gruel-like blood freezing in place in the frigid near vacuum. The brain case was worse for wear as well, the transparent alloy now completely opaque across one side. A single eye glared with hate, the other hidden by the marred container.

Parasite rose, one arm hanging by its side, the baton still clenched. It glanced over and saw Ally up against the bulkhead. Ally's suit appeared damaged, leaving Parasite to wonder how long the creature would last. Like Parasite, Ally appeared to be at the end. If they didn't finish the chimera soon, it would be over for them both.

Ally returned its stare, its own weapon back in its hands. The "other" thought the situation was perfect, somehow satisfying regardless of the outcome. Parasite didn't recognize such thoughts. It only knew that if it were to survive to finish its task, Ally would have to survive too.

Parasite gestured backward to the open panel. It mimicked dropping down, although it couldn't raise its damaged arm. Ally shook its head. The "other" interpreted the gesture, and Parasite repeated the movement.

Its human eye caught motion. The entity controlling Chimera must have recovered control over its patchwork, vat-grown body.

The "other" told Parasite to jerk its head, and it followed the suggestion. Ally finally took a step backward, and Parasite faced the chimera. The giant dragged its left leg in slow steps. Every movement told Parasite about the damage done. The nerve clusters on that side below the waist were mostly inoperative, the arm damaged beyond repair, although it could still be used to bludgeon or ram if the chimera used its good arm for support. A good shot to the brain case might further damage it, perhaps even crack the case itself.

The neural connections, kilometers worth of ganglia analogs, an entire nervous system encapsulated in a box, spread throughout its grown body. The two were inseparable once combined, but that was a boon of sorts. Enemy couldn't control it directly. Enemy had sacrificed some of its regenerating tissue to create this abomination. Enemy was weak. The chimera might be the last organic unit it had.

The chimera was nearly close enough to take a swipe. Backing up a step, Parasite slapped the air with one of the batons. The chimera didn't break its stride. Parasite took two steps backward for every lumbering step the giant took, each one a little to the side, a little more of a stutter. Establish a rhythm and break it, confuse, confound, disrupt inexperience.

Enemy might not have had time to load all the memories and experiences into the chimera's entity, or maybe many of the combat routines had been lost to the massive attack that almost destroyed this ship and Enemy along with it. Or the abomination had been feinting all along.

Parasite stutter-stepped backward and gave Ally a glance. Near the lip's edge, Ally stood in a less than graceful combat stance. Parasite felt the impact tremor and knew the chimera had taken a larger, longer step, no doubt hoping for a backstab. Parasite felt the rumbling vibration of the dragging leg and steeled itself.

It anticipated the killing blow and rolled to the opening in the floor, wrapped its good arm around Ally, and dropped down. Ally squirmed in Parasite's tight grip, but Parasite wasn't letting the creature move. The six meter drop might have hurt Ally, but it was nothing to the Parasite. Its bad arm, however, no longer functioned at all. The impact of their combined mass striking the deck was enough to jolt it out of place. Something important had torn there, nerves destroyed or no longer functioning.

Parasite half carried, half dragged Ally a few meters into the level before turning around to face what it knew was coming. Parasite took one long step forward and tensed, waiting for the shadow. It had to time the strike just right, or the chimera would probably kill it and do so rather easily.

The chimera dropped in front of Parasite with a relatively slow speed in the 1/3 G. Parasite crouched and sprang in one fluid movement, its body twirling, its good arm clutching the baton to its side. It timed extending its baton at the same time the creature's brain case came into view.

The hunk of metal smashed into the weakened, transparent shielding around the left side. The brain case broke free of a bone holding it in place, tearing a vital connection.

Parasite landed awkwardly, its own damaged arm hanging by flesh, tendons, and ligaments, the limb completely dislocated. It stumbled a few steps before finally regaining its balance. It stared at the chimera, one baton raised in a blocking stance.

The chimera's left side sagged as though the muscles there had atrophied or were barely functional. Both of its upper arms seemed useless, the pair's fingers still twitching and flexing but ultimately impotent. It took a step forward, wobbled, and fell to one knee.

Parasite didn't move but remained where it was, its human eye glancing to make sure Ally didn't attack. It needn't have worried—Ally was staying a good five meters from the fight, well beyond the range of both Parasite's and the chimera's weapons and limbs.

The chimera raised its brain case so that it made eye contact with Parasite. Parasite reacted by walking two meters closer, its human eye returning the glare, the remains of its cheek bones rising to sneer, a gesture of which it was no longer capable. The creature leaned forward and blasted a stream of vomit. The liquid splattered against the brain case, and the creature's arms twitched as it tried to raise them in defense.

This time, Parasite attacked. It leaped and smashed the baton once more into the brain case. The acid had finally weakened the alloy's lattice structure, and the hunk of metal pierced the entity's true brain.

Blue liquid dribbled down the creature's damaged chest, vapor rising from its dissolving flesh and bone. Its own conglomeration of mutated organs and attributes from multiple species had begun to fail or disintegrate. The entity inside was dying, the fierce color draining away as the ganglionic network failed.

The chimera crumpled to the deck, its upper chest still dissolving.

Parasite stepped away from the mostly dead thing, its human eye darting as it looked for another threat. It didn't find one, but when it turned to see Ally, Ally was gone.

* * * * *

Jordan watched the Til thing take down the giant creature with a blow to its brain after hosing it down with more gunk. The sight had made him want to retch, and he turned from the inevitable end, staring in the opposite direction. Multiple meter-and-a-half-high metal structures stood on the deck, arranged in some design that made no sense to him.

He finally saw a figure standing at the far bulkhead. The colors were all wrong in the blue light with patches of bright yellow and soft green covering an abnormally shaped profile. Jordan stepped forward cautiously, his brain finally catching up with where he was and what he was seeing.

The silhouette hadn't moved, although with each step, the shape was becoming more normal, if you accounted for a damaged suit of some kind, or tattered, stiff clothing. Jordan continued moving until he came to the first of the metal structures.

He'd thought they were alien sculptures at first, but he couldn't have been more wrong. The structures had both nozzles and needles, an automated nest of tools that could be raised to any height, and a number of drains. His mind screamed the word "morgue," but somehow he knew that was not what this place was.

Jordan turned around to see where the Til thing was and found it creeping through the blue light, approaching Jordan cautiously, one arm hanging limp and useless, colored liquid splashed upon its neck and chest. The creature had to be nearly dead.

It waved to Jordan but not in a "hello" gesture. It was beckoning him to retreat and to do it fast. Confused, Jordan took a step backward and turned to face the far bulkhead once again. The colored silhouette was no longer standing there but had quickly walked across the deck.

As it neared, Jordan finally understood what he was seeing. It had been a mining suit at some point, but portions had been burned or cut away. Alien flesh growing from its shoulder pulsed with a slick sheen. The helmet had been cut away, the scalp peeled back and the side of its skull removed.

In its stead was a bright blue eye. The rest of the face was a horror show of gnarled, rugose, and raw, red flesh. It moved too mechanically, its human eyes dead and glazed in their sockets, looking completely frozen. Even with all that damage, he knew it was Aryana.

"No," Jordan said softly, his mind not quite believing it. "No." More emphatically this time. As the Aryana thing closed on him, Jordan screamed the word loudly enough to make his ears ring and swung the mining hammer. It smashed into the skull just as its hands touched Jordan's shoulders. The damaged head splattered into frozen liquid, its alien eye bursting.

The body stayed there for a moment, arms jiggling and twitching mindlessly. At last, it fell over, blood welling out and immediately freezing. Something glowed at the base of its neck, flickered, and died. The body didn't move.

Jordan fell to one knee before her corpse, head lowered. An alert flashed across his HUD, something about leaking atmosphere. It seemed to fade from his mind, just as everything that had kept him going finally crumbled. He'd been telling himself she was probably dead. He'd been telling himself he was fighting to save Chu. But Aryana, dead, mauled, mangled, and mutated, had experienced the ultimate assault, transformed into something hardly anyone would still recognize as human.

He hadn't been able to save her. He knew that. She was more than likely doomed the moment she and the others had landed on the planet. There was nothing he could have done to save her unless he'd taken the drop.

And then you'd be dead, too, he said to himself. And she'd be right here experiencing this in your place, if she was lucky.

### OXYGEN AT 10%

Suit was telling him he was fucked. He peered down at his left shoulder and saw a rip there, the hint of his jumpsuit visible through the exposed fabric. Without the armor, he was more vulnerable than in an EVA suit. The Aryana thing reaching for him, touching him, had been enough.

*You can do something about that,* he told himself. *You can patch that.*

Why? Why not asphyxiate here? Take off his helmet and make it fast? He'd rather die than end up like Aryana.

Vapor rose from the rip like steam, the auto sealant unable to repair it quickly enough. No matter what he did, he was going to die here. Jordan took in a deep breath and grinned. He'd done his best to make sure Chu was safe. Maybe he'd at least managed that.

He reached forward to touch Aryana when something grabbed him around his chest and lifted him. Jordan found himself staring into the Til thing's ruined head. The human side, its remaining eye rimmed with broken veins that pulsed with the same hellish green the eye cluster had, was little more than eye sockets, a nub of a nose, and the hint of cheekbones. Its upper teeth were gone, leaving serrated, tortured flesh, edges blackened and burned.

The eye glared at Jordan in a silent accusation before glancing in the direction of his waist.

Jordan, still grinning, shook his head no.

The creature shook him.

Jordan giggled. His atmosphere was almost gone, and he felt high as a kite, flowers blossoming before his eyes. It was getting cold, and everything felt so blissfully far away.

# CHAPTER FORTY-FOUR

Parasite held Ally, watching its color change through the transparent visor. The "other" had sent the word "asphyxiation," but Parasite had no understanding. An image appeared over the neural connection a millisecond later, that of Ally dead and clutching its throat, eyes bugged out, tongue lolling. It was more than enough to get the point across.

The second image it sent was of the pack on the suit's hip. Parasite needed something inside the container. The something was shiny and rectangular. Parasite placed Ally carefully on the deck and opened the pouch. The object it sought was there in a slot. Parasite freed it, popped the top, and touched it to the rip.

It felt a vibration through its fingers, and the strange tool's end glowed bright white. Parasite's human eye traced the path, its fingers carefully following the pattern. Between the loss of depth perception and the damage to its nervous system, it had difficulty at first but improved with each movement.

When the "other" stopped sending instructions, Parasite lifted the tool away from the suit. The fabric had healed, and it could no longer see Ally's delicate, inner skin. Ally's face had gone ashen, the "other" panicked and frantic about the lack of color. Parasite waited to see if Ally survived, as did the "other."

* * * * *

Jordan's head pounded as if a pair of ancient miners were swinging their pickaxes against his brain. His lungs burned, and his heart beat too fast. After taking in a deep breath of air, followed by another, he managed to clear his vision.

The Til thing stood over him, its mangled face peering down with its lone human eye. The remains of Til's face implied concern or maybe anger. The creature stepped back, bent down, and picked up its baton. It walked back to Jordan and tapped one of his feet with the piece of metal. A gentle tap, yes, but it got the point across.

Jordan groaned as the suit told him he had two percent oxygen reserves. He was surprised it was that much. He rose to one knee and winced as he stood, his joints complaining and his calves feeling like molten steel. On shaking legs, he turned and looked at the Til thing.

It had walked to the metal structure and stood before it. The thing gave Jordan a come-hither gesture, the same one he'd seen Til make a thousand times.

That's not Til, some part of his mind told him. Remember that.

But did it really matter at this point?

Jordan walked forward on numb feet, his arms tingling as though not enough blood circulated through his body. Aftereffects of losing atmosphere? Or was he finally just succumbing to exhaustion, pain, and the constant drain of flight and fight?

He reached the machine, Aryana's mangled face drifting into his mind.

The Til thing dropped its baton to the deck, where it bounced in silence.

Jordan watched the creature bend with some effort and grasp something from the tool rack. Jordan couldn't see what it was doing, but the thing seemed to be inspecting it or maybe trying to figure out how to use it.

The creature finally rose and regarded Jordan with its single human eye. Its eye cluster had gone dark except for a single node that occasionally flickered with an eldritch glow. Its damaged arm seeped fluid that didn't freeze but sizzled when it hit the deck. Jordan glanced down at the creature's good arm.

It held a short, thin cylinder with a pronged end of some kind. Well, "pronged" wasn't quite the right word. The shape didn't make much sense to him. He raised his eyes back to the creature's as another alert flashed on his HUD.

### OXYGEN RESERVES AT 1%

Jordan took a deep breath as though it might be the last good one he had left. "What do you want?" he asked the thing, although he knew it couldn't hear him.

The creature did nothing, simply stood there, its purple blood seeping from a fresh wound in the remains of its human face. The liquid looked too turgid, too much like a pudding that had gone over, threads of orange and green running through it. The creature's human eye blinked slowly at Jordan, as though it were heading off to sleep.

Jordan cocked his head as if to ask a question, and the creature's good hand flashed upward, the tool in its hand puncturing the exposed fabric of his suit and his dermis. He was so surprised by the move that it took his brain more than a few seconds to feel an icy sensation spreading outward from his heart.

The creature stepped back and tossed away the tool. It regarded Jordan in silence for a moment, although Jordan barely realized it was still there. The synapses in his brain fired again and again, or rather misfired, in trying to make sense of what was happening. Darkness crept at the edges of his vision, the suit telling him he was out of oxygen, although his suit had sealed the new micro perforation.

Jordan's lungs burned then froze then burned again. Breathing became more and more difficult. He sank to his knees and wavered, hands clutching at his throat as he suffocated. At the last moment before the lights went out, he told himself it was the best he could have hoped for.

* * * * *

Parasite watched Ally fall to the deck. The "other" continued shrieking in anger, betrayal, and a dozen other emotions Parasite didn't understand. The "other" made thinking difficult, and so Parasite finally sent it images barely comprehensible to the remains of the human mind but somehow understood.

The "other" ceased its frenetic bursts of thought for a moment, leaving Parasite relieved. As it turned to begin its task, the "other" sent a different image, one Parasite didn't at all understand. It looked like

Ally holding another, smaller Ally in its arms. The small Ally, pink and blemish free, misshapen as though it were abnormally small, destined to become much larger, had an all-too-piercing green eye.

Parasite didn't understand but didn't need to. It was something the "other" had thought and nothing more. The creature walked away from the machine with a relaxed, wounded stride and headed to where the abomination had appeared. What hadn't been visible when the semi-suited figure had stood against the bulkhead was the outlet from an oversized tube. The tube itself had a number of instruments and devices embedded in it similar to the one Parasite had destroyed earlier, back when it had fed.

The mission was at an end. Parasite reached for a transparent, flexible alloy hose that ended in a thick needle. Parasite punctured its flesh with the needle and flexed its arm.

Somewhere inside the bulkhead, a pump came to life, the suction draining the fluid from Parasite. Strangely colored bubbling liquid rose through the hose and into the bulkhead. Parasite didn't know what was happening, only that it was dying. Dying was, after all, part of completing the mission. It only knew it had to wait until it knew no more.

*　*　*　*　*

Enemy was a cancer. Its progenitors had evolved in both technology and biology to the point of bioengineering themselves and their progeny. Upon discovering other species, they began incorporating $H_2S$, silicon, arsenic, and carbon lifeforms into their physiology and biological neural networks.

The progenitors merged their thoughts and their biology until they became a singularity—a communal brain composed of countless neural connections from thousands of races, all becoming part of Enemy.

It used automatons, genetically designed and engineered lifeforms, and captured races, subverting their anatomy as well as their minds, to build, to protect itself, and to spread.

Enemy had survived for countless millennia until the great war when multiple races finally found one another, made alliances, and destroyed Enemy's colonies. Enemy built a great ark ship, one with millions of potential servants and enough food and power to survive for millions of years while it searched for new, less well-armed sources of food and technology.

For a hundred millennia, it traveled the stars without fear. The other races, those it had preyed upon nearly to extinction, finally chased it down. Hypervelocity weapons destroyed Enemy's outer shields, the debris ultimately forming three ice giants that wound up orbiting a dying star.

Enemy responded by firing beam weapons and multiple missile assaults against the oncoming ships and deadly munitions. It destroyed most of the fleet, but Enemy didn't count on their final weapon.

The system's mid-sized, low-mass star detonated in an outrush of EMR (electromagnetic radiation) that bombarded the entire system and its outreaches. Instead of going nova, the majority of the star's remaining energy had been transformed into a fatal blast meant to destroy Enemy once and for all.

Enemy had had nearly an hour to protect itself from the moment its quantum entangled probes saw the star seem to explode. The ship's outer defenses had been mauled and nearly destroyed by the fleet's attack. Knowing the wave of radiation would annihilate its colonies, Enemy severed them.

Three identical colonies drifted apart, two forming a rudimentary shield for the third colony. It didn't matter which one survived. It only mattered that one did.

The outer colony took the blast head-on, the radiation assault transforming it into a ball of radioactive alloy too dangerous to ever be harvested.

The other colony spun off from the blast, its artificial atmosphere deflecting much of it, but the powerful weapon caught at least enough of the moon-sized colony to send it spinning.

The third colony, the one least damaged by the blast, lost nearly all its atmosphere in the sudden rush of stellar wind. Enemy had prepared this colony for the damage, had closed all access points and evacuated the surface. The damage, however, had been catastrophic.

Enemy's remaining colony had just enough power to keep Enemy partially alive. The radiation weapon caused enough damage to force Enemy to feed upon itself as it struggled to rebuild its damaged support systems using a few operable automatons.

The fleet had been destroyed by the weapon as well, leaving nothing but particles in their wake. Before Enemy's sensor network completely collapsed, it detected several minuscule energy sources entering the system. Shortly afterward, Enemy lost its ability to see beyond its remaining colony.

The fact that no fleet returned to destroy Enemy meant it had won. It had survived. It would take thousands of more years for another fleet to arrive, and by that time, Enemy would have rebuilt at least enough to protect itself, if not escape the system. It had time.

Many of its biological sources had been damaged during the power outage, causing them to perish in their malfunctioning stasis pods. It took an enormous amount of energy to engineer one of its specimens, so it consumed as many of the dead as possible. The process was slow, but Enemy had time.

A century or so after it managed to repair a drone factory and reconstruct a portion of its sensory network, Enemy detected an energy source on its surface. One of its drones found a roaming machine, looking as though it was searching for something.

The machine looked crude and poorly constructed, although it had little trouble navigating the rocky shield covering the colony. When one of the alien robots sent a pulse through the ship, Enemy knew some new race had discovered it. It only had to wait.

Some time later, the creatures arrived. Enemy was well prepared for them, with dozens of drones and two new sentries, one of which was still trying to get from the levels on the other side of the colony to help protect Enemy.

Moments after capturing the new arrivals, however, a new weapon rained down an EMR burst similar to what the star had generated but far less intense. The burst knocked out two of Enemy's power nodes, further handicapping it and preventing most of its factories from coming to life.

Enemy responded by re-tasking many of its drones into surveillance mode. They saw the new orbital come online, its tether falling from space. Enemy, the latest EMR attack fresh in its collective mind, remained cautious, unwilling to greet the newcomers or let them know they had been detected.

It allowed them to move freely and chose to observe rather than capture. It needed to know what was happening. By that time, it had dissected one of the creatures, studied its biology using less than optimal sensors, and received the tissue, absorbing it, adding it to its essence.

Enemy could use this species more easily than many. Carbon organisms were by far the most susceptible to its engineering techniques; they were mere clay awaiting the sculptor's dexterous touch.

By the time Enemy had decided to take the newcomers, another had arrived. The moment its drones saw the parasite, Enemy knew what it was and what it would try to do.

The chimera had been its last best hope. If it could stave off the Parasite long enough, its other sentry would arrive, but it had hastily converted one of the new creatures, accelerating the mutation process, in hopes the mutant would have time to grow before it had to fight the interlopers.

No such luck. The pair defeated the sentry, its lone chimera, and its last hope. Enemy watched through its sensor network as the genetically designed creature hooked itself up to the feeding tubes and fed itself to Enemy.

Enemy could do nothing but watch the creature deflate like an exhausted goiter as its being dissolved into the hose. The fluid, engineered just like the rest of Parasite and, in turn, its host, spread through the ganglia, dendrites, and crystalline lattices. The more it spread, the more of Enemy's mind dissolved.

The contagion progressively multiplied, a hellish virus converting all the healthy alien tissue into factories for more of the deadly virus. Just as Enemy itself been a cancer, it died in much the same fashion as it had extinguished countless races of beings over its billions of years of existence.

# CHAPTER FORTY-FIVE

Chu felt a little better. The hellish radiation sickness was finally under control and his fever had gone down substantially. For a while, he'd floated in and out of consciousness, occasionally hearing Jordan calling for him or someone else. Sometimes Jordan's suit sent an alarm for some reason. Good thing he was back on the Kirkland.

Back?

Chu opened his eyes, practically feeling the snap of his mind coming back to itself. He was in the emergency medical bay on MacReady, not the *Kirkland*. The holo-displays filled with his physiology reports, improving status indicators, and updated prognoses. It also had a flashing warning—

**LIFE SUPPORT SYSTEMS FAILURE**

**ENTER STASIS IMMEDIATELY**

Chu wasn't going to argue. He walked to the cylinder, already feeling the chill coming on. Reactor failure, meaning this place was going to get cold in a hell of a hurry. Long before he ran out of oxygen, in fact.

He made his way to the pod, stripped out of his jumpsuit, and climbed inside. The door closed, and the HUD came to life. Systems nominal. Ready to go night-night.

If Jordan came back, he'd have to get into the other pod, and they'd both have to hope the company wanted their ship back. Or what remained of it.

Standard procedure. When the *Kirkland* didn't report in by the required six-month mark, the company would send a search and rescue vessel to investigate. It had taken the *Kirkland* over a year to get to MacReady. An S&R ship, with its low relative mass, high engine output, and designed for speed and short missions, could blaze here from Proxima in just a few months.

His stasis pod was good for a year of uninterrupted sleep. At least if they never came for him, he'd die without knowing. He'd die in a blessed, dreamless sleep.

Chu activated the pod, and a moment later, he knew nothing more.

# CHAPTER FORTY-SIX

Jordan came to with a harsh cough, his eyes flickering and fluttering, dim, unfocused bluish light occasionally finding his optic nerve. Every part of his body ached with a deep throb, and his heart felt as though it was barely beating. To make matters worse, his head pounded.

He slowly raised himself, having to get to all fours before sitting up on his knees. Aryana's corpse looked decayed. Either the thin atmosphere had something that corroded unprotected flesh, or there was another mechanism at work. Something chemical, perhaps.

Jordan touched her left cheek, the one less affected by whatever had taken her over. He didn't bother speaking, only said, "I'm sorry," in his mind.

Before he tried to get to his feet, he turned to the bulkhead and saw a hunched shape leaning against it. His slightly blurred vision made it difficult to know for sure, but he thought it was the Til thing. Jordan knew it was dead, but he needed to be sure.

He stumbled past the machine and headed to the bulkhead, his vision not quite clear, and his balance less than stable. His leg tried to buckle halfway there but recovered with a tingle of nerves and a jolt of pain in the muscle.

When he reached the tube, Jordan halted a meter away from the dead body that had once been Til, his friend. The creature looked completely deflated, or maybe "desiccated" was the right word, as if every drop of moisture had been squeezed from it. The creature's flesh had eroded in places, giving Jordan a view of a thin slurry pooling where lungs should have been.

He retched, managed to hold in the bile, and swallowed hard. The action felt strange, as if his throat didn't remember how to do it. He nearly panicked when his throat vapor locked, his lungs refusing to expel air or ingest it. He closed his eyes, ready to scream, afraid he would choke and die, and finally, blessedly, his body seemed to remember how to do everything, and the feeling passed.

Jordan turned away from the mess. He didn't want to see Til now. An image of Til leaning against the *Kirkland*'s bulkhead, his face set in a wide smirk after making a joke that didn't land, was what he wanted to hold on to. That was the Til he wanted to remember.

Jordan took a deep breath but heard nothing and felt nothing. His lungs didn't expand. Confused, he activated the HUD, and a slew of statuses over the last few hours appeared on the screen.

**SUIT PERFORATION DETECTED**

**PERFORATION SEALED**

**ARYTHMIA DETECTED**

**SEEK MEDICAL ATTENTION IMMEDIATELY**

**OPERATOR HEARTBEAT LOST**

**OXYGEN RESERVES AT 0%**

According to the suit's chronometer, that last alert had occurred more than three hours ago.

Confused, he blinked through the interface until he found **OPERATOR STATUS**.

**--> HR: 0**

**--> BP: 0/0**

**--> OA: 0%**

No heart rate. No blood pressure. No oxygen absorption. As far as Suit was concerned, Jordan wasn't alive.

Without air in the suit, he couldn't hear anything. It was as though he were trapped in a vacuum within a vacuum. But the suit was right. He couldn't hear his heart, and he couldn't feel his lungs taking in breath.

He tried to remember what happened, but he couldn't. He had followed the creature to the machine, and then—

Everything was so hazy, so disjointed, so removed from how he normally felt, yet his limbs responded, he was thinking, he was seeing, and he could feel. The back of Jordan's neck tingled, and he quickly turned in response.

There in the shadows behind one of the machines, a spider thing—"drone," a part of his mind insisted—had entered the room the same way he and Til had. It had crept up behind him, probably hoping for a sneak attack.

But the drone was hesitant, almost as though it didn't know what to do. *Poor Enemy's toys are broken.*

Jordan frowned. Where had that thought come from?

The thing skittered toward him. Jordan deftly leapt aside with an agility he didn't understand, the drone moving as though it were in slow motion, and his eyes seemed to see everything at once, his mind studying every joint of the automaton, its movement, its routine motion, dissecting it all in order to anticipate, building a catalog of information to draw on in an instant.

The drone's forward leg lunged at Jordan and smashed through his helmet. Without knowing he was going to do it, he ripped it off and stared the robot down. When the robot began to move, his insides felt a warm, comforting liquid boiling where his stomach might once have been.

Jordan spat vomit at the leg's final joint before savagely punching it with a fist that felt far too large for his gloves. The hardened armor shattered, as did the drone's joint. He tumbled forward, his hand grabbing the thick hunk of metal, and he jumped to his feet and waited for the drone to make the next move.

In the distance, he saw five more skittering inside. They didn't look as confused as this one, and Jordan knew why. A sentry, a large robotic machine with an entity inside, had connected to them. It was commanding them, and it was bringing the remaining horde to bear.

Which meant a part of Enemy, a clone coming out of suspended animation, perhaps, still survived somewhere on MacReady. It also meant Jordan was going to have to eat to heal, to fight, to survive. Good thing there was a lot of food on the upper level.

# ABOUT THE AUTHOR

A full-time author and podcaster from Houston, Texas, Paul E Cooley produces free sci-fi, suspense, and thriller fiction, essays, and reviews available from **shadowpublications.com** and iTunes.

His best-selling novel, *The Black*, was released in 2014 and won the 2015 Parsec Award for Long-Form Fiction. Since then, he has published six novels in both the urban fantasy and hard sci-fi genres, including *The Derelict Saga* as well as two sequels to *The Black*.

He has collaborated with New York Times Bestselling Author Scott Sigler on the series *The Crypt* and co-wrote the novel *The Rider*. In addition to his writing, Paul has contributed his voice talents to a number of podcast productions.

He is a co-host on the renowned **Dead Robots' Society** writing podcast and enjoys interacting with readers and other writers.

For more information about current and upcoming projects, please visit **shadowpublications.com**.

To contact Paul:
    Mastodon: @paul_e_cooley@vyrse.social
    YouTube: https://youtube.com/paulecooley
    Email: paul@shadowpublications.com

Want to know when a new book or podcast presentation is released? Join the Shadowpublications.com mailing list:
    http://mailinglist.shadowpublications.com